THE HIGHLANDER'S

THE HIGHLANDE
BRIDE
The Hardy Heroines series (book #3)

By Cathy & DD MacRae

PRINT EDITION

PUBLISHED BY
Short Dog Press

www.cathymacraeauthor.com

ISBN-978-0-9966485-5-4

License Notes

This book is licensed for your personal enjoyment only. This book contains copyrighted work and may not be reproduced, transmitted, downloaded, or stored in or introduced into an information storage and retrieval system in any form or by any means, whether electronic or mechanical, now known or hereinafter invented, without the express written permission of the copyright owner, except in the case of brief quotation embodied in critical articles and reviews. Thank you for respecting the hard work of this author.

This book is a work of fiction. The names, characters, places, and incidents are products of the writer's imagination or have been used fictitiously and are not to be construed as real. Any resemblance to persons, living or dead, actual events, locales, or organizations is entirely coincidental.

BOOKS IN THE HARDY HEROINES SERIES

Armenian and Arabic words of interest:

Albarun - baron
Ari – brave, spunky
Barev – hello
Destry - daughter
Ditel – (to) watch
Haryry – father
Hijab – head scarf
Im dustry – my daughter
Morak'uyr - aunt
Orhnut 'yunner – blessings
Sher, asad – lion
Singha – courageous lion
Thawb – loose, flowing robe
Asasiyun – a disciple of the Hashashin order
Hashashin – an order formed in the late 11th century primarily as a counter-movement to a political coup in the Seljuk Empire. They were practitioners of asymmetric warfare that negated most of their enemies' advantages, and specialized in covert operations.

Jan – (pronounced *j-ar-n* in Persian) A unique word which expresses love and tenderness toward the person addressed. It is used as a suffix only when referring to family or close friends.

Scottish and Gaelic words of interest:

Addis – flame
Amadan - fool
Beannachdan – blessings
Beannachdan air ar taighean – Blessings on our house
Dunfaileas – Reflection fort
Langa – fish
Leannan – sweetheart
Maon - hero
Slainte mhath – good health (a toast)
Slainte mhor – great health (reply to a toast)

THE HIGHLANDER'S CRUSADER BRIDE

Born in the Holy Land only a few years after the Third Crusade, half-Armenian, half-Scot Arbela MacLean is a true daughter of the desert, beautiful and untamed. Trained to be a warrior to avoid her gentle mother's fate, Arbela has honed her skills with Turkish bow and arrow, sword, and throwing darts—and dreads the day her father choses a man for her to marry.

After more than thirty years in the Holy Land, Donal MacLean, Baron of Batroun, is recalled to Scotland, the last son available to take up leadership of clan MacLean. He brings with him knights, treasure, trade—and a daughter of marriageable age.

Caelen MacKern, known as the Bull of the Highlands, is cynical about women. His first marriage formed an alliance, and he did not grieve when his spoiled, immature bride passed away. He has agreed to marry again—against his better judgement—for the men, means, and coin to recover from a devastating pestilence that all but wiped out his clan.

More than a little resentful at finding himself forced to remarry, Caelen's proposal to Donal MacLean's headstrong daughter nevertheless piques her interest. Each will receive what they want most from life—the ability to live as they please without interference from a meddling spouse. But their marriage of indifference will soon change to one of passion that neither Arbela nor Caelen could have predicted.

Chapter One

The Holy Land
County of Tripoli
Late fall, 1221 A.D.

The pungent smell of burning pitch and the screech of steel on steel dominated the afternoon. Crouched behind a merlon, Arbela MacLean took aim at the siege tower inching toward the castle and launched another flaming arrow toward the lumbering wooden target. Consumption by fire endangered the poorly constructed battlement. The men pushing it crowded behind shields to avoid arrows, stalling their advance.

The group manning a battering ram at the gates fared no better. Screams pierced the sounds of battle as a cauldron of heated sand tipped, pouring its burning contents through a chute built into the barbican, showering the men below. While enemy shields deflected much of the sand, Arbela knew it didn't take many grains to slip into clothing, searing skin as if on fire.

"Remember Jerusalem!"

Her father's men repeated the oft-heard battle cry from atop the wall. Ever since Saladin had retaken Jerusalem and slaughtered all the inhabitants, this had become the call to arms of all Latins in the Levant.

"Arbela!" her brother Alexander shouted, drawing her attention from the gates.

He and Phillipe de Poitiers fought several Turkish warriors who had scaled the curtain wall, a ladder propped against the top. Arbela pulled four arrows and placed them in her right hand for rapid firing. Drawing her bow, she hit the enemy atop the ladder under the arm as he reached for the wall, sending him tumbling backward, disrupting his follower's ascent. She fired the next three arrows in rapid succession, striking an equal number of warriors, her movements fluid and deadly. Alex and Phillipe finished off the remaining invaders who had achieved the wall's summit.

Alex offered her a brief salute of thanks, then used his war hammer to shatter the top rungs of the ladder. He, Phillipe, and two other men pushed the ladder along the wall until it fell, its occupants plunging to the rocky ground below. As Arbela fitted another arrow and sought a target, the Turks abandoned their tower, fire consuming it as they fled. She turned to the gates and struck down the few remaining fighters. Their tenacity was to be lauded—their tactics, however, were not.

In the distance, the remnant of the invading army withdrew over the hills, likely headed from whence they came. After four days of attempting to breach the gates and walls, it appeared they'd given up the fight. This marked the third such attack they'd endured this year, each more desperate than the last. The Turks seemed to grow overconfident and more numerous as the months passed.

Alex removed his helm and coif, a triumphant grin beaming across his face. His black hair and deep brown eyes sparkled. As twins, he and Arbela shared the same coloring and similar features.

"I look forward to a hot meal and soft bed tonight, sister mine."

Phillipe strode toward them, sword in hand, enemy blood spattered on his tabard. "Aye, 'twill be a welcome change to a cold supper and keeping watch on the wall."

"I long to trade my haubergeon and gambeson for a long soak in a hot tub." Arbela pulled the short mail shirt and padded jacket, wet with sweat, away from her skin. She led the others down the stone stairs of the outer wall toward the keep. As soon as her feet touched the bailey, two dogs, one black, one sable, tackled her.

"Off! Ye two beasties! Leave off!"

Phillipe and Alex laughed as they left her rolling on the ground with the dogs and strode toward the hall.

"Toros, Garen, sit!"

The two dogs dropped their haunches in obedience, tongues lolling, anticipating her next command. Arbela rose and dusted herself off.

"Come." She snapped her fingers and each dog took up position beside her—Toros on the right, Garen on the left—nosing her hands. Each dog's shoulder reached slightly above her knees, their furry tails and bodies wriggling with delight. Thus flanked, Arbela made her way toward the chapel where she would pray for the dead and ask forgiveness for taking life. She prayed to never grow so callused that killing—even in self-defense—would become commonplace. After cleansing mind and soul, she rose to do the same for her body.

* * *

"You look lovely, my lady, considering you've spent the past several days fighting the cursed Turks. I prayed for your safety daily, and the Almighty saw you through the siege without so much as a scratch."

The older woman crossed herself then finished braiding Arbela's hair and affixed her hijab. Arbela, dressed in a flowing thawb—the one-piece garment commonly worn by both men and women—and loose salwar pants, sat patiently on a cushioned stool. Her clothes, constructed not of linen or cotton, were of embroidered silk, marking her as nobility.

"Thank ye, Aunt Zora. Ye are a treasure."

Arbela flashed a look of gratitude to her mother's elder sister. After Arbela and Alex's mother passed, Zora had offered to live with them and provide female guidance to Arbela. The thought brought a smile to Arbela's lips. She had spent most of her childhood chasing after her brother, the two of them making a goodly amount of mischief. Aunt Zora had the patience of a saint, though, at her age, Zora was more grandmother than aunt.

After finishing Arbela's ablutions, the two women descended the stairs, the noise from the hall expanding with each step. Supper in the great room carried a joyful mood as the residents of Batroun gathered to celebrate their victory. Donal MacLean, Baron of Batroun, had ordered a pair of fatted sheep cooked on a spit and a cask of his best wine to be served to all, as each played an important role in repelling the infidels.

Her father occupied the central chair at the high table with Alex seated on one side, and Farlan, his captain, on the other. Phillipe, the third son of Bohemond IV, Prince of Antioch, Count of Tripoli, and her sire's liege, sat next to her brother. He had fostered with them for years, growing up with Alex, the two of them inseparable. Truly, Arbela viewed him as a second brother, though not as close as her twin. He was a good man and a better knight.

Arbela sat at Farlan's side as her sire stood and raised his cup. The hall grew quiet in anticipation.

"To victory!"

"To victory!" the people roared.

"A MacLean!" Gordon, one of her father's knights toasted. The cheer was chanted thrice by everyone in the hall.

Her father drained his cup, then sat and turned to his captain as the crowd returned to their festivities, disquiet etched on his face. "The attacks grow bolder."

Farlan, who had accompanied Donal from Scotland years earlier and had as much experience as any in Saracen tactics, paused before answering. "We protect the pass of Saint Guillaume. Its worth is well known to both pilgrims and traders."

"Och, 'tis plain enough why we attract attention from the Turks. The question is, who is behind these assaults, and why do they keep coming?"

"Likely a nobleman wishes to make his reputation as a powerful caliph. By attacking holdings in the region, they may find a weakness and draw more followers with their success, no matter how small. Papal attention remains on Egypt and ridding the Iberian Peninsula of the Moors. This is widely known, so there is no expectation of another crusade on this soil in the coming year."

Donal scratched his whiskers, dark red now peppered with gray. "Aye, but with each attack, the castle's reputation of being impenetrable grows."

"Begging yer pardon, Laird, but no fortress is impenetrable."

The baron grinned widely. "Agreed. But the Romans knew what they were about when they laid the foundations for this keep. Sheer cliffs on all sides with a small approach from the east gives the advantage of spotting an enemy well in advance, with only one option for entrance. 'Tis mayhap a wee barony, but we have the most secure holding in the Levant. Only size limits how much food we can store over a long siege."

Arbela entered the conversation. "Who fancies himself the next Saladin?"

The older men turned their attention to her question, a frown marring her father's face.

"Mayhap the better question, daughter, is who among the Turkish leaders *doesnae* wish to emulate Saladin by driving out all Latins from the Holy Land?"

Firm in her da's confidence of her logic, Arbela met his gaze. "Aye, but all three attacks have been undertaken by the same leader."

Her sire's dour expression gave way to a knowing grin. "What makes ye say that, lassie?"

Arbela nodded at his challenge. "Each attack learned from the previous. The men we faced in the past few days did not make the same mistakes the others did, nor did they use the same tactics. The important question is, how will this leader maintain his ability to draw followers to his cause if he continues to be defeated? I would think this aspiring warlord will pick lower hanging fruit for his next attack. Mayhap a holding further inland."

Donal clapped Farlan on the back. "Now ye see why I need to find her a husband. When Prince Bohemond realizes her worth, he'll replace me with my daughter, here."

Arbela dropped her head to her hands and groaned aloud. "Marriage again? I do not wish to be married, Da."

"'Tis a woman's fate to marry and breed sons, Bela." Alex sat upright, arms folded, his smug expression telling the story they'd had this argument before. Arbela narrowed her eyes at him, wordlessly threatening retaliation. Phillipe remained quiet, taking neither side, though his lips twisted in a partial smile.

"And who would have guarded yer back today, dear brother?" Arbela quipped. "The Prince and Clan MacLean would be in mourning this eve had I not been ready with a bow to even the odds."

A knight in her father's service approached her da from behind, a missive in his hand, interrupting any further talk of marriage and women's duty. The baron broke the wax disc and opened the parchment.

"My sire's seal," Phillipe observed.

Donal nodded agreement as a frown replaced his previous mirth.

"What does the Prince say, Da?" Alex leaned close to get a glimpse of the message.

"It says we are to leave for Antioch on the morrow. Phillipe is to be wed and the Prince seeks my counsel on a matter of some importance, though what, he dinnae say." Donal lifted his head and called to another of his men. "Amhal!"

"Yes, *Albarun*?" Her da's dark-skinned castellan bowed briefly.

"Sir Phillipe, my family, and twenty knights are to depart for Antioch at first light. See to the preparations at once."

"As you wish, *Albarun*." With a turn, Amhal shouted orders in rapid Arabic, putting all servants within hearing into motion. Though an Arab, Amhal was Copt rather than Muslim, and had proven his worth a thousand times over, easing the way for her father to hire people to work the land and to establish local connections for trade. They now turned away people seeking work due to her father's reputation, as few Latin nobles treated their servants as well.

Donal's pronouncement muted the celebration as news of Phillipe's nuptials spread, and speculation about the Prince's summons began.

Arbela rose from the table. "Da, might I be excused?"

Her sire stood and waved for everyone to continue, then gestured for Arbela to follow him. He escorted Arbela to his solar on the second level. He indicated a chair and poured them both wine while she sat, arms crossed, preparing for the lecture certain to come.

"Arbela, ye know ye are as precious to me as my next breath. After yer ma was cut down by a Turkish sword, I swore I'd never allow ye to be helpless. I've encouraged ye to train alongside yer brother. Ye take to the training like a hawk to the wind. Ye've a keen mind for logic and tactics. However, 'tis time ye considered yer future, and 'tis not as one of yer da's men-at-arms. Yer brother and Phillipe both earned their spurs this year and will soon go their own ways. 'Tis time for ye to seek a husband."

Arbela twisted her archer's thumb ring and calmed her breathing as she attempted to push emotion aside and gather her thoughts. "Aye, Phillipe and Alex earned their spurs, and were I a son instead of a daughter, I would have earned them as well. I am better with a bow and dagger than either of them and have skills they know nothing of."

Donal shifted uncomfortably in his chair and ran his fingers through his thick silver-shot auburn hair. "But ye arenae a man, ye are a woman. No matter how much ye wish otherwise. Dinnae remind me of the Hashashin training ye received from yer ma's kin. Had I known yer uncle practiced the black fighting arts, I wouldnae have allowed ye to spend so much time with them."

"What need do I have of a husband, Da?" Arbela asked, attempting to distract her da from his speech against training she'd found fascinating. "What have I to offer a man? Do ye think a husband will allow me to fletch arrows? Lead the hunt? Sharpen his sword or mend his armor? I cannot embroider, nor can I weave." She knew she was running out of time before her sire lost his temper and ended the conversation.

14

He dismissed her arguments with a wave of his hand. "Ye have followed Amhal about since ye were a wee lass. He has taught ye all ye need to know to run yer own home. Ye love Farlan and Elspeth's children like they were yer own."

Arbela shook her head and opened her mouth to reply, but her father halted her with a lifted forefinger.

"I may have been a poor younger son of a Scottish laird when I took up the cross and followed King Richard, but I am now a baron of a small but important holding, serve a powerful lord, and have made a fortune twice over in trade. Ye have royal blood from yer ma's side, and a very large dowry to ensure ye are considered by every nobleman's son in the Levant."

The look in her father's eyes and the determination he wore marked her defeat. She would have to consider another strategy. "My dowry will ensure men will see only what they stand to gain, and ignore the woman." Melancholy filled her voice.

"Ye are approaching twenty summers, daughter. 'Tis past time for ye to marry. I will find ye a husband who willnae try and break yer spirit, but ye will obey me. I will seek the Prince's counsel on the matter and see ye married before the next year is out."

Arbela rose, made her curtsy, and quietly left her father in his solar. She padded down the hall to her chamber, Toros and Garen in her wake, her heart throbbing painfully. Marriage would mean she'd have to give up the life she loved and submit to a man who cared naught for her—only for the color of her father's coin. Briefly, she considered running away to her mother's people but knew they would allow her fewer choices than her sire had. Misery threatened to settle like a shroud. The journey to Antioch she'd greatly anticipated only an hour before, now loomed like a trip to the gallows.

Chapter Two

Loch Linnhe
Western Highlands of Scotland

Caelen MacKern glanced around the hall at the solemn remnant of his people. Little more than half his clan remained alive. The worst of the outbreak was over, but Clan MacKern had been devastated by what their healer called *mezils*. They'd spent the day burning bodies as winter made the rocky earth too hard to dig proper graves for all. As laird, he could not risk seeing more of his people sickened by this scourge from allowing the bodies to linger for burial, so they bid fare thee well to kin the old Viking way.

He nodded thanks to the serving lass whose sweating brow and flushed face suggested she was barely out of the sickbed. The smell of pottage wafting from the bowl she set before him was a welcome change from the stench of disease and death lingering in the castle. Caelen reflected on the faces now gone, many he'd known since childhood— either theirs or his own. Though the pestilence had affected everyone, it hit the eldest and youngest the worst. He pulled a long draught of ale to wash down the bitterness of loss before devouring his humble meal.

The door to the keep opened and closed with a *snick*. Spurs jangled on the flagstones. Caelen glanced up. "Rory. 'Tis good to have ye home. What news do ye bring from the MacLean?'

Caelen nodded to the serving lass to bring his captain a bowl and mug. Rory offered her a smile of appreciation for the food and drink. "Thank ye, lass."

He dropped into his seat. "The MacLean is dead." He allowed the words to settle before continuing.

Caelen scowled. "Dead? How?"

Rory took a bite then gestured at the near-empty hall with his spoon. "Same curst affliction that ravaged our people."

"Damn. We dinnae need our agreement with MacLean to get pushed aside whilst they sort out a new laird. Any talk about who 'twill be?"

"I spoke with their elders. Two on the council died from the illness, and another recovers slowly. They sent word to the Prince of Antioch inquiring of Donal MacLean."

Caelen absorbed this news, trying to remember the man behind the name. "A younger son who took up the cross, aye?"

Rory nodded. "They say he attached himself to Antioch after Richard returned to England and has served him ever since. They have nae idea if he lives, and if he does, if he be willing to return and lead his clan. The elders say he is next in line and the last of his da's blood. If not him, things get a wee bit murky, and mayhap bloody."

Caelen frowned as he considered Donal MacLean. Caelen would have been merely a gleam in his da's eye at the time Donal went on crusade. He had no personal recollection of him.

"After more than thirty years living amongst Franks and Saracens, is the man still a Scotsman?"

"Fair question, Caelen. Fair question. I dinnae think the MacLeans know the answer. Howbeit, they dinnae have a good alternative handy. The auld laird's first two sons cocked their toes up afore they did more than breed a daughter each. Both lassies married outside the clan. With so many sick or dying, I think the MacLeans are content to tend their own and wait to hear word from Outremer. If not Donal, many cousins with equal claim to the title will fight like dogs over table scraps. A Clan MacLean distracted by internal strife leaves us vulnerable."

"What answer did they give about aiding us against the MacGillonays?" Caelen braced himself for the answer.

Rory's lips tightened at the question. "They said if auld Keith

MacGillonay comes knocking on our gates with a host of men, they'll gladly uphold their side of the agreement."

Caelen rose and paced, opening and closing his fists in a mix of anger and despair. "Damn! Did ye tell them it has grown beyond thieving a few cattle and sheep?"

"Aye. I did. They say if MacGillonay declares open war on the Bull of the Highlands, they'll be at our backs, but they willnae stir over stolen livestock and a burned croft."

Caelen's neck and face heated and he clenched his jaw, ignoring the nickname settled on him for his headstrong nature. "That croft had a family still in it when they fired it."

"Och, dinnae ye think I told them this? It dinnae sway them. What will we do now?"

Caelen stopped his pacing and stared at the beamed ceiling above. "We will move our people on the northern outskirts into the keep for the winter and make certain we patrol our borders. Make the rounds random so we dinnae become easy to predict."

Rory shrugged. "Our patrols will have to be only two or three men. We've nae enough men to send more and keep enough here to repel an attack."

"'Twill have to do. Be certain to pair the younger lads with seasoned warriors."

"Having our people close is what spread this damned sickness, auld Maggie says."

"It has run its course. Better to take yer chance here than alone with a MacGillonay raiding party. There arenae crops to tend in winter, and their livestock can join the rest at the keep." Caelen slumped in his chair, fighting off despair.

"Ye willnae take it amiss if I leave my wee sister, Brinna, with her great-uncle rather than bring her to the castle?"

"She has, what, six summers?"

"Nearly eight. After our parents died, Coll was the best choice for her. She loves the mountains and the sheep. I believe she is safe there."

"'Tis yer decision," Caelen grunted, his thoughts straying far from one wee lass to the larger concerns of the clan.

Rory slurped another spoon of porridge. "I hear wee Bram is feeling better, aye?"

Caelen smiled at the mention of his son. "Aye. The wee imp will be back to terrorizing the keep within a day or two. He had nae trouble telling his nurse he dinnae wish broth for supper and wouldnae stay abed."

Rory ducked his head and drank deeply of the watered ale, avoiding Caelen's gaze. Caelen tilted his head.

"Spit it out. I know ye've something in yer craw."

Rory offered a grim expression, warning Caelen whatever his friend had to say, he wasn't going to like.

"I dinnae wish to offend, Laird."

Caelen drew his brows inward and shook his head. "Ye call me laird? Rory, ye and I are foster brothers. Whatever is on yer mind, say it."

Rory took a deep breath. "Have ye considered marriage as a way to strengthen our clan and mayhap gain new allies?"

Caelen crossed his arms and stiffened in his chair. He should have expected such a statement. However, Rory knew how he felt about marriage—and why. After Bram's mother died, he swore he'd have nothing more to do with marriage. 'Twas worse than a prison sentence. At least a dungeon was honest about what to expect.

Caelen's hand struck the table, startling everyone in the hall. "Nae! I willnae submit to that piece of purgatory again."

"Laird, ye know not all women are like Ruthie."

Caelen glared at Rory. "I dinnae wish to hear that woman's name again."

"Aye, Laird. But consider yer own mother. She was a sweet woman with a kind heart and plenty of courage."

"My da was a lucky bastard, though they fought often enough. If I make a new alliance through marriage, I will have no say in the woman's character, but must take what is offered. Why would a clan give away a good woman when they can rid themselves of a viper? Such women promise one thing at the chapel then deliver something else entirely once the vows are made and cannae be broken."

"Caelen, ye are my laird and my friend. I will do whatever ye command. But as yer friend, I have to say MacGillonay's daughter clouded yer thinking and turned ye bitter toward women."

Caelen grabbed the pitcher and refilled both their mugs. "'Tis where ye err, my brother. I am not bitter against women, only the curse of marriage."

"Yer arrangement with Euan's widow isnae what I speak of and ye know it."

Caelen drained his mug and rose from the table. He had duties to attend and their conversation had done nothing to alleviate his dark mood.

"Be that as it may, 'tis the only relationship with a woman I am willing to have."

Chapter Three

City of Antioch, The Holy Land

Arbela surveyed the high walls surrounding the beautiful citadel, home of the Prince of Antioch, Bohemond IV, with its ornate towers, arches, and fountains. As the only woman in the group, she was given a private chamber, a waiting bath and a serving girl to assist her. Zora had remained at Batroun as she had no desire to make the five-day journey north, even if it meant coming close to her ancestral country of Armenia. After refreshing herself from their travel, Arbela left to join her family.

The Byzantine influence was readily apparent in the architecture and artwork, plaster and brickwork replacing worn stone, and mosaics adding brilliant color and design. The palace made her home look penurious by comparison. She spotted Phillipe on one of the many balconies overlooking the city. His back rigid, hands gripping the carved railing, he stared into the distance.

"Phillipe! What has happened?" she cried in alarm.

He turned at her question, his face hardened with strong emotion. "It appears ye are not the only person who must wed where ye do not wish."

He turned and resumed staring at the vista provided by the citadel's vantage point. Arbela touched his arm in sympathy.

"Whatever do ye mean, Phillipe?"

His glance fell on her hand, his features softening. "It seems Armenia wishes to restore relations with my sire after laying siege to Antioch whilst father was away quelling a rebellion in Tripoli."

"The battle in Tripoli where yer da lost his eye?" Arbela asked.

Phillipe grimaced. "Aye. 'Twas bad enough to return gravely injured, but to learn the King of Armenia had taken advantage of his absence and attacked whilst his back was turned made my father's anger burn hot, indeed. Now that the Seljuks are at their door, Armenia wishes to make amends."

"And offers what?"

"Marriage to Zabel, Queen of Armenia, King Leon's daughter. I am to be crowned king through marriage."

"But, Phillipe! Ye are yer father's third son. Is this not a loftier position than could be expected?"

"Did ye not hear me, Arbela?" he exclaimed, his eyes dark with anger. "I am to be king of the cowardly Armenians. The daughter of the man who attempted to stab my sire in the back is to be my wife."

She bristled. "Ye know as well as any, a daughter has no say in her father's decisions. I am half Armenian and am no coward. Do ye not see? This could be a chance to create greater unity in the north."

Phillipe's harsh chuckle spoke of irony rather than humor. "No, Bela, ye have nary a cowardly bone. In truth, ye have more courage than any I know. What other woman would take the abuse Alex and I delivered as boys and keep challenging us? Ah, but I have yet to tell ye the best part. In addition to ruling these people, I must turn my back on the teachings of the Church in Rome and embrace the Armenian way. It stands alone outside of Rome and Constantinople. How can I lead a people I despise and follow a religious path I do not believe in?"

Arbela embraced Phillipe, her heart breaking with pain at his confession. "I know ye, Phillipe. Ye are the best of men. Ye will find a way to make this work for the peace and strength it brings our people. The Turks continue to take more territory. With Antioch and Armenia united, the Saracens shall think twice before invading either. I know this is not the future ye had hoped for, but 'tis a significant task yer father puts before ye. He would not do so if he did not believe ye able. Ye are capable of great things, but ye must put this hatred behind ye and embrace yer new mantle. The fate of many will soon rest in yer hands."

Phillipe bent and kissed her full on the lips. The unexpected move stole her wits and her breath.

"But 'tis ye I love," he whispered.

All thoughts fled at his confession and kiss. Her mind blanked, her legs shook, and she feared collapse if Phillipe's hands did not rest on her upper arms, providing support.

"I sought your father's permission to court ye last year, but he bade me wait until we heard from my sire. The Prince's response was noncommittal. Now I know why. He anticipated a political alliance even with a third son. I had hoped to marry where I wished. Now I know what I dreamed of shall never be."

Arbela's heart thundered in her chest. Phillipe's thumbs stroked lightly over her arms.

"Now ye will marry another, and I must set my feet on the path the Prince dictates." His use of his sire's title held no affection.

His hands rose to her shoulders, and he eased from their embrace. His resigned smile lit a slow burn of emotion Arbela didn't recognize.

His manner became formal, distant. "Thank ye for your kind and wise words of support. I shall dearly miss ye. Prepare yourself, Arbela, as I fear your life will soon change as drastically as mine has."

Still stunned by Phillipe's declaration, near panic grabbed her throat. Surely her sire had not contracted her marriage without consulting her first. Phillipe shook his head at her wild look.

"I have not much to tell. My sire only says a missive has arrived for your father. It seems the baron is faced with a decision about your family's future."

He grimaced at her expression of dismay. "Go. My sire and yours have requested your presence. I shall see you later."

Arbela resumed her passage through the halls, seeking her father and brother. A man she recognized as the prince's castellan approached and bowed.

"My lady, the Prince requests ye attend him in his private chambers. Your sire and brother are already present and await your arrival."

Arbela nodded, hiding her fearful anticipation with a tilt of her chin. "Please lead the way."

He bowed again and motioned her to follow. They wove their way through the lavish palace, passing several guards before arriving at an ornately carved set of doors. The castellan pushed open the panels and bid her enter. Arbela stepped into an opulent room filled with artwork, beautiful tapestries and rugs that begged her leave her shoes at the door and tread barefoot upon them.

"My son does not exaggerate your daughter's beauty, MacLean."

Arbela's attention turned to the tall man wearing a patch over his missing eye, though the patch did not cover his terrible scar. This was the Prince of Antioch, the Count of Tripoli, the man people referred to as *le Cyclope* due to his disfigurement. She offered him a deep curtsy.

"Rise," he commanded. "Rise and dine with us. Your sire has some news he wishes to share with ye."

Arbela rose gracefully. "Thank ye, my lord."

She took a seat in the heavily carved chair next to her father and Alex. Though he smiled indulgently, her father's mien suggested his thoughts were miles away.

"What is it, Da?" she asked, her voice low.

Her words seemed to draw him back into the room, his expression one of deep contemplation. "It seems I am to be the MacLean chief if I wish to return to Scotland. Both my brothers have passed and the lairdship has fallen to this auld man." He gestured vaguely at himself.

Though she hadn't known what news to expect, this revelation certainly wasn't something she'd considered. The County of Tripoli was their home. "What about Batroun?" she asked.

The Prince responded. "If your father decides to accept, we would agree upon a seneschal to oversee the holding and protect the road, but the

24

title remains with your father. We have discussed Alexander staying behind to take control once he reaches his majority."

"I told Father I prefer to accompany him to Scotland, but will serve the Prince if requested." Alex nodded to their father and bowed to the Prince, telling her they'd already discussed this and come to an agreement.

Bohemond smiled at this diplomatic response and turned his intense gaze to her. "Your father has requested I assume your guardianship. Ye would live here in Antioch until a suitable marriage can be arranged."

Arbela's heart plummeted yet again at the mention of marriage, and the same fear that gripped her on the balcony returned with a vengeance. The thought of being separated from her father and her twin was too much to bear.

She dipped her head to the Prince, her gaze on the floor. "'Tis quite generous, my lord, but I wish to remain with my sire and brother." Her gaze rose until it met the one eye of the Prince and held it, willing him to cede to her wishes.

His face broke into a grin, and he handed over a coin to her da. "Ye were right, MacLean. Most young noblewomen would leap at the chance to have my sponsorship and pick from among our best young noblemen. But ye know your daughter well."

Donal winked at her and tucked the coin into his belt then turned to his liege. "Then it is settled, my lord? We return to Batroun with fifty knights to replace the ones who will travel with me to Scotland, and my sister by marriage, should she wish to travel with us. I will install Giordy as seneschal."

"That is acceptable, MacLean. If Zora wishes to remain, she will have my protection." The prince grimaced. "Though I do not have to tell ye, I dislike the idea of not having ye at my southern flank when the Turks finally decide to rid themselves entirely of Latins."

Donal grinned. "Och, ye've gotten the best fighting years I've to offer. I'm more of a burden now that I'm entering my dotage. As agreed, I will recruit lads to yer cause once we arrive in Scotland. My ship will carry them back, along with what trade goods we can gather."

"Ship? Ye have a ship, Father?" Arbela's brows rose at this bit of news.

"Aye. A new design of Venetian construction. Ye will get to know her well, as we will spend the rest of this year and part of the new aboard her."

Arbela inhaled deeply, filling her lungs with the rich scents of myrrh and jasmine incense. A dull throb shot through her neck and shoulders as she released all the fear and worry she'd carried the past five days. However, she knew her sire, and this news merely brought her a short reprieve. More than injury or death itself, she feared facing a lifetime under a husband's rule. She must find a way to maintain her freedom. If she failed to produce a plan, her father would eventually have his way.

Chapter Four

Four months later
Near Ayr, Western coast of Scotland

Wintery winds carried no promise of spring, though they were already three months into the new year. White mists hovered low over the sea, weakening the sun's rays, robbing its warmth. Arbela huddled within a heavy velvet cloak lined with luxuriously fine mohair, but the damp, cold air slipped its icy fingers through the fabric as surely as a dagger through diaphanous silk. Her brocade tunic over thickly-woven silk trousers hardly provided protection in this cold, damp climate.

"Does it ever warm in this godforsaken place?" she muttered. She gritted her teeth to keep them from chattering, looking forward to a fireplace and warm bath once they reached the king's residence at Ayr. She eyed her brother and father with disgust as they stood, feet braced apart to absorb the swell of the ship, cloaks thrown back over their shoulders, embracing the cold.

"We will be ashore soon," her da replied, noting the discomfort she struggled to hide. He surveyed the coastline. It appeared first as a dark stain against the fog, then the breeze parted the mists, revealing the shore. He inhaled deeply, shoving his chest outward. "'Tis a fine Scottish morn!"

"Refreshing," Alex agreed. "Though I keep waiting for the day to heat, and it ceased doing that some time back."

"It isn't home," Arbela murmured sadly, adjusting her hijab to cover her ice-cold nose.

"'Tis yer home now, lass," Donal said. Arbela frowned at the sympathy in his eyes "A right proper woolen plaide to keep out the wind and ye'll be right as rain."

"Do not mention rain, Da," she moaned. "'Tis all this sky offers. Cold and rain. In more abundance than I've seen in my entire life."

"Keeps the land green," he replied cheerfully.

"I think ye would look grand in the checkered wool I've seen the ladies wear," Alex teased. Arbela lunged at him, striking a glancing blow to his shoulder.

"Plaide!" their sire roared.

"I do not see ye changing your attire, brother," Arbela groused. He wore full trousers of linen, and an overtunic of dark red velvet, embroidered in gold at the neck. His cloak was made of a heavier version of mohair than her own. He looked dashing and youthful and vibrant—and totally at ease with his new environment.

A grin split his face. "The ladies like my clothing just fine."

Arbela sighed. 'Twas plain to see he and their da relished the trip to their new home. And if she did not wish to be sent back to Prince Bohemond's care and choice of a husband, she would learn to live in the cold, damp reaches of this wretched place called Scotland.

* * *

The fire roared, but its warmth dissipated only a few strides away from the hearth. Arbela had the serving girls place her tub within this space, and steam from the water rose to mingle with tendrils of smoke that escaped a poorly drawing chimney.

She was careful to keep her thoughts to herself, but her first days in Scotland were not pleasant. The other women dressed differently, their skin a pale contrast to her own dusky complexion, enhanced by the kohl she used to rim her eyes. The close-fitting sleeves of their linen-lined woolen gowns covered their arms into points down the backs of their hands, while Arbela's full-sleeved cloak fell away reveal the intricate henna designs Zora had painstakingly applied to her hands—a decoration the court women had viewed much as if she had leprosy. She was rarely warm, and the food lacked the spices she enjoyed.

Arbela leaned her head on a thickly folded towel she'd placed on the narrow rim of the tub. Her dressing gown hung from a peg near the hearth to warm, the silk threads of the heavy brocade shimmering in the firelight. This was their last night at King Alexander's castle in Ayr, and she knew well enough the evening would be raucous and long, with feasting continuing into the night. With a sigh, she rose and began drying herself, henflesh prickling on her backside as she faced the hearth. Toros and Garen entered on the heels of the maid assigned to her during her stay. Garen stepped forward for Arbela's pat.

"Ye are a good girl—oh!" Arbela jumped as Toros's cold nose touched her bare backside. "Naughty boy!" she complained. "Your nose is colder now, and no more appreciated than it was when the air was hot and dry."

The maid hurried across the room and helped Arbela into her robe. Warmth from the heated fabric enveloped her, and she breathed a blissful sigh.

"Which shall ye wear, Arbela?" Zora asked, glancing pointedly at the garments laid out on the bed. Arbela padded across the tapestry she'd pulled from the wall two days earlier and spread on the floor, hating the bare, cold wooden boards under her feet. One more thing for the courtiers to gossip about when she was gone—if they didn't already.

She halted beside the bed, toes digging into the heavy fringe border of her invented carpet, as she perused at her choices. "Someone has offered her gown so I will feel less awkward?" she asked, eying the unfamiliar robe.

The dark rust velvet tunic was lined with fur, its linen kirtle a soft cream devoid of embellishment. Compared to Arbela's court dress, it rested on the coverlet like a sparrow next to a peacock.

"Did my da or brother suggest this?"

Zora shook her head. "No."

Arbela considered the only other person whose opinion she would entertain. Twelve-year-old Joan of England, bride of King Alexander of Scotland, had clapped with delight when introduced to Arbela and her finery the day before. Dizzying hours later the queen had at last tired of peppering Arbela with questions about the Levant, thrilled to hear Arbela's tales. 'Twas unlikely the queen had invited a change of clothing.

"I will dress as befits the daughter of the Baron of Batroun," she declared quietly. The serving girl leapt to sudden usefulness, clearing the proffered gown from the bed, setting a large candelabrum close to the table where Zora would help her dress.

Arbela fingered the heavy silk garment, finding fault with the intricately woven blue and cream pants and tunic. "I wish to wear the red."

"But, Arbela, 'tis for your wedding!" Zora objected, shocked.

"I doubt any here will attend my wedding. And I do not intend to leave this court without making an impression. If they wish to turn up their noses at my attire, let them do so with envy. I weary of disapproval."

With a slight incline of her head, Zora whisked away the blue salwar and thawb and produced the requested garment, brushing her hand lovingly over the heavy embroidery sparkling with tiny gold discs and precious stones.

Zora helped her into the salwar, the heavy silk brocade trousers cool against her legs. The yards of fabric fell gracefully, caught at her ankles in embroidered cuffs.

The tunic stopped mid-calf to reveal the lower portion of the trousers, its silk shimmering in the candlelight. The cloth was weighty with embellishments, the modestly sweeping neckline a' twinkle with gold thread and pink and green stones surrounding large, perfect pearls like petals of magnificent flowers. At Arbela's nod, Zora placed a priceless choker of pink sapphires, diamonds and pearls about her neck. Zora reached inside a chest for the matching veil, but Arbela stayed her hand.

"I will save that for my wedding." Meeting Zora's gaze, she indicated

30

a deep pink hijab. "That will do. 'Tis too cold for a thin veil."

Zora wrapped the silk about Arbela's head and neck, nestling it beneath her chin in a narrow swath, the better to show off the incredible necklace. Pink and white stones dripped from the choker in tiers on either side of a single, spectacular pink sapphire that touched the tops of her breasts. A wide band of stiffened, embroidered fabric with a fringe of small gold beads fell across her forehead. Zora bent close, applying a smudge of kohl around her eyes.

She held up a small, framed piece of mirrored metal. "Does this please ye?"

"Yes." Arbela's short reply earned her a hard look from her aunt. "I am very pleased," she amended. "And I do not believe I shall put the house of Batroun to shame."

* * *

Late the following day, off the coast of the Isle of Mull

"Sails ahoy!"

Arbela raised a hand over her eyes and gazed upward at the man in the top castle. His arm stretched toward the south and west where two single sail vessels approached. Making her way to the weapons rack, Arbela collected her bow and climbed the ladder to the aft castle where her da and the captain of the *Falcone di Mare* stood.

"What is it, Da?" Garbed in a warmer version of her normal fighting garb, Arbela again shielded her eyes to better see the approaching ships.

"Likely birlinns. 'Tis similar to the pirate galleys we saw near Gibraltar. They are a long boat, low to the water with a single large square sail. Twelve to sixteen oars."

She peered across the water. "Pirates again?"

"Aye. Without a doubt. Probably laid in wait in a cove off Mull for a lumbering merchant cog to come by. Easy pickings for men who are willing to work the oars. They've yet to meet a ship like our wee *Sea Falcon*. We shall teach them the same lesson the Moorish pirates learned."

Her father smiled like a child full of mischief. They both knew what Captain Benicio and his ship could do. They were well prepared.

"Alex! Kade! Man the ballistae."

Alex and Kade unlocked the machines, allowing them to be tilted and fired. Two giant crossbows mounted on stands to the aft castle deck hurled five-foot-long bolts with either iron heads, stones, or iron balls. The creak of the windlasses turning, drawing the oversized bows back, cut through all other sounds on deck. A third ballista awaited on the fore castle. They sailed prepared.

"My lady?"

Arbela leaned over the rail amidships. Shaw, her father's squire, had attached a bucket of fire arrows she'd made to a rope hanging from the railing. She smiled at him and pulled the bucket up. One of the crew lit a small brazier for archers to light the arrows when the time came.

Ten of her father's knights joined her along the aft rail, bows at the ready once the ships drew near. Arbela glanced at the aft mast, the triangular lateen sail taut and pushed out to starboard. This new design, coupled with the massive square mainsail, allowed the Venetian ship to sail into the wind, a feat most ships were unable to accomplish. The wind blew mostly from a westerly direction. Since the birlinns approached from Mull, the wind was directly at their backs, allowing the smaller, faster ships to gain on them at a frightening pace.

"Steady now, lads. The only difference between these sea rats and the ones we sank in the Mediterranean is the color of their skin. Make no mistake, they have chosen the wrong ship to approach. We shall send them to a watery grave and let them explain their choice of vocation to their Creator."

Several faces broke into smiles. 'Twas something her father did well, boosting his men's confidence and easing the tension before the coming storm of battle. Gordon, her father's largest knight, drew his great bow and nocked an arrow. Aiming high, he released the bolt toward the approaching ships. It landed a few boat lengths in front of the birlinn's prow. Archers drew fire arrows and prepared to light them.

"Release the first volley, Alex."

Alex triggered his ballista at his father's calm order, sending the rounded stone flying through the air. The splash a few feet from the lead boat meant battle was close at hand. The windlass creaked as Alex reloaded his weapon, the sound twisting the anticipation as surely as it did the sturdy rope. The wind was to their advantage. Though the smaller boats traveled faster, their hands must continue to row while the MacLean crew could fire at will.

"Fire!" Donal MacLean roared over the thundering flap of wind in the sails. Alex's next shot landed on the deck of the lead ship amid screams of injured men and those who were at once shocked and furious at the seaborne ambuscade racing toward them. Kade's shot immediately followed, the creak and crash of splintering wood ringing across the water.

The first volley of fire arrows, aimed at the sails and rigging, met with partial success. Half landed harmlessly in the water, trailing wisps of steam to mark their fate. Arbela refrained from firing as the distance was yet too great for her. Though she could not fire a bolt as far as the men beside her, she was as accurate as any in her da's company.

Each arrow bore a small wrap of linen soaked with a combination of saltpetre, sulphur, and charcoal just below the broadhead. The resulting mixture was highly flammable and would continue to burn for more than a minute after being lit.

"A MacLean!"

The cry rose from the *Sea Falcon* as three arrows struck the massive square sail of the lead pirate ship and two others struck the men still rowing. The stricken ship took on water and dropped behind the larger, half its crew in chaos. Arbela released her first arrow at the second ship, hitting the sail. Alex's next volley ensured the first ship would never make it to shore, its hull breached at the water line. Men dashed about the deck, attempting to lower their sail before it was consumed by flames. Kade's next shot splashed wide of the larger vessel. Both men readied their weapons for another round.

The second ship, recognizing the fate of its companion, slowed pursuit and concentrated on lowering its sail, now aflame, into the sea. Another volley of arrows from the *Sea Falcon*, and many of the crew abandoned ship to avoid the deadly onslaught. The last round from both ballistae landed, shearing off most of the aft portion of the smaller ship, ruining their rudder, causing the vessel to flounder.

Arbela assessed the distance to Mull and realized they would likely drown in the frigid water before making shore.

"Will they all die, Da?"

Her father placed an arm about her waist. "Aye. I dinnae see how any will make land. 'Tis the price ye pay for a life of treachery and murder. Make no mistake, my kind-hearted lass, the pirates would have killed us all, save the women and children—though they would wish for death before it eventually came."

She nodded once before slinging her bow over her shoulder and descending the ladder amidships, seeking a quiet place to pray for the dead . . . and the soon-to-be-dead.

* * *

The wind freshened, cold and damp on her face as they, at last, slid through the Sound of Mull to the strait that led to Loch Aline—and Arbela's new home. Long shadows darkened the shores on both sides, raising the hairs on the back of Arbela's neck as she searched for attackers hidden in the trees.

"Relax, lass," her da chuckled, approaching to stand with her on the fore castle. We are on MacLean land. We shouldnae come to harm here.

We've MacLeans on both sides of the Sound."

"'Tis as likely the cold as it is suspicion prickling my neck," Arbela grumbled. "But the strait is narrow and we've encountered too many pirates to become complacent."

"Cease worrying yer pretty head," Donal said, his condescending tone taking Arbela aback as if he'd struck her.

"I do not recall your minding what my *pretty head* worried about when we repelled the pirates only hours ago," she replied, shock and anger coloring her brittle words.

"Och. Dinnae fash, lass. Yer days playing at being a warrior are over. 'Tis time ye settled into gentler arts."

"Gentler arts?" she seethed. "Trade my sword for a needle so I might prick the finger of any attacker—as Ma would have done?"

Donal's face clouded. "Ye are capable of defending yerself. As soon as I see to the affairs of the clan, I will see to yer husband. Dinnae mistake my leniency as permission."

He averted his face, his gaze on the approaching shore where a looming pile of stones lit with torches atop the single wall around the tower house awaited. Arbela choked back her frustration, the path before her growing narrower by the moment.

Chapter Five

Caelen slammed his mug on the scarred table, sending ale sloshing over the sides.

"Damn him!" He tossed aside the missive he'd just read. It snapped once in the air then fluttered to the table boards, a corner soaking up the spilled ale. Rory rescued the parchment from further damage, blotting it before rolling it and re-tying the strip of leather that held it closed.

Rory hazarded a guess. "MacGillonay makes demands?"

Caelen slung a look of rage at his captain. "He insists on his rights as Bram's grandfather."

Rory's eyebrows lifted. "No good can come of this."

"If that bastard gets his hands on my son, I will never see him again."

"Can he force the issue?"

"He could try force, mayhap petition the king. But I will never turn my son over to him."

"How do ye propose to keep the lad away from him?"

Caelen surged to his feet, anger gripping him, his father by marriage's words from the missive hovering before his eyes like a thrown gauntlet. Pacing the floor, he pounded out his fury on the flagstones.

"The bastard cared naught when we were under threat of *mezils*, but now that we are struggling to get back on our feet, he sends condolences. Does he offer foodstuffs or sheep?" He swung to face Rory.

"Nae! He offers to take one wee lad off my hands." His right hand gripped the pommel of his sword. "I will rot in hell before I allow Bram to fall into MacGillonay's hands!"

Rory nodded. "I dinnae blame ye, Laird. If his sons are any judge of the man, he raises sycophants, nae warriors."

"Something I should have remembered before I married his

daughter," Caelen growled, resuming his pacing.

"Bram is a good lad," Rory interjected.

Caelen inhaled a deep breath, releasing the anger building inside. His step slowed. "Aye." A faint grin tugged the corner of his mouth. He released his grip on his sword. "I am grateful the sickness dinnae take him."

"How fares his nurse?"

"She will recover. Though at her age, 'twas close. One of the serving lasses minds him until Ilene recovers."

A giggle erupted behind Caelen and he whirled to peer in the shadows behind a wooden pillar. He shifted his gaze to a bit below hip level and spied a single brown eye in a pale face, and a familiar nose—the other eye hidden behind the post.

"I see ye, lad," Caelen announced gruffly. "Where is yer nurse?"

Bram glanced over his shoulder. "I dinnae need a nurse, Da. I want to practice swords with ye."

"Ye are but a bairn," Caelen replied.

"He's five summers," Rory reminded him in a low voice.

"Da!" Bram whined over Rory's comment, slithering sideways around the post.

Caelen clenched his jaw. He knew Rory and Bram were right. The lad was old enough to learn the basics with a wooden sword. But his heart bid him wait another year. He glanced away, torn with indecision.

"Can I have a pony, then?" Bram asked, popping out from behind the pillar, breathless as though he sensed a different answer than he'd been given for the past season.

"I will see about a pony when I have time," Caelen said, hardly agreeing, but earning a look of profound disappointment from his son. His heart twisted at Bram's discouragement as the lad raised morose eyes to his.

"I will be 'specially good, Da. I promise. I will eat my veg-ables and not hide from Kirsty." He cast a worried glance over his shoulder as his nurse tacked across the hall, her small charge in her sights. "Even if she fusses more than Ilene."

"Ye are a good lad, Bram," Caelen assured him. "I will see about the pony soon." He glanced about, looking for Kirsty to resume the lad's care. "'Tis near yer bedtime."

Bram sent him a last pleading glance. "Will ye tell me a story?"

"Wee Bram!" Kirsty exclaimed as she sailed to a halt. "Ye are a naughty lad, stealing away and making me worry so." She bobbed her head to Caelen. "'Tis sorry I am, Laird, that the lad has bothered ye."

Caelen saw his son's stricken look and sought to reassure him. "The lad is nae bother. But I dinnae like that ye are fashed over him."

Guilt flooded Bram's face and his shoulders drooped. Without another word, he turned beneath Kirsty's guiding hand and shuffled from the hall.

"I dinnae know how to care for him," Caelen sighed.

Rory canted his head. "Carve the lad a wee sword. Find him a pony. Tell him a story. 'Tis nae difficult. The lad but craves a kind word from ye."

"I dinnae know how to be a da," Caelen replied bitterly, recalling his own forbidding father. "If I follow my da's lead, I will surely estrange the lad. Yet I dinnae wish to coddle him." The dilemma tore at him, leaving him uncertain, prodding him to take the easier route and leave the child in the care of his nurse.

"'Tis true yer da was no shining example of fatherhood," Rory agreed. "But yer ma was a kind woman."

"I only remember the bitter arguments between them on how to raise me."

Rory shrugged. "The lad is growing fast. Now that he is past the *mezils*—"

"Ye dinnae understand," Caelen interrupted. "He almost died. I

38

couldnae face such anguish again."

"So, rather than risk injury, ye protect him at all costs?"

"He is still a bairn," Caelen argued stubbornly.

Rory's challenge rose. "Then tell him a bedtime tale."

* * *

Bram's hair, damp from his bath, gleamed in the firelight. He held his arms in the air, waiting for Kirsty to drop his sleep tunic over his head. Spying Caelen, he leapt from his spot near the hearth and charged across the room.

Caelen caught his son's wiry body. "Have a care, lad," he admonished, instantly regretting the commanding tone of his voice as Bram's step faltered. He attempted to gentle his voice. "Let Kirsty finish dressing ye so ye dinnae catch a chill."

Bram reluctantly retreated to the hearth, casting repeated glances back as if to reassure himself his da remained.

Caelen caught Kirsty's eye. "I came to see to the lad's bedtime," he said. Bram jumped up and down, hindering Kirsty's attempts to dress him. "I have a few free moments this eve."

Despite his implied warning this was a one-time offering, Bram continued to surge up and down, managing to aim his arms and head through the proper openings. Kirsty tied a haphazard bow at the drawstring neck and threw her hands into the air.

"He's all yers, Laird. Though I wish ye luck getting him to sleep." She rose to her feet. "Were I a few years older, I'd never keep up with the lad. Ilene will have her hands full when she resumes her duties."

"Mayhap Ilene should be relieved of her burden," Caelen answered, glancing pointedly in Kirsty's direction. She sent him a look of alarm.

"I've enough work to do, thank ye just the same. Chasing after this lad will age me afore my time." She stepped to the doorway, giving Bram a meaningful look. "Be a good lad. Yer da has little time to deal with foolishness."

With an abbreviated bob, she took her leave.

Bram was silent for all of one long breath before he exploded in a flurry of movement. Eyes dancing with excitement, he grabbed Caelen's hand and dragged him across the room. "Tell me a story!" he demanded as he leapt onto his small bed. The mattress sagged beneath the onslaught and Bram shrieked as he bounced.

"Settle," Caelen commanded, his bark dissolving Bram's glee. The lad scrambled beneath the blankets.

"Will ye tell me a story?" he wheedled softly.

Caelen frowned. "I've told ye a tale before."

"I like the story of St. George," Bram replied. "Do ye know another?"

Caelen thought hard. In the years of Bram's short life, he'd told him a bedtime story perhaps a dozen times. It was always St. George and the dragon—the only one he knew.

"Nae. I dinnae know another," he admitted.

"I dinnae mind," Bram avowed. "I want to hear about the dragon!"

Buoyed by his son's eager acceptance, Caelen settled onto the chair next to the bed and began the tale.

"St. George traveled many months 'til he reached a far-off country. He encountered a hermit who told him the sad tale of a dragon who lived nearby, poisoning the water if he dinnae receive tribute from the people."

"What's a tribute, Da?"

"I've told ye. A tribute is a payment for a debt."

"What debt?"

"The dragon accepted payment and in return dinnae poison the water," Caelen replied. Bram frowned but didn't pursue his question.

Caelen resumed the tale. "Every day the people sent a beautiful maiden to the dragon. Only the king's daughter remained, and the king was very dismayed."

"'Cause the dragon was going to eat her?" Bram's question hovered between relishing the power of dragons and the sinister plot of eating people.

"Aye. But St. George dinnae like this, and vowed to slay the dragon. He rode to the lake where the dragon lived and saw the princess waiting beneath a tree."

"Did she look like a faerie princess, Da?"

"Who tells ye tales of faerie princesses?"

Bram shrugged.

Caelen resolved to give his story a more manly bent. "The dragon burst from its cave, roaring louder than thunder. Its head was larger than St. George's horse, and its tail was longer than the stride of five horses."

Bram's eyes widened appreciatively.

"Its scales were harder than stone, and St. George's spear splintered when he struck the dragon. Leaping from his horse, he rushed the dragon and pierced it with his sword beneath its wing where there were no scales, and the beast fell dead at his feet."

Bram stared at his da. "He was a good fighter, wasn't he? Will I be a good fighter someday, Da?"

Caelen considered the lad. He was only a bairn. Caelen knew other lads his age already fought mock battles with wooden swords. But he could not bring himself to admit the lad was growing up. Was it because he wished him to remain young and innocent? Or because he had little time for a lad at his heels?

Shamed by the realization he had no idea how to deal with the lad and his unending curiosity, he rose abruptly, angry at his lack of skills where his son was concerned.

"Ye will be a fine warrior," he replied gruffly. "Get to sleep." He strode to the door, then paused. "Even mighty warriors need sleep."

But closing the door to his son's chamber did not close the door on his dilemma.

Caelen made his way to the hall and tucked a chair by the hearth. With so many still recovering from the illness that ravaged the land, he had the place to himself. The fire in the great hearth was banked for the night, though the coals offered enough heat to keep the spot cozy. Edgy, he considered seeing if Cook had left any food laying out for a wee snack, but realized 'twas not hunger that drove his restless spirit.

What the devil did a man do with a wee son? He'd been told to sire one, not how to raise him once he arrived. If the boy were a bit older, the problem would mostly solve itself by turning him over to Rory and the other men who trained the lads. At five, Bram was still a bairn, not ready for the rigorous tussling among older lads. And with the fiendish MacGillonay nipping at their heels, the urge to lock the boy away rose.

Caelen scrubbed his face. If nothing else, he should learn a new bedtime story. Perhaps auld James knew a few. As one of the few elders who'd survived the cursed *mezils*, he'd be a good choice to glean a story from. A man with as many grandbairns as he surely knew a good bedtime tale or two.

He drew a hand across his close-shorn head. With as much work needing to be done, finding time to listen to an auld man spin yarns seemed frivolous. Deep in thought, Caelen didn't notice Alesta until she placed a tankard of ale on the table at his elbow.

"M'laird, ye seem to be lost in thought this eve. Is there aught I can do to ease yer mind?"

Alesta slowly unlaced her bodice, revealing her ample breasts. The white mounds bulged over the top of her undergown as she squeezed them together, drawing his interest. Caelen felt the first stirrings of his manhood. At least something he could depend on. Alesta lifted her skirts, revealing her woman's flesh and his interest caught fire.

The low glimmer of the coals did nothing to enhance her fading beauty, but Caelen's dead wife had been a beautiful bride. Alesta's charm was the passion she possessed, something significantly more appealing than lovely Ruthie's ice-bound comportment.

"Ye understand this means naught?" The last thing he needed was a serving woman using her body to elevate her position in the clan.

"Aye, M'laird. I've no schemes. Ye look like a man who could use a hard rutting and I'm rather fond of what ye keep beneath yer tunic. Mayhap we will both sleep better after," she added with a sad smile.

Alesta's husband, cold in the ground nigh on three years, had been a lusty man—the two well paired. Caelen wondered why his dead wife couldn't have been more like Alesta.

He took Alesta's hand and allowed her to lead him toward her small cottage. Even in the lingering twilight, the desperate state of the holding with its sagging buildings and curtain wall in disrepair was evident, and his inability to set things to right burned in his gut. With little funds to pay for improvements and fewer men to do the work, Caelen didn't know how he could see to the restorations needed. He'd spent almost every waking moment cudgeling his brain for ways to fix the situation he was in—that they all were in.

For tonight, however, he'd lose himself in Alesta's body and let his troubles wait until the morrow.

Chapter Six

Arbela opened the shutters to the single narrow window in her room, allowing the stale, smoky air to escape. Fresh air whipped inside on the heels of a gust of wind and chill bumps leapt to immediate attention on her arms. She closed the panels with a decisive click. Pulling a heavy velvet tapestry over the window darkened the room, but blocked the damp, cold air of late March.

Crossing the room to the fireplace, she rubbed her arms, warming her chilled skin. Her feet sank into the plush comfort of a rug that spanned much of the width of the room. Candlelight reflected off a myriad of polished metal discs hung about the room to magnify their glow. Copper-colored circles of light and faint echoing shadows danced on the walls, and a curtain of strung glass beads tinkled as she pushed past.

"We've been here nearly a month and I believe I've seen the sun twice," she complained to Zora. Her aunt, swathed in a mohair-lined cloak of shimmering brocade, glanced up from her sewing. Her heavy layers of robes all but hid her petite frame, and the tip of her nose held a decidedly pink hue.

"'Tis our duty to follow where our men lead, niece. But I would not object if we returned to the Levant. I have yet to see anything to recommend this place."

Arbela nudged a chair closer to the hearth and sank into its cushioned comfort, absently rubbing Toros's ears as he left his spot by the hearth to beg attention. Garen yawned widely and settled back to sleep.

"I am not allowed to train with the men when rain falls." Arbela fingered her silk tunic, not liking the petulance sliding through her voice. "How was I to know the men would object to clothing I have always worn?"

44

"'Tis not yer clothing. 'Tis the way the fabric clings to your body when wet. You have a figure men lust after. The women here are tall and thin, and do not have the fullness of breast and hip ye possess."

"If I am so different, why should they care?" Arbela struggled to keep the peevish tone from her voice, but it frustrated her to watch her brother and the other knights train whilst she wasted hours needlessly indoors.

"I do not know. But the men eye ye—some with furtive glances, others more openly." Zora set her mending aside. "Ye are of an age where men do not wish to best ye on the field of battle, but in the privacy of the bedroom."

Arbela fluttered a hand in the air. "I care naught for that. I do not chafe beneath the strictures of my trousers, but beneath the unjust treatment of my father. I am as able as any man on the training field. I can outwit and out-shoot the best MacLean has to offer."

Zora shrugged delicately. "Be that as it may, ye should put aside yer bow and sword and turn your brilliant mind to housekeeping matters."

Arbela surged from her chair, outraged to find no sympathetic words from her aunt. Zora waved her back to her seat.

"This is my council, should ye care to heed it. 'Tis only a matter of time before your father chooses a husband for ye. Become comfortable with your new role before that time, for your new husband will not likely give ye time or opportunity to vent your spleen in his presence."

Arbela frowned and chewed her lower lip, not happy with the advice she knew was well meant—and true. "I am not like other women," she finally admitted. "I rejoice in children, but do not long for my own. I find court dress—in Antioch—beautiful and flattering. But I do not care to spend my days choosing which gown and jewels to wear. My pride is in a well-fletched arrow, and in a sword pass well executed."

Zora smiled. "And I will bear witness to your lack of personal awareness when I have seen ye in disarray and besmudged far more frequently than clean and with your hair properly combed and oiled."

Arbela surrendered to a smile at her aunt's teasing. "I am not adjusting well into Scotland, am I?"

Lifting sculpted eyebrows, her aunt tilted her head. "Did ye mean to?"

* * *

Supper was a grand affair for all its informality. Eager to impress the new laird, some women dressed in their finest gowns, with veils, fresh and white, held in place by fillets of stiffened cloth showing a bit of embroidery and other fine needlework. Other women chose their traditional dress, woolen and warm—and completely unlike the ladies Donal had come to know over the past thirty years. But they were a familiar part of by-gone days and the sight warmed his heart.

However, clan affairs heated his blood in a different manner, making the dinner of stewed venison and dried fruits bland and unappetizing. He stared at the men seated to his left, lairds accepting his hospitality, lingering to beg his favors. Crossing oceans hadn't changed that aspect of his title.

He leaned toward Alex. "Have ye seen yer sister?"

Alex glanced up, startled. "No. Not all day, actually."

Donal sat back in his chair, surveying the gathered crowd. "A fine pick of men—some unwed—and she chooses tonight to tarry in her chambers. Bah!"

He drained his mug and rose, motioning for the others to follow. Four men left their seats and accompanied him to his solar. Closing the door effectively silenced the merrymaking in the great hall. Donal strode to his desk, waving the others to chairs.

"Does any among ye have aught to say that cannae be voiced before the others?"

And so it began. Two hours later, there remained only Laird MacKern, a man with broad shoulders and a way of carrying his head slightly lowered, chin a bit forward, as though capable of plowing directly through any obstacle foolish enough to stand in his way. Donal had heard him called *Bull* by more than one man this evening, and he could imagine how he'd earned the nickname. Stubborn though the man might be, Donal noticed intelligence in his eyes, capable of thoughtful consideration of the petitions presented thus far. He'd answered abruptly yet creatively when asked his opinion on Laird MacHugh's dilemma, earning a chuckle and easing the tension in the room.

There was much to be done to alleviate difficulties in the region, hostilities building in the long months since Donal's elder brother had passed away, but for the first time since they'd arrived at MacLean Castle, Donal could say he'd made significant headway. Now, only Caelen MacKern remained. One by one, the other lairds had taken their leave, their problems solved or at least recognized and shelved for later discussion. The hour grew late, but Donal did not wish to ask MacKern to come back another day. Something about the man intrigued him.

He motioned him closer and the laird scooted his chair forward until his knees nearly bumped the heavy oak of Donal's desk. A scowl marred the lines of a strong face, beard stubble thick across his jaw, piercing blue eyes beneath a furrowed brow. His clothing was clean but well worn, and his leather belt appeared older than the man himself. Donal hazarded a guess. Twenty-five summers? A year or two more? He could recall little of the man's father other than a stern visage and a reputation for fierce loyalty.

"How may I be of help to ye, Laird?" Donal asked.

A light rap on the door interrupted them. At Donal's permission, the door opened, silhouetting Arbela in the light of the torchlit hall. Her dogs flanked her.

"I was asked to bring refreshment," she said, hesitating, glancing from the MacKern to her da.

Donal noted his guest's flared nostrils, his quickened breathing. All gone within an instant as if the MacKern's interest in Arbela never existed. Donal motioned her into the room and she glided across the floor, all lion-like grace and balance, with none of the mincing steps of a pampered lass. Her long tunic of figured silk did not hide her voluminous trousers—likely something Caelen had never witnessed before. Her robe was slashed front and back, exposing the tunic beneath and edged in a wide band of gold embroidery that sparkled with tiny gold discs. A long veil covered her hair, but raven-dark wisps escaped to curl about her forehead, accentuating her kohl-rimmed eyes.

Donal nodded appreciatively. *A vision. And lucky the man who weds her.* His gaze drifted to his guest, but the man remained rigid in his chair, though his eyes tracked Arbela as she crossed the room and deposited her tray on Donal's desk. With a wave of her hand, she sent the two dogs to sit beside the door.

As host, Donal poured them each a dram of whisky then settled back in his chair, his glance ordering Arbela to remain. Caelen accepted the drink with a nod and a quick sip, pulling his attention back to the matter at hand.

"Six years ago, I married Laird MacGillonay's only daughter. She died not long after our son was born, little more than a year later. Though 'twas not by my hand, MacGillonay seeks revenge for her death, plundering our small herds and firing outlying crofts."

Donal gave a casual shrug. "Sheep and a croft or two?"

Caelen's eyes darkened. "Crofts—with the families inside."

Arbela gasped. Garen whined and shifted her forefeet, but did not rise.

Donal leaned forward, placing his elbows on his desk, steepling his fingers. "Ye are certain 'twas MacGillonay?"

"As my life depends on it."

"A handful of crofters matter to ye?" Donal observed MacKern through slitted eyes, taking the measure of the man's honor.

48

"They are my clan, my kin," Caelen bit out. He gathered himself to stand. "I'd heard ye were an honorable man, for all ye've spent the last thirty years with the Saracens. It appears my information was wrong."

Arbela's weight shifted forward on her toes. Her hands clenched and Donal wondered how many blades she had hidden beneath her tunic.

"Sit," Donal commanded Caelen, allowing a thread of steel in his voice, seeking to keep Arbela at bay despite the insult from their guest. They locked gazes over the expanse of the desk and a muscle twitched in Caelen's jaw.

Giving the laird and his daughter both a moment to settle, Donal eyed him thoughtfully. "Ye are called Bull of the Highlands by some."

MacKern did not reply. Silence stretched. "Is there a question, Laird?" he finally asked.

"Mayhap. I wondered if it referred to a persevering nature—or inability to see reason."

"I am certain ye would get a different answer depending on who ye asked."

Donal barely halted the smile the man's answer provoked. "Ye wish protection from MacGillonay?"

"I seek an alliance, Laird," Caelen replied. "The scourge that killed yer da and brother nigh devastated my clan, leaving me with too few men to protect what is mine. We require only to be left in peace so we may see to repairs and tending what livestock remain."

Donal's eyes narrowed. "What do ye have to offer in return?"

Caelen's scowl reappeared. "My pledge that we will support ye as best we may should ye have need."

"In exchange for the possibility of the support of what few men ye are able to spare, ye require full protection from MacGillonay?" He leaned forward. "How desperate is yer clan?"

Caelen's face flushed. "We have no way to hold longer than a few days should MacGillonay besiege our keep."

The admission was costly, and Donal noted the fine flush to Caelen's cheeks. "Why do ye defend such a place?"

"'Tis my son's inheritance. I will do anything for my son."

"Men and their land," Arbela scoffed. "No matter the importance or the value of their rocky footprint, men sell their souls for a bit of scorched earth."

Caelen turned in his seat, his gaze sliding roughly up Arbela's frame. "And what would a wee lass know of the value of land?"

"I mean no disrespect—'tis the same the world over. We defended one of the most valuable strips of land in the Levant for many years," she replied, scorn for his easy dismissal forcing her voice into a lower range. "Our land's value as well as our honor was measured by the safe passage of travelers and merchants from the Silk Road to the sea."

Caelen grinned, a baring of teeth with little humor and less tolerance. "*We?*" he mocked.

Rage flooded Arbela and she forced it deep within where it would not control her. She lifted her chin, setting the gold fringe on her hijab jingling. Ignoring the delicate chimes, she addressed Laird MacKern's question. "Indeed. *We.* I have lifted both bow and sword in defense of our land. I have sent as many men to their creator as any of my father's knights."

This time Caelen's amusement overcame his scorn, twitching his lips in the faint echo of a smile. "Ye arenae big enough to lift a sword nor bend a bow. Dinnae take me for a fool."

His glance fell to Donal in appeal. Laird MacLean shrugged. "My daughter does not lie."

Arbela shifted her gaze to her da. "I'll have no stain on my honor. Nor will I suffer being called a liar." She raked Caelen with a haughty glare. "I'd heard Laird MacKern was an honorable man, for all he's spent his entire life in this land called Scotland. It appears my information was wrong. There is but one way to settle this."

Caelen came upright in his chair, his amusement gone. "What is it ye wish, *lass*?"

"To broaden your education," she stated. "*Man*."

Again Caelen appealed to Laird MacLean. Donal tilted his head, a mild look of disquiet on his face.

"I believe she has challenged ye to a duel."

Chapter Seven

Bram grumbled sleepily as Caelen slid from the bed. He splashed cold water on his face, wondering how, by St. Andrew's crooked toes, he'd managed to get himself into such a predicament. As a guest at MacLean Castle and with no pressing duties, he should give in to the impulse to sleep past the first hint of dawn. But he somehow found himself preparing for an archery competition. With a lass.

Shite! A lass who doesnae know when to speak and when to be silent. Enters conversations not about her. He paused in his musings, water dripping in his eyes. *And doesnae know how to clothe herself properly.*

The memory of Arbela intruded, her small yet buxom form wrapped in a patterned cloth in colors he'd never seen before, metallic fringe—was it gold?—tinkling on her headdress. And in trousers!

The sheer grace of her as she moved still took his breath away.

He scowled. *Idiot! Women are naught but a burden. Weak, willful, and treacherous.*

He rubbed his head vigorously with a square of linen and dropped the damp cloth carelessly over the edge of the bowl. He turned to gather his weapons and halted at the sight of his son struggling to wrap his leggings beneath his tunic.

"I'm going with ye, Da!" he said, a pinched look of intense concentration on his face as he picked at the laces. With a grunt of frustration, he leaned against the bed and shoved his legs toward Caelen. "I cannae do these."

Caelen strode across the room. "Ye dinnae need to. Crawl back into bed, lad. 'Tis verra early and ye need yer rest."

Bram kicked his feet. "No! I want to go with ye and Rory!"

Caelen propped his fists on his hips, a frown on his face. "And where is it ye think Rory and I are going?"

"To a contest to best a wee slip of a lass who doesnae know how to act around men," Bram replied, clearly mimicking Caelen's and Rory's conversation of the night before.

"Ye were supposed to be asleep."

Bram shrugged. "I was. Ye were noisy." He tilted his head. "Can I go, Da? I want to see the archers."

"'Twill be no archers. Only me and the lass. No contest and 'twill be over quickly. I'll send a lass upstairs to see ye get a good breakfast and are ready to leave right after."

"I'm going," Bram declared, the stubborn set to his jaw an exact imitation of his sire's.

"Best let the lad ride with us," Rory chimed in as he entered the room. "We dinnae have all day to change his mind, and from the looks of him, 'twill take that long at least."

Bram leapt to his feet. "Thanks, Uncle Rory!" He beamed as he gazed at his favorite uncle. But his face fell as he saw Caelen's frown.

Caelen bit back a snarl at Rory's meddling. "I am not taking a bairn to the field and . . . .." Words failed him as he could not garner a single plausible argument for not allowing Bram to come with him. Other than he simply didn't know what to do with the bairn.

"And let him watch ye shoot an arrow?" Rory finished the statement for him, his bland voice softly mocking.

"I'm not a bairn, Da," Bram prodded, all seriousness. "I've five summers."

"He's yer lad, and 'tis yer decision," Rory continued. "But ye brought him with ye to ensure MacGillonay dinnae take him whilst ye were away. 'Tis time the lad saw a bit more of men's work and a little less of women."

Caelen agreed with a short nod, not liking the idea of keeping up with a wee lad, and liking the idea of arguing with him even less. "Then lace up yer leggings, lad. I dinnae have time to wait on ye."

Rory knelt and fastened the ties on Bram's leggings. Caelen faltered, unsure if he should take charge of Bram's clothing or not. But Rory finished before Caelen could object and Bram leapt about, shouting for his boots. He stomped his feet inside and was tugging at the door as Caelen slid his dirk into his belt.

He let Bram dash ahead, following at a more sedate pace but with a close eye on the lad's whereabouts. Bram darted through the hall, lingering long enough to snatch a chunk of bread in one fist, a bit of cheese in the other.

"'S goo'!" he mumbled around a full mouth, nodding his head vigorously. Caelen made short work of his own meal, downing a mug of warm cider as Rory lifted Bram in the air, pretending to drop him only to catch him once again. The hall, slowly filling with people, rang with Bram's gleeful shouts.

"Come, Bram. Let us saddle Addis and ride to the archery field."

Bram fisted the hem of Caelen's tunic as they entered the stable. Evidence of the new laird's wealth reached even this place. Noble equine heads pushed over open half-doors, fine ears pricked forward at their approach. Arched necks and slender legs bespoke their exotic bloodlines, and Caelen paused a moment as he approached a stallion whose hide glistened like the purest gold.

"There's a fine lad," he crooned, stroking the slim yet well-muscled neck. The horse tossed his head, dancing lightly out of Caelen's reach. Caelen peered inside the stall, noting the stallion's narrow chest and short silky mane and tail.

"Ye could use a good bag of oats," he said. "What wouldn't I give to take ye out for a good ride and test yer mettle?"

"Is this Addis's bridle, Da?" Bram skipped toward him, legs tangling in the trailing leather straps.

Caelen left the golden stallion to gather the bridle from Bram, the leather old but supple from daily care. "Aye. And I'll ask him to take the bit, not ye, lad. Ye will keep yer fingers, please."

Bram fell into step beside him. "Addis wouldnae bite me," he scoffed. "I like him. But I still want a pony," he added quickly, a stubborn tilt to his head.

Caelen reached Addis's stall, relieved to have a distraction from the pony discussion. Settling Bram on the edge of the wooden trough, he quickly tacked up his horse. Placing his son in the saddle, stirrups flapping gently well below the reach of the lad's feet, Caelen led Addis into the hall.

"Ye are almost big enough for yer own horse, Bram," Rory chuckled as he met them, his horse trailing behind.

Easing his white-knuckled clutch off Addis's red mane, Bram gave Caelen a hopeful look which Caelen ignored.

"I will leave the lad with ye when I am on the field," he reminded Rory. "It shouldnae take long and we can leave for home shortly after."

They walked through the double doors into the sunlight and swung into their saddles. Bram leaned against Caelen, fitting solidly between his arms on either side. The sturdy horse, Caelen's pride and joy, the product of generations of the Fjord horse descended from Norwegian stallions and mares blended carefully with the Highland pony, was fast and agile, even over the forbidding, rocky terrain.

With a slight flick of his hand on the reins, Caelen directed Addis through the main castle gate and to a nearby clearing within view of the castle wall. Two thick piles of straw backed white cloth squares fluttering briskly between wooden stakes. Small crowds of people dotted the field. The late-night challenge hadn't gone unnoticed as he'd hoped.

He drew Addis to a halt and dismounted, handing the reins to Rory. "I'm going to pace the distance," he said.

"Can I come?"

Bram's voice held a faint note of panic, and Caelen patted the lad's knee. "Nae. Ye will be fine here with Rory to look after ye. Addis willnae let ye fall."

Bram's nod was hesitant, his eyes wide, the wee lad nearly lost in the big saddle. Caelen strode away, through the milling people, to the painted targets. The center mark was smaller than the palm of his hand and the wind would play havoc with his accuracy. The breeze frolicked about, altering direction as often as it changed strength. Caelen carefully paced the distance from the targets to a post in the ground marking the spot he'd shoot from. Pivoting, he stared back over his path, pondering the variables of wind, sun, and distance.

He peered at the sky. The sun topped the hills on the far side of the Loch Aline inlet, its rays sparking off the water like diamonds. He scowled.

Spoiled lass isnae taking this seriously. Stomping back to his horse, he snatched the reins from Rory.

"I dinnae have time for this," he growled.

"Have ye the promise from MacLean?" Rory asked.

Caelen swallowed a curse under his breath. "Nae. But I dinnae like standing around, waiting on a—"

"Faerie princess!" Bram breathed, lifting his arm to point over Caelen's shoulder.

Caelen followed his son's direction and the vision before him shocked him to the soles of his well-worn boots.

The glint of sun off the loch paled in comparison to the gleam of well-groomed horseflesh beneath the petite rider's flowing cloak of chatoyant silk, its colors changing and merging as the cloth billowed in the breeze. Her two dogs followed at her heels, and Caelen recognized her instantly—indeed there could be no other like Arbela in all of Scotland. He immediately quelled the surge of interest—and lust if he only allowed himself to admit it—she engendered.

"She *IS* a faerie princess, Da!" Bram insisted, though Caelen had not corrected his assumption.

"The lad may be right, Bull," Rory chimed in, a husky burr riding his voice. "I have never seen cloth change color like that before, nor have I seen such confidence in a lass."

"She is only a lass," Caelen grumbled. But his attention did not waver from Arbela as she approached. The edgy stallion he'd greeted in the stable earlier submitted to her control, though he champed his bit and danced on eager hooves, as if the slightest inattention from his rider would see him airborne.

His coat glistened with a metallic sheen, but even Caelen's deep appreciation for horseflesh did not override his reluctant appreciation of the lass atop the beast. She reined the horse easily to a halt a length or so away. The threads of her cloak shimmered pink, then brown, then gold and back again. Caelen shook his head.

Arbela stared down her long nose at him, dark brown eyes sparkling cold welcome.

"Good of ye to attend," he growled, unable to find anything to like about rising from his bed to duel with a lass he'd just met. Ironically, that sparked too much of the early days of his marriage—which had only gone downhill from there.

"'Twas my challenge," she replied. "Good of ye to accept."

Donal MacLean approached, his superb horse with its thickly arched neck and high-stepping gait a marked contrast to his daughter's high-headed, slender mount.

"I believe we can settle this quickly," MacLean said, his manner guarded.

Does he worry I will harm his daughter? "Quickly and without bloodshed," Caelen agreed.

"Och, ye are lucky ye dinnae choose swords," Donal replied, nodding his head as if Caelen should count himself fortunate to not be facing Arbela over a blade.

"Can we get on with it?" Caelen asked, taking a step toward the mark.

He set the end of his bowstaff on the ground. Stepping between the bow and string, he propped the lower end against his instep. With an effort, he flexed the longbow enough to notch the string at the upper end. He checked to be certain the string would not slip, then faced his opponent. His jaw dropped, but no words passed his tongue.

Arbela stepped lightly from her horse, handing her reins to her father. Slipping her cloak from her shoulders, she emerged garbed in a leather jerkin over a silk tunic and leather trews beneath. Her hair spilled down her back in a thick braid that surrendered curling wisps to the wind. She caught his gaze and her winged brows arched upward in reprimand.

"Have ye paced the field?" she asked, directing him to the challenge.

Caelen recovered his voice. "Aye. I will allow ye first shot."

She tossed her head. "Hardly fair since I challenged ye." She gave a regal nod. "Please take the first shot."

"And allow ye to see what the wind does at my expense?" He mocked her, certain such a thought had never entered her lovely head.

She returned his taunt. "I know what the wind does. It creeps past yer defenses and spoils yer aim. Do not let it hinder ye."

Anger stirred in his belly and he breathed it out in a long sigh. It would not do to allow emotion to spoil his shot. Touching two fingers to his forehead in salute, he accepted her offer. He turned his back to her and drew an arrow. Taking a moment to finger the feathers, the pads of his fingers sliding the length of the shaft, testing for signs of weakness, he set the arrow against the bow.

Pointing the bow upward, he nocked his arrow, bringing the tip to bear on the target in a sweeping downward motion as he drew back on the string. Sighting along the shaft, he released the string, sending the arrow streaking through the air. It landed with a resounding slap in the center of the painted circle.

Arbela rubbed the shallow groove in her archer's thumb ring as the

MacKern laird nocked his arrow. His stance straightened from his habitual slight crouch, the traditional, six-foot bow nearly as tall as the man. His grip was powerful yet light enough to allow for slight adjustments of movement, and heavy muscles shifted beneath his tunic as he drew back on the bowstring.

It did not surprise her when the arrow hit dead center of the target. Caelen MacKern did not appear to be a man who took his training lightly. It was not his skills she challenged, but his narrow view of the world—and her ability to knock the condescending smirk from his lips.

"Are ye a faerie princess?"

The question pulled Arbela's contemplation of her opponent to glance about for the speaker. Her gaze settled on a young boy atop a red dun horse, its flaming mane and tail a marked contrast to the lighter chestnut coat. The child regarded her with wide eyes.

"Ye look like a faerie princess. Ilene tells me stories about them. Are ye one?"

Arbela smiled. "I am mayhap a princess from a faraway land. Will that do?"

The boy nodded. "I'm Bram, Laird MacKern's son."

Arbela glanced over her shoulder and found the laird staring at her, an unreadable expression on his face. "My name is Arbela. I have come to teach your father some manners."

She unhooked a small bow from her saddle and, with deft movements, strung her Turkish bow. Its *C*-shape pulled backward as the string grew taut, giving it an appearance quite unlike the longbow Caelen had used. The laird's eyebrows lifted, but he kept his thoughts to himself.

Arbela strolled to the mark and Caelen yielded the spot.

"Very nice shooting," she murmured. A small shake of her head negated her words. As she'd hoped, it provoked Caelen.

"Ye can do better than dead center?" he demanded. "Yer bow is naught but a toy—too small to be accurate, and ye've not enough strength to cover the distance." He sent her a patronizing look. "Do ye wish to step a wee bit closer?"

She leaned in. "Tempt me to come closer and ye may find a knife in your belly," she warned. "I do not need an easier target."

Plucking four arrows from her belt, she gripped three in her right hand, placing the fourth against the bow. In two swift, fluid moves, she pushed the arrow forward, nocking the arrow as she then drew it back against the string. The arrow scarcely left her hand before she had the second nocked. She sent the last three arrows in rapid succession with no pause to determine her success or adjust her aim.

A ripple of applause swept the crowd. Used to her father's moderately paced Gaelic, Arbela understood little of the rapid-fire words of excitement. But she did not need them explained. Caelen's face was translation enough.

She cast a swift look at the target. Her four arrows ringed his single shaft in a tight circle, feathered ends bristling together.

"Will I hear your apology, M'laird?" she murmured, fighting the glee threatening to force a smile on her face. "Does this demonstrate my skills adequately?"

Caelen swallowed and shifted his gaze to hers. "Ye are swift and accurate with a bow. But when it truly counts, can ye look in a man's eyes and deal him death?"

Glee changed to brittle challenge.

"Test me."

Chapter Eight

"My most sincere apology for doubting yer ability with a bow, m'lady." Caelen bowed stiffly from the waist, but Arbela sensed the acknowledgement was sincere—even if the words appeared difficult to speak. Though she managed to lower her chin in an accepting gesture, her gaze was anything *but*.

"I have spent my life protecting Batroun and its people. I do not care to be besmirched simply because I am a woman. My height and gender have nothing to do with the abilities I train hard to achieve."

"Point taken. But in our country, a lass knows her place. When it comes to hand-to-hand combat, ye must agree yer strength cannot compete against a man." He eyed her speculatively. "And that is *not* a challenge."

"I would not accept," Arbela informed him. "As ye say, I cannot compete with ye on such a physical level. I have other skills—"

"—Such as managing a home and servants. The lass has a quick brain and makes short work of bookkeeping as well."

Arbela turned a skeptical eye on her father as he approached, uneasy with his cheerful interruption of her words with the MacKern laird. Her suspicions increased as he continued, turning his affability on Caelen.

"Ye may turn yer lad over to Arbela whilst ye and I finish our conversation begun last eve. We dinnae come to terms with our alliance proposition."

Relegating me to a woman's duties, excluding me from something I was privy to yesterday, and using big words. Donal MacLean was a learned man, with a vocabulary that put scribes to shame. But his use of them often meant he hid an ulterior motive. Her eyes narrowed, wondering what he was up to. But Donal's smile never wavered.

Keeping a wary eye on her da, Arbela stepped lightly into her saddle, gathering her reins, a comforting hand on Voski's shoulder as he pranced backward.

"I'll find a lass on foot to care for Bram," Caelen said, stepping between Arbela's horse and his son. "Thank ye all the same."

"Voski is spirited, but will obey my command. He will carry your son and sooner come to harm himself than allow young Bram to fall." Arbela lifted her chin. "Ye may hand him to me."

"I would as lief place my son under yer horse's hooves as atop his back," Caelen declared, crossing his arms over his chest. "That beast isnae meant for children."

"We shall walk to the stable together," Donal said, silencing Arbela's retort. She glanced at the boy's pale face and realized Caelen protected Bram from his own fears as much as the child's.

She slipped from Voski's back. "He may walk with me," she said, ending the confrontation.

With a stern look, Caelen turned reluctantly to his son and lifted him from his sturdy horse. He set the boy on his feet and spoke in his ear, though the words drifted easily for all to hear.

"Ye may go with Lady Arbela and see to yer meal. A morsel of bread will keep yer belly full and we will ride home soon."

Bram ignored the adults in favor of Arbela's two dogs who sat at Voski's side. "Can I pet them?" he asked eagerly. At Arbela's nod, the dogs raced to the lad's side, tails wagging, tongues marking him as their newest friend amid Bram's hysterical giggles. His hands fisted in their thick, wiry coats and he beamed happily.

Caelen sent a warning glance to Arbela as he released his shoulder. "Keep him safe."

She held her hand to Bram and closed her fingers over the small hand. "He will be safe with me. I do not harm children, and neither do my dogs."

His piercing gaze locked onto hers. "Believe me when I tell ye, there are people who would take my son, and all yer flippant words would come to naught. This is neither yer desert, nor yer people. Ye have much to learn about Scotland."

* * *

Caelen stalked away without another word, knowing full well to deny the laird's daughter the right to care for his son was tantamount to forcing another duel—though he couldn't decide who would be the lesser threat, Arbela or her da.

Showing his easy-going manners, Addis tagged at his heels, and Caelen shuddered to think of his wee son atop the excitable horse Arbela called Voski. Bram's pleadings aside, he needed to teach his son to ride soon. Instead of embracing the challenge of the horse, there were signs Bram was beginning to fear them.

Donal and his son, Alex, flanked Caelen on his right, Rory on his left. Slowing his pace allowed Donal to reach his side, and Caelen reminded himself he was a guest in the MacLean's castle, not the other way around.

None of the men spoke on the short walk to the stables, and Caelen's ears picked up the excited chatter of Bram's voice several paces behind. It was enough to drop his anger with Arbela to a manageable level, and allow him to enter the laird's solar with his attention on the alliance he meant to form.

Alex poked the fire on the hearth into greater life, adding a bit of warmth to the room. Donal sat behind his desk and motioned for Caelen to be seated. Alex took a chair and fixed his attention on Caelen, his look interested rather than hostile—though Caelen couldn't have called it friendly, either.

"I have need of men to help patrol my boundaries," Caelen began, not waiting for an invitation to start. "Only then can we see to shoring up our defenses, and spare backs to work the fishing nets and the fields."

"Yer castle rests on the edge of Loch Linnhe?"

"Aye. About twenty or so miles from here."

"Yer father by marriage lives at the western tip of Loch Eil," Donal noted.

Caelen clenched his jaw. "I no longer claim him as kin."

Donal raised his brows. "Nonetheless, he is yer son's grandda."

"An accident of blood." Caelen's fingers gripped the arm of his chair. "What does his relationship have to do with our alliance?"

"I dinnae wish to become embroiled in the squabble over the living arrangements of a bairn," Donal replied.

"I willnae allow that bastard to take my son!" Caelen exploded, half-rising from his chair. "Will we make an alliance or not?"

Donal gave a light shrug. "I think we need to consider strengthening our position." He waved Caelen back into his chair.

"What do ye have in mind?" Caelen asked warily as he lowered to the chair.

"I have looked into yer request. And yer ability to follow through on yer end of the bargain. Och, I have no doubt ye mean to make good on any promise ye make. Others have said that of ye. But the fact remains, yer clan was hit hard by the scourge and ye have little resources to accomplish all ye wish in a timely manner. There will always be fish to catch, crops to plant and harvest. But all for naught if ye cannae defend what is yers, and building defenses doesnae put food in bellies."

Shame slid through Caelen's veins like a poison. Though he'd done what he could, the disease had spread through his clan like wildfire before a strong wind, and in the time it took to collect their dead, last summer's harvest had been lost—ruined in the fields. The past winter had been hard.

"What is it ye wish from me?"

"I want ye to marry my daughter."

Caelen bolted up in his chair. "Yer daughter?"

Alex slid forward in his seat, clearly as startled by his sire's words as was Caelen.

Donal chuckled. "I certainly dinnae think ye should marry my son!" His smile did little to allay Caelen's alarm.

"Yer daughter and I dinnae get along." It was an understatement, but the truth and diplomatic.

"My daughter has a mind of her own, but she is caring, smart, and fiercely loyal. I know her faults, and they are few. Adjusting to life here hasnae been easy for her. She is more inclined to fly in the face of convention than worry overmuch what others think of her."

He leaned forward. "But, consider what her dowry brings."

Still reeling from the idea of accepting the exotic, free-thinking lass as his wife, Caelen allowed his business sense to take over. Giving a stiff nod, he invited Donal's explanation.

"It should come as no surprise that her dowry will contain much gold and other items of wealth. But ye also need men to help rebuild yer keep, and seasoned men-at-arms to work with yer warriors to guard yer borders. I can supply these men, including four knights who are battle-hardened and verra skilled. Who knows? They mayhap teach yer men a thing or two and learn from them as well."

"Ye must know by now, my sister is an accomplished warrior," Alex interjected. "She can wield a bow with speed and accuracy as ye saw for yerself not an hour past. Her skill with a sword is surpassed only by her knowledge and shrewd evaluation of tactics. Not long before we left Batroun, we were besieged by Saracens for the third time that year, and she was the first to point out the invaders were likely led by the same man." Alex turned an eager look to his da.

"She is brilliant. And she was quick to save my and Phillipe's hides when the Turks came over the wall. And when the Moorish pirates attacked off the coast of the Iberian Peninsula—"

Donal waved him to silence with a tolerant smile. "She is quite useful," he agreed. "But yer sister has other, more womanly qualities."

Caelen's ears perked up. Not that Arbela's womanly qualities were of great interest, but because so far he'd seen little evidence of such.

"She is, as I believe I have mentioned, skilled in numbers and bookkeeping. I have no qualms about allowing her to handle my household accounts. In fact, I am initiating a shipping venture from here to Europe and beyond, similar to what I ran whilst living in the Levant. Arbela would be invaluable in suggesting to ye what goods to develop in trade, and setting up the books for ye."

"Ye would bring me into yer venture?" Caelen asked, suddenly overwhelmed.

It was an offer too good to be true. Not that he doubted Laird MacLean's willingness and ability to see to the bargain once struck, but Caelen had listed his reasons for not remarrying to Rory not that long ago, and they hadn't changed.

"Laird, I respect yer offer. And 'tis verra tempting. But ye must know, after my first marriage failed—and it failed long before Ruthie died—I swore I'd never enter the bonds of matrimony again." He glanced away, disliking to recall the memory, the recounting of it as bitter as an unripened gooseberry.

"Ruthie MacGillonay was a bonny lass, full of fun and smiles. I willingly entered the marriage arranged to form an alliance between our clans, certain she would become the light of my life. For reasons I willnae disclose, we dinnae find ourselves in accord, and she quickly turned bitter. I hoped the bairn would see a return to her sunny disposition, but she rejected him, and her only delight seemed to be in causing as much strife in my house as possible."

He pulled his gaze back to Laird MacLean. "I swore after her death I wouldnae enter into marriage again."

Donal returned his stare evenly. "I willnae lie and say life with Arbela will be without strife. But she doesnae willingly cause it, and she is honest and careful in her relationships."

Caelen opened his mouth, but Donal raised a hand. Caelen yielded the floor.

"I married a lass from Armenia," Donal said, his voice low, cadence set to a long-ago tale. "She was a princess from a noble house, and I, the third son of a Scottish laird, wooed and won her. By then I was Baron of Batroun and worthy in her father's eyes.

"She bore twins not long into our first year of marriage. She was so happy. I could scarcely contain myself with pride. When Alex and Arbela were not quite past their first summer, she felt 'twas time to introduce them to her family." Donal's face darkened and a muscle in his jaw twitched.

"They journeyed by caravan, and I felt 'twas secure enough I only sent two of my knights with her. They were set upon by a Saracen raiding party, and they killed my wife."

Silence deadened the room, the air thick with remorse. "The bairns' nurse escaped with them and two others and managed to make their way home, arriving at Batroun exhausted and filthy—but alive." Donal leaned back in his chair, his movements as if he'd aged far beyond his years. "I swore Arbela would never be helpless as her ma had been. Beautiful, delightful, a woman to be proud of—but not helpless. 'Tis my fault Arbela is confident, willful, learned, and skilled in weapons far beyond what is considered feminine or right. But I wouldnae have it any other way."

A smile crept across his face and settled in the creases at the corners of his eyes. "Will ye accept the money, the workmen and the knights? Will ye accept my daughter—and the challenge?"

Caelen took his time considering his options. He could decline MacLean's offer and though he wouldn't have his alliance, he doubted MacLean would completely turn his back on him. He sensed an honor in the older man that went deeper than kinship. But the facts were, his clan could use the help, the masons and men-at-arms. And his coffers were alarmingly empty, though his clan had never before faced such a time of poverty as they saw ahead of them.

But did he need the gold and men enough to take a wife? Arbela?

"I have seen the way ye look at my sister," Alex said. "Sometimes as a man looks at a beautiful woman, and other times as if she were something ye'd rather not approach. I will add my own qualification, MacKern.

"My sister is a princess by blood of one of the oldest houses in Christendom. Given another path, she would likely be pampered, soft, and not facing marriage to an impoverished Scottish laird. But she is fierce. And she worked harder than I or Phillipe, our foster-brother, learning her skills—be they sword, bow, or keeping records. She speaks more languages than do I, and she will be at work long after ye have retired to yer bed, if there is a need. The only contention she brings is a distaste for intolerance. Her love of children is well known amongst those at Batroun, and Farlan and Elspeth's children—who returned with us from the Holy Land—are very fond of her.

"But hear me well, Laird. If ye harm my sister, I will gut ye like a landed fish."

"I promised her I would not marry her to a man I thought would try to rule her," Donal said. "She will step into yer authority easily if offered instead of required of her. I, too, willnae sit by and see her broken. That is, out of all ye have been offered, the unnegotiable part of the contract."

Alex's words rang in Caelen's ears. He did not doubt Arbela's brother would check on her regularly and give him challenge were he to find his sister less than content.

"What if I say nae?"

Donal sent him a curious look. "I willnae deny ye protection from MacGillonay."

"I dinnae think he is good enough for my sister," Alex muttered.

Caelen leaned forward in his seat, forearms on his knees, hands clasped tight. 'Twas a business arrangement like any other—with a wife added in the bargain. But the words of acceptance hovered just beyond the reach of his tongue.

"I have one more offer to make ye, MacKern," Donal mentioned.

Caelen glanced up. "What is that?"

"I noticed yer horse, earlier. He's a fine, sturdy animal, with clean lines and well-cared-for. Ye are a noted horse breeder in this area and many praise yer stables." Donal leaned forward in his chair, forearms braced on the desktop, the gleam of challenge once more in his eyes.

"If ye can convince Arbela that ye are her best choice for a husband, if she goes willingly to this marriage, I will add a Lusitano stallion and mare to the dowry."

Chapter Nine

Arbela strolled to the stable, Bram chattering nonstop at her side, the horse and dogs following obediently.

The child perched on a nearby wooden bench, Toros and Garen on either side.

"*Ditel*," Arbela ordered. She knew the command to watch ensured neither dog would leave the child's side, nor allow anyone to approach. She untacked Voski and ran a cloth over his gleaming coat. His energy by no means depleted after a short walk to and from the archery field, the horse nipped at her sleeve with his thick lips as often as he could get away with it. Arbela laughed and shoved at his shoulder.

"*Ch'yen karogh linel himar,* Voski-jan." Caressing his silken nose, she gazed into his unusual crystal eyes.

"What did ye say?" Bram wanted to know.

"I told him not to be so silly," Arbela replied. "He is a young horse and does not always understand how strong he is."

"Does he frighten ye?" Bram asked, his voice hesitant.

"I would be foolish indeed if I said no. However, I respect the fact he is so much bigger than I am. He is not a malicious creature, merely high-spirited, and we are learning each other's ways."

"Does it hurt when he bites ye?"

"It would if he used his teeth. But he is only teasing, and his big lips are annoying, not hurtful."

Bram hopped down from his bench amid anxious whines from the dogs. Ignoring them, he dragged the wooden seat across the aisle to Voski's half-door. He climbed atop the bench and hung over the door.

"What's his name?" he asked.

"Voski," Arbela replied. "It means *golden*."

"But ye called him Voski-*jarn*," Bram argued, repeating the word as he'd heard it. "I heard ye."

Arbela smiled. "Jan simply means I like him. A bit like a sweet nickname." She took a step toward Bram and tweaked his nose. "I could call ye Bram-jan."

"*Bram-jarn*?" Bram scrunched his face. "I dinnae like it."

"Ye do not like having a new friend?" she teased.

"I like ye," Bram admitted. "My friends willnae believe I know a real princess, though."

He looked so forlorn, Arbela smothered her smile.

Bram's face brightened. "I like yer horse, though he is verra skinny."

"Hmm. Ye may think he is skinny, but 'tis his nature."

"Da says he needs more to eat."

"I agree he appears thin next to yer da's sturdy horse. But Voski is a son of the desert and his tall legs keep him farther from the hot sand, and his thin skin and sleek muscles help cool him when he is active. Yer da's horse would be much too hot where Voski is from."

Bram tilted his head. "Will Voski not like living here, then?"

"Actually, he is bred to be very hardy—even in cold weather, and on very rocky soil. I think he will do fine."

She rubbed the tall horse's golden neck, leaning into his shoulder, her head not cresting the top of his withers. Giving Voski a final pat, she had Bram move his bench then stepped from the stall.

"Do ye have a pony?" she asked the lad at her side.

Bram heaved a big sigh with a crestfallen look. "Nae. My da doesnae think I am big enough." He turned anxious eyes on her. "Do ye think I am?"

"Are ye afraid I will say yea or nae?"

Bram dropped his gaze, a stricken look on his face. "I think I am afraid of horses." His cheeks colored as embarrassment bloomed.

"Truly afraid? Or simply not used to them?" Arbela asked carefully.

"I dunno," he replied, a thoughtful look on his face.

"Mayhap ye do not know much about them," she offered. Bram shrugged. "Or perhaps ye simply are shy around them—like a person ye have not met before."

"Mayhap." Bram tilted his head as though a thought occurred to him. "Do ye think if I knew them better, they wouldnae bother me as much?"

Arbela gave him a fond smile. "I think ye will be a superb horseman one day. The sooner ye start, the better." She peered down the stable hallway. Interested heads peered over half-open doors. Determined, she strode to a doorway where no head peeked out. "Let's have a chat with Ari."

Bram skipped at her side. "Who's Ari?"

"Ari is a brave boy much as ye are," Arbela replied. She halted at the empty doorway.

"I dinnae see anyone," Bram complained, glancing about.

Arbela opened the bottom half of the door. A sturdy pony, his winter-rough coat revealing patches of slick black summer fur, faced them. He chewed his hay in a lazy manner, one ear pricked forward, the other twisted and much abbreviated. He stared calmly at them, one eye clouded.

"What happened to his ear and eye?" Bram exclaimed.

"Ari once belonged to a boy about your size," Arbela said. "But the boy grew too big, and there were no other children to ride him, so Ari was sent to live in the hills with the sheep where the shepherd could keep an eye on him."

"So he wouldnae be lonely?"

"Aye. After he'd lived with the sheep for a year or so, the shepherd went into the hills searching for a lost ewe. She was due to have her lamb and could not be found. The shepherd put a small pack on Ari's back and off they went. But a wolf had found the ewe, and thought she'd make a nice snack."

"But he dinnae know about Ari, did he, Arbela?" Bram's eyes shone with the light of a warrior.

"Nae, the wolf did not know about Ari. As the shepherd tells the tale, Ari flew at the wolf, his ears pinned back, teeth bared, squealing like an enraged boar. And everyone knows how fierce they are! The wolf attacked Ari, and though he tore one of the pony's ears and scraped the side of his head, Ari grabbed the beast by the scruff of his neck and shook him— hard! When the wolf fell to the ground, Ari stomped him with his hooves, and the wolf ran away."

"Good for ye, Ari!" Bram approved. "Can I pet him?"

"I'm certain he would like that." Arbela led Bram inside the stall and the pony greeted him with gentle snuffles.

Bram laughed. "He's a nice pony."

"The two of ye would get along well together. Would ye like to sit on him?"

With a moment's hesitation, Bram took a deep breath and gave an emphatic nod. "Aye."

Hoping to bolster Bram's confidence, Arbela gave him simple instructions on approaching the pony, noting the pony's damaged eye and the need to avoid startling him on that side. Bram soaked up her words eagerly, even offering Ari half of a winter-wizened apple in eager friendship.

"He is a brave pony and ye are now his friend," Arbela said as she lifted the boy into the air. Bram swung his legs wide to encircle the pony's girth, gripping the wiry mane with both fists.

"Ye may use the mane until ye feel comfortable with your balance," she told him. "But do not pull so hard. Take your time and sit up like a warrior. Ye are not a sack of flour."

With her encouragement, Bram gained confidence, and he at last demanded to ride Ari on his own. Arbela smiled. "I will lead ye to the paddock, and ye may guide Ari there."

Silent as ghosts, Toros and Garen slid through the barn at the pony's

CATHY & DD MACRAE

heels. Unperturbed, Ari plodded along, his gait easy and slow. Arbela thrilled to the triumphant smile on Bram's face as he directed his mount with nothing more than a tug of the rope on the headstall Arbela drew over the pony's head. She let him ride until he moved freely with the pony's motion, then called a halt.

"Ye are developing a good seat, Bram-jan," she told him. His cheeks, flushed with accomplishment, darkened at her praise. "But we must not tire Ari. He has not had a rider in some time, now."

She saw the argument in the set of Bram's jaw and the downward tilt of his head—so like his sire—but he agreed without comment and they returned to the barn where she then instructed him in the pony's care.

"All riders care for their horses," she informed him. "Ye must always see to your horse yourself."

"I did it, dinnae I, 'Bela?" Bram asked as he wiped a rag down Ari's sturdy legs.

"Indeed ye did. I believe ye are about ready for your own pony."

Bram grinned, his face shining. "I'll talk to my da again when we get home!"

"Finish, then, and we will see to our morning meal before the food is gone."

Ari's care dispensed with, Bram grabbed Arbela's hand as they departed for the hall. A curious thrill lit a small smile at his easy acceptance of her, and Arbela hoped fervently the boy's father would see to his riding lessons soon.

The aroma of freshly baked bread and spiced ale met them at the door to the hall. Steam rolled above bowls of porridge, sending hints of cinnamon and anise to mingle with the other kitchen smells. Arbela sighed. It had taken time to convince the cook these spices were now available to be used at liberty, not hoarded for special occasions. She placed a generous pat of butter on her and Bram's bowls of porridge, then stirred in a generous portion of dried fruit.

74

Bram eyed his skeptically. "Do ye like those?" He nodded at the crinkly fruit.

Arbela gave him a surprised look. "Aye. Do ye?"

Bram shrugged. "We had some, but it dinnae last the winter."

She studied the child as he tucked into his porridge. Thin, wiry. Active? Or underfed? Caelen's words drifted back to her. *The scourge that killed yer da and brother nigh devastated my clan . . . ..* The affliction she'd heard called *mezils* had struck at the end of the summer. Had they not gotten their harvests in?

Her heart went out to the lad. He was motherless, facing a clan of dwindling numbers, and one with limited supplies. His dead mother's father was a man not to be trusted if she believed Caelen. And she couldn't imagine being the center of so much personal strife.

She snorted lightly, suddenly amused with the thought. Each time she'd visited her mother's family, she'd faced the possibility of an attack by Saracens—and being sold into slavery—and her day-to-day existence had been dependent on her family's ability to defend itself. Death was a reality she had dealt with all her life. Though she'd always trusted and counted on all her family—something Bram could not do.

"What would ye like to do whilst we wait for yer father?" she asked, wishing to give him a few carefree hours.

He swallowed quickly. "Can we go outside and play with Toros and Garen?" He gave the dogs a hopeful look.

"Well, they are not exactly used to playing," Arbela cautioned. "They are Aidi, good hunters and bred for protecting sheep."

"Like Da's sheepdog?"

"Not exactly. They can herd, but they are better at protecting the flock against wild animals."

"Like wolves?"

"Or perhaps lions—or bears," she teased.

"What's a lion?" Bram asked, a puzzled frown on his face.

"Finish your porridge and I'll tell ye about the large cat with a mane of hair all around its neck."

"A mane? On a cat?" Bram laughed.

Arbela pointed to his half-empty bowl. "Eat. Special tales are better on a full stomach."

"Ye are making that up," he accused her, but he grinned and gobbled a glob of porridge atop a chunk of bread, the bite threatening to leak from the edges of his mouth. Arbela motioned to a serving girl to clear their table and pretended not to notice when Bram slipped a handful of the thick bread to Toros who waited eagerly beneath the bench.

Arbela moved them to a seat by the great hearth. Pulling a half-burned stick from the embers, she set it carefully aside to cool. Bram settled next to her, and Toros and Garen took their places beside them.

"Have ye ever seen a lion, Bram?" she asked.

The child shook his head. "Nae. I dinnae know what a lion is."

Arbela wrapped a linen napkin from the table around the unburned end of the stick and picked it up. With quick strokes, she used the burnt end to sketch a rudimentary lioness on one of the stones of the hearth.

Bram crept close. "That just looks like a big cat. It doesnae have a mane!"

"Ah, but the lion did not always have a mane," she said.

Bram's eyes widened. "He dinnae? How did he get it, then?"

"Well, the lion is a large animal, bigger than a wolf, and as fierce as a bear. Because of this, he is known as the king of all the animals. But one day, Horse came prancing into Lion's territory, tossing his head and telling all the other animals how grand it was to have a mane.

"Lion thought the mane was spectacular, and decided he wanted one for himself. He announced to the animals that they would provide him— their king—with a mane. Well, the animals were very unhappy. How could they give Lion a mane? They discussed it among themselves, and the next morning, approached Lion with all manner of leaves and twigs, and arranged it around his head, using mud to make it stick." She drew stubby lines from around the lion's head, sketching in a few leaves to add to the silliness. Bram giggled.

Arbela waved her arms in the air. "Lion was thrilled! He had a mane—and it was better than Horse's! He stalked about, boasting about his new mane. And it looked glorious—until the mud dried and it all fell off."

Arbela rubbed her drawing with the cloth, erasing the twigs and leaves. She then dropped her hands into her lap and fell silent.

"What happened?" Bram asked. He edged closer. "Was Lion angry?"

"Yes," she whispered loudly. "He was SO angry! He roared and roared and rushed about in such a state, until he ran headlong into a tree with silky golden leaves."

Bram's gaze followed her hands as she drew a flowing mane about the lion's head and neck. "What happened then?"

Arbela sat back on her heels to survey her artwork. "He hit the tree so hard, it fell on top of him. All the animals rushed to help him, but he crawled from under the tree and shook to rid himself of his headache."

"Did the golden leaves fall off?"

"They did not! Miraculously, they stuck to him. Lion was so proud, he tossed his head over and over, just to feel the sweep of his glorious new mane. And because Lion is, of course, King of the animals, everyone knows his golden mane is the mark of royalty."

Bram laughed. "That was a good story! Tell me another one!"

"Arbela!"

She glanced up as Alex called her name. His hooded look gave her pause. "What is it, Alex?"

He shook his head, a smile ghosting his lips. "Da wishes to speak to ye in his solar. I can see to Master Bram. Looks like Toros and Garen are guarding him well."

"I dinnae need a guard," Bram informed him. "I've five summers and

I'm braw. The dogs protect sheep."

"They certainly do," Alex agreed. "But I saw one put Arbela on her butt . . .er, backside the other day."

"Tell me!" Bram crowed. Arbela rolled her eyes and stalked to the laird's solar.

"Boys!" she muttered. She braced a hand on the closed door and tapped gently. A voice bade her enter, but it wasn't her father. A flash of caution slid through her. She opened the panel, but did not step inside the room. Light from the fireplace and a large candelabrum lit the room, and she stared at the only person within.

"Yer da stepped out," Caelen told her. "But I believe we should talk before he returns."

"Oh?" Arbela arched a brow. "What could we possibly have to discuss?"

Chapter Ten

Light-headed, as if he'd just purchased the Lusitano stallion outright—and spent far more gold than he had a right to—Caelen sipped a glass of warmed ale as he waited for Alex to return with Arbela.

She arrived at the threshold, dressed as she'd been at the archery field at daybreak. Her choice of leather trews and a vest over a pale pink tunic still startled him. The supple leather clung to her generous form, tailored to fit her slender waist between the swell of her bosom and hips. Black hair down to her hips shone like a raven's wing, the braid thicker than his wrist. Dusky skin and full lips beneath dark, tilted eyes added to her exotic appearance.

"What could we possibly have to discuss?" she asked, her expression cool and aloof.

Left on his own to convince her they should wed, Caelen struggled for the right words and tone. "Ye look lovely, Arbela."

Her brow arched higher and Caelen hid his scowl. Could she not accept his compliment? Ruthie had sought them endlessly. He turned his attention to the archer's thumb ring she absently rubbed. It was something he'd never seen before. Perhaps he could study it more closely—later.

"Ye shot well today." That should please her. But her eyes narrowed and she crossed her arms over her chest.

"What do ye wish to say?" she asked, her voice silky smooth.

Caelen propped his hands on his belt, then realized he loomed over her, and that hardly engendered the agreeable attitude he sought. Rather than causing her to step back or duck her head in deference, her only response was to tilt her chin to stare up at him. He did not wish to approve of her, but a small part of him did. *She's a strong lass.*

"Mayhap we should go where we willnae be disturbed," he suggested, motioning at the door.

Her chin took on a stubborn angle. "I will wait here for my father."

"He willnae return until I've spoken with ye." He again motioned to the door.

She refused to budge. "Oh? Why is that?"

Her stiff tone annoyed him, but he held his temper. "What I wish to say to ye is private."

Arbela raked him with a searching look. "I need to turn Voski out in a paddock. Mayhap ye could walk with me."

She led the way along the passageway. They crossed the hall, and Caelen noted Bram chatting excitedly with Alex, pointing to a stone near the hearth. The dogs Arbela had with her earlier in the day took notice of her. With a motion of her hand, she brought one of the dogs to her side. The other remained with Bram and Alex.

"Why do ye bring one of the dogs with ye?" Caelen asked.

Arbela glanced at the sable dog, its coat rich with colors ranging from dark gold to russet against a nearly black background. Its head rose a bit taller than Arbela's knee, its build muscular and athletic. "She guards me. If I did not allow her to come, she would be unhappy."

He glanced at the black-coated dog sitting next to Bram. "The other doesnae fash?"

Arbela stole a look over her shoulder. "He is protecting Bram."

"What sort of dogs are they?"

"Aidi. They are bred to guard flocks of sheep and other livestock. They are fierce, loyal, and highly intelligent, and have an excellent nose for tracking." She brushed the dog's head affectionately. "I've raised this pair since they were weaned."

She had a way with horses, dogs, and apparently young lads. This alone was more than Ruthie had brought to their marriage.

They finished the short walk to the stable in silence. "Thank ye for keeping my son company whilst I spoke with yer father."

80

Arbela grabbed a silken headstall from a peg near the door. "He is a charming boy. I enjoyed our time together."

She opened the top half of the door and the golden stallion shoved his head into the hall. Arbela's lips curved into a smile and she stroked the shimmering coat. "Ye are a charming boy as well, Voski-jan."

Caelen marveled at Arbela's firm yet casual handling of the horse that towered over her. His head, carried high on a long neck, reinforced Caelen's opinion of the animal's temperament, and blinked his surprise when the beast nipped Arbela's sleeve and received nothing more than a murmured reprimand for his behavior. She pulled his head to her chest and slipped the headstall over his ears, then released the door latch.

The stallion bolted from his stall, making a show of fighting the control of a mere wisp of a lass. Snaking his head low to the ground, he then rose on his hind legs before deigning to stand on four feet like a horse should. His antics caused Arbela to simply step out of his way, allowing him to dance on the end of his lead until he'd blown off his excess energy.

"He needs a good bit of exercise every day," she commented, though it scarcely sounded like an apology.

"My ponies arenae so active," Caelen muttered, careful to remain beyond reach of the dancing hooves. "They are sturdy and reliable."

"Voski is bold and brave and fierce. Yet he is a prince with children. Believe it or not, he can be quite gentle." Arbela's face softened as she gazed at the horse. "His kind was bred in the desert mountains and none compares to their size, strength, speed, or beauty."

Caelen eyed the stallion as Arbela led him to a paddock set back from the stables. She fussed with the horse, murmuring to him in an unknown language before she set him loose. Voski flew across the small field, tail high, coat aglow with a sheen Caelen had never seen on an animal before. Resembling the burnish of a priceless piece of gold, each hair seemed to quiver with life.

Drawing back to his purpose, Caelen glanced about for inspiration, gaze alighting on a patch of small white flowers near the base of a tree. He quickly stooped and plucked several stems, twisting them together, their creamy faces clustered in a wee bouquet. Crossing to the paddock gate, he held out his woodland offering.

"For ye, m'lady."

Arbela gave him a puzzled look—one that did not hold even a hint of feminine fluster.

"What is this, Caelen?" she asked, her dark eyes flashing.

"I wish to speak with ye," he grumbled.

"Then I ask ye to speak plainly," she insisted.

"I have complimented ye and offered ye flowers." Caelen's tone paused just short of complaint. "Other women like such things."

Her chin rose. "I am certain ye have noticed—I am not like other women."

Something tugged in Caelen's chest, but he shoved it aside irritably. This was not progressing as he thought it would.

"Ye wish only for plain speaking? As if ye were a man?"

"Why do men think only they may speak so?" she asked. "I have no reason to lead ye about with pretty words, and I daresay ye have no reason to play at such with me."

Caelen laid the flowers aside. "I have no true right to speak of such things to ye, but I would ask ye hear my words before ye reply."

She nodded and leaned against the rail fence.

Caelen marshaled his thoughts and spoke plainly. "I wish for ye to marry me."

Arbela gaped at him, her wits scattered. Only a few months earlier, she'd received an avowal of love from a young man she cherished as a brother, and now faced an offer of marriage from a man she'd only just met—and challenged to a duel. Nothing in her life thus far had prepared her for such events, for she felt certain these words were not meant to be

THE HIGHLANDER'S CRUSADER BRIDE

met with swords or flaming arrows. Flustered, an uncomfortable state for her, she groped for the words she needed. Not only did she simply not wish for a husband, she certainly did not wish to bind herself to *this* man.

"Is this why ye wished to speak with my father?" she asked as soon as her tongue could shape the words.

Caelen peered at her from beneath thick brows. "Nae. We hadnae finished our talk of alliance. He is the one who mentioned marriage."

Her heart thudded in her chest. *Father already plans my betrothal?* Panic threatened. She swallowed, pushing past the rising fear. "If he has spoken truthfully of me, ye know I am not a biddable woman, nor do I willingly seek the authority of a husband."

A corner of Caelen's mouth quivered, but his eyes remained impassive. "Neither he nor ye have ever given that impression."

"Then what about me gives ye reason to think ye want me as a wife?"

"I know ye dinnae wish to marry. Howbeit, 'tis a woman's lot to wed—to form an alliance between clans, to run a home—to bear children."

"Is this to settle the bond between our families?" Arbela asked, shrewdness winnowing through Caelen's flowery words. "I am to be nothing more than a reminder our clans will remain faithful?" Resentment replaced fear and Arbela ground her teeth. Garen whined at her side, and Arbela knew her hostility upset the dog. She patted the furry head and the dog subsided.

Caelen, also, appeared anxious, running a palm across the back of his neck. "Yer da cares for ye more than that, it would seem. So does yer brother, if his words of warning are to be believed."

Curiosity piqued her attention. "What did Alex say?"

"He warned he'd gut me like a fish should I ever mistreat ye."

The tightness in her chest loosened. "He means it."

"Och, aye, he does," Caelen agreed. "Lass, I cannae think of two people less likely to seek marriage than ye and me. My first wife wasnae a pleasant woman to be around, and I willnae willingly bind myself to such a life again. Ye and I each have something the other wants."

"Oh?" Despite her convictions otherwise, his words piqued her willingness to hear more.

"Between us, we would have a marriage in words only. I dinnae seek a wife and ye dinnae seek a husband. Howbeit, I need a woman to care for Bram and his nurse is aged. He seems to like ye. I also need a woman to run my home, tend to the duties therein. And yer da has promised an alliance between our clans, as well as men and tools to help rebuild the keep and protect my borders."

He paused, and Arbela considered his words. "Ye have quite a bargain to strike, Laird MacKern," she noted drily. "How does this benefit me?"

"I would make no demands on ye. Ye would be free to dress and act as ye will. Ye will marry as yer da wishes, and secure yer future. Make no mistake, there are few men who would permit such freedoms once the vows are spoken. My land isnae so far ye couldnae visit yer da when ye wish, though I will require ye care for and protect Bram."

Arbela released a small breath. "I would marry—and yet, be free to do as I wish?"

"Ye would first and foremost protect Bram. Ye know his mother's da seeks to take him from me. I dinnae wish the lad closed up within the castle, but there can be no chance of MacGillonay kidnapping the bairn."

Caelen's gaze shifted from serious to piercing. "And ye willnae fill his head with anything but Christianity."

The implied charge caught Arbela off-guard. "Do ye question my faith?"

He gave a slight nod to her clothing. "I cannae concern myself with the manner in which ye dress, as long as 'tis modest, but yer appearance isnae like those of other Christians here. I willnae have Bram raised a Saracen."

"I have walked the very streets our Lord once trod." Fury bubbled out of her mouth before she could halt it. "As a child, I was blessed by the Bishop of Antioch, and have touched Holy Relics. My father fought with King Richard to regain the city of Jerusalem and he was present when Saladin and King Richard created a truce. My mother's country is one of the oldest Christian nations in the world, and the first ever to adopt Christianity as its religion. How dare ye question my faith?"

Caelen did not respond and tears of fury pricked the back of Arbela's eyes, hot and prideful. "I will not marry ye."

Caelen faced the paddock as Voski trotted over. "I dinnae mean disrespect, but ye are foreign to me. For all that yer da is Scots, ye have been raised verra different from anything I've known—or imagined. I dinnae ask for anything more than yer word ye will protect my son, keep my home running smoothly, and raise Bram in a Christian manner."

Her heart racing, Arbela sought to still her shaking hands by stroking Voski's neck. Caelen spoke the truth. If her fate was to marry, how could she do better than marry for the sake of a boy who needed a mother—and whose father wanted nothing more than a business arrangement?

"If I agree . . .." Her voice trailed off, unwilling to commit to this tremendous step. The temptation of having a marriage in name only was powerful. Rather than being the property of a man, subject to his whims and chained by the traditional roles demanded of women, she'd be free to pursue her life as she saw fit. And Bram. What a delightful child. Would it not be a boon to step into the boy's life at a time when he still needed a woman's touch, but would also benefit from her knowledge as a warrior?

To hear MacKern speak, he likely lived in a hovel. Nothing more than a pile of stones, much like the many tower houses they'd passed along the coast once they sailed into this land called Scotland which the sun had apparently forsaken. Though her home in Batroun had been well kept, it had been nothing like the sprawling MacLean keep. She had no need for so many servants or so much space. In fact, she found the attention quite stifling. A more modest home would prove no hardship. Caelen obviously wished her approval—and likely her father wished it also—which put her in a position to negotiate.

"If ye agree," Caelen continued for her, "we will hold the ceremony within the next month. Ye will become part of my household, and I will be known as yer husband. We will be polite in public, and see little of each other in private. Should ye have concerns, ye will bring them to me."

"If I agree, I will have reassurances from ye, as well."

Caelen's expression grew guarded, but he gave a short nod.

Arbela began her list. "I will hold ye to your statement of allowing me to live as I will."

He nodded again and turned slightly, his profile stern. Arbela's cheeks heated as she considered her next question, but she pursued it nonetheless.

"Do ye expect children from this . . . arrangement?"

He swung about, eyes hooded, face emotionless. "Nae."

Though she currently had no great desire for motherhood, the finality of his denial left an ache in her heart. Dreams of someday holding her own child, while fleeting, had always appeared as a certainty in the distant future. To hear those dreams would never come to fruition left her unsettled. Could she trade this for a lifetime of assurance her life would be her own?

She leveled an even stare at the man who wished to marry her, yet live a separate life. A vision of the problems that could arise cautioned her.

"Ye will swear ye will never act in a way as to embarrass me before your people or your son. I will hear no rumors of other women striving to take my place, nor will ye consort with questionable women in my presence."

"Ye cannae agree to a business alliance, yet think to forbid me comforts of my own choosing?"

Caution fouled with confusion. What she knew of men and women were gleaned from stories told in the women's quarters. And aside from Phillipe's unexpected kiss, no actual knowledge at all. How much could she bargain for?

"I have lived in tents and palaces, and I know how gossip spreads. I will not be disgraced by ye or the manner in which others whisper. Inasmuch as ye will hold me to a celibate state, I will expect ye to honor no less."

Caelen's face darkened, and for a moment Arbela wondered if she pushed too far. But she was not his wife yet, and she would start this alliance with her expectations firmly in place. He pivoted on a booted heel, wrestling with his decision.

"We will speak of this to no one," he growled.

"There should be no reason to," Arbela agreed.

He faced her, brow lowered, eyes flashing. He shoved a hand at her and she gripped it firmly. "Agreed."

Chapter Eleven

"Och, Arbela, *barev, dustry.*" *Hello, daughter.*

Caelen glanced up at Donal's words, their cadence foreign to his ears. Laird MacLean beamed at his daughter as she entered the hall for the noon meal. She had obviously taken time to refresh herself and change into clean garments since Caelen had parted from her more than an hour earlier. As exotic as ever, her heavy pink brocade tunic shimmered with pearls sewn amid the silver embroidery. A long scarf of the same bright color wound about her neck, a perfect foil for her night-dark hair which was secured off her face with a fillet of woven silver, a large pink stone resting on her forehead.

"*Barev, hayry,*" she replied. *Hello, father.* Donal tilted his head to Caelen. Her brown eyes flashed, but she greeted him civilly enough. "*Barev*, Laird MacKern."

Donal led them to the head table, seating Arbela immediately to his left, Caelen next to her. A few heads lifted as Arbela took her place next to her father—and Caelen assumed a position of power within the family.

Alex entered the hall, Bram skipping beside him, the black dog tagging at his heels. Bram looked up and, releasing Alex's hand, bolted across the room to Caelen's side.

"Da! I've found ye!"

His pleasure was infectious, and Caelen allowed a brief smile. "Have ye been a good lad for Alex?" he asked.

Bram beamed. "I have been verra good! Alex said if I was, he'd give me his berry pasty to eat!" He climbed into Caelen's lap and wriggled about as he surveyed the table. "We're having berry pasties, aye?"

Caelen gently but firmly shifted Bram to the empty seat to his left. Bram sat for an instant before he spied Arbela. Scrambling to his knees in the chair, he leaned over the arm rest.

"Hi, Bela!" he cried in a whisper loud enough to reach any ear at the laird's table. Arbela leaned back and sent him a pleased smile.

"Hello, Bram-jan," she replied with a wink.

Bram squirmed, leaning farther across the slim wooden rail. "Alex said I could have his pasty. Did Cook make any?"

"Dinnae bother Lady Arbela, lad. If Cook made pasties, ye may have *one*." Caelen stared down the distraught rebellion in his son's eyes as he dispelled the hope of extra servings of the coveted berry pies. "Seat yerself, lad."

Bram slumped in his chair, then wriggled upright at Caelen's reproving look.

Around them, people began the meal. The mouth-watering aroma of succulent meats filled the air, undercut with the bold yeasty scent of fresh bread. Colorful vegetables floated in various sauces, and foods Caelen couldn't name graced platters on the laird's table.

Bram sat up further, eying the unusual offering. "What's that, Da?" he asked, pointing to brown balls that could have been meat, though they appeared to have been dusted with sand before cooking.

"Come sit with me, Bram-jan. I will tell ye about the food," Arbela said. With a quick glance at Caelen, Bram slid from his seat and climbed onto Arbela's chair, the pair of them fitting the grandly carved seat quite well. As discreetly as he could, Caelen turned an ear to Arbela's tutelage.

She selected one of the balls from the platter and placed it on her trencher. "This is called *falafel*," she told Bram. "They are made with fava beans and spices, and deep-fried until they are crispy." She broke one in half and ate it, encouraging Bram to try the other half. The lad took a bite and chewed it slowly, curious expressions crossing his face.

"I *think* I like it," he ventured. "'Tis different."

Arbela laughed. "It is a favorite of mine. Ye may grow to like it more." She spooned a bit of paste from a bowl in the center. Taking a small portion of what appeared to be a flat bread, she dipped it in the paste and handed it to Bram.

"Try this one and I'll tell you the name."

Bram sniffed it, then took a cautious bite. "I think I like it, too," he said. "The bread is good," he added with certainty.

"This paste is *baba ganoush*."

Bram giggled. "Baba noosh."

"*Ga*-noosh," Arbela corrected. "Another favorite of mine. My Aunt Zora has been teaching the cook a few recipes since we arrived."

Bram eyed the remaining food on the table. "Do ye not eat Scots' food?" he asked.

Arbela ruffled his hair. "Of course, we do. But I like other food as well. What do ye like best?"

"Pasties!" Bram crowed.

"Besides that."

Bram thought, a frown crossing his face. "I like roasted meats, and porridge—with lots of butter and honey."

"Vegetables?"

Bram wrinkled his nose. "Kirsty says I must eat them, but I dinnae like them."

"I will have our cook roast eggplant for ye. We will eat it together. We must plant the vines this summer."

Appearing skeptical, Bram gave a slow nod. "Does it taste like eggs?"

"Nae," she laughed. "It has a flavor all its own."

To Caelen's surprise, as Arbela spoke, she'd added roasted carrots to Bram's trencher—and the lad was eating them without a fuss. Uncertain if Arbela had beguiled the lad or if the carrots had a seasoning that enhanced their flavor, Caelen added a few to his own trencher. The aroma that drifted up set his mouth to watering, and he took a bite.

The flavors filled his mouth, nose, and throat. Light and vaguely sweet, nutty and perhaps slightly bitter, the unusual spices surprised him.

He stole a look at Bram's trencher. It was empty.

"What does yer cook season the carrots with?" he asked, drawing Arbela's attention with the tip of his knife, pointing to the rapidly emptying platter.

"Coriander, cumin, and fennel, mostly," she replied. "And honey. Do ye like it?"

He nodded. "We dinnae have such spices at Dunfaileas."

"I will bring them. Dunfaileas is your home?"

Our home, he was tempted to remind her, but decided against it. "Aye. 'Tis the name of our castle."

"What does it mean?" Arbela's voice, while soft, sounded eager, and Caelen remembered Alex mentioning she spoke several languages.

"A *dun* is a fort. *Faileas* means reflection. The castle sits on the edge of Loch Linnhe and ye can see its reflection in the water."

Her head tilted slightly. "It sounds lovely," she murmured.

Donal's chair scraped the stone floor as he rose to his feet. Caelen and Arbela glanced up, the fleeting moment of accord gone. Laird MacLean lifted his goblet, candlelight catching the glow of silver. Conversations in the hall slid to a halt as people gave him their attention.

"I have enjoyed living again amongst ye for the past month and more, my clan. As the youngest son, I sought my fortune in fighting. Farlan and I took up the cross and traveled to Outremer with King Richard. After King Richard left the Holy Lands, Bohemond IV of Antioch accepted our service, bestowing upon me the title of Baron of Batroun. I lived at Mseilha Castle, on the road between Tripoli and Beirut at St. William's Pass until I received word of my da's and brothers' passing."

He glanced about the room. "I recognize many of ye, and grieve to realize there are faces no longer present who knew me as a lad. I have spent the past weeks re-acquainting myself with the affairs of the clan and will remain open to suggestions or hearing of difficulties ye may have. 'Tis my honor and privilege to serve the MacLean clan."

Fists thundered on the wooden tables in an approving cadence and voices rumbled low. Donal paused then spoke again when the noise receded.

"One alliance I wish to announce this eve is the one between the MacLean and MacKern clans, and formalized by marriage between my daughter, Arbela, and Caelen, Laird MacKern."

Caelen's heart thudded as he glanced at the woman next to him. For all of his avowed claims to the contrary and his certainty he'd never remarry, he was about to take Arbela MacLean to wife. Unease slid through his veins, curling his toes. Flashes of memory, of shrill complaints, sobbing accusations—the woman he'd once loved refusing him, his touch, their son. Caelen shook his head. 'Twas a business arrangement this time. No expectations beyond two people filling positions that would benefit them both and require nothing from either other than distant, polite discourse when the need arose. He wanted nothing more from her, and she'd made it clear she expected nothing from him except to be left alone. That should be easy enough.

A jolt as alarming as the sudden din of a hammer tensed Arbela's muscles. How had she come to agree to this marriage? Caelen MacKern was a Scot—a barbarian—a man with no use for her beyond her skills at managing his home and his son. Her glance slid to Bram and something inside her softened. A ready-made family. She was free to continue living her life as she pleased, with no condemnation for her preferred style of dress or her less-than-ladylike skills. No condemnation other than the bunched brow and narrowed eyes of the man soon to become her husband. Her lord and master.

The memory of a sweet kiss, stolen on a balcony in Tripoli, crossed her mind. Phillipe had said he loved her, and though she had not been ready to explore his words, she would never know what his love could have meant to her. If things had been different, if she and Phillipe had married, would Phillipe have insisted she give up her warrior's ways? Become a wife, a mother?

Her words to Phillipe came back to mock her. *Do ye not see? This could be a chance to create greater unity in the north.* Instead of following his heart, Phillipe had become a pawn, advancing an alliance against the Turks. And she, Arbela, would unite the MacLean and MacKern clans.

She knew Phillipe would find a way to make his marriage to the Armenian princess work to bring about peace. She faced less of a trial than he, as she did not despise the MacKerns, but simply found little common ground with them. They were Scots. Her father's people. Now *her* people. Like Phillipe, it was not the future she'd imagined, but it was not the death sentence she'd envisioned months ago when her father had taken up the idea of her marriage once again.

Arbela rose to her feet and lifted her goblet. "May we be blessed with peace and a prosperous alliance." She tilted her head to Caelen. "*Orhnut'yunner.*"

"Blessings," her father replied, then took a sip of his wine.

"*Orhnut'yunner.*" Alex tossed the contents of his goblet back and a serving girl quickly refilled it. He stood and surveyed the crowd. "My sister is a woman of priceless value—and Caelen MacKern the most fortunate of men. May their union be a blessed one." He gave Arbela a short bow. "*Orhnut'yunner.*"

"*Beannachdan.*" Donal changed the words to Gaelic and lifted his goblet to Caelen who slowly stood.

"I am honored to join our clans. May there be blessings on both our houses. *Beannachdan air ar taighean*" He lifted his goblet to the people. "*Slàinte mhath!*"

"*Slàinte mhor!*" the crowd roared as drinking vessels clinked and the toast became the finality on the announcement and her future.

The heated room shortened her breath, and Arbela sank slowly to her seat, hiding her unsteady hands in a fold of her scarf. She bumped against

Bram who stared at her with big, questioning eyes. Struggling for a smile, Arbela leaned her head close to his.

"I do not suppose your father has mentioned our plans?" She cast a quick look at Caelen in deep conversation with one of her father's knights.

"Nae," Bram replied, his lower lip slightly forward, indicative of his distress.

"Do not worry, Bram-jan," she reassured him. "Your father and I have agreed to marry and that means I will live at Dunfaileas."

Bram's eyebrows bunched together, his features more angry than confused. "I dinnae like it," he stated.

Taken aback, Arbela schooled her face into a smooth mask. "Why do ye object to this?"

A mulish expression clung to Bram's face and he turned away. Picking up his wooden spoon, he shoved the remainder of his meal around on his trencher, sending small pieces over the edge and onto the table.

"Bram! Be mindful of what ye are doing." Caelen's rebuke sounded low but unmistakable through the din. Bram flung his spoon to the table and slumped back in the chair.

"What has gotten into ye, lad?" Caelen scooted his chair back. Arbela lifted a hand, stalling the reprimand certain to come.

"There is some reason he does not wish us to wed—though he has not said why," she murmured. Caelen relaxed his weight onto his seat.

"Lady Arbela has agreed to become my wife," he said, placing a hand on Bram's shoulder. "Do ye have something ye wish to say?"

Bram continued to stare at his lap. The soft curve of his cheek glistened. Arbela's heart clenched.

"Why does this distress ye so, Bram?" she asked. "I thought we were friends."

He kicked the table leg. Caelen cleared his throat and Bram hunched lower in his seat.

"Would ye care to speak of this in the laird's solar?" Arbela motioned

94

to the room off the great hall. Bram shook his head, mute.

"I will have an answer, Bram," Caelen insisted. Bram resumed swinging his legs, the toes of his boots tapping the table leg ever so gently. Arbela shook her head slightly as Caelen opened his mouth.

"When I come to Dunfaileas, I will bring Toros and Garen, as well as Voski," she murmured in a low, soothing voice. "Ye and I will spend time together and give your nurse time to rest. I have been told my stories are exactly right for a boy who will soon pass his sixth summer." Arbela sighed as Bram continued to refuse her overture. "Your father and I have an agreement. I believe ye and I should have one as well."

Bram slanted her a look from the corner of his eyes.

"In exchange for the fun we will have, I will expect ye to mind yer table manners, try at least two bites of any new food I offer ye, and to speak when something momentous is on your mind."

Bram slewed around in the chair, facing Caelen. "Da, if Bela marries ye, will she be my ma?"

"Aye," Caelen replied, sending Arbela a look over the lad's head. "It doesnae mean we have forgotten yer ma."

Bram climbed to his knees and over the chair arm, into Caelen's arms. He buried his head against his chest. "I dinnae like it."

"But, ye like her, aye?"

Bram nodded, rubbing his face against his da's tunic.

"Then why do ye not want her to come to Dunfaileas with us?"

Bram peered at Arbela over his shoulder, a wealth of sadness on his face. Arbela swallowed past a lump in her throat, her heart hurting.

"I dinnae want her to be my ma," he hiccupped, "'cause my other ma died."

Chapter Twelve

Bram had seen too much of death in his short life. Arbela's heart went out to him, but she could not bring herself to promise she would not die. Life was too uncertain for promises that were not hers to keep.

"I plan to be around a long time, Bram-jan," she whispered. "Ye will likely grow weary of lessons and manners long before I am ready to quit this earth. But ye are a brave boy and smart enough to know people are not meant to live forever. Let us be the best of friends whilst we have the chance."

He lingered against Caelen's chest, looking very young and fragile. With a shuddering sigh, he at last nodded and relaxed. "Can ye bring Ari as well?"

"Who is Ari?" Caelen asked.

"Ari is a brave pony I introduced Bram to this morning," Arbela replied. "Bram was feeling a bit less than certain and Ari convinced him he has nothing to fear."

"I like Ari, Da. Can she bring him? I need a pony."

Arbela sent Bram a cautioning look. "'Tis up to your father, Bram. But Ari *is* in great need of a boy to look after."

Caelen's eyes narrowed. "Lady Arbela and I will discuss this." He slipped Bram to his feet. "Go with Rory, now. We leave for home as soon as I finish here."

Bram glanced at Arbela. "Are ye coming with us now?"

She smiled fondly. "Nae. I will come in a few weeks after I have settled things here. There are things for me to do and people to say good-bye to. I expect ye to come back for the wedding wearing your finest clothing and with a small gift for me," she teased.

"Will ye have a gift for me, as well?" The idea apparently put all thoughts of death aside—as Arbela had intended.

"Mayhap," she laughed. "Now, mind your father, and I will think of the first bedtime story I shall tell ye when I come to Dunfaileas."

"Da always tells the story of St. George and the Dragon," Bram supplied.

"Mayhap I tell it better," she whispered. Bram giggled and darted off to Rory's side.

"Have ye chosen a date for the wedding?" Donal leaned past Arbela, inserting himself into their conversation.

The brief shiver of panic was gone almost before it registered, and Arbela lifted her chin against its return. "I see no reason to wait over-long," she answered. "I have no desire for the rigors of a formal wedding."

"Shall I tell Father Sachairi four weeks, then? At the next full moon?"

Rather than consider the planning a wedding entailed, Arbela realized a full moon would make for easier travel to her new home.

"'Twill be in time for Beltane," Caelen noted, obviously pleased with the timing.

"Beltane?" Arbela queried. "What is this?"

Caelen flashed her a look of mild irritation and his face flushed. "It marks the beginning of the growing season," he said as he rose to his feet. "I will see to things at Dunfaileas and return at the full moon. 'Tis a pleasure to have such a bonny wife."

"I am sending Alex and Kade with ye to assess yer needs," Donal said. "They will report back to me so I may know how to best aid my soon-to-be son by marriage." With a nod, Donal sent the two men to Caelen's side. Alex clipped Caelen's shoulder with a jesting clout.

"Must see to my sister's new home, aye?"

Caelen's nod of leave-taking warred with Arbela's sense of incompleteness. She darted to her feet, past her father's outstretched hand. "Wait!" Caelen came to a reluctant stop, his quarter-turn clearly indicating a desire to avoid further conversation. Arbela ignored it.

"Why does our wedding at the start of your growing season please ye?" she asked. "What does Beltane mean?"

Their halt positioned them next to Donal's oldest friend and companion throughout the Crusade, and Arbela and Alex's godfather, Farlan. The knight rose from the table. "Beltane simply means *return of the sun*, and is one of our ancient festivals, lass. Long before man came to understand such things, it was believed the sun was held hostage during the winter and its return was celebrated with fire and feasting."

Arbela turned incredulous eyes on her soon-to-be husband. "Ye wish us married during a pagan festival?"

"It does no harm to find good cause to celebrate. Our wedding is an excellent reason, and for the clan to remember it as the mark of a new season cannae be a bad thing. We have seen too much evil of late."

It seemed much to take in. The man who demanded she raise his son in a Christian manner and who had been misinformed as to her own beliefs, saw benefit in aligning their nuptials with pagan rituals? Arbela sent her father a wild look.

"We will rejoice in the holy joining of our clans, daughter," he said. "And if the houses are decorated with the yellow flowers of May, we willnae regard it. The church has ignored this celebration of new life and season of hope after a long winter. We will rejoice in the promise of new alliances as well."

"There will be a Christian priest, Arbela. Not a druid," Caelen admonished.

He *chided* her? Arbela's head slewed around so quickly to face him she thought it would fly off her neck. "Ye will not question my faith," she informed him. "But ye *will* give me leave to question *yours*."

"'Tis about blending our past with our present—and our future," Caelen replied. "For many 'tis a way to mark the new season, to rejoice that all dark things are past and the brightness of the future is before them. Dinnae deny them the chance to embrace a new season of life."

Arbela fought her outrage to a manageable level and gave a strained nod. "As ye wish. I will not cause strife in my new home."

Caelen's brow crumpled with suspicion. "Until the full moon, m'lady." His brief pause could hardly be construed as a mark of respect, but he offered nothing further. His footsteps faded as he followed Rory and Bram from the room.

Arbela accepted the congratulations from those around her, forcing a brittle smile to her face. Two unmarried girls she'd developed a passing friendship with dragged her to a vacant spot at a nearby table and collapsed onto the benches, twittering excitedly.

"Ye must have a new gown made," Caitriona said, eyeing Arbela's tunic.

"I think her clothes are lovely," Agnes demurred. "And they look so nice on her," she added with a wistful slide of her hand over her own thin contours. She shoved a hank of shockingly red hair from her face. "I have never seen such colors or embroidery in my life."

"But she is a Scottish bride, now," Caitriona insisted. "Why wouldnae she wish to please her new Scottish husband?"

"I do not have to please my new husband," Arbela replied absently, not particularly engaged in the girls' conversation, but unable to let Caitriona's remark pass unchallenged. "I am as much my own person as he is, and I will not change my clothing—or anything else—simply to appease a man."

Agnes nodded encouragingly. Caitriona drew back, apparently scandalized.

"I understand ye wish to show off yer jewels," the plump daughter of the castle seneschal drawled. "But, could ye not do it in a less . . .." An airy flurry of fingers indicated either a lack of proper wording or condescension toward Arbela's *accoutrement*.

Affronted to find the girl who had befriended her apparently hid a low opinion of her appearance, Arbela leaned forward, laying her forearms on the scarred table top.

"When I decide 'tis time for me to wear a formless, itching dress such as ye have determined 'tis proper to wear, I will do so. Until such a time, ye will find kind, helpful suggestions are appreciated. Shrewish, baiting tactics are not."

With a huff, Caitriona rose from the bench. She sent a pointed stare to Agnes, who gave a small shrug and refused to follow.

"It scarcely matters what she thinks of me, as I am the laird's daughter and will be leaving in less than a month's time," Arbela said, offering Agnes a chance to reconsider her choice to remain.

"'Twill do no harm to tweak her nose," Agnes replied. "Her rank is often all she has to cling to. I will be back in her good graces soon, never fear. Too many others refuse her friendship."

"She should not struggle so."

"She can be thoughtful when she wishes, but I fear there is usually a hook hidden within the proffered kindness."

"What is your opinion of my clothing, Agnes?"

Agnes laughed. "I have no belief ye will heed my comments should they differ from yer own. Why do ye ask?"

"Do ye merely pretend to admire my attire?" Arbela insisted, ignoring the request.

"If only other people would be as direct as ye," Agnes sighed. "I dinnae pretend. Nor do I merely shield ye from the worst of Caitriona's barbs. I admit I am fascinated by yer clothing, but they suit ye."

"How do they suit me?" Arbela questioned.

"They are made of fabrics I have either never heard of or only imagined. The auld laird's family was wealthy." Agnes swept her leveled hand around the hall which was spacious and boasted carved beams and pillars. "And some of the ladies have worn silk undergarments and veils. But brocade is something I havenae seen, nor the lining of yer cloak which ye call mohair. Not to mention the casual way ye wear jewels and gold and silver sewn into the embroidery."

She shrugged. "Such things are fascinating, and so are ye, a lass born of two worlds."

Arbela blinked. "I am as unlike ye as possible. The women here favor striking red hair, porcelain skin and slender bodies. I am short, with ample curves. My skin is dusky, and my hair is as black as soot. Hardly your Scottish ideal for beauty."

"Hmm. Should I find myself in your homeland, I daresay I would be an item of interest. But I would feel as though I stuck out like a sore thumb. Being an object of curiosity and gossip can hardly be a comfortable feeling."

Arbela stared at Agnes. "Come with me to Dunfaileas," she blurted. Warmth heated her cheeks. "Forgive me. Ye have ties here. I should not have said that."

Agnes laughed merrily. "I am flattered ye did. But ye speak truth—I am needed here by my family." She blushed prettily. "I have a suitor," she confessed quietly. "He is braw."

"Braw?" Arbela latched on to the word, hoping to turn the conversation away from her unprecedented plea for companionship. "How so?"

"Do ye know this word?" Agnes asked.

"Aye. I spoke Armenian with my mother's people. Court Persian with others of high-rank. Latin with many of the Antioch court. But my father spoke Scots when we were in private, as did Farlan and Kade. Gaelic, also, from time to time, though I only know a bit of it."

"There is, then, *one* thing I know better than ye do." Agnes smiled. "I was born speaking Gaelic, and Scots—or, as some term it, *Inglis*." She leaned toward Arbela, her smile reaching her eyes. "My man, Dubh, is a bonny man," she confided.

"Dubh?"

"His nickname because he is black-haired—like ye, though 'tis not a lassie's name."

"Tell me about him," Arbela invited, a bit out of her depth, for she'd never entertained such thoughts about a man before, nor felt the lack. But Agnes piqued her curiosity.

"He is verra strong." Agnes suppressed a giggle—mostly. "He can lift me in his arms—not that I'd allow him that much familiarity." Her giggle broke through. "Once or twice," she admitted, her face flaming almost the color of her hair. She glanced about, but no one appeared to pay them any attention.

"He trains as one of yer da's soldiers, and he is nimble-footed. But when his eyes light on me . . .." With a sigh, Agnes melted on the bench. "Have ye never known what a man's eyes tell ye when he finds ye bonny?"

Startled, Arbela shook her head. "Nae. I have seen what a man's eyes tell me when I have bested him. Before he meets God."

Agnes placed a palm lightly over Arbela's left hand. "I know lairds' daughters dinnae always marry for the pleasure of a union," she began delicately. "But I saw Laird MacKern stare at ye—as if he finds ye intriguing."

"More likely as if he doesnae know what to do with me," Arbela corrected. "I have no reason to believe he finds me of interest beyond my dowry and my ability to put his household in order and care for his son."

Agnes gave a slow shake of her head. "Nae. Ye have his attention. But I dinnae believe he knows what to do about it."

Arbela considered Agnes' words. If he found her attractive—as a man to a woman—would it break the contract made in private between them? If he wanted her for a wife in more than name only, would he then expect her to become like the other women of his clan? It did not bear considering.

"'Tis my belief we will have a contented marriage," she said softly. "He has promised he will not strive to change my manner of dress nor thwart my routine weaponry practices. He will not change my life, and I will not change his overmuch."

Tiny frown lines marked Agnes' brow. "If 'tis any consolation, Laird MacKern is known as a fair man. If he has said he willnae challenge yer clothing, he willnae. Some call him the Bull of the Highlands. 'Tis true he is headstrong, but 'tis also rumored he is a favorite among the women of his clan." A sly smile smoothed away the wrinkles. "I would imagine ye will soon discover what about him causes the lasses to blush."

Heat rushed through Arbela's veins, settling in her cheeks and breast. "I do not believe Laird MacKern wishes other children. He has an heir."

"Och! All men want children. And they will lie on both sides of the blanket to get them. Children are not guaranteed to live to adulthood, and a laird especially needs others to ensure his lineage. Yer hips should bear up nicely in childbirth, so dinnae fash. 'Twill likely come easily to ye."

Something foreign pooled low in Arbela's belly and she struggled for words.

"I've made ye blush!" Agnes crowed. "Has yer auntie not told ye of men and women?"

Arbela's eyes widened. "I know enough. Ye could help me with another matter," she said, diverting Agnes' interest. "My wedding is to be at the next full moon."

"Beltane?"

"Aye. I know nothing of the festival. I would very much appreciate your knowledge." Arbela settled a coaxing smile on her friend. "Tell me what ye know of Beltane."

Chapter Thirteen

The differences between the horses he raised and the ones the MacLean had brought with him struck Caelen anew. From Lusitania? The region was as little known to him as the horses it produced. Alex's mount, a high-stepping dark gray, arched his neck against the bit, his full mane rippling across Alex's hands. Despite his antics, the stallion's gait appeared smooth and flowing, his rider moving easily in the saddle.

Though Alex's horse stood nearly two hands taller than his own, Caelen did not have to tilt his head much to look the young man squarely in the eye. A good thing, for he felt somewhat compelled to question the tale Alex spun. From the intent way Bram listened to the story, he feared the lad already had an enormous case of hero-worship. Only Caelen wasn't sure if Bram was more fascinated by Alex's tale, or of the part Arbela played in it.

"I appreciate ye entertaining the lad," he said, giving Addis a wee nudge to move him closer to Alex's horse. "But ye dinnae expect us to believe yer sister—*Lady* Arbela—was much help when the Turks attacked, do ye?"

Alex and Kade exchanged looks. "Aye," Alex said. "Ye have seen her—"

"Och, with a bow," Caelen interrupted. "Likely carefully out of harm's way on the battlements. Not at the gate, knocking back siege towers."

"'Twas one of her arrows which struck a Saracen beneath his arm, felling him before he could attain the top of the wall, knocking his companions down as he went." Alex added a fluttering movement with his hand, delighting Bram.

"Bela is verra brave, isn't she, Alex?" the lad asked—insisted.

Alex gave a solemn nod. "Aye. Very brave. I've seen her stand her ground even whilst an enemy Saracen raced toward her, a javelin in his hands and death in his eyes."

"And he obliged by keeping his horse in a steady canter so she could knock him off with one of her wee arrows?" Caelen hadn't meant for his words to sound so mocking, and he met Alex's stare with a carefully blank look.

"Nae. He crouched low over his horse's neck, spear at the ready." Alex leaned across his horse's neck, mimicking the rider in his tale. "'Twould have been impossible for any to accurately aim an arrow, such a poor target did he present. At the last possible second, Arbela stepped before the horse and to the other side, spoiling his aim. As the rider wrenched his horse to a halt, Arbela drew one of the knives at her belt and sent it straight into the base of the infidel's neck. A second blade followed the first, severing the great vessel in his neck, killing him within moments." He slipped to his horse's side, hanging dangerously low, much to Bram's amusement.

"Where, might I ask, were ye, Lord Alex?" Caelen couched his words politely.

Alex resumed his seat. "I was fighting off an unhorsed Saracen. Arbela and I were en route to visit our mother's people in Armenia, some days' travel from our home at Batroun. We traveled by caravan, with several of Da's knights and men-at-arms for protection." He winked at Bram and returned to his singsong story-telling cadence.

"But the Turks had heard of a beautiful half-Armenian princess who traveled to Sis, the Armenian capital, and they greatly desired to capture her."

"Bela?" Bram asked breathlessly.

"Aye. Known as *Sirun Aghjik*, The Beautiful Girl, she would have made a fine addition to any sheik's household."

"Nae!" Bram shouted, a clenched fist in the air.

Alex nodded. "They would have hidden her away like a treasure too wonderful to be seen by others, and she would have spent the rest of her days pining for the life she could have lived in Scotland."

Caelen fought the urge to laugh.

"She would have gutted them first!" Bram crowed.

Caelen glanced at his son, startled. "Why would ye say such a thing?"

"Bela isnae afraid of anything," the lad assured him.

"Er, 'tis truth," Alex muttered, clearly just as surprised by Bram's observation. Caelen sent him a mildly questioning look. Alex took a deep breath.

"Would ye like to hear about animals ye dinnae have here?" Alex asked, obviously hoping to lure Bram from his bloodthirsty thoughts.

"Aye!" the lad agreed. "Are they ferocious?"

"Some are," Alex replied. "We have lions, and—"

"I know about lions!" Bram interrupted. "They're big cats with a mane like Addis's all around their neck. They are king of all the animals!"

"Where did ye hear about lions, Bram?" Caelen wanted to know.

"Bela," Bram stated succinctly, as if Caelen should have known. And he should have. "She even drew one on the hearthstone for me."

Alex nodded. "Aye. I had forgotten ye showed me the drawing earlier."

"And she told me how the lion got its mane. It dinnae always have one, but one day . . .."

Bram's chatter continued as he regaled them with Arbela's story and Caelen wondered again what he had agreed to.

* * *

Alex surveyed the castle from his position atop the western tower, observing the crumbling weaknesses in the outer wall, victim of the ages. Fields to the north were only half-plowed, though he could see the rounded backs of men and women doing their best to get seeds in the ground. A lone fishing boat bobbed on the surface of the loch, lines stretching into the water from the vessel, giving it the appearance of a large water bug, legs spread to balance it atop the gentle waves.

He had a good idea of what was required to repair the structure, and of the men needed for plowing, planting, fishing and hunting. The scourge had been unkind to MacKern's people, and without help, the clan would likely founder—soon.

His thoughts ranged over the home his sister would soon inhabit. The size of Dunfaileas did not bother him, nor did he imagine it would concern Arbela. Indeed, it was closer to their home in Batroun than the enormous MacLean castle at Morven where they now lived. But its ancient bones were apparent in the ten-foot-thick walls, slender windows—when there were any at all—and lack of even the basic comforts they had been raised with.

Food was lean, though he'd see to it enough staples were sent with Arbela to greatly bolster their pantry. And his sister already knew to bring spices for cooking if she wanted familiar flavors at the table.

He wrinkled his nose, recalling the pall of the privy that hung over the castle. That was something he could set men to repairing before his sister arrived. Perhaps he would insist on fresh reeds and herbs on the stone floors before he and Kade quitted themselves of Dunfaileas on the morrow. And insist on a thorough cleaning before their new lady arrived. Of a certainty, the wedding would be held at MacLean Castle. Dunfaileas would not support a large gathering in its present condition.

Alex stepped to the edge of the tower walk. 'Twas obvious where the laird's heart lay. Of all the outbuildings either within or without the castle wall, the stable alone had been kept in satisfactory condition. Soiled hay, piled to one side, readied to be carted to an area close to the fields where it would rot and enrich the soil. Fresh straw in each stall kept the horses's hooves clean and free from disease. And, though sparse, the oats were of excellent quality.

'Twas clear Caelen MacKern cared for his horses. His people greeted him warmly and without reservation. His attitude toward his men was open and jesting. Only with his son did he seem reserved. He treated him with distant care, perhaps afraid others would claim partiality should he favor his child over another. Perhaps afraid to form too close an attachment to one so young.

"Are ye ready to present Laird MacLean with yer report?" Kade settled next to Alex, arms braced on the stone wall.

"There are many needs here," Alex said. "Protection must be our first priority, for without it, all else is for naught. But I shudder to think of my sister living here. Eager to please, the MacKerns may be, but none appear to be miracle workers."

"Och, the place has potential," Kade assured him. "'Tis a bit old and neglected, but Arbela will have the place running efficiently in no time."

"Whilst she makes wedding preparations, I will have Da send carpets, incense, and oil lamps. Silks to line the bed hangings—which we will also replace. Arbela may survive quite well mired in dirt and sweat—and ye and I have both seen it—but I will have her live here in at least modest luxury."

"What do ye think of the laird? Arbela's soon-to-be husband."

Alex swiveled on his heel, placing his back against the wall. "Laird MacKern is a fair man. That said, I will add he is stubborn. I have done what I could to make my suggestions without running afoul of his notion of what is good or even good enough. He either does not care or mayhap does not understand he is taking a princess to wife, even if she is half-Scots. Arbela will not demand special treatment, but she will condone nothing less than fairness, and I am not certain the two of them will always agree what that is."

Kade gave a light laugh. "The Bull of the Highlands doesnae know what our Desert Flower is capable of. He will soon find out."

"I warned him once of his fate should he cause my sister distress. I do not wish to restate myself and possibly cause a breach between them before they are even wed."

"I dinnae believe him to be so dull-witted as to mistake yer meaning," Kade noted. "Ye have never been one to mince words. As twins, ye and yer sister are much alike."

Shadows lengthened on the hillside and a tendril of smoke drifted upward. Alex peered at the dark column. Something wasn't quite right—

"Alex!"

Alex spun about, leaning over the wall to view the yard below. Caelen raced to the stable, Rory and two others on his heels. Stable lads drew horses outside, saddled and ready to be ridden, heads flung high in protest of the melee.

Without a word, Alex and Kade sprinted down the stairs, reaching the yard as Caelen and his men mounted up.

"MacGillonay raids a croft not far from here," Caelen snarled. "Will ye ride with us?"

Alex and Kade exchanged glances. *The smoke.*

"Aye." Alex nodded, intercepting his horse from the stable lad as he led the pair into the yard. He and Kade leapt aboard their mounts and wheeled them about, following Caelen's charge from the keep. The heavy gate swung closed behind them, jarring an unpleasant thought from Alex's mind.

Could this be a diversion?

He cast a look at Kade who needed no words to understand the worried expression on Alex's face. They reined their horses to a halt.

"I will return and keep the men on high alert," Kade said.

"I will help the laird," Alex replied.

With no other words necessary, they parted, hooves kicking up dust as their horses strained at their bits. Alex drew even with Caelen. Laird MacKern's face was dark, his jaw set. His woolen cloak flapped across his shoulders as he crouched over his horse's withers.

"Hold up." Alex raised his voice to gain Caelen's attention. Caelen shot him a furious look. After a moment, he pulled to a stop, his horse snorting as he champed the bit.

"Tell me what we are going in to."

"MacGillonay attacked an outlying croft," Caelen snarled, his anger at being held from pursuing the raiders clear.

"I saw smoke," Alex confirmed. "Will he have a large force?" With a quick glance, he tallied their men. Eight.

"A young man, half-dead, brought the tale. He counted no more than twenty."

Thirty. In Alex's experience, there were always more than a frightened boy knew. "The odds are against us."

"Ye waste my time. Do ye suggest we turn back?" Caelen sneered. "Do ye fear Highlanders more than Saracens?"

Alex laughed. "I suggest we split our group and approach from two sides. Charging straight into the enemy camp wastes men and I have no desire to find myself wishing I'd been more cautious."

Caelen betrayed his roiling fury by yanking on his horse's reins. The red horse spun about, crouched low on his haunches. Nodding to his men, Caelen sent three men with Alex, taking Rory and two others with himself.

With a salute, Alex and Caelen parted, thundering toward the source of the smoke, haste leaving them no room for stealth.

Undergrowth grew dense as Alex and his party left the widened trail and burrowed deep into the forest. Alex waved the men close, slowing his horse to a sweeping walk.

"Someone must lead. I do not know the way. Bring us to the outskirts of the croft, but not a blind rush inside."

Keeping their pace slow enough to accommodate the heavy underbrush, hooves muffled on the soft earth, carpeted thickly with damp moss and dead leaves, they approached the raided croft.

Shouts and the clang of steel rang out, alerting them to the conflict. In accord, Alex and his men swerved to meet the threat. Within moments, they entered a small clearing, Caelen's force rousting a group of at least twice as many men from their villainy. A line of men on horseback approached from Alex's right, swords out, aiming for Caelen's soldiers.

With a raised hand, Alex held his men back until the riders passed them, then closed in from behind, trapping them neatly and killing the men at the rear of the column before those in the lead knew there was an enemy behind them.

The battle was over minutes later, bodies littering the forest floor. The MacKern men fought well, killing more than twenty soldiers. Caelen's force suffered one man dead and another who would need care as soon as they returned to Dunfaileas. Alex's men were unscathed beyond a few minor cuts and likely a few bruises as well.

"We wouldnae have returned to Dunfaileas this day had ye not been more cautious," Caelen admitted as Alex rode up. "Ye were right to flank the bastards."

Alex simply nodded. "It would behoove ye to remember, if MacGillonay—or any other—attacks Dunfaileas, to do as my sister advises ye. She is much better at strategy than I."

Caelen wiped his forehead and sent Alex a disbelieving look. Alex canted his head. "Do not dismiss her opinions."

"Laird!" Rory rode up, a lass of perhaps eight summers in his arms. "She was wrapped in a plaide and tied to one of the bastard's horses. She is too frightened to speak, and I dinnae know how badly she is injured." His eyes flashed. "MacGillonay will pay for this!"

Caelen and Rory exchanged looks. Sending one of his men to scout the holding, Caelen dismounted. He strode among the fallen men. He nudged one with a boot and the man gasped.

"Where is yer master?" Caelen asked. Alex edged his horse closer. The injured man glared at Caelen.

Alex lifted a small leather bag from a strap over the man's chest with the tip of his sword. Flipping it into his hand, he emptied the contents with a flourish. Four coins, dull with age, fell into his palm.

"Ye did not get this from the croft ye fired. Who paid ye?"

The dying man spat feebly in Caelen's direction. Caelen nudged the man again and he groaned, turning his head to the side.

"Speak," Caelen commanded. "Was it MacGillonay?"

For a moment, the man neither moved nor spoke and Alex wondered if he had passed. With a sudden inhale of breath, the man nodded. Caelen stepped away.

A shout alerted them as the scout returned.

"I spotted MacGillonay on his gray horse on the ridge, heading north. I counted eight, mayhap ten riders with him."

Caelen mounted his horse and called Alex to follow with a jerk of his head. Smoke drifted through the trees as they approached the croft. A cottage, its thatched roof blackened from the attempt to fire it, sat in the middle of another, larger clearing. A short distance away lay the carcass of a cow, its long-haired hide a dull red hump on the churned ground. Disheveled piles of clothing lay on the ground. Closer inspection revealed a man, woman, and young lad perhaps a year or two younger than the lass they'd rescued.

Alex's stomach churned.

"See the work of MacGillonay," Caelen growled.

Alex's jaw tightened. The feud between MacKern and MacGillonay was real. And his sister was about to wed the MacKern laird. This day, their feud became personal.

Chapter Fourteen

Arbela kicked the small, leather-bound ball across the floor of her bedroom and Toros bounded after it gleefully. He pounced on the toy and snatched it up, working his jaw muscles as he chomped on the firm yet somewhat spongy surface. Losing interest in their game, Arbela faced her aunt.

"Ye heard what Agnes had to say," she blurted. "Beltane is naught but a pagan ceremony to welcome summer. I still think there are better days on which to perform a Christian wedding."

Zora sighed and rose to her feet, graceful despite her age and the swollen joints the cold, damp weather had exacerbated. "Ye concern yourself overmuch with these things, Arbela. There are rituals and feasts the world over to celebrate and mark the seasons of the year." She strolled to the hearth and sank onto the cushion placed there. Closing her eyes, she lingered near the warmth of the fire.

"I agree people often set their planting and such to these ceremonies," Arbela pursued the subject. "I simply do not agree a Christian wedding should have pagan rituals attached to it."

"What is it ye find objectionable to Beltane—aside from its origins?"

Arbela became thoughtful. "There is the belief that passing through fire—or in most cases, between two bonfires—protects against evil."

"Fire has always been deemed to have purifying powers. Even John the Baptizer spoke of our Lord as one who would baptize *with the Holy Spirit and fire*."

Arbela abandoned that argument, knowing her aunt's knowledge of the Holy Bible far exceeded hers. "Aunt Zora, am I creating too much of a mountain of this?"

Zora opened her eyes, fine lines marking the years on either side of her tilted brows. "My daughter—and yes, that is how I think of ye—these are the things men fight over. Whose religion is better, what can and cannot be done. I find women to be much more practical. Does it truly matter so much what names we utter if our children are not fed? If ye notice, God puts up with the nonsense of men, and gives His rewards in plentiful crops and strong children—which are both under the care of women."

Arbela sank into the chair next to her aunt.

"Have ye thought much on the symbolism behind the rituals we follow in wedding ceremonies?" Zora asked.

Arbela shook her head.

"In Armenia, attendants stand behind the bride and groom, bearing candles or torches. Do ye know why?"

A grin bloomed on Arbela's face. "To keep either from *backing* out of the ceremony?" she ventured.

Zora smiled. "Nae. 'Tis to ward off evil. Even in our enlightened age, this is still done. The veil placed over the couple has the same symbolic virtue. The belief is that it will keep evil eyes from viewing the bride and groom whilst the priest gives his blessing."

"It seems all religions seek to keep their people from evil, no matter the ritual performed."

"That is truth, my child. I do not believe one should offer blood sacrifices, but wearing a veil or a symbolic use of fire does no harm."

"And I am aware many marriages are simple exchanges of intent, neither said before witnesses nor accompanied by a ceremony."

"Most weddings do not include a priest," Zora agreed. "Indeed, the church has little to do with the marriage vows unless a priest is present and blesses the couple. For a young woman of your station, marriage is more a business transaction than a Christian sacrament."

Arbela frowned. "Aye. MacKern stands to gain much from this marriage."

114

"Ye will as well, Arbela," Zora chided gently. "Ye will have a home, your own family. Caelen MacKern is a man well-liked here, and he has a strong, commanding presence. He is very pleasing to look upon, with a firm body and well-cut features to draw a young girl's eye. Ye could do far worse."

"I am grateful he is in good standing with those who know him," Arbela replied, carefully skirting Zora's remark of Caelen's physical attributes. "It puzzles me that he is so aloof with his son."

Zora gave a delicate shrug. "It could be he does not wish to attach himself to the child as young as he is. Many children do not grow to adulthood. Or, mayhap he only acts as his father did, and does not know how to behave differently."

"But he brought Bram here to ensure MacGillonay did not kidnap the child whilst he was away. That would suggest he cares for him."

"It would. As ye will soon have the boy's care, what difference does it make? In a couple of years, Bram's training will be in others' hands, as I believe fostering is common here."

Disappointment flooded Arbela's chest. "I will miss him," she murmured.

"There will be other children," Zora reassured her.

Arbela sent her a startled look. "I am not certain—" There was no way to broach the subject of her and Caelen's intent to lead separate lives. She knew her aunt would never approve of such an agreement, and she did not wish to enter an argument.

Zora's eyes twinkled. "Ye do know the symbolism of the orange blossom?"

Arbela shook her head again. "They are beautiful and smell wonderful. Though I scarcely believe they could grow in Scotland, as cold as it is."

"They are one of the few plants that both blossoms and produces fruit on its branches at the same time. Therefore, when a bride weaves her bridal crown of fragrant orange blossoms, it is said to confer fruitfulness on the union."

"I am afraid, no matter the rituals performed or the symbols invoked, orange blossoms will have no effect on *this* marriage."

"Do not fear," Zora soothed. "My own barrenness should not concern ye. There is no reason ye should not find yourself with child before many months have passed. Do not forget twins are common in our family."

She leaned forward and patted Arbela's hand.

"Twins!"

* * *

Bram stared at the small leather-bound box then lifted his incredulous gaze to Arbela. "This is for me?"

His voice squeaked slightly and a lump rose in Arbela's throat. "Aye. 'Tis a gift, though I hope ye will share." The laird's solar was silent, anticipating the lad's reaction. Zora had deemed it fit for Arbela to greet Bram—and his father—in private before the wedding, and Arbela was grateful to not have a crowd surround her as Bram opened his gift.

Bram nodded as he fumbled with the silver clasp holding the two halves of the box closed. Freeing the latch, he opened the box, revealing a flat surface of alternating black and red inlaid wooden squares arrayed in a checkered pattern.

"Look beneath this side," Arbela coaxed him, pointing to the indention along one edge, carefully hiding all but the tip of her forefinger within the sleeve of her coat. Zora had spent the majority of the previous day drawing the delicate hennaed designs on her hands, and they were to be viewed by her groom at the wedding—not by those gathered around her hours before the vows.

Bram slid his forefinger along the smooth surface to the small depression and pulled the section up. A velvet-lined cavity held a cloth bag, a water stain faintly marking the satin. She knew if he turned the case over, he'd find a similar blemish on the leather, a reminder of long ago when she'd spilled a cup of watered wine on the table where she'd left the box.

Bram lifted the bag from its place, tilting his head at the clink of objects inside. Tugging at the drawstring, he opened the bag and peered inside.

"What is it?"

"This is a game I played a lot as a young girl, no older than ye. It originated in Egypt more than two thousand years ago. It was called *Alquerque*. But a hundred years ago, a Frenchman changed the game somewhat, and it is now known as *Fierges*."

Arbela motioned to the satin bag. "The markers for the game are in there. Twelve for each player. One person will use the obsidian, the other the ivory. I cannot wait to teach ye to play!"

Bram's quizzical look broadened the smile on Arbela's face. It was clear he'd never played the board game before. "Go ahead and look at the pieces if ye like. Create your own game until I have a chance to show ye the rules of *Fierges*."

He plunged a hand inside and drew out three markers. The ivory glowed palest yellow, the obsidian's black shine enhanced by years of wear.

Bram grinned. "I like them!" He ran his hand around inside the bag, clinking the markers against each other.

"'Tis your game, now, Bram-jan," Arbela said. "But be aware rough handling can chip the markers and mar their beauty. And the leather and wood playing case must be occasionally cared for as well. I will show ye. I am happy ye now have something I have always cherished."

She tilted her head to Caelen. "Such a game will teach him many skills such as strategy, competitiveness—without bloodshed—confidence, and respect. And, 'tis fun when weather dictates we remain indoors."

"This is a tremendous gift, Arbela. I thank ye," Caelen intoned, a look of interest crossing his face.

Bram slowed his hand, merely flicking his fingers through the markers. "I thank ye, Bela," Bram echoed, his father's response reminding him of his manners. "I will take care of it. When can we play?"

"I believe 'twill be a few days. We have a wedding today, and travel on the morrow. Mayhap a day or two after I arrive at Dunfaileas?"

At Bram's nod, Caelen touched the boy's shoulder. "Ilene is ready to help ye dress. Go with her."

An older woman who must have arrived in the wagon with others from Dunfaileas, held her hand out to Bram.

"Come, lad," she said. "Ye mustnae bother yer da or his bride this day. I will see to ye."

Arbela bit back an arch reply. This was a more difficult day than she'd anticipated, and having Bram at her heels as she finished preparations would prove most distracting. And it would not do to alienate Bram's nurse, even if Arbela would soon see to the majority of Bram's care. But she did not like the woman's assumption Bram was a bother.

She turned to Ilene, a slight smile on her lips. "Thank ye for yer help. I know he will make ye and his da proud with his manners at the ceremony. I expect him to be with us as we enter the chapel."

Ilene gave her a startled look. "A bairn at yer wedding? 'Tis not proper."

"He will be my son. It is my wish he attends." Arbela's voice remained sweetly modulated, but none could deny the thread of steel that brooked no interference from the boy's nurse and whatever idea of *proper* she had.

Ilene sent a look to Caelen, but he refused her silent plea. "He will be there, m'lady," the nurse said, her eyes downcast. Taking Bram's hand, she followed a servant from the room.

"I must finish preparing," Arbela said. With a graceful nod to Caelen and her father, she left the hall, Zora and Agnes in her wake. Behind her, the men took up welcoming shouts, and though the hour was before noon, Arbela expected ale and wine to flow freely.

Toros and Garen met her as she opened her bedroom door, whining eagerly after her absence.

"Agnes, find someone to take the dogs to the stable," Zora instructed. At Arbela's startled look, she replied. "This is now your bridal chamber. Your pets are not needed here and will only get in the way."

Arbela swallowed hard to remember this night would mark the first of her married life with Laird MacKern, but gave a nod to Agnes who hurried from the room, dogs leashed beside her.

Zora approached the tub beside the hearth and dropped handfuls of dried rose petals on the steaming surface. "We will let those linger whilst we prepare ye for your bath," she said.

Arbela removed her clothes and pulled on a heavy robe. Seating herself on a stool, she opened a small jar on the low table at her side.

"The cream and honey will give your skin a lovely glow," Zora approved as she took the jar from Arbela and dipped her slender fingers into the blended substance. She applied the thick mask carefully to Arbela's face then reached for the cask of costly castor oil. Arbela's eyes closed as her aunt massaged the oil into her scalp.

Agnes returned, closing the door softly behind her. "They werenae exactly happy to go to the stable, but went with yer brother willingly enough."

Arbela released a sigh of relief to hear Alex had dealt with the dogs. Sending her two companions from her side was almost like sending children away. There were other things she needed to occupy her mind with this day, however.

"If ye wouldst be so kind as to brew the tea I have set out," Zora requested. Agnes busied herself with the chore, measuring the tea and steaming water as Zora had instructed her previously.

"The bath is ready, daughter," Zora murmured, assisting Arbela from her seat.

Used to servants in the room, though she preferred to attend her own needs, Arbela slipped out of the robe and into the tub without remarking the others' presence. She sank into the warmth then placed her hennaed feet upon the far lip of the tub as the heavy scent of roses rose in the steam. Zora brought a warm cloth and a dish of sea salt mixed with olive oil and began bathing her arms as Arbela relaxed as much as she could.

"What do ye bathe with?" Agnes asked, fascinated with the ritual she'd been part of for the past week. Zora described the bathing oil.

"These items Arbela has kept in her wedding chest since she attained womanhood, and we have added to it over the years."

"I scarcely remembered the chest," Arbela noted wryly. "Aunt Zora has kept up with it far better than I."

Agnes giggled. "Ye would likely have stocked it with arrows."

"I am glad ye are coming with me," Arbela laughed. "Even if only for a short time. Ye are a good friend, and I hope to make another like ye at Dunfaileas."

"Och, ye will," Agnes protested, but her cheeks pinked and Arbela knew she was pleased with the compliment.

"I will be along soon enough, child," Zora reminded her. "I believe the next two weeks are a time for a couple to bond without one who has been as your mother in attendance. A maid is sufficient, and since ye have none, Agnes will see to your clothing and such."

"I am happy to assist," Agnes said. "A couple of weeks apart from Dubh will do neither of us harm. And if he is prone to wander, I need to know this."

Zora collected a clean cloth and wetted it in a basin of rose water and wiped the mask from Arbela's face, silencing her question of what to do with a wandering suitor—or husband.

After cleaning the mask, Zora laid a warm, damp cloth over Arbela's face.

The door to the bedroom opened, and, even without seeing, Arbela knew Caitriona had entered the room. The girl had insisted she would assist on Arbela's *special day*—Arbela could still hear the young woman's condescending voice as she made her announcement, and even how Caitriona's strident voice set her teeth on edge. Arbela had counted it her great fortune the girl had been tardy in this endeavor today as she was in many others. However, she had arrived at last, and peace fled the room.

"I am here!" Caitriona announced with a clap of her hands. "I will see to the bride's clothing and jewels."

"Bring that basin, and ye may wash her hair," Zora corrected her.

"But I—"

Arbela's lips curved. Whatever Caitriona had been about to say disintegrated beneath one of Zora's firm looks. Arbela had known neither free person nor slave to utter another syllable after receiving one of Zora's silent reprimands.

Creaking sounds ensued as the wooden basin was dragged across the floor. Standing behind Arbela, someone—Caitriona, most certainly—pulled Arbela's hair over the edge of the tub and wetted it.

"I will require an apron for my dress," Caitriona whined. "I dinnae consider being a lady's maid today. I'd rather tend to her clothing—Ow!"

"Wet fingers should never touch silk," Zora admonished. "I will inspect Lady Arbela's hair when ye have finished."

Arbela hid her laugh beneath the cooling linen and settled a bit deeper in the warm water. Hands picked up her hair and began massaging a generous quantity of rose-scented soap through the strands. Arbela did not worry Caitriona would play foul with her hair—not beneath Zora's eagle-eyed gaze.

It was at last time to move from the bath—*lest ye ruin the henna on your hands and feet*, Zora fussed—and Arbela once again slipped into a heavy robe, averting her eyes from the elaborate costume laid out for her on the bed. Caitriona combed out Arbela's long, thick hair, brushing it gently as it dried while Zora inspected the beautiful, intricate patterns in henna on Arbela's hands and the tops of her feet.

Agnes knelt beside Zora. "Ye spent all of yesterday applying the designs—or several hours of it. Tell me of them again."

Zora leaned back and pointed to Arbela's hands. "The flowers represent love, happiness and fulfillment, whilst the leaves and vines show devotion and dedication to her new life." She turned Arbela's hands palm up. "We add the designs to the palms of a bride as a blessing for her, and on the back as a talisman of protection."

Arbela stilled. "I did not know there was so much symbolism in these designs." She swiveled her hands, surveying them front and back. "I thought they were pretty and meant to enhance the beauty of the wearer."

"Ye need nothing to enhance your beauty, *hayat alby*," Zora said. Arbela's heart warmed at the familiar endearment—*my heart's life*. "Ye will find many things have multiple meanings, depending on the time, execution or simply who ye ask."

"I thank ye for your devotion, Aunt Zora," Arbela said, finding a sudden hole where her most cherished beliefs of right and wrong lay. "I am humbled to find I should guard my tongue when tempted to malign another's religion or practices."

"As long as 'tis not the black arts, mayhap 'tis best to spend time in another's shoes before declaring the fit to be imperfect." Zora smiled. "Let us finish your preparations. Your groom will await ye soon."

Chapter Fifteen

Caelen glanced about the room as he lifted his left shoulder, giving it a bit of a massage. A man could become a wee bit sore from all the congratulatory clouts he'd endured. He rotated the arm experimentally, loosening the muscles tense from the inexplicable apprehension this visit to MacLean castle brought. Everyone around him was happy with the marriage—but they weren't the ones pledging themselves to a life with a young woman raised to state her mind and choose her weapons with equal ease.

Donal MacLean was pleased with the arrangement. He'd toasted the upcoming nuptials several times this morning, and if his jovial attitude was any indication, 'twas likely he'd been toasting for some time previous.

Bram was cheerful enough, though 'twas clear he viewed Arbela as something between a faerie tale princess and a bosom playmate. Caelen wondered what the lad would think when Arbela proved to be more exacting than his nurse.

His captain and milk brother, Rory, viewed the marriage with a bit more solemnity. Initially pleased with the arrangement and all it meant for their clan's well-being, he'd become a bit more skeptical when Caelen had at last admitted the constraints of the agreement between himself and Arbela.

Rory's eyebrows had disappeared beneath his shaggy forelock, and his whistle of disbelief sliced through Caelen's composure. "Ye dinnae stop to think what a life of celibacy will be like?"

"Och, once she doesnae quicken with a bairn, no one will think it amiss if I take a mistress. Quietly, of course."

"Caelen, yer *wife* will take it amiss, I can state with certainty."

"By then, she will be content in her life and have come to her senses—"

"Come to her senses? Did ye fall off yer horse and land on yer head? Have ye lost every bit of sense ye ever laid claim to? If Arbela doesnae gut ye, her brother will. And I'd take on Alex sooner than I would yer wife. She is likely to draw her blade a wee bit further south."

Rory's words rang true. A pledge was a pledge. Unless Arbela agreed to dissolve or amend it, he was stuck in an unenviable position. Alesta had taken word of his impending marriage philosophically and bid him good life yesterday morn, refusing to bed him the night before his wedding.

His marriage was a business arrangement. Nothing more. How he and Arbela spent their time apart should be no one's business but their own. He held no desire to bed the strong-willed woman whose manners and appearance were foreign to him. Ruthie had been tall and willowy, her green eyes startling in her pale skin. 'Twas the image he'd always admired, and even Alesta, her beauty mostly a thing of the past, fit his ideal more than Arbela did. And even on their wedding night, Arbela was unlikely to agree to a shared bed.

The sudden skirl of pipes snatched him from his musings. Glancing up, he spied a procession coming from the end of the great hall to his position near the enormous double doors of the keep. Even Bram, who'd begun to fidget, stood straight, grabbing at Caelen's tunic as he peered around his legs.

"Bela?" he asked.

Caelen caught a glimpse of scarlet fabric trimmed in gold and glittering in the candle light. "Aye," he breathed, awed in spite of himself.

Deep in a crowd of well-wishers, Arbela's short stature made her an elusive target. But Caelen's eyes followed her as she approached. Reaching a point only a few feet away, she halted and the party around her drew back, allowing him to see his bride clearly for the first time.

Arrayed in a gown of dragon's blood red, her glittering necklace of rubies and diamonds appeared worth a king's ransom. Her dark eyes flashed, their tilted lines accented with a dark liner, adding to the exotic mystery that was Arbela. Her face, framed by a gossamer-thin veil, invited his touch, and he checked his impulse to caress her cheek.

"Do we continue to the chapel?" she murmured, one eyebrow raised in mild mockery. "Or admit our folly?"

Caelen glanced at the expectant faces gathered around him. With a deep bow, he offered his hand, accepting the startlingly patterned one she placed in his. He cleared his throat.

"I am as willing as ye."

Eyes bold and challenging, Arbela inclined her head toward the door, and they began their walk to the chapel.

The crowd followed. Pausing at the door to the castle's small chapel, Arbela and Caelen exchanged their vows. Caelen's voice flowed solemnly to Arbela's ears.

"I receive ye as mine, that ye become my wife and I yer husband."

She repeated the words back to him. "I receive ye as mine, that ye become my husband, and I your wife."

As they stepped inside the chapel, Arbela fingered the ring Caelen had placed on the third finger of her right hand. The red and gold cabochon jasper was smooth beneath her thumb as she twisted the beaten gold band on her finger. Though she had jewels aplenty—and of much greater worth than the semi-precious jasper—this one would never leave her hand. The idea drew her thoughts away from the nuptial mass.

She moved through the responses with little awareness. She stood, sat, and knelt as prescribed. With effort, she pulled her attention to the priest's words. Her father, Zora, Rory, and a second representative from Dunfaileas stepped forward and held a shimmering veil over Arbela and Caelen's heads as the priest spoke a blessing over them. His hand rested lightly on her head and she peered at Caelen from the corner of her eye.

"*Ego congelo vos in matrimonium in nomine Patris et Filii et Spiritus Sancti. Amen,*" Father Sachairi concluded.

Arbela jerked her gaze to the priest and Alex's shoulders shook. Caelen made to rise, but Arbela did not budge. He sent her a look of surprise.

"'Tis a bit late to balk, my lady," he murmured.

"The priest . . . he . . .." Arbela's voice trailed off. She leaned forward, catching Father Sachairi's gaze. "With respect, Father, ye must repeat the declaration." She leaned further still, and he bent his ear close. "The verb is *conjungo*, not *congelo*."

The priest gave Arbela a startled look. "What right have ye—"

Donal silenced him with a small wave of his hand. "The lass is correct, Father. Dinnae fash. 'Tis easy to mistake the Latin. But my daughter speaks it well."

Red-faced, Father Sachairi mumbled the words. "*Ego* conjungo *vos in matrimonium in nomine Patris et Filii et Spiritus Sancti. Amen.*"

"Amen," Arbela responded, head bowed. She hoped she appeared demure—correcting a priest at one's own wedding was not something done lightly. But she kept her head bent until she could control the mirth that threatened to erupt wildly at the error.

I stiffen ye in wedlock . . .. From what she knew of the act that passed between husband and wife, stiffening was needed, though it shouldn't take a priest's command to make it so. The traditional *I join ye* was much preferred in a public setting, though it seemed she and Alex and her father were the only ones who'd noticed. She bit her lip as she idly wondered how many other couples the good priest had *stiffened*.

Hilarity at last under control, Arbela rose and accepted Caelen's binding kiss.

"Go in peace to glorify God with yer life," came Father Sachairi's dismissal.

The gathered crowd replied, "Thanks be to God."

126

The skirl of pipes once again filled the air and people encircled the couple, congratulating them and ushering them outside. Children scampered about as small coins were tossed in the air. The mood was jubilantly festive and Arbela's heart lifted. Bram marched at her side, clutching her gown as they crossed the yard to the open doors of the keep.

Cut flowers spilled from swaths of fabric draped from pillar to post. More bouquets graced large vessels on the tables, their scent mingling with the aroma of roasted meats. Arbela sat in the chair Caelen offered, the wooden back draped with more garlands of the sweet-smelling flowers. Bram gave her a hopeful look and she invited him to share her seat. He climbed up and leaned against her, his sweet weight going straight to Arbela's heart.

If nothing else, I will have the joy of raising his child. Encouraged, she hugged Bram against her briefly, then released him to his exploration of the laden table.

Tray after tray was brought to the cloth-draped boards, adding to the already crowded surface. Arbela filled her plate and Bram's, and she noted Caelen's attempt to sample a few of her favorite dishes. Pleased, she turned her attention to the tumblers in the center of the room.

"Have ye tried that particular stunt?" Alex's voice unexpectedly filled her ear. She looked up to find her brother standing at her shoulder. He grinned and indicated the agile men who tumbled about. "Remember the time ye spent with our uncle?"

Arbela shushed him and glanced quickly at her father who was far too busy regaling Laird MacHugh to pay heed to Alex.

"Until father found out, ye mean," she said, her words for Alex's ears only. "To answer your question, I perfected the forward roll on a tightly strung rope. Our tumbler today is somewhat more secure on the pole his two assistants are holding."

"Ye always were agile," Alex commented.

"Were?" Arbela arched a brow at him. "I still am agile, brother."

"Who knew our uncle's castle was a safe retreat for members of the *Hashashin* order?" mused Alex. "As the area was in a bit of upheaval, he amused himself by allowing ye to train alongside his recruits. In disguise, of course."

"Ye and Phillipe were too busy becoming knights to bother with how your sister spent her time. Ye were glad to have me away from Batroun," Arbela teased.

"We thought ye safe enough with Mother's family," Alex frowned.

"I was," Arbela claimed. "Amid a cult trained in the use of poison, stealth, and disguise, I could not have been safer."

Alex rolled his eyes. "The tumblers made me think of yer special skills. I'd forgotten how upset father was when he discovered Uncle was training ye to be an Asasiyun."

"He forbade me from visiting there again. But I have kept my skills honed, never fear."

The performer in the center of the room exchanged his horizontal pole for an upright one and scurried to the top. Alex and Arbela shared a look.

"Easy," Arbela scoffed.

Alex shook his head. "Ye should have little need to continue these skills, sister," he said. A frown crossed his face.

"What is it?" Arbela asked, sensing his disquiet.

"Ye know MacGillonay attacked whilst I was at Dunfaileas."

"Aye. Father has taken great care to have ye see to the defenses in the past weeks."

Alex nodded, his face grim. "The man is vicious, Arbela. Should he attempt to breech the walls of Dunfaileas, waste no mercy on him. He will have none for ye."

* * *

Caelen held back from the free-flowing wine and whisky. He walked among his new clan by marriage, accepting the toasts and accolades, his bride on his arm, his blood little tainted by alcohol. He had no desire to enter his marriage a drunkard. The night ahead already held too many questions for him to willingly add to the discomfort and regrets.

A wedding night was anticipated by the guests and family. What did Arbela expect?

Bloodied sheets would be displayed on the morrow. Whose blood would it be?

Weeks ago, they'd set the tone of their marriage—a business arrangement only. Neither was attracted to the other and he had no desire for more children. Arbela had made clear her wish for no physical relations between them, and other than forcing the role on her of broodmare and a convenient body on which to slake his lusts, there was no reason to visit her chamber after this night. And he did not believe himself such a brute.

But *this* night . . ..

Her perfume drifted to his nose. Something he could not place. Ruthie had favored heavy floral scents, but Arbela's was earthier, warm, spicy, and intoxicating. *Sensual.*

Caelen risked a look at his bride. She faced away, speaking to one of her da's knights. A pang shot through Caelen's midsection. Jealousy? Ridiculous. The man had likely known her all her life. 'Twas natural they spoke together.

Candlelight glinted on her blue-black hair. She'd set her veil aside some time ago, and her heavy locks hung below her waist, inviting him to gather it in his hands. Her gown sparkled with beads and gold embroidery. Caelen scarcely knew whether to describe the gown as red or gold. Below the gauzy sleeves, her painted hands made gestures in the air as she spoke.

Caelen had no idea what to think of his new wife.

The noise level of the crowd grew and Arbela glanced up. For an instant, Caelen imagined a look of panic crossed her face. He leaned down, his lips beside her ear, ignoring her intoxicating scent.

"How do I get to yer room?" he whispered.

The look she sent him confirmed his suspicion. There *was* something in this world that frightened Arbela MacLean. The thought of bedding him. He squeezed her fingers.

"If ye dinnae wish us both paraded to yer room before the wedding guests, we must separate. I will tarry near the privy and ye will find a way to yer room alone. Unless ye think I should ask yer da how to find ye, ye need to tell me now."

"Third level. Last door." The lines marring her brow vanished as she faced her fears without complaint or question.

Caelen took a casual step toward the table, dropping her hand to reach for a tankard. He downed the contents and moved further away, putting distance between them, dividing the crowd's attention. Someone spoke to Arbela and she laughed. Beckoning the woman to accompany her, she strolled unhurriedly from the room. Wending his way through the crowd, Caelen marked his path with jokes on finding the privy.

Alone at last, he quickly ducked around a pillar and edged toward the stairs. The couples seeking privacy and partly cloaked in the shadows paid no attention as he slipped past. Within moments he found himself at Arbela's door.

He tapped on the doorframe and she allowed him inside, closing and latching the door securely behind him. He stared at her, enigmatic in her wedding finery, clothing meant to draw a man's eye. The scooped neckline was demure, but she'd removed the fantastic ruby necklace, and her skin glowed, bare and heaving gently as she breathed.

"How do we go from here?" she asked. "Shall we endure one another's company and present bloodied sheets on the morrow? I do not mind a lanced finger."

"Is that yer wish?" he asked, disappointment surprising him with its prick.

Arbela arched a brow. "What do ye ask of me? Allow ye into my bed this night and never think on it again? Do ye chafe against our agreement so soon?"

Her words slammed into him, rejection an emotion he was all too familiar with. "I dinnae enter this marriage to add discord in the form of a nagging wife," he growled. "Keep yer bloody virtue. I have nae need for it."

Her eyes flashed. "I ask only the manner of man ye are. 'Tis in our best interest for each to speak our mind. This night, no matter how we spend it, will set the tone for the rest of our lives."

"The two of us alone, this entire night?" Caelen cocked his head. "When we last spoke, we agreed only on the manner in which we would live our lives once wed. I havenae changed my mind. We dinnae specifically agree on this night where the expectations arenae entirely our own."

"They should be," Arbela pointed out. "What others think of us should not influence how we live our lives, or how we treat each other."

"I had no expectation of bedding ye," Caelen replied bluntly. "I will admit the thought crossed my mind, but I leave the matter to ye."

A noise akin to thunder rumbled through the heavy door as fists pounded the boards, demanding entrance.

"The guests have noticed our absence," he said. "'Twill be some time before they admit their disappointment and return to their drinking." He glanced at the door, reminding himself Arbela had latched it. "What is yer wish, Arbela? How would ye prefer to spend our first night together?"

She glanced about the room, her attention lighting on a small leather box on a nearby table. Laughter lit her eyes and curled her lips as she lifted her gaze to his.

"Someone brought this here, though I gave it to Bram earlier. Should I teach ye the game of *Fierges*?"

Caelen gently rested the back of his hand on the soft curve of her cheek. "Mayhap there is a better game I could teach ye?"

Chapter Sixteen

A streak of longing shot unexpectedly through Arbela, leading her—where? She could not deny the appeal of Caelen's muscular charm, his air of complete confidence—though her challenge of the wedding night activities appeared to deliver a slight blow to his composure. Playing a board game on one's wedding night likely was not commonly done.

She did not care to give her body where her heart did not lie. Though, as of only a few hours ago, she no longer had the privilege of choosing another path for her heart. She had spoken her wedding vows, and the consummation was as much a part of the ceremony as any words of binding.

"I will stand by our agreement," she finally said. "I will not intrude on your life after this day, as I know ye will not intrude on mine." She lifted her chin as Caelen's hand fell away. "And yet, to begin our marriage with the lie of consummation—even if 'tis my blood on the sheets—is distasteful to me."

Caelen's eyebrows jerked skyward. "Ye agree to the bedding?"

Panic chased cold through her veins and she drew a firm breath against it. "Aye. However, mayhap we could get to know one another a bit first?"

With a nod, Caelen indicated the cushioned chairs by the hearth. Arbela arranged her wedding finery about her, using the tactile distraction to ground herself, preparing for the hours ahead.

"Tell me about Bram," she coaxed, seeking to fill the silence with a topic of interest to them both.

"The lad has five summers," Caelen replied.

"He will be in my charge, will he not?" Arbela asked, disappointed in his blunt answer. "Ye can give me a better answer."

"His mother's da is a bastard who wishes to take him from me," Caelen bit out. Clearly the subject of his former father by marriage vexed him. But he warmed to the subject. "If—or rather, when—he decides he has destroyed enough of Clan MacKern, he will arrive at Dunfaileas for Bram." His challenging look struck a chord in her warrior's heart.

"Ye willnae give the lad to him, no matter the cost," Caelen ground between clenched teeth. "Should it mean yer life, ye willnae give the lad over."

"I once told ye I do not harm children," Arbela reminded him softly, though the ring of steel vibrated through her words. "As long as Bram is in my care, he will remain safe."

Caelen regarded her, apparently finding her assurance acceptable. He leaned forward and clasped his hands, forearms on his knees. "Within the laird's—my—chamber is a secret passage. 'Tis hidden behind a tapestry and ye must be able to move the chest that sits before it." He tilted his head then gave a confident nod. "Ye can do it. There must be a signal between us, one that ye willnae disobey, to take Bram through the passage. None others remain alive who know of the secret, other than Rory, and he willnae speak of it. But I will have yer promise to leave whatever is brewing and save Bram."

Arbela considered the request. "I will not say I approve this plan," she began, holding a palm up for silence when Caelen's face darkened and he opened his mouth.

"But, if I see no other course, I will do as ye bid. And I will place Bram's safety above all other considerations."

Caelen's jaw clenched and his brows jammed together in withheld argument.

"My brother told me of what he witnessed whilst at Dunfaileas and what MacGillonay is capable of," Arbela continued. "I also know he told ye I have a quick mind—though he is more likely to tease me than praise me for it. Strategy is something that comes quickly and clearly to me."

134

She lightly touched his hands. "And I do not fear death."

"What shall the word between us be?" Calen asked. "The one which tells ye to flee with Bram."

"If I imagine the situation correctly, 'twill be when I am uncertain the path to take. If we are blatantly attacked, ye will be free to command I flee with the child—indeed, 'twill be expected. Our concern is the time treachery is involved and codes are necessary to keep others from guessing what we truly mean."

Something flashed in Caelen's eyes. A slight narrowing of his lids telling her he'd just changed some assessment of her. He inclined his head. "Go on."

"In such a time as I should remove Bram from a potentially dangerous situation, ye should bid me take him to his room and keep him entertained." She glanced at the board game resting on the table. "*Fierges* was created from an Egyptian game called *Alquerque*. Tell me to teach Bram *Alquerque*. Call it a *damned board game* if ye wish. 'Twill call less attention to the action if ye dinnae appear to approve."

Caelen's slow nod increased to full acceptance of her idea. "*Alquerque*." He gave her a wry smile. "And if I dinnae recall the name, I shall simply call it *that damned game*."

"'Tis the beauty of the code. It has a plausible backup."

Silence fell, hanging between them as fragile as the bond they sought to forge. With a heavy sigh, Caelen straightened in his chair, drawing his hands away. A peculiar sense of loss rippled beneath Arbela's fingertips. Caelen listed to the side, elbow on the chair arm, chin in his palm.

"Tell me of this beast named Ari ye wish to give my son."

Will he not be my son as well? But Arbela shelved the question for another time, anxious to move them into a more lighthearted conversation.

"Ari, which means *brave* in Armenian, was a child's pony for many years. When the youngest child outgrew him, rather than give him over to taxing work as a draft animal, or simply turn him loose to make his own way, he was given to a shepherd."

Arbela wove her tale of the one-eared pony, pleased to see the interest spark in Caelen's eyes. "I allowed Bram to sit on Ari's back only after he requested it and I saw him to be sincere."

"Ye must ask me first," Caelen said, pleasure in the story waning in the frown that crossed his lips. "I have not yet given him a pony. He is too young."

Arbela raised a brow in contest. "Bram has five summers. He should be caring for his own pony."

"I will raise him as I see fit," Caelen stated. "Ye will teach him his numbers and letters. I will teach him the things of a warrior. If it is yer wish, ye may bring the pony along. Contact with such a sturdy beast will do Bram no harm."

His narrowed look warned her from argument. He may have married her, and he may expect her to exchange her life for Bram's, but Caelen clearly did not trust her—her ways. She tightened her lips and neither promised nor denied.

Caelen ran a hand over his close-shorn head. His gaze lit on the game board on the table and he motioned toward the case.

"Teach me this game ye call *Fierges*."

Relief from the change in topic washed over her and she seated herself next to the table and waved at Caelen to join her. Opening the leather case, she quickly showed him how to arrange the pieces and recited the simple rules. He studied the board carefully before each move, saying little as she coached him.

She bested him in fewer than twenty moves.

He scowled at her and she offered a slight grin of apology. "I am not very good at losing," she admitted.

"Yer brother said ye were verra good at strategy," Caelen muttered, but his mouth quirked in a half-smile as he reset the board. He waved at the markers. "Again."

Arbela rose. "I must remove this outer gown," she said, stepping through the beaded doorway. "'Tis stiff and uncomfortable."

"Ye dinnae wish to be distracted," Caelen called. "Or I will certainly win this game."

Arbela muffled a laugh as she released the fasteners on her heavy outer robe of stiffened brocade, embroidery and precious stones. She draped the fabric over the edge of the empty tub with a sigh and quickly slipped out of the silk underdress as well. Exchanging it for the satin-lined velvet dressing gown was an enormous relief. Finger-combing her hair, she pulled it into a loose braid and tied a ribbon around the end. Tossing the braid over her shoulder, she pushed through the beaded curtain.

"I am much relieved—at hearing your arrogance at supposing I am that easy to best, and also to be rid of that gown."

Caelen's eyes stopped her in her tracks. His intense stare resembled a lion's determined gaze before it pounced on an unsuspecting lamb. Blood iced in her veins, then roared with heat, leaving her lightheaded and confused. Caelen rose to his feet.

"Do ye wish another game?" he asked, his voice husky and low.

"I believe," she considered carefully, "I believe I would have this constraint between us at an end. It has been a long, tiring day, and playing *Fierges* into the night may prove exhausting, leaving us little desire for intimacy."

"Ye ask me to take ye to bed?" he asked, approaching slowly, his words more clarification than question. He halted an inch before Arbela's resolve broke. She nodded.

"Aye. This will change nothing, yet it will provide the honesty our vows require."

With a smile of confidence Arbela did not understand, Caelen reached for the belt tied about her waist. "Will ye trust me?"

"Of the two of us, ye alone know what we are about," Arbela commented. She managed a halting half step at his gentle tug on her sash.

The knot in the thick silken cord unraveled almost magically in his hand. Denied the belt's firm support, the robe slid over her skin, trailing sensuously across her bosom as it drifted open. Arbela felt every warp and weft of the heavy fabric across her strangely sensitive skin and she shivered.

"Cold?" Caelen asked, his eyebrows flicking upward.

"Nae. Unused to being stared at by a man without my sword at his throat," she quipped.

Faint amusement flickered in his eyes, and a corner of his mouth twitched. "I should have insisted the bedding take place without weapons. Would ye be opposed to the amendment?"

Something akin to pleasure at his responding humor washed over her, easing her breathing once more. "Are ye prone to *mutationes sine causa?*"

Caelen's startled gaze leapt from her partially-exposed chest to her eyes. Arbela hid her smile.

"*Changes without cause.* Och, I forgot ye speak Latin. Enough to challenge the priest at our wedding. Ye will have to forgive a poor Highlander his *labitur in lingua.*"

"Your grasp of Latin seems fine," Arbela said. "I hear no *slip of the tongue.*"

Caelen closed the distance between them, his body warm through the narrow opening in Arbela's velvet robe. The luxurious fabric slid from one shoulder and she scarcely caught it before it completely exposed her. Her skin heated. Caelen loomed over her, yet his only hold on her was the robe's cord, which hung all but useless at her waist, and the two fingers he chucked beneath her chin.

"My command of Gaelic, *Inglis*, and Latin are fine," he murmured. "As is my understanding of Norn." He dropped his lips to hers, only a fraction of space between them. "'Tis this slip I am referencing."

His tongue rode the crests and valleys of her lips, the unexpected move betraying Arbela into a shocked gasp. Instantly, he plunged inside her mouth, teasing her, coaxing her to his seductive dance. Her hand shot up to fist the front of his tunic, twisting in the fabric as she fought to keep her balance.

Obligingly, he crooked an arm around her, pulling her against him, supporting her. Every hard, muscular inch of him blazed hot against her thighs, her belly, her breast, crushed against him as though she no longer belonged to herself.

She didn't. She belonged to *him*.

Sparks of heat fluttered low in her belly, welcoming the hard ridge of flesh pressed at the juncture of her thighs. Arbela had heard enough gossip in the women's quarters at Batroun and other places to know the rudiments of what passed between a man and a woman, but the innuendoes and sly looks canted her direction by the gossiping women did nothing to reassure her of the surge of desire sapping the strength from her limbs, clouding her brain, leaving her befuddled as the first time she'd taken a direct hit from an opponent on the training field.

Only now there was no shocking pain as a prelude. Only the breathless sensation and grasping recall of thought.

This is what other women sigh over? Losing control in a man's arms?

It wasn't unpleasant, but it went completely against her nature. Arbela struggled to relax, fought the urge to crook a foot behind his heel and dump him to the ground. He swept his arm beneath her knees, lifting her against his chest, and carried her across the room, tangling them briefly in the beaded fringe of the doorway to her private chamber. Kneeling against the mattress, Caelen deposited her onto the bed and stepped back to strip away his clothing.

Arbela slid across the bed, her back against the thick pillows at the head, barely noticing the rose petals scattered across the cover someone—Zora?—had placed there. Their bruised scent wafted upward. Caelen dropped his tunic and trousers to the floor.

The mattress sagged with his weight, bobbing Arbela as though she were a small boat in a choppy sea. Caelen advanced, stripping the covers back, revealing the white sheets—pale gold in the firelight. Arbela bounced her bottom obligingly, allowing the bedclothes to shift beneath her. The sight of his naked form startled her and she clenched her jaw to keep from voicing her thoughts.

Firelight played bronze and shadows along his limbs, emphasizing his muscles, glowing warmly against his skin. She wanted to touch him, but held back, uncertain how he would respond. Unlike the languid dalliances she'd heard gossiped about, Caelen was direct and confident, his desire for her evident. Bold and hungry.

He settled next to her, half on his side to face her. With a gentle move, he swept the robe from her other shoulder. Cold air rushed over her, banished in an instant beneath his heated gaze. He dropped a kiss to her shoulders, slowly moving from one to the other. His hand slid inside her languishing robe to cup her breast, his thumb flicking across her taut nipple.

Excited, frightened, Arbela no longer knew what she desired. Her breast throbbed in his hand and she leaned forward to place it more firmly in his grasp, seeking to assuage the troubling ache. Caelen pushed her robe aside, sliding it from her arms, and Arbela slipped free. Nuzzling her neck, Caelen pulled her beneath him, and she gave herself over to his kisses.

Her legs quivered as he slid between them, and she drew her knees up, daring to touch her core against his heated length. Caelen groaned and rubbed his cock against her, and she quickly caught his rhythm. A thrum of pleasure tingled and Arbela did not object as he pulled back slightly, positioning the head of his cock at her opening. He hesitated, then pushed.

Arbela's knees tightened against his flanks at the unwelcome sensation. All pleasure fled as he broke through her maidenhead. He thrust back and forth, panting, suddenly a stranger to her. She willed away her tension and the burst of pain eased.

Her vows. It was but this once. She could do anything *once*.

Caelen shouted, his body stiffening over her. He groaned, bucked his hips and stilled. After a moment, his head dropped to her shoulder and he lay atop her, breath slowing to a more normal pace. He moaned.

"I know it is uncomfortable for ye—the first time," he muttered. "I should have gone slower. Eased ye more."

Arbela firmly shoved his head off her shoulder, and he rolled to his side, slipping easily from her body.

"As ye are finished, do not worry yourself. 'Twas my burden to bear."

Caelen rolled to an elbow, eyebrows plunged together in alarm. "Yer *burden*? Ye call *this*," he swept a hand over their naked bodies, "a *burden*?"

"What do ye think, Caelen?" she asked, tears stinging her eyes. "No matter the how or the why of it, the consummation is complete." She sat, grabbing her discarded robe and wrapping it about her. "Or is one of *this*," she mocked his earlier movement, "not enough? Should I have stipulated a number?"

Caelen rolled to his feet and stalked across the room, snatching his clothing from the floor. "Nae. Henceforth, ye may wear yer weapons to bed. 'Twill be no concern of mine."

* * *

Caelen threw a cushion from a chair to the floor and rolled himself in the woolen expanse of his cloak. It was warm and scratchy, but he'd take its known discomforts over his wife's rejection.

Shite! He didn't know how to woo a wife. His first marriage was proof of that. Why, by St. Andrew's mismatched ballocks, did he think this marriage would be different?

Because Arbela was different. The problem, then, was him. He'd suggested a business arrangement, never dreaming she would allow him to touch her this night. At the time, given her exotic boldness, and the memories of Ruthie he knew better than to dredge up, keeping Arbela at arm's length seemed a brilliant idea. He'd gotten more than he hoped for in help for his clan, and taking her to wife, yet not a wife, was a good fit.

But for a short time this evening, he'd enjoyed himself. And it wasn't only the bedding. Conversation with Arbela was intriguing. The game of *Fierges* had been of interest to him, even if his eyes had strayed more to the delicate tracery on her hands and the nearly blue glimmer of light on her hair. To the generous curves of her hip and breast beneath the fanciful attire. And the bedding had been very good—for him. Even Alesta, for all her willingness and knowledge, hadn't sparked the sensations in him Arbela had. Spending time with his wife hadn't been the burden he'd imagined.

Burden.

Her word for lovemaking. Her word for him. The word—God help him—for the rest of their life together.

Chapter Seventeen

Bram twisted on the mattress, eyes too bright for a child ready for sleep. Arbela perched on the edge of the narrow bed, aware of the long hours ahead of her before her own rest. Though the journey to Dunfaileas had not been arduous, the events of the previous day had left her exhausted, yet with much left to be accomplished.

"Are ye not sleepy, Bram-jan?" she asked, brushing a stray lock of hair back from his forehead.

"The lad will drift off," Ilene snapped, her voice and manner brusque. The old nurse busied about the room, tidying the small mess the lad had created in an effort to show Arbela everything as soon as they entered his chamber. "Ye needn't stay," she added over her shoulder as she slammed the lid of Bram's clothing trunk. "Dinnae fash yerself."

"He's no bother," Arbela murmured, wondering how many times she'd say the words before others—and Bram—believed it. She'd heard Ilene fuss over Bram's care one time too many.

She gave the boy a smile. "I believe I promised ye a bedtime tale, did I not?"

Bram beamed, nodding his head vigorously.

"Ye must prepare for sleep, then. After the tale, ye will find your rest." Arbela dragged a wooden chair close and moved onto its wickerwork seat, making a mental note to add a cushion to give it comfort. "Let us see how ye like my tale of St. George and the dragon."

"'Tis a short tale," Bram objected.

"Not as I tell it," she assured him. Taking a deep breath, she laced her fingers in her lap and began.

"St. George was a very brave knight, born in Cappadocia, in the mountains to the west of Armenia. One day in his travels, he came to a city with a small lake where the people obtained their water. But an enormous dragon had taken up residence there, poisoning the water and the entire surrounding region."

Bram's eyes widened with excitement and he clutched his bedclothes to his chest.

"Da says a hermit told him about the dragon."

"Mayhap he did," Arbela agreed. She paused, waiting for his nod to continue.

"More fearful was he than any monster anyone had ever seen, and upon his back were roughened scales harder than iron or steel. His teeth and nails were like the sharpest swords, and his breath stank of char and death. Everything he touched withered and died, and the area around the lake, his new home, reeked of decay. None dared approach. Indeed, the townspeople had begun feeding the fell creature two sheep daily, and in return, the dragon pledged not to poison the water in the pond. But soon, the dragon insisted on a villager each day to eat, in addition to the sheep, and the king submitted to the foul dragon's demand."

Bram furrowed his brow. "Yer dragon is meaner than da's."

Arbela smiled. "People were chosen by lots to feed the dragon, and every day, another was chosen to meet a terrible end. Days passed with no recourse, until the king's own daughter was chosen. The king offered much silver and gold for someone to change places with his beloved child, but the townspeople insisted her fate would be no different than any among them."

Bram scrambled to a seated position, knees tucked beneath his chin, but this time he did not interrupt.

"Greatly saddened, the king dressed his daughter in her finest clothing, kissed her, and led her to the lake near the dragon's lair where he left her to await her doom, alone and frightened. St. George rode up and, spying the beautiful princess, asked her why she tarried alone so far from town. She told him of the dragon and the terrible price he exacted from her people.

"And St. George said, *Fear not, fair maiden, for I shall help ye in the name of Jesus Christus.*"

"Yay, St. George!" Bram shouted. He kicked at his covers but settled quickly beneath Arbela's mild reproach.

"The princess wept and pleaded with him to flee, for she was convinced none could save her from the evil dragon and she did not wish St. George to be eaten as well. As they spoke, the dragon appeared and swooped down from the skies, plumes of smoke befouling the air. The princess fell to the ground in fear, but St. George held his horse firm against their foe, drew his sword and, making the sign of the cross, rode hard against the dragon. He smote him with his sword, throwing the beast to the ground where he lay, dead, at St. George's feet."

"'Cause he had no scales beneath his wing, and St. George knew where to stab him!" Bram shouted, the light of a warrior in his eyes. Arbela gave a nod of agreement.

"St. George drew the princess to her feet, lifted her onto his horse, and delivered her to her father, the king. After hearing St. George's tale, the king was baptized, followed by all his people. The king erected a church of Our Lady and Saint George, and a fountain sprang up before it, and all who drank of its water were healed of their infirmities. The king offered St. George as much money as he could carry, but the noble knight refused the reward, giving it instead to the poor. Then St. George requested the king honor the priests, hear their services diligently, and have pity on the poor and sick of his town."

"I dinnae know about the money or the fountain," Bram mused. "He really was a good knight, wasn't he?"

"Aye, he was. Do ye know the rest of the story?"

Bram shook his head, eyes wide with interest.

"Many years later, in the history of Antioch, when the Christians set out to conquer Jerusalem and wrest it from the Saracens, a young man appeared to a priest and advised him to carry some of the relics of St. George. During the siege of Jerusalem, a man wearing the white armor and red cross of St. George, led them all to victory."

Bram tilted his head. "St. George killed the bad people who captured Jerusalem?"

"He certainly helped," Arbela said. "He was a knight of renown whose fame brought victory to those who honored his ways. Shall ye tell me the story as your father does next time?"

"Mayhap," Bram said. "I'll think about it."

Arbela rose. "Sleep well, Bram-jan. I will find other stories and interesting things to do on the morrow."

"Will ye stay with me?" he asked, grabbing her hand. She squeezed his fingers gently and drew away.

"I have yet to find my bed," she told him. She sent a glance to his nurse. "Mind Ilene, and go to sleep."

His little body fairly bristled with objection, but Arbela placed a light kiss on his forehead and padded from the room, closing the door softly behind her, ignoring Ilene's glare.

Agnes rose from a bench against the wall in the passage. "I will help ye prepare for the night," she said, falling into step at Arbela's side. Arbela hesitated.

"The laird's room is here," Agnes said, gesturing to a door only a few feet away. "There are few private bedrooms in a tower house," she added.

"Laird MacKern is still below stairs—I've been watching," Agnes giggled as she pushed open the door. She bustled inside. "I made certain the fire was stoked and the room warm for ye. And here's a tub waiting. I'll add the hot water to it now if ye are ready for yer bath."

Fighting back the overwhelming sense of events spinning out of control, as though Agnes pushed her into a new life she wasn't certain she was ready for, Arbela reminded herself of the arrangement between herself and Caelen. She would allow Agnes to see to her evening routine, and then, once Agnes retired for the night, consult Caelen for other sleeping arrangements.

"I thank ye, Agnes," she said, forcing calmness into her words. "A bath sounds lovely. Ye may seek your rest once I am in the tub."

Agnes' eyes danced, her demeanor merry as she helped Arbela disrobe. "I know Dunfaileas isnae what ye are accustomed to," Agnes whispered. "But 'tis neat enough, and the laird is grand to look upon."

Arbela sank into the heated water, allowing it to soothe her. "The size of the keep is fine. It reminds me of Batroun. Howbeit, there are many things to be done."

Agnes handed her a linen square and a chunk of soap she'd brought with her. "Oh? What will ye do?"

Lathering the soap into the linen, Arbela reflected on her initial thoughts as she entered the Dunfaileas keep. "Alex and my father have already sent men who have begun work on the walls, and 'tis apparent the privies need attention. I will put those on a regular maintenance schedule. The keep appears to have been recently scrubbed, and I will see to it someone is in charge of that as well. Once I have viewed the pantry, kitchen and such, I will know more about what I should implement, improve on, or learn from." A wry smile caught the corner of her lips. "There will be much to do on the morrow."

"A new bride should enjoy a few days with her husband before settling into such things," Agnes chided gently.

"This new bride will get a good night's rest and set about learning her new home after the morning meal," Arbela corrected.

"I wish ye'd had more time to know Laird MacKern," Agnes said, wringing out the linen cloth. "When ye dinnae know each other well, it can take time for ye to become comfortable with one another and enjoy spending time together." She patted Arbela's shoulder. "I will say no more. Except, I dinnae think ye will have a full night's rest this night!"

Her laughter followed her from the room, and Arbela sighed. As much as she enjoyed Agnes' company, it was proving difficult to hide her arrangement with Laird MacKern. Rising from the water, she quickly dried and donned the velvet robe Agnes left laying across the chair next to the hearth. She sank into the chair and drew her feet beneath her, tucking her toes beneath the generous folds of her robe. Drawing a blanket over her shoulders, she closed her eyes.

A soft thud awakened her. The fire had burned low, casting little light beyond the stone hearth. Arbela remained motionless as she surveyed the room.

A few feet away, Caelen stripped away his clothing, his back to her. The side of him turned to the fire glowed like an ancient golden idol, compelling yet forbidden. He dipped a hand in the water then turned to the empty buckets on the floor. A scowl narrowed his eyes, turning them into dark, unfathomable pools in his bronzed skin.

Dragging her gaze from its wide-eyed wanderings, Arbela focused on her husband's face. "I did not know where I should set my things and ye were not here to ask. This seemed appropriate for the night, though we can sort it out on the morrow."

Caelen grunted, but other than his right hand fisting at his side where his sword should have been, he gave no indication she'd startled him. "Sleep there," he said, giving a jerk of his head toward the curtained bed. "I will bed down in the stable."

"Is that how ye wish to portray our marriage?" Arbela asked. "I am comfortable in this chair, and can have a cot moved to Bram's room later. Mayhap that would draw less attention—and speculation."

Caelen stood motionless as Arbela silently urged him to take a step or two back into the shadows. Even one step would hide most of the jutting evidence that he could easily join with her again. Did he truly desire to lay with her? Arbela drew back, hoping the meager firelight did not betray the blush heating her cheeks. She had no wish to become a broodmare, and the consummation of their marriage the night before had been painful and unsatisfying. Certainly nothing resembling the rapture prattled about in the women's quarters in Batroun. Then why the deep pulsing stirrings in her belly urging her to touch him. To invite him to touch her?

"As ye wish, wife," Caelen at last answered. "I dinnae mind sharing my sleeping space if ye are cold." He motioned to the blanket she gripped tight in both hands. "'Tis a wee bit warmer to share."

"I will last the night," Arbela replied drily. "Sleep well."

With a shrug, he turned away. He bent over the tub and sluiced water over his head and shoulders, scrubbing himself quickly with a scrap of linen stacked on a small table pulled close for the purpose. He dried himself and strode to the bed. Arbela's view was unhindered as he climbed onto the soft mattress, and she wondered about the various textures of his skin, roughened and smooth, firm and soft. Her fingers twitched.

Suddenly irritated with the drift of her thoughts, she jerked the blanket higher over her shoulders and firmly closed her eyes.

* * *

By St. Andrew's teeth! I'd thought the woman would sleep in Bram's room. Caelen drew the curtains around the bed partly closed, allowing the resulting box to capture the warmth from the hearth. He sprawled on his back, a plaid blanket pulled to his waist.

He'd made no special provision for her living arrangements. In his defense, Alex had given him little time for idle thought, pushing hard night and day to repair the wall. Caelen appreciated the effort—he'd no wish for MacGillonay or any other to consider Dunfaileas easy to assault. The work had kept him too busy to consider the fact he was adding a wife to his household. One who would not be sharing his bed.

He'd failed his wife. Given her less thought than for her horse which had a stall of its own. Arbela slept curled on a cursed hard chair whilst he lounged in cushioned luxury. He eyed the bed hangings. Were they new? He recalled a wagon of household goods arriving several days ago, but he'd paid little heed to the contents. Rising to his knees, he fingered the curtains. Two layers. One heavy and plush, the other silky fine—like the tunics Arbela was fond of wearing.

He jumped as if stung and scrambled from the bed. Crossing the floor, he gently shook Arbela's shoulder. Her eyes flashed and Caelen felt something prod his leg a bit higher than his knee.

A dagger. She held a bloody dagger point at his thigh.

"Do ye always arm yerself?" he asked, his voice husky—and he didn't care to wonder at the reason. Her dark eyes, a wealth of expression, rimmed in kohl—he'd been told—met his, the thick braid of her midnight hair draped over her shoulder, glistening in the scant light. She withdrew the dagger.

"Always."

"I came to bring ye to bed."

A thick brow arched high. "And what of the agreement?"

"Damn the agreement. This is about ye not freezing out here simply because ye dinnae wish to sleep next to me." He drew a breath against the unexpected twist in his gut. "I willnae touch ye. But it willnae look good for my wife to catch a chill her first night here."

She eyed his proffered hand and he fought the urge to snatch it away. "I offer warmth, nothing more."

Unfolding slowly, gracefully from the chair, Arbela strode to the bed. She motioned for him to precede her. "'Tis warmer on this side, aye?"

"The far side is safer," he argued, not liking the idea of her being between him and the door should they come under attack.

"Ye offered warmth, not safety," she reminded him.

"I dinnae wish to bound over ye should we be attacked," he explained.

"I should hope not. I am likely to have a blade out. It could prove dangerous."

Caelen scowled. He caught a twinkle in her eye and a corner of her mouth twitched. The vixen teased him? No woman had ever presumed as much.

"I suppose I can trust the guards this night," he growled, not quite certain how to tease her back.

"Oh, ye should never trust your guards," Arbela admonished him. "They can be bought. Your wife, however—*this* wife—cannot be bribed or coerced. I assure ye, we will be quite safe no matter which of us is nearest the door. But this side *is* warmer."

Caelen gave a curt nod and climbed into bed, moving to the far side, making certain his sword leaned against the far bedpost. A position he was unfamiliar with.

Arbela waited until he settled, then rose gently onto the mattress, robe and blanket still wrapped about her. Within moments, she burrowed beneath the covers, facing the hearth, her back to him.

From this view, she appeared as any other woman. Long braided hair, rounded bum. Her scent caught him off-guard, triggering a memory of the previous night, and lust instantly flooded his groin. He stifled a groan and turned away, quite shackled by his unexpectedly desirable wife—and their damned agreement.

* * *

Arbela had a cot brought to Bram's chamber, and within the day, her personal belongings followed. Caelen knew he had no grounds to argue, but something tugged deep within, though he knew she was only a room away. Her maid clearly did not approve, casting speculative looks between Arbela and him. Agnes would be leaving within a sennight or so, and for that, he was grateful.

Late evenings were often the only time he had to speak of the day's events with Arbela. Before their marriage, he couldn't imagine voicing his activities and concerns with her, but now he almost looked forward to this time. Though proximity with his forbidden wife—alone—in his chambers, brought its own perils. He'd risk it.

Caelen had not spoken with Arbela in two days, and expected her in his room this evening. He poked his head inside Bram's chamber and found the lad fast asleep. Agnes slumped in a chair, her gentle snores a whispering counterpoint to the crackle of the fire.

He closed the door, a grin on his face as he entered his chamber. It was empty. Casting a glance about the room, his gaze lit on the chest against the far wall. A handsbreadth of darkness between it and the wall indicated it no longer remained in place. He approached it cautiously. The tapestry hanging behind it billowed slightly, exposing the hidden door behind it.

Arbela stepped through, seemingly unconcerned to find him there.

"Ye know 'tis a *secret* passage, aye?" he asked.

"Aye. But 'twas necessary to discover where the tunnel leads and to ensure nothing blocked it." She smiled. "After a good sweep, it appears to once again be in working order."

Arbela leaned a willow broom against the wall and dusted her skirts with a few quick swipes of her hands. "A few stones had fallen onto the walkway, but I have moved them and added two candles and a striking kit wrapped in heavy cloth just inside the door. 'Tis dry enough inside and I doubt moisture would be an issue."

Caelen stared at her, trying to keep up with her list of improvements to the passage—approving, yet wondering why he'd never thought of such.

"I have a waterskin on a small table I moved next to the door in Bram's room," she continued. "'Tis where we wash of a morning and 'tis replenished daily, yet 'tis handy should we need to escape. I do not suppose ye have noticed the tray of snacks in his room? Doubtless Bram sleeps too deeply to be bothered with hunger during the night, but an apple or two, cheese and chunk of bread could be useful if we were forced to flee."

Her head tilt challenged a reply. His mouth opened once or twice, uncertain whether to praise her or berate himself for not believing she could mount such strategy. Curious about the wisdom of maintaining food in the sleeping quarters, he settled on a question of his own.

"Mice?" he asked a split second before he recalled a striped feline haunting the upper stairs.

Her withering look assured him nothing escaped her notice.

"Cat."

Chapter Eighteen

Bram dashed about the yard, circling the lone tree near the wall before racing back to Arbela. She smiled indulgently at his youthful energy.

"I am fast as Toros and Garen!" he declared, eyes bright with energy. "Fast as Voski! Fast as a *dragon*!" He darted away.

"Ye are indeed the fastest young man I know. But can ye tell me how many rocks I have placed beside me?" Arbela tossed a small, rounded stone in the air and caught it in one hand, snagging Bram's attention. He whirled about and glared at the line of rocks arranged in the dirt. Storming over, he scattered the stones with two swift kicks, then nailed Arbela with a fierce look.

She returned his glower evenly. "There will never be a time when it is appropriate to destroy someone else's work. Such behavior marks ye as a brute, and an unlettered one at that. If ye do not know the answer to my question, ye may say so. But such a childish display will not be tolerated."

"I dinnae wish to do lessons," Bram declared. "Why must I learn things I dinnae wish to? I wanna learn how to kill dragons!" He leapt about, jabbing his arm about as if he wielded a sword, his war cries filling the air.

"We shall slay dragons, Bram-jan," Arbela replied. "We will require two sturdy sticks, a length of sinew—which we will measure later— several thin strips of wood, a narrow length of leather, a scrap of linen, and hide glue."

Bram sent her a dubious look. Arbela arched a brow, challenging his response. "Do ye wish to learn how to aim a sword at a dragon? Or would ye think it wise to also learn to use a shield?"

The boy's eyes widened. "Truth?"

Arbela shrugged. "For practice only, as ye would need something much sturdier should a real dragon arrive. But ye must begin somewhere. Do ye know where to find these items?"

"I can find two sticks!" Bram exclaimed. He frowned as Arbela held her hands a short distance apart. "That isnae a verra big sword."

"No longer," she confirmed. "We will make larger swords as ye grow. This will do for now. What of the other items?"

Bram rattled off the places to look for the rest of the required objects as he bounded down the path to the cooper's shop. Arbela followed along as he wheedled the items from the indulgent clansmen, giving an approving nod to the cooper who requested Bram sweep up after himself in return for cutting the thin boards into shape.

"When there is a job ye cannot do for yourself, it is proper to pay or exchange labor for the work." Arbela praised his decision to accede to the cooper's request, pleased Bram did not simply stomp his foot and remind him he was the laird's son.

The sun dipped toward the horizon and after promising Bram to spend the following day creating his sword and shield, Bram agreed to dinner, a bath, and a bedtime tale.

Once he was abed, Arbela slipped outside, a cloak wrapped about her as clouds hastened the day's end. A brisk breeze promised an evening rain, but a few minutes to herself was worth the risk of a sprinkle. She was growing used to the persistent rains and the crisp air, though she frequently longed for the warmth of strong sunlight and bone-searing heat. She sighed. Such a thing was in the past, for she did not think she would see her beloved desert again.

"Might I have a moment?" Caelen's voice rose to her ears.

"Aye," she replied evenly. They'd hardly spoken in the past sennight, though they'd spent the required hours together before the clan at meals, pleasantly tolerating each other with words and small gestures. It was doubtful there were any who thought their marriage a love match, but at least none showed animosity toward her. Indeed, they'd listened to her prompts regarding items from the larder to the privy, and she noticed a discreet crowd gathered by the hearth each night as she told Bram a tale. Small, progressive steps as lady of the clan. Acceptance. It was enough.

She propped a shoulder against the parapet, one eye on the land surrounding the castle, the other on her husband. "What is it ye wish, Caelen?"

"I received a report from the cooper, tanner, fletcher, and blacksmith today," he stated.

Arbela sighed. So much for acceptance. But such intrigue had been common at Batroun. Why had she not expected it here?

She gave him her full attention, without replying as she waited to hear what the craftsmen had told him.

"It seems my son is now a sweeper for the cooper to repay him for wood, a water-fetcher for the tanner in exchange for a scrap of leather, feather-collector for the fletcher in exchange for bits of sinew, and will clean stalls for the blacksmith for a handful of iron nails and a shallow metal cup." Caelen cocked his head. "Do ye care to tell me why my son has hired out to these men?"

"He did not care to learn his numbers," Arbela replied, stifling a grin.

Caelen ran his palm over his shorn head. "What has learning his numbers have to do with these chores?" he demanded.

"When asked to count rocks I lined up for him, he not only refused, he kicked them, scattering them across the yard. Rather than punish him outright, I set him a task that will not only teach him to count, but will also teach him to expect to return service to those from whom he gets supplies." She allowed a small smile. "And he will have crafted his own small shield—to better fight dragons."

"Dragons?"

"He is rather fond of the tale of St. George and the dragon."

Caelen pondered Arbela's words, a frown tugging at his lips. "The stable master tells me Bram cleans Ari's stall each morn."

"And feeds him before he breaks his own fast. He will learn to care for others before himself," Arbela said. "A good quality in someone who will one day lead his clan."

His gaze took on an approving gleam, and something warmed inside Arbela. "I forget he is growing," Caelen admitted. "One day soon, I will allow him to practice with the young lads. Swords and such," he added, as though Arbela wouldn't have known what he meant.

She stifled the urge to roll her eyes, afraid they'd pop right out of her skull. *He still does not believe my skills have worth. He has gained a woman he can trust to watch over Bram and keep order in his home. Naught else.*

"Was there aught else ye wished to discuss?" she asked, her words clipped.

Caelen's eyebrows rose. "Has what I said offended ye?"

"I find myself quite weary this eve," Arbela evaded. *Weary of being ignored. Weary of being nothing more than a housekeeper.*

"The hour grows late," Caelen said. "I agree with yer actions with Bram. Thank ye. He thrives in yer care."

Taken aback by Caelen's unprecedented praise, Arbela stared at him, silent for the moments it took her to gather a response. "Ye are welcome. 'Tis good to know I have yer support."

With a curt nod, Caelen spun on his heel and hurried down the parapet stairs.

* * *

Sounds of scuffling, punctuated with shouts and grunts, burst through the open kitchen doorway. Arbela glanced up, instantly alert, aware she'd sent Bram outside to play only minutes earlier. Setting the ladle beside the pot, she strode to the door, the pitch of the voices telling her this was a youthful spat, not one between adults—or an invasion of MacGillonays.

It was not difficult to discover the source of the commotion. Four or five youngsters Arbela knew as Bram's friends surrounded a pair writhing in the dirt. She stepped closer to see Bram sprawled atop the other lad, using his weight to keep the larger boy pinned. Hands fisted in the lad's hair, Bram shouted above the noise of the gathering crowd of youngsters.

"Ye will take it back!" He smacked the lad's head against the ground. "Ye willnae say that again!"

Arbela stirred the other boys aside and planted her feet next to the combatants.

"Ye will stop this instant," she barked.

Voices fell to a murmur then halted. Two lads hauled Bram and his red-headed foe to their feet, avoiding Arbela's stern gaze. Bram glowered at the ground as he swiped a sleeve across his nose and mouth. His lower lip sported a cut from which trickled a tiny line of blood, the skin already beginning to swell. His opponent's left cheek was scuffed, the back of his tunic coated in bits of dirt and grass. Neither lad appeared seriously injured. Arbela glanced from one to the other.

"Explain yourselves."

The boys exchanged looks, then dropped their gazes to the ground.

"Well?"

The red-headed lad sighed. "I'm sorry," he said, nudging Bram's arm. Bram nodded, but did not meet the boy's gaze, his jaw clenched, clearly unappeased.

"Scrapping in the yard is for dogs. If ye have hurtful thoughts ye consider speaking aloud, come to me and I will keep ye busy enough ye'll have no need to share them." Arbela sent each lad a quelling look.

"Aye."

"Nae, my lady."

Murmurs drifted about the small group. Arbela shooed them away. "Be gone before I task the blacksmith with giving each of ye a job."

The boys scattered like sheep before a wolf. Bram lingered, Arbela's fingertips on his shoulder. "Care to tell me what that was about?"

Bram shrugged, not quite hard enough to dislodge her hand, but his reticence was clear.

"Have we not spoken of the warrior's rules of conduct?" Arbela asked gently. "It does not require ye to tell me what this brawl was about, but it does require ye to not take matters into your own hands."

"He said ye were black-skinned, like a Moor." Bram lifted his gaze. "I thought a moor was a bit of grassland. But Aiden said it in a mean way and that ye werenae fit to be Lady MacKern."

"Well, I agree ye should not speak ill of someone. And 'tis clear his claim is faulty. Do I look black-skinned to ye?" She filed away the comment, wondering which adult was responsible for putting such ideas in the boy's head. Who among the MacKerns found her lacking?

"Ye are darker than me," Bram answered honestly. "But ye arenae black, are ye?"

Arbela laughed. "Nay. I have seen people of many colors, from pink-white albinos to those with skin so black ye cannot see them on a dark night."

Bram's eyes widened.

"I am not that dark," she teased. "And a Moor is someone of possibly Arab or Berber descent, who may live in northern Africa, Iberia or other areas such as Sicily or Malta. Many Moors have very dark skin. I was born in a castle on the road between Tripoli and Beirut, but my mother was Armenian, and my father a Scot. I am not a Moor."

Two young boys crept back to Bram's side. Arbela recognized them from the small group that often gathered when she told Bram stories in the evening by the hearth. One elbowed Bram. "Ask her."

Bram frowned. "They dinnae believe ye are a princess."

"Oh? Then I will tell ye my story, for my mother was a royal princess of Armenia, but being the youngest of four, she was much petted and loved. When she declared she had fallen in love with the Baron of

Batroun—a Scotsman!—her parents were horrified. But there were no royal princes of an age to marry her, as her sisters had snatched them all up. And so, seeing how much in love she and the baron were, and what a very good man he was, they allowed the marriage."

"So, ye *are* a princess?" the smallest of the lads asked, eyes wide.

"I am. Though not one in any danger of inheriting the throne of Armenia," she laughed. "I am quite settled here. My aunt will arrive here in a sennight, and she *is* a royal princess, raised in a palace of unimaginable beauty, where flowers and fountains abound, and everyone eats off silver and gold and drinks from jeweled goblets.

"She was not blessed with children, and when her husband died, my brother and I were newborns. She decided to live with and help care for us. Since my older two aunts have scores of children and grandchildren between them, Aunt Zora is not expected to inherit the crown, either."

The boys gazed at her, adoration on their faces. Though that had not been her intent, it hopefully meant they would strive harder to behave—at least in her presence.

"Come, Bram. We will continue our lessons."

* * *

Arbela thumped the surface of the small shield. "Ye have done excellent work, Bram-jan." She eyed the narrow strip of leather that encircled the shield, held in place with sinew lacings. "The leather will help hold the slats in place, as will the sheet of linen—which ye did a grand job gluing to the boards." She turned the piece over, inspecting the leather grip on the back. "The small bowl made an excellent boss and ye helped pound the flange, aye?"

"'Twas hard work," Bram admitted, but his eyes glowed. "But fun!"

"The iron nails will hold it in place, and your fist will fit just so." Arbela nodded. "I believe any dragon will think twice before confronting

160

Bram the Brave!"

Bram could scarcely contain his excitement. He bobbed up and down, accepting the shield from Arbela in a mix of enthusiasm and reverence for the evidence of his hard work.

"Ye became quite good at measuring and counting," she teased him. "Do ye see why such things are not mere work to annoy your brain, but skills ye will use daily?"

"Aye. Though this was much easier to learn than counting rocks."

"Ye can do both, but this was mayhap a more interesting route. Let me see your sword."

Bram slung his shield over his shoulder as if born doing so, and drew his short wooden sword from a leather sheath at his belt. Pleased that he remembered to hand it to her hilt first, despite the fact it was of no actual danger to her, she accepted it solemnly, checking the 'blade' for nicks or other defects.

"Ye have a fair piece for practice, now, Bram-jan. And ye are learning to respect it, even if 'tis made of wood. Ye crafted it yourself, and I am very proud of ye."

They practiced holding the sword, both defensively and a few parries and lunges, then moved to footwork, instilling balance in the young lad. Arbela was pleased to note he was quick, and eager to learn.

"Do ye think Da would like to see me do this?" Bram asked, executing a forward roll, his sword and shield tucked away. He sprang to his feet and immediately focused on the line Arbela had sketched in the dirt, arms outstretched as he walked quickly down its length, toe to heel.

Arbela laughed. "'Tis not something I've seen warriors here practice," she told him. "They seem to rely on brute strength to gain the upper hand. But as a boy these skills ye are learning will be of more use until ye are a man grown. Even then, ye will be more agile than your opponents. Practice, practice, and more practice," she admonished, demonstrating a back flip in perfect parallel to Bram's line, falling smoothly into a crouch, sword arm at the ready.

"I want to learn that," Bram insisted, awe etched on his face. With careful guidance, Bram practiced leaping up and back into Arbela's arms.

"I am glad ye are no older, Bram-jan," she declared after a short time. "My arms grow weary of catching ye. I believe 'tis time to show me what ye remember of throwing a dagger."

His attention immediately captured by the promise of more lessons, Bram caught her hand, dragging her to the small grove just outside the keep where they practiced. Men at work on the wall waved as they passed and Bram tossed a brief wave back as he hurried to the wooded copse.

Arbela drew a slender dagger from the sheath under her sleeve and held it flat. Bram held his fingers at his sides, though they tapped against his trews, impatient to touch the smooth steel. He recited the rules of handling the blade in a clear voice, then took it gently from her hands. Stepping to their practice area, he placed himself at an angle to the target. Once again, he recited the steps for throwing the blade, walking slowly through the paces, dagger firmly in his hand.

"Well done," Arbela approved, her eye keen for any misstep. "Ye may practice."

Bram's first throw flew slightly off the mark and landed with a thud on the leaf-covered ground. He darted off to retrieve it, then paced back, dagger at his side. He drew a deep breath and set himself again for the next attempt.

"Imagine exactly the path your blade will take," Arbela murmured. "It is an extension of your arm, of your mind."

His next throw pierced the thin wooden target inside the outer circle. He spun about, quivering with excitement. "I did it!"

"Ye certainly did. Your aim and strength improves daily. Fetch it again, and this time, count off your paces. Ye must learn to judge your distance."

Shouting his numbers aloud, Bram stalked to the tree, not missing a beat.

* * *

Caelen reined his horse to a stop. Ahead lay fields planted by the men Alex had sent, straight lines of new green growth pleasing to the eye as the oats burst from the plowed ground. Four boats bobbed gently on the water of the loch where only one had sat only a few weeks earlier, fishing for the evening catch. Meals had improved, as fresh fish and the occasional hart graced the tables, and the herbs and spices Arbela brought with her lent the dishes an exotic but tasty flavor.

She also brought new life to Bram, who now rarely spent time with Ilene, his ma's elderly nurse. He'd never seen the lad so eager to learn. He knew Arbela taught him basic sword drills, though he had not sanctioned it, and it would soon be time to turn Bram's training over to Rory with the rest of the young lads who would become warriors. He thought of their last conversation. Bram's split and swollen lip had caught his attention, though Bram's nonchalance told him he had not been seriously injured.

He defended my honor, Arbela had said. *Though the other lad started the argument, and was the larger of the pair, Bram had the upper hand.* Her faint smile flashed and was gone. *I do not believe the boys will be squabbling again soon, though I seem to recall idle hands make the greatest mischief. I have offered to send the next batch of miscreants to the blacksmith for extra chores should they feel the need to roll about in the dirt.*

Things had certainly changed since she arrived at Dunfaileas.

"'Tis not a sight I thought to see at the turn of the year," Rory said, as though reading some of Caelen's thoughts.

"Aye. 'Tis a welcome sight," Caelen agreed.

"Warms a man's heart," Rory replied. "Yer wife brought new life to the clan."

"Her dowry is much appreciated." Caelen's voice, flat and pitched low, did not invite further comment.

"Yer *wife* is much appreciated," Rory returned, ignoring Caelen's implied request to drop the subject. "Och, there are those who see her as foreign, but others who are coming to appreciate the Scots side of her." He stacked his hands over the pommel of his saddle. "The question is, do *ye* appreciate her?"

Caelen's scowl darkened, calculated to elicit an apology from Rory for asking such a personal question, but the man simply lifted an eyebrow, challenging Caelen to answer.

"What a daft question," he snorted. "Of course, I appreciate Arbela."

"Ye seem to spend a lot of time avoiding her."

It was Caelen's turn to raise his brow. "Ye remember the bargain between us, aye?"

Rory shrugged and grinned. "I have known ye to be persuasive. And the lass is comely. Bram likes her. Yer clan likes her a bit better each day." He pinned Caelen with a stare. "Why does it appear ye merely tolerate her?"

"She scarcely invites my attentions," Caelen retorted.

"Have ye asked?"

"Asked? Have I asked a woman—*my wife*—if she would welcome my attention?" Caelen sent Rory a disbelieving look. "I groveled enough with Ruthie. Arbela and I have made our wishes clear, and we will abide by our agreement." He scowled. "I willnae beg a woman for her favors," he muttered.

"I dinnae say *beg*. But getting to know yer wife a wee bit better isnae a bad thing. The two of ye may decide to give a real marriage a try." Rory's grin did not improve Caelen's bad humor. Rory made an exasperated sound. "Ye are aptly named, Bull," he growled. "Bullheaded ye are in truth."

"Do ye believe I should have a desire for such a foreign wife?"

Caelen challenged. "She was not my choice. I had no desire to marry again, but circumstances forced my hand. Ye have seen her, dressed in trews like a man. Painted eyes. Dark skin. She is nothing like other Scottish lasses."

Rory hooted with laughter. "I *have* seen yer wife! And if ye think she looks like a man in her trews, ye and I need to have a different conversation. Aye, her eyes are painted, though I would argue they are mysterious, not foreign. And praise St. Andrew's favorite hound she isnae like the other lass ye married."

"Enough! We have an agreement, and it suits us both," Caelen insisted stubbornly. "You and I have better things to do than discuss my married life." He urged his horse forward, ignoring Rory's grumbled reply.

"Wait!" Rory lifted his voice. Caelen turned in his saddle. Rory pointed to the loch where galley ship, ten oars to a side, rounded the shoreline and approached the beach.

Caelen stood in his stirrups, straining for a better view. The ship landed and a breeze caught the flag hanging from the top of the center mast. His gut clenched as he recognized the bright red and blue pattern.

MacGillonay!

Chapter Nineteen

Crouched low over his horse's neck, Caelen drummed his heels against his mount's sides, sending him down the rocky trail at breakneck speed. Surefooted, Addis plunged over fallen limbs as he swerved off the path, picking a more direct route down the hillside. Rory's horse's hooves clattered behind, then pulled alongside as they raced neck-and-neck to the gates of Dunfaileas.

"A MacKern!" Caelen shouted, seeing the gates swing closed. The men at the wall changed direction, bracing against the heavy doors to halt their inward track. The opening between the doors was enough to admit Caelen and Rory as they rushed inside amid a thunder of hooves and shouts.

Caelen swung from the saddle, reins flying through the air as a stable lad struggled to capture Addis who still clattered across the yard. "Close the gates. Place guards on the walls. No one enters without my command."

"It is already done, Laird."

Caelen pivoted to face the calm, but firm voice. "Where is my son?"

Arbela tilted her head to the tower house. "Inside with Ilene. I have placed most of our soldiers, including our knights from the MacLean, at the front wall, bows at the ready. There are others watching the rear approaches. Though MacGillonay comes from the loch, in broad daylight, I do not trust him to not flank us whilst our attention is on the beach."

Caelen opened his mouth, torn between startled appreciation for her clear thinking, and anger to find her outside instead of with Bram. "Thank ye," he managed, distracted by a call from a soldier on the wall. "I now have command. I need ye to see to Bram." Not waiting for her response, he strode to the rock stairway leading to the parapet. Attaining the heights, he peered at the orderly line of men striding the path to Dunfaileas.

MacGillonay sat astride his unmistakable gray horse, his men maintaining pace with him on foot. Caelen's gut twisted, hatred for the man boiling through his veins.

MacGillonay halted several lengths from the gate and glanced up, his gaze sweeping the walls before lighting on Caelen. A wolfish grin split his face.

"Caelen! Son by marriage! Is this any way to greet yer wife's da?"

"I no longer claim ye as kin—as ye well know," Caelen replied.

"And I know ye have taken a new wife—a Saracen, so the rumors say," MacGillonay shouted back.

"*Zadeh* . . .." A hiss of sharply indrawn air told Caelen his wife had followed him to the parapet rather than doing as ordered—and disapproved of MacGillonay's comment. Caelen wasn't certain he would approve of Arbela's reply, and perhaps it was as well he didn't understand the language she spoke. Given the circumstances, he let it go.

"Hie yerself inside," he told her. "Protect Bram."

The very air around Arbela bristled at his brusque command. She hesitated only a moment before replying, her eyes flashing her displeasure.

"As ye wish." Reaching the first step on her downward trek, she paused, casting a look over her shoulder that burned with the intensity of an unguarded flame. "If he persists, I will be happy to instruct him on the difference between a Saracen and a Christian."

Realizing the depth of her passion on the subject, Caelen merely gave a small shake of his head. "Heed him not, Arbela. He is an old wolf who causes what mischief he may with his words."

"A wolf whose hide can be stretched on our outer wall in warning to others," she countered, eyes dark with warning.

Caelen hid a smile. "Care for the lad. I must know he is safe."

Arbela's boots made little sound as she raced into the keep.

"Yer wife doesnae like being compared with a Saracen," Rory noted, his voice a carrying whisper from the corner of his mouth.

Caelen tore his gaze from Arbela as she entered the keep. "Nay," he agreed thoughtfully. "I made the mistake once and she ripped into me. I, for one, willnae make the same mistake a second time. I wager, if allowed, she would make MacGillonay pay dearly for shouting it so all could hear."

Rory raised a brow. "Mayhap ye should turn her loose on yon wolf. I have little doubt she would come out ahead. His hide would make an interesting addition to our new wall."

Caelen shot Rory a quelling frown then turned his scowl to the gathering clouds overhead. The first drops of rain spattered on the stone. More followed.

"Is this Highland hospitality?" MacGillonay called. "To leave kin standing outside whilst a storm brews? I have come to see yer new wife— the woman who has the care for my grandson. I wish to give her my blessing."

"Even if she is a Saracen?" Rory chuckled under his breath.

The wind picked up, wrapping cloth about bodies, snapping the pennant on the distant ship. Rain began in earnest, a drumming sound on the stones.

"Shite." Caelen started down the stairs. "Strip the inside of the keep of anything of interest—let none linger who are not required to serve," he called to Rory over his shoulder.

"Ye'll let the bastard in? On the grounds of hospitality?"

Caelen grunted, too angry to speak further. "Aye."

* * *

Arbela stormed into the keep, boots pounding the stone floor, her anger carrying her past the startled soldiers at the door.

"Clear the room," she commanded, her voice crisp and carrying. "I want no unnecessary people visible. If ye can wield a weapon, get it and keep it at your side. Wrap others in blankets and place them in the corners

168

out of sight. Set a guard on the stair."

Her pace carried her through the hall and to the interior stairs. She noted—not for the first time—they spiraled upward to the right, the wall hampering the sword arm of most warriors who would fight to gain the upper levels, the open side leaving clear fighting space for those who would defend the castle. Her gaze swept the hall, noting the dearth of faces as most disappeared from sight at her command.

"I have a weapon!" Bram's sudden presence halted her step. He fisted his wooden sword, a scowl on his face, his shield hanging across his back. His feet planted firmly on the ground, weight slightly forward as Arbela had taught him. Had he been older, his sword of steel, she might have considered his help.

"Aye, ye do," she agreed, placing her hands on his shoulders and turning him down the hall. "And we need every able hand we possess. Do ye know who has arrived?"

She steered him into Caelen's room and partially shut the door behind them, leaving it slightly ajar, hoping to catch sound from below.

If possible, Bram's frown deepened. "Auld Man MacGillonay, the bastard," he said.

Arbela drew up short. "Where did ye hear such a thing?"

Bram shrugged, and his shoulders sagged. "He's my ma's da, isn't he?"

"MacGillonay is your grandsire," Arbela confirmed. "I dinnae know much about your ma, except she was unfortunate enough to miss seeing ye grow. But MacGillonay has not been very nice lately, and we will remain here, out of the way, until he is gone."

Bram's look slid from ferocious to angry challenge and finally to heartbreaking bewilderment. "My grandda is a bad man, isn't he?"

"'Tis important we do not allow him to cause us unnecessary grief. And that means letting your da handle things and keeping ye safe—away from potential trouble."

Bram's expression firmed, his hand gripping his sword. "'Tis my duty as a MacKern warrior to protect the clan. Even if it is from my grandda."

"A warrior must do what his laird commands. Your laird commanded us to wait here," Arbela countered.

"But, what if—?"

"What if I tell ye a tale of the Moorish pirates we encountered on our voyage to Scotland?"

Bram tilted his head, obviously weighing the option of having his questions answered over hearing a new story. With a slow nod, he agreed to the tale.

Arbela settled him on a bench near the hearth, taking the chair for herself.

"Our ship was three months from Messina, Italy, and storms had beset our travel across the Mediterranean. Had we simply been intent on traveling to Scotland, we could have made port at Marseilles and traveled overland until we reached the northern coast of France. But we had valuable cargo aboard we wished to bring with us, and so our path led us to the narrow sea passage called the Strait of Gibraltar."

"What's a strait?" Bram interjected.

"In this case, 'tis a small strip of water between two land masses that leads from one body of water to another. And the passage is so narrow, and full of hidden coves, 'tis like creeping down a hall full of closed doors—with pirates waiting to jump out at ye, and ye with no place to go."

Bram's eyes widened and he drew his legs up in a protective motion.

"Our ship is a wonder of Venetian shipbuilding, its sails designed to give her the ability to move both with and against the wind whilst carrying great loads. She is among the first of her kind, and of course the pirates had never seen such a vessel before." Arbela's voice lowered in pitch.

"*The ship's a beauty,* the first mate growled to the captain. *She is a queen among lesser vessels.* The captain nodded. *She will bring us much gold when we make port. See how she glides across the water like a living thing, and the wind gives her homage.*"

Arbela gave Bram a sidelong glance. "Our ship, the *Sea Falcon*, is a marvel of engineering and a feast for the eyes. In addition to the main sail amidships—which all cogs have—she has a smaller sail, a lateen, which allows the ship to move in virtually any direction." She bladed her hand upright, using it to visualize the movement of a ship in the water. "With the wind." She blew on her hand, moving it away from her. "Angled to the wind." She blew across her hand, keeping it steady on.

"And into the wind." She nodded, inviting Bram to blow her hand away. He puffed out his cheeks and blew, and she sent her hand leaping forward, into his *wind*, and fluttered her fingers at him, tickling him as she made contact with his tummy. Bram shrieked in glee and pushed her hand away.

"I'm a hurricane!" he declared. "I can blow yer ship across the ocean."

Arbela sighed. "Aye. Even the *Sea Falcon* cannot sail against such a storm as Hurricane Bram." She settled back in her chair. Bram giggled, all worry of MacGillonay forgotten.

"The pirates swarmed us from the coast of northern Africa as we reached the narrowest part of the strait, and Captain Benicio skillfully tacked the *Sea Falcon* across the wind, away from our pursuers." She leaned forward, her voice dropping.

"But the pirates had another ship lying in wait, and suddenly it appeared off our port bow, a Moorish dhow with ten oars to a side cutting through the water, its sail furled, heedless of the direction of the wind. It sped toward us whilst the other pirate ship gained on us from behind, their small size and shallow draft making them swift as eagles after their prey."

Arbela raised an open fist to her mouth and gave a fair imitation of a manly bellow. "*Man the ballistae!* Laird MacLean cried. Alex and Kade leapt to the aft castle where two massive crossbows awaited them. The creak of the windlasses as they prepared to fire tore through the air. Farlan manned the single ballista on the fore castle, and Lachlan and I prepared the flaming arrows."

"They were faster than the Sea Falcon? What is a ballista? When can I make flaming arrows?" Bram asked, rapid-firing his questions.

"Aye, they were faster. But they did not count on the fact we were so well defended. A ballista is a very large crossbow that fires bolts as big as spears. It can even fire great stones. The pirates were only familiar with the merchant cogs which floundered without a steady wind to fill their sails. The *Sea Falcon* is agile for such a large ship."

"And has ballistae and flaming arrows!" Bram shouted.

"Aye. We were prepared, and willing to fight off the pirates."

"Ye werenae afraid?" he asked.

Arbela considered his question. "I think fear can be replaced, or at least tempered by determination. Once ye decide on an action, fear will no longer control ye. Exchange your fear for courage, and do what needs to be done."

"Did ye kill the pirates?"

Arbela nodded. "They will no longer stalk the seas, taking prisoners and bounty, killing any who resist. Others doubtless replaced them, but those pirates who sought to capture our ship met their end that day at the bottom of the sea. I prayed for their souls, as is proper."

A knock sounded at the door, startling them. Arbela had heard no footsteps in the passage. She rose, drawing a dagger from its sheath at her belt. Motioning for Bram to the bed where he scrambled to peer around a curtained post, Arbela flattened herself beside the door.

"Aye?"

Rory's voice rumbled through the slight opening. "Bring Bram to the hall. His da wishes his presence."

"Has MacGillonay retreated?"

"Nay. He requested hospitality—from the rain." Rory's disdain for such action was clear. "Caelen couldnae deny him. MacGillonay claims he comes only to meet Caelen's new wife and ensure Bram's well-being."

Arbela laughed softly. "The wife he claims is a Saracen." Her words more statement than question. She opened the door, admitting Rory. He stepped inside the room, his gaze finding Bram.

"I'm here to take a braw lad to see the MacGillonay," he said. "Will ye come?"

Bram slid a questioning gaze to Arbela. She gave a single nod. "Decide on your course of action, and fear cannot stop ye. Ye are Laird MacKern's son and heir. My son. Ye are equal to the task before ye."

Bram nodded once, then again, vigorously. His small frame straightened and he slid from the bed. "I will come."

He placed a hand on the hilt of his wooden sword, giving it a reluctant stare. "Warriors dinnae bring their weapons to a peaceful gathering, do they, Bela?"

"No, Bram-jan they do not."

With a sigh, he slowly removed his belt and placed it and his shield on the bed. Straightening his shoulders, he turned to Rory. "I am ready," he said evenly, nary a quiver marring his bravery.

Rory gave him a respectful nod and motioned the lad to precede him through the door. Arbela followed, keeping Bram within arm's reach. Rory leaned close as she passed.

"Have ye left yer weapons behind, my lady?" he murmured.

"Do ye believe MacGillonay comes in peace?" she countered.

"I dinnae," Rory admitted.

Arbela did not miss a step. "Neither do I."

Chapter Twenty

Caelen's gaze flashed over his wife as she and Bram entered the room. Her silk tunic, supple leather vest and leggings stood out among the other women's simple woolen dresses, but were not as exotic as the brocades and jewels he'd seen her dressed in on other days. Her clothing bespoke a warrior, not a woman whose main job was keeping a wee lad out of trouble.

Rory followed in their wake, staying in the shadow of the second level gallery, drawing little attention to himself. Bram and Arbela halted at Caelen's side, her hand firm on the lad's shoulder. Caelen's heart warmed at the even look Bram settled on his grandda. No fear or nervousness from *his* lad.

MacGillonay took a step forward. Bram upped the tilt of his jaw, but made no move to avoid his grandda. MacGillonay chuckled. "A braw lad ye're raising, MacKern." Somehow there was no approval in the man's voice. "How does he fare with a sword?"

"He attends his lessons," Caelen growled, clenching his fists at his side to keep from smashing the smug grin from the older man's face. "Ye've seen the lad is well. Ye are now free to leave."

MacGillonay cocked his head. "'Tis still raining and I havenae met yer new wife." He turned a malevolent gaze to Arbela. "Yer Saracen wife."

Arbela's eyes narrowed slightly, and she, too, closed a fist, keeping it firmly at her side. Otherwise, she gave no outward sign MacGillonay had spoken.

"Does she not understand Scots?" The older man questioned, disdain in his voice. "What barbaric tongue does she speak?"

"*Tha mi gad thuigsinn,*" she replied in flawless Gaelic. *I understand ye.* "When ye can keep a civil tongue in your mouth, I will answer."

"Barbed-tongue wench!" MacGillonay swung to Caelen. "I trust she is not in charge of teaching my grandson manners. A good thrashing should straighten her out." His eyes gleamed as he returned his gaze to slide up and down Arbela's form. "If ye arenae man enough to do it, I will be happy to show ye the how of it."

"If ye were not under my husband's hospitality, I would invite ye to try," Arbela returned evenly, and Caelen was amazed he did not see flames shrivel MacGillonay where he stood.

He sent Arbela a cool look, neither condemning nor approving, and the faint arch to her brow told him she would not back down. *Good lass!* Shocked at his thought, he made an effort to defuse the situation, acutely aware of his son in the room, but it was already too late.

"Disrespectful Saracen!" MacGillonay shouted as he lunged a step forward, hand going to the empty scabbard at his side. His captain placed a restraining hand on his shoulder and MacGillonay halted, shrugging off the grip, his face dark with anger.

"Arbela." Caelen's voice cut through the air as he placed himself between her and MacGillonay. "Take Bram upstairs. Teach him that damn board game ye've harped on. I've business with MacGillonay."

Arbela stepped firmly around him, placing herself at his side. "I believe MacGillonay and I have a lesson to conduct. Thrice he has called me a Saracen, as well as barb-tongued and disrespectful. Clearly, this godless barbarian has little idea how to phrase his words when speaking to a woman. I will happily tell my sire the quality of MacGillonay when next I see him. He will be quite keen to know of the brood of snakes which borders his land."

"Give her to me, MacKern!" MacGillonay spat. "Devil's spawn!"

Bram slid to Arbela's side, shoulders pitched slightly forward, a glower for MacGillonay on his face.

"Arbela!" Caelen growled. "Take Bram upstairs."

Tension flowed thick, binding the three of them together. Arbela made no move to withdraw, her dark eyes boring into MacGillonay. Caelen cursed under his breath, unwilling to attempt to manhandle her out of the situation. With a shrug, Arbela stepped back, her voice light.

"Come, Bram. We will await your father in your room. I am certain he can discuss what hospitality means with his guest whilst we play *Alquerque.*"

Caelen's stomach unclenched as she referenced the game by its ancient name. *She understands. 'Tis a misdirection stating where she and the lad will be. She knows the passage is in my room.* He waited, hands at his belt, as she and Bram left the hall. At Caelen's slight nod, Rory positioned himself with two other men at the bottom step. It would not be easy to follow the pair up the stairs.

"Ye allow that woman to speak in such a manner?" MacGillonay demanded.

"When faced with bald-faced disrespect and taunts, I willnae insist she apologize. I believe an apology should come from *ye.*"

MacGillonay's face darkened, white spots at his temple, spittle in his beard. "I will apologize to no woman! Especially one such as her!" He pointed to the empty stair. "Bring her back and I will punish her insolence if ye havenae the guts to do so."

"Ye are out of line, auld man. And ye have overstepped the bounds of hospitality. Rain or not, ye will take yer men and leave my home."

"A tumble-down pile of stones," MacGillonay sneered. "I dinnae know what my Ruthie saw in ye, and I curse the day I agreed to the marriage. Ye are a bull of a man with no grace and little wit. She bemoaned her mistake of marrying ye until the day she died.

"When I heard ye had married the MacLean's girl, I knew 'twas time to retrieve my grandson from ye and the godless hands of the Saracen witch. I am here to collect Bram. Send yer man up after him. I will give him a quarter hour to collect his things."

176

Caelen shifted his weight forward on the balls of his feet, anger dulling everything but the man before him. "Get out of my home, MacGillonay. Ye will never get yer hands on my son."

MacGillonay's face split into a malicious grin. "Think not? My men are ready to see my request is met."

Caelen's laughter barked. "Yer men were disarmed at the gate. Ye are surrounded by soldiers loyal to me, well-armed and prepared to escort ye to yer ship."

"Yer men are loyal, but all it takes is one disgruntled crone to create a chink in yer wall. Look around ye. My men are armed. And if ye wish yer soldiers to live out the hour, ye will instruct them to hand over their weapons."

Startled, Caelen glanced at Rory. Two men stood over his captain's prone form, a line of blood trickling across the stone beneath his head. A scuffle sounded as MacGillonay's men quickly disarmed three other men in the hall. Two other MacKerns stood back-to-back, swords out, defying the order to surrender.

MacGillonay crossed his arms over his chest. "Have them put away their weapons."

Stunned at the attack he hadn't seen coming, Caelen glanced about, seeking a different solution. At MacGillonay's nod, one of his men stepped to a captured MacKern soldier, knife pressed to his throat. Blood ran freely down the column of his neck from the careless press of the blade.

"Ye can watch them die, or ye can obey me."

Caelen gritted his teeth, refusing to give the command, stalling. Arbela needed time to get Bram away from the castle. Once MacGillonay realized they were no longer at Dunfaileas, he would send his men out to hunt them down. On horseback, they would capture them quickly.

How long before MacGillonay made good on his threat to kill? Could Caelen stand by and watch his men die? How far would he go to save his son?

"Ye plunge to the depths of idiocy, MacGillonay," Caelen warned. "By insulting my wife, ye have incurred the wrath of Baron MacLean, who commands the strongest force in this region. He has the power to wipe ye off yer land."

"That Saracen?" MacGillonay scoffed. "He's no true Scot."

"Those whom ye term *Saracen*," Caelen seethed, "have trod in the very footsteps of Our Lord, even to the hill of Golgotha. My wife, a princess of Armenia, was baptized by the Bishop of Antioch before Holy Relics. Their lives have been spent in service to God, keeping the Holy Land open to sinners such as us. Have a care for yer words, laird. They give great offense."

MacGillonay's lips twisted in a leer. "That's what I do best."

* * *

"Hurry," Arbela whispered, the word harsh, betraying her anger. Her palm pressed on Bram's back, urging him down the hall.

She should *not* be backing down from MacGillonay's insults. He was up to no good, of that she was certain. Such a man did not toss out abuse of this nature without knowing he could get away with it. Something was terribly wrong.

"I will take the lad." Ilene stepped from the darkened doorway. "There is nae need for ye to bother yerself with him."

Arbela barreled through the open door, passing the older woman without pause. Agnes looked up from the mending in her lap as Ilene followed them inside, protesting.

"She has harped on ye all eve," Agnes reported, eyes narrowed in disapproval. "She willnae cease, the auld biddy."

"Bram is with me," Arbela stated, sparing Ilene no look. "Agnes, put yer mending aside and come with me."

178

Toros and Garen milled about her feet. Toros broke away to stand next to Bram who shoved a hand into the dog's ruff, clearly needing the dog's reassurance. Arbela grabbed the waterskin and tossed the strap over her shoulder, adding the small bag of food. "Take only a change of clothing, Bram," she said, handing him an oilcloth pack and a length of wool. "Here is your plaide."

Bram's lower lip quivered and Toros wiggled his back end and tail, adding a swipe of his tongue across Bram's cheek for good measure. Bram hugged the dog to him then squared his shoulders and filled his bag.

Arbela gathered her sword and bow, adding three daggers from her chest of belongings to a set of sheaths on her belt, bringing her total blades to eight. She slipped a few other small packages into her bag, too quickly for the others to remark.

"My lady?" Agnes ventured, puzzlement on her face as she glanced from Bram to Arbela.

"I will explain," Arbela assured her. "Trust me. Come now."

Ilene rushed to her side. "Ye must not take him away!" she cried, tugging at Bram's sleeve. "Not now! There are armed men at the gates!"

Arbela spun on her heel, staring at the woman. "Whose men?" she demanded. Bram jerked from Ilene's grip.

Ilene wrung her hands. "Ye cannae leave," she moaned. "He is my lad. My precious Ruthie's lad."

"He is under *my* protection. Do not delay us further." Arbela grasped Bram's hand and turned to the door.

Ilene leapt forward, surprisingly agile for a woman her age. The dogs, alerted to her abrupt movement, growled low in their throats.

"Nae!" the old woman cried. "Ye arenae worthy to care for him! Ye have turned him against me, taken him from me." She spread her arms before the door. "Ye Saracen witch!" she spat, unknowingly echoing MacGillonay's words. "Ye touched my lamb with yer black hands, darkening his precious soul. 'Tis time he came back to me. Time ye returned to the godless lands ye came from."

Garen slid a step forward, her growl deepening.

"That answers the question of who is spreading unkind rumors," Arbela quipped, holding Garen at bay with a hand motion. "But I do not have time to instruct ye. Move aside now. Ye and I will have a talk soon." She reached for the latch.

"Nae!" the woman shrieked. She whirled and pressed her face to the wooden panel. "Help me!"

Arbela's fist curved upward, fast and powered by a single forward step. She clipped Ilene on the point of her chin, crumpling the old woman to the floor. Agnes gasped. Bram stared at the woman at his feet. Arbela knelt and checked the woman's pulse.

"She will wake, though her jaw will be sore for a day or two." She caught Bram's gaze. "I could not allow her to summon help, for I fear she has betrayed us. We must leave now."

Bram nodded solemnly and stepped around his nurse to follow Arbela from the room. Toros remained at Bram's side, a whine and a lick for the lad in encouragement. Agnes tread close on their heels. Arbela led them unerringly to the secret passage, collecting a candle as they crossed Caelen's room. She made quick work of opening the hidden panel, urging Bram and Agnes into the dark space. Bram darted past Arbela to retrieve his sword and shield from the bed, then joined Agnes and the dogs.

"How did ye know this was here?" Bram asked, running his hand over the stones.

"Your father told me of it. 'Twas to be used if he suspected ye were in danger. He told me a few minutes ago to bring ye here."

Bram sighed, his relief apparent that his da knew where they were. "Where does it go?"

Arbela ignored Bram's question. She gripped Agnes' arm, gaining her full attention. "I suspect Ilene has assisted in some treachery and fear she has helped MacGillonay into the castle. Bram must be protected. Ye must take him to my father."

"Me? I dinnae know the way." Agnes' eyes were wide and frightened. "I would do anything for the lad, but I would only wander in circles—and likely lead him back here. Ye must come with us."

"MacGillonay and I have business to finish," Arbela said. "And I cannot leave." She hazarded a look at Bram, wondering how much she should reveal. "If there is a fight, I am needed."

Agnes shook her head. "I would be no help if we were captured before we reached MacLean Castle. My life is his, but would avail him nothing." She also sent the lad a look. "He would be as good as caught."

Arbela gritted her teeth. What would happen if she left with Agnes and Bram? What would happen if she stayed? She did not doubt Agnes' stout heart, but it was true Agnes would protect Bram for the entire five seconds it would take for MacGillonay's men to cut her down. Or worse.

She paced the narrow confines of the passageway, impatient with the indecision and the time she wasted.

"I will go with ye." The words tore something inside her, but she set it aside, concentrating on getting them moving as quickly as possible.

"Why—?"

Arbela silenced Agnes with a wave of her hand. "I will explain later. We have no more time. I must set the doors behind us so none will follow. Remain for me here."

Not waiting for their nod of obedience, Arbela darted as silent as a wraith across Caelen's chamber. Easing the door open, she glanced down the passage. Seeing it clear, she moved to Bram's room. She dragged Ilene to the far side of Bram's bed, hiding her beneath a carelessly thrown blanket, then reduced the fire on the hearth to a faint glow.

Stepping back to the door, she withdrew a thick leather package from her bag and scattered a swath of thick metal wires, each approximately an inch long, twisted together in pairs and then splayed so that at least one sharp, barbed end pointed upward. If MacGillonay's men came to search

Bram's room, they would encounter the barbs which would slice through their leather boots, inflicting great pain and possibly resulting later in infection or even death.

She drew a small jar and brush from her bag. With a dagger's blade, she ripped a splinter from the wooden latch to Bram's room, leaving it anchored by its nether end, and jutting out to catch the hand of a heedless person. Prying the lid from the jar, she dipped the brush into the contents and painted a bit of the mixture over the wooden barb. The splinter would be a nasty surprise to the next person who attempted to open the door, and the belladonna coating the sliver would soon bring about symptoms of a dry mouth, racing heart, and possibly a terrible case of hives. There were other poisons at her disposal, but though she believed Caelen would follow them to his room, not Bram's, she decided on a poison that would incapacitate, not kill.

Garen met Arbela at Caelen's door with a soft whine. The dog at her heels, Arbela then arranged the chest and tapestry to appear as undisturbed as possible before entering the dark passage where Bram, Agnes, and Toros awaited.

They rushed down the dark corridor, feet and paws a faint scuffle on the stone floor, punctuated by soft panting from the dogs. Arbela led the way, Bram between her and Agnes, Toros' sturdy frame lending support to the young lad. A thin trail of smoke billowed back from the candle she carried, which she shielded from the air draft with a cupped hand. They wound down short flights of steps interspersed with level stretches. The walls, only a few feet apart, hemmed them in, creating a stone tunnel that seemed to never end. Agnes' slippers faltered, but she made no sound as she resumed the headlong pace Arbela set.

After what seemed like a lifetime, they halted. Other than acknowledging the end of the hall with a slight broadening of the passage, there was no indication of a door. Arbela opened a small chest and handed out cloaks and another waterskin, this one empty. Pulling long leather leads from the box, she snapped a leash on each dog's collar.

"I am sorry about your slippers," she said to Agnes, knowing they would prove worthless long before their journey was over. "I have no boots for ye."

"Yer magical chest is empty?" Agnes jested, a strain in her voice. "No matter. At least there is no snow on the ground. I will be fine."

Fine was stretching matters a bit, but Arbela left the subject. "Cover yourselves as much as possible. Remember your faces and other exposed skin will appear bright in shadows. If you hear someone, pull your hood over your face and look down until the danger is past."

With a glance to ensure Bram and Agnes were sufficiently covered, Arbela handed each of them a leash, leaving her hands free. She placed her palm against a stone at the level of her head. With a near-silent *whoosh*, the stones moved in unison, revealing the door. Instantly struck with the aroma of the stables, it was clear where the passage had led them.

"We will ride?" Agnes asked, her eager voice a faint whisper.

"Nae. Though 'twould be faster, we would create too much noise and I do not know where our enemy lies." Arbela's heart lurched, understanding she left Voski behind. She nodded to the open space before them as her eyes adjusted to the faint moonlight. The soft lap of water against the shore greeted their ears. Silver lines marked the ripples on the loch. Stone walls stretched to either side, the castle behind them.

"And the stables are on the other side of the wall. We are now beyond the protection of Dunfaileas."

Chapter Twenty One

Arbela could have predicted the rain. What weather other than *cold* and wet did this land offer? If she had not been hampered by a five year old and a young woman facing a long trek, she would not have allowed the inconvenience to hinder her. But neither Agnes nor Bram was adequately prepared for the trip, and beyond tightly woven wool cloaks, they had little protection from the downfall that plagued them shortly after they left Dunfaileas.

"We can stop and rest, but we cannot light a fire," Arbela said, eying the sullen skies and the rain that had at last withdrawn to a light drizzle. Agnes gave her a wan smile, the gray line about her lips marking her fatigue. Bram dropped to the ground. Toros and Garen surrounded him, lending him warmth and protection.

"He is exhausted," Agnes murmured.

Arbela handed Agnes the waterskin and bag of food. "Use this sparingly. I hope to be at MacLean Castle by nightfall, but this is all we have. I will fill the other waterskin and return in a moment." She disappeared deeper into the forest.

The results of the rain dulled the normal sounds of the forest. Birds whose chirps would have alerted her to another's presence, huddled on their nests, feathers puffed against the damp. The sodden ground absorbed all footfalls, limbs made a faint *swish* as she passed. Arbela knelt beside the burn that bubbled from the hillside and filled the waterskin, eyes scanning the surroundings.

Nothing stirred.

She disliked taking the direct road from Dunfaileas to Morven, and had kept them off the path as much as possible. But the rise and fall of mountains made striking off across the land dangerous—and nigh impossible. And even at the slower pace she'd allowed for Bram's sake, he hadn't lasted half the trip.

Securing the mouth of the waterskin, Arbela turned back, relieved as the drizzle faded to a fine mist. She collected three sturdy sticks and as Bram and Agnes watched, arranged them roughly as a triangle, the apex two handbreadths apart. Trimming a narrow strip of leather from the bottom of her long vest, she used the supple length to lace the limbs together, filling in the center space with smaller branches which she then lashed into place.

Toros stood at her command and she fitted him with a harness of strips of wool torn from her cloak. Arbela noticed the faint gleam of interest in Bram's eyes.

She motioned to Agnes. "Help me run the poles through these straps."

Agnes held the loops steady as Arbela secured it behind Toros. The dog's tail swayed gently.

"Climb aboard, Bram-jan," Arbela urged, her voice gentle. "I believe ye must rest whilst we trek."

Bram gave a skeptical look, but carefully maneuvered onto the sled, hesitating as his weight caused it to sag.

"Toros is quite sturdy," Arbela reassured him. "He has pulled heavier loads than ye."

Toros whined and wagged his tail encouragingly. Bram jerked his gaze to the dog. Arbela laughed. "He is not disagreeing, merely asking ye to hurry. He is looking forward to a dry spot by the hearth."

Bram settled and Arbela tucked his plaide about him securely. She grasped Toros' leash and the dog paced at her side as they continued their journey.

Within moments, Bram was asleep.

"I dinnae suppose ye have one of those for me," Agnes sighed as she maintained the grueling pace. Though they'd slowed to keep the sled from bouncing over the rocky terrain, the steepness of the trail quickly tired them, creating spasms in leg muscles, and laboring their breathing. Agnes sent a half-hearted glare to Toros who surged ahead, his tail high.

"Cheeky bastard," she stated, without heat.

Arbela glanced at the sky, noting the position of the sun, a bright spot behind thinning clouds. "We will take a short break," she said. "We are on MacLean land, though far enough out we may not see a patrol for another hour."

She released the sled gently from Toros' harness, allowing him a brief respite. She lowered the traces to the ground as he bounded to Garen who ignored his invitation to play.

Agnes sank to a flattened boulder with a sigh. "That dog has endless energy," she half-complained. She closed her eyes and leaned her head back, soaking in the smattering of sunlight.

Arbela did not waste her breath debating the merits of her dogs. That was a luxury for another day, one when they were not being pursued by MacGillonay and his men.

* * *

MacKern soldiers exploded into action. The two armed men sprang apart. A quick stab at the MacGillonay holding his blade to a MacKern soldier sent him to the ground, his dagger skidding across the floor, released by useless fingers. There was no time to sort out the melee that erupted. Caelen dodged to the side, shoving Rory's motionless form beneath a bench, then rolled to a crouch facing the room, hands spread, sword ready—having unexpectedly found a cache of weapons in the corner next to the stairs. *Arbela's work?* He didn't have the time to pursue the how of it as a dagger whipped past his ear.

The clash of steel, *thud* of bodies struck, and cries of anger and injury rose and echoed in the hall. Someone had obviously helped smuggle weapons—and possibly men—for MacGillonay into the keep. Caelen counted many more heads than he'd admitted through the doors an hour earlier. He would seek the traitor out later. And hope the old woman MacGillonay referenced had not encountered Bram or Arbela.

He joined the battle, the room too small a space to allow much freedom of movement. Men grunted, shoved, grappled, slipping on the reeds and herbs scattered on the floor—and in widening pools of blood. He struck a soldier who challenged him, sending him to his knees with a blow to the side of his head. A following strike to the back of his skull ensured he stayed down.

Caelen stalked across the floor, elbowing men out of his way as he pursued MacGillonay. The older man met his approach with a challenging leer, accepting a sword from the man at his side. A sense of disbelief washed over Caelen before he could banish it at the appearance of the weapon. He loosened his muscles with a shrug of his shoulders, rotating the sword in his hand, putting thoughts of treachery from his mind. A path cleared almost magically between him and MacGillonay.

"Ye cannae have my sword," Caelen growled.

MacGillonay laughed. "I dinnae want yer relic. It would be better consigned to the dung heap." He stepped confidently forward. "I want my grandson," he said.

"Ye have an heir," Caelen snarled. "Leave mine alone."

"Ruthie's brothers willnae inspire men to follow them," MacGillonay replied. "Bram has much potential, and many years to bend to my will."

"Ye will never get him. Not whilst I draw breath."

MacGillonay's predatory grin drew his lips past ruined teeth. "A choice I can live with."

He lunged forward, a lightning-fast move unexpected from a man of MacGillonay's years. Caelen twisted, sending a shaft of torchlight off the flat of his blade into MacGillonay's eyes. The attack missed Caelen with a whisper of steel past his ear and Caelen completed his turn, catching the tip of his sword in MacGillonay's billowing cloak.

The auld laird snatched at the cloth, yanking it from Caelen's blade and wrapping it about his arm for protection. Caelen wound a section of his own plaide about his forearm as he circled, looking for an unguarded moment. He disregarded the uproar behind him, his sole focus on his bitter enemy.

Caelen feinted, drawing MacGillonay closer. He leapt forward, blade flashing where MacGillonay had been only a moment before. The sting on his belly told Caelen he'd not gotten away unscathed as his adversary swept his sword beneath his guard.

Shite! Who'd have thought the auld man could move so fast? Caelen plowed ahead, forcing MacGillonay back beneath a heavy barrage of attack. Steel clanged on steel, faster as MacGillonay faltered, unable to withstand the abuse. Caelen's sword rose and fell, then slid the length of MacGillonay's blade as the older man's grasp slipped.

Sparks flashed as the tip of Caelen's sword struck the stone floor. He absorbed the shock, sweeping the blade up to counter MacGillonay's thrust. The auld laird pressed forward, seeking a way inside Caelen's reach. The pair broke apart, panting lightly.

"Give me the boy," MacGillonay demanded, switching his sword to his opposite hand. He shook his empty fingers, holding them at a peculiar angle.

The auld wolf may be spry, but his bones willnae take the stress. Caelen grinned and wiped a trail of sweat from his brow.

"Nae."

MacGillonay straightened. "So be it."

Pain exploded through Caelen's skull and his world went black.

* * *

Caelen struggled to awareness. Bone-biting cold. Pain shrieking down every limb, bursting in a flash of white light in his head. A groan bled from his lips and weights pressed against his shoulders.

"Dinnae move," a voice murmured in his ear.

A dim thread of light appeared before one eye, and Caelen realized the other lid would not open. He slowly raised his hand to his face, puzzled by the effort it required.

"Bram is missing, and MacGillonay dinnae take well to the news. When ye scarcely could speak, much less answer his questions, he gave ye over to his men for a bit of fun." Rory sighed. "I am sorry they surprised us. I had no idea Ilene had spiked the postern gate for them."

"Ilene has been too attached to the lad. She came here as Ruthie's maid—had been her nurse since she was a bairn. I'd told Ilene 'twould soon be time for Bram to move beyond the nursery."

"Clearly an unpopular decision," Rory drawled. "I wonder if MacGillonay promised her she could remain with Bram?"

"Whatever he promised her, 'twas enough for her to commit treason," Caelen growled. "Her life is forfeit once we escape."

Rory nodded. "MacGillonay's men apparently slipped inside whilst he hurled insults at yer bride and held our attention."

"He certainly had mine," Caelen muttered. His fingers slid gingerly over lumps and crusts—the swollen areas of bruised and split flesh, and old blood. Every inch of his head pained him, and he placed a palm on the floor, levering himself to a seated position.

His stomach instantly rebelled, and he fell to the side, retching. Other hands caught his shoulders, low voices murmured in the dark. When the sensation of being on a pitching horse subsided, Caelen straightened as much as he could and surveyed his surroundings.

Dark forms, rounded on top, appeared as shadows in the nearly lightless room, indicating he and Rory were not alone. Old straw released foul odors as he shifted his position on the cold floor.

"Should've had someone attend to the pit," he said. "'Tis rarely used, and I cannae say I am pleased to be the first down here in a while."

189

"Aye. And the *amadans* dinnae use the ladder when the MacGillonays dumped us here. Most of the lads they simply pushed in. Young Alan broke his leg when he fell, and I dinnae doubt Wee Erik would have as well, had he not landed on Fergus."

"How many . . .?" Caelen couldn't bring himself to finish the question.

"From what I gather, six died either in the yard or in the hall. There are ten of us in here, including the MacLean's knights, and all sport a bash or two."

"Do ye believe anyone escaped?" Caelen asked.

"I cannae say, though 'tis doubtful. The attack was too unexpected. I cannae account for everyone from down here, and have only told ye what I've pieced together from what others have said."

"MacGillonay doesnae have Bram?" It seemed important to ask, though Rory'd already said so and Caelen doubted he would still be alive if Bram had been captured and returned to his grandfather.

"Och, it seems yer wife has disappeared as well." A smile softened Rory's voice. "And MacGillonay is quite beside himself. Yester eve's insults were mild compared to what he has called her of late."

"How long before he realized they arenae simply hiding and look outside the castle?"

"I dinnae know for certain—as I was out of my head for a bit—but when he came for ye, demanding to know where ye'd hidden the lad, 'twas still dark. When they returned ye to the pit, a bit of light was peeking over the wall. They've had a bit of time to get away, Caelen."

A shout from above jerked Caelen's attention.

"Dinnae fash," Rory advised. "They do that every little bit. I believe 'tis more to agitate us than from any real happening. If they capture the lad, we'll know it."

* * *

Arbela roused Agnes from a light doze. "Gather your things and hide in the brush. Something has alerted Garen and Toros."

Bleary-eyed, Agnes rolled to her feet and Arbela woke Bram and the pair disappeared deeper into the underbrush. Arbela unsnapped the dogs' leashes and waved her arm in Bram's direction. "Toros, guard," she said, sending him after the boy. Garen stood firm at her side, the rumble in her chest vibrating against Arbela's leg. Arbela slung her bag over her back and vanished into the shadows.

Woodland noises faded, the beat of her heart the loudest thing in her ears. A flock of birds burst from the trees to her right, arcing overhead to land a good distance to her left, cawing their displeasure. Within moments, the clop of hooves thudded nearby, shuffling atop the wet leaves.

Arbela breathed deep against the thud of her heart, straining her ears to sift through the sounds. She could not detect the distinctive four-beat pattern of a single horse's hooves, the heavy shuffle indicating several mounted men. There was no relaxed bantering among them, which meant they had grown weary of each other's company—or they hunted something, or someone, to whom they did not wish to announce their presence.

Sinking on level with Garen, Arbela watched the trail. She withdrew a length of twine from her belt and attached it between two saplings a few inches off the ground. Taking the small jar from her bag, she carefully swiped two daggers in the poisonous mixture. She replaced the lid and eased the jar back into her pack, stowing the blades in a sheath on her belt, away from an accidental touch.

Time stretched as she waited. At last the brush of leaves caught her attention as a slender shrub swayed. The hoofbeats ceased. A light *thump* drifted through the trees and Arbela imagined a rider dismounted. She knew they'd left signs, though she'd backtracked as far as she dared earlier as the others rested, gently brushing the trail. But the ends of the sled Toros pulled had dug into the debris of the path under Bram's weight, and her efforts had done little to confuse their followers.

Garen's growl increased, then softened beneath Arbela's restraining hand. The dog crouched, her legs poised for a leap. Arbela eased the pair of throwing blades from her belt and moved some of her weight onto her right leg. She snapper her head around at the crack of a twig to her left. Garen lunged forward, barking furiously. A shadowed figure burst through the trees to her right, swooping down on her.

Arbela dodged between her two attackers, sending one blade into the shoulder of the noisy one to her left. Landing in the open area of the trail, she rolled once and came up on one knee, primed to throw the second blade. The shadowed man's cape billowed about him, suggesting no good target. She slid the dagger into its sheath and drew her sword, swinging it in a low arc, catching the back of the man's knee. He fell with a cry, leg twisted beneath him.

Blood poured from the wound in the other man's shoulder, but he advanced on her, a snarl on his face. "I willnae put up with insolence from the likes of ye," he spat. "Save yerself and give up the lad. 'Tis the lad he wants."

Arbela didn't bother to ask who *he* was. No one but MacGillonay sought Bram. The man crept toward her, one wary eye on her sword. Garen rushed him, slashing his legs with her fangs, only to retreat as quickly as she'd attacked. His attention now divided between the two, the wounded man backed against a tree and cupped a hand to his mouth.

"Over here!" he shouted as three other men burst into view. Garen danced back and forth, barking, nipping, trying to drive them away from Arbela. One man chased the dog away, sword swinging as they wove through the trees.

"Give us the lad," the largest of the rogues demanded. "We can make this go hard or easy." His grin betrayed the lie of his words.

Arbela shifted her weight, unlocking her muscles, but did not give up her defensive position. Eyeing the three men remaining, Arbela kept them in sight.

"Och, I'm hard already!" one boasted. "She looks sturdy enough for all of us. Catch her and let's have a bit of fun!"

"Son of . . .." Arbela whispered low, not moving her gaze from the men who shuffled their feet as though waiting for the others to instigate their plan. A cry of pain blurred with Garen's savaging growl. *One more down*. She spared a quick look at the man who dragged himself away from the fight, one leg half-severed. *Two gone*. The man she'd pinned with her dagger scratched himself. Then again. He swatted the back of his neck and rubbed his eyes. Arbela allowed herself a small smile as she watched the poison take effect. *Three*.

Two remained. For a moment they seemed undecided, apparently not anticipating the resistance she'd offered. A silent word seemed to pass between them and they both darted forward, their war cries rising in the air, the shorter of the pair closing the distance to Arbela first. The one to her right struck her trip line, sending him crashing facedown into the wet, leaf-strewn ground.

In a graceful swirl, Arbela brought her sword and dagger to play, stepping directly into the taller man's path, nicking the downed man on the arm as she whirled past him. She dropped to one knee, head down, inviting the taller man to vault over her. Completely taken aback by her tactics, he tried to stop, tumbling into Arbela rather than over her. She clenched her jaw against the impact and drove her sword into his side as he fell, flesh giving way to the scrape of steel on bone.

Arbela leapt to her feet, instantly catching sight of the shorter man. He'd gained his feet and stumbled to the side, one hand clenched on his arm. He pulled his hand away, a puzzled look on his face as he realized there was very little blood on the long, shallow gash. He gripped the wound again, blinking his eyes furiously as he staggered against a tree trunk.

"No tolerance for belladonna? A shame." Arbela centered her attention on the other man.

"Ye bitch!" the taller man spat, hand clenched to his side where a stream of blood and other liquids told their deadly tale. "There will be others after ye. Ye cannae hide much longer. 'Tis too far to MacLean Castle. Ye'll never make it."

"We already stand on MacLean land."

"I am MacGillonay's younger son. Ye cannae hope to escape my father's wrath."

Her heart double-tripped as she absorbed this information. Killing the laird's son—even a younger son—was certain to incite a clan war. Not that MacGillonay hadn't already crossed that line, but this was simply fuel for the fire.

Hooves pounded up the trail. Arbela leapt to her feet and vanished into the trees.

Chapter Twenty Two

Horses came to a halt with shuffling hooves and the undisguised creak of leather. Shouts filled the small glen and the distinctive scrape of steel slipping from scabbards reached Arbela's ears. Torn between the expectation of more pursuers and the desire to discover a MacLean patrol, she slipped closer. Men—she counted eight—perused the MacGillonays, prodding those who could walk into a group, leaving the one with the slashed tendon and MacGillonay's son where they lay.

One knelt beside the lad with the gash in his side, peering at his wound.

"Ye have acquired lions in Scotland?" he asked. Arbela knew him instantly.

"Kade!" she cried as she leapt from the brush.

He spun about, sword ready. A look of puzzlement crossed his face. "What are ye about, Arbela? Should ye not be at Dunfaileas?" His brow furrowed deeper as he took in her disheveled clothing. "I will personally hang the man responsible for this."

Arbela drew a hand through the air. "These are MacGillonay's men." She indicated the lad on the ground. "That is his younger son. MacGillonay invaded the castle last night. I escaped with Bram and my maid, and these men have been on our trail."

"Ye have done well to have made it this far," Kade noted. "And they were unwise to try to take ye." His voice held a mix of pride and amusement. "MacGillonay willnae be pleased to lose his son, though I've heard naught good of him. We must get ye to yer da. Where are the lad and Agnes?"

Garen shoved her nose into Arbela's hand. With a cry of relief, Arbela stooped and hugged the dog to her, noting the fur along one shoulder matted with blood and bits of leaves and dirt. "Garen will find them."

Arbela stood and cupped the dog's chin. "Find Toros." Garen hesitated only a moment, then was off, tail high, only a slight limp betraying her wound. Arbela dashed after her, sword drawn. She cut the tripline before any could see her handiwork. Though she knew her da made allowances because of their history, she thought it best not to leave snares lying about for all to see.

They burst through the trees several lengths from the road. Toros bristled, head lowered, hackles up, a snarl on his lips. A single bark sounded as Garen bounded toward him and Toros dropped his guard, tail swinging madly. Agnes and Bram crept from behind a fallen tree.

Arbela grabbed Bram's shoulders and pulled him tight as relief flooded her. Bram burrowed close, then shoved away, a scowl on his face.

"Agnes wouldnae let me help ye," Bram complained. "She made me hide in the bushes—like a lass."

"Careful, my boy," Arbela cautioned. "Girls are neither weak nor cowardly."

"I heard fighting," Bram persisted, ignoring her correction. "I had my sword. And I can use it."

Arbela squatted on her heels. "Bram, ye will one day be a fine warrior. Ye will have the sword to match your skills, and your bravery will be well known. Until then, ye are bound to others who will do their best to keep ye safe. No one doubts your heart, merely the years of training all warriors need."

"Did ye kill the bad men?" Bram asked, his voice small.

"Aye, Bram, I did. Death is often the fate of those who do evil in this world. Ye and Agnes were at great risk, and I had no other choice."

Bram was silent for a moment. "Can we go home, now?"

"We will continue to my father for help. Then we will go home." Arbela glanced at Agnes' wan face and grinned. "The MacLeans are here.

196

We will ride the rest of the way."

"Saints be praised," Agnes replied, a wealth of weariness flooding her voice. "If ye can manage a warm bath and a few hours' sleep, I'd kiss yer feet." She peered around Arbela as men appeared through the trees. "Definitely *his* feet," she murmured as Dubh stepped forward.

"*Leannan*—are ye well?" he asked, hurrying to her side.

Delight lit her face, erasing the tiredness. "I am blessed ye found me," she replied. "Though I will require a new pair of slippers," she added, wincing as she shifted her weight on her battered feet. Dubh instantly swept her into his arms, halting abruptly at the sight of the other MacLean soldiers.

Silence reigned for two beats, then laughter erupted. "I suppose Agnes rides with ye?" Kade queried, his voice balanced between humor and mild reproach.

Dubh's face reddened. "Aye. If ye will allow it."

"Mount up!" Kade ordered. "Arbela, choose a horse."

"Bram is with me," she said. Kade gave a brisk nod of agreement.

They hurried along the trail to where the rest of the MacLean patrol had made short work of securing the MacGillonays. Arbela noted the laird's son was missing from the group of prisoners. She spied a wool-wrapped bundle draped across the back of one of the MacGillonay ponies. It hadn't taken long for his wound to prove fatal. She bowed her head and murmured a prayer for the dead man's soul, stooping to Bram's level so he could hear her words.

"Even though he died conducting evil against innocents, he was a child of God," she told him.

"He tried to kill ye?" Bram's voice trembled.

"And I stopped him," Arbela replied. "Though he showed no mercy in this life, it is right to pray for your enemies." Taking Bram's hand in hers, she led him to the tethered ponies.

She inspected the MacGillonay horses, surprised to find them sturdy and in good condition. Choosing a leggy bay, she swung aboard. "Split our group," she advised. "Captives will slow us down, and we must make haste."

Kade tasked four of his men with conveying the prisoners to Morven. The rest formed around Arbela and Bram, their horses dancing nervously as they scented excitement—and blood. With a silent signal, the small group sprang down the trail, riders crouched low over their horses' necks. Dubh and Agnes brought up the rear, but would not be left behind. The horses toiled beneath the heels of their riders as their great speed ate the remaining miles.

They thundered down the approach to Morven, the towers of MacLean Castle bold against the gray sky. Sunlight glinted off Loch Aline in the distance. Arbela's heart stuttered.

Home!

"We're here, Bram-jan," she said, jostling the boy gently to wake him. "I will make certain ye are fed, and after, ye may have my old room for the night."

"Can Toros sleep with me?" he asked. "I feel safer when he's with me."

Arbela glanced at the boy's upturned face, worry lining his brow, the sheen of tears bright in his eyes. He had seen too much evil in the past hours, and the small concession would help keep the night's insecurities at bay.

"Aye. Toros would like nothing more than to guard ye after ye both have eaten a hearty meal. He may stay with ye."

"A MacLean!" Kade shouted as they urged their flagging horses down the last stretch to the castle. Gates that had begun to close swung open again, activity boiled on the parapet, and cries echoed in the bailey. People halted on the side of the road, staring at the riders as they swept past.

They dragged their horses to a halt amid a cloud of dust, eager hands reaching for the reins. Toros and Garen headed for the low trough beside the stable several lengths away. Toros climbed in and lapped the water as he wallowed to cool himself. Garen drank sparingly then hobbled to the shade of the wall and plopped down, tongue lolling. Arbela sprang from her mount as Alex raced across the open yard. He sent her horse a bewildered look.

"Where is Voski? And what are ye doing here? Are ye hurt?" He accepted Bram from Arbela's arms and set him on the ground. "What has happened?"

"One question at a time, brother," Arbela said, bracing a hand against her mount's shoulder, her legs unsteady after the long trek and ride. She approached exhaustion, but could not spare the time to rest. "I must speak to ye and father together. Do ye know where he is?"

Alex wasted no further words. "This way." He pivoted on his heel and led her to the hall. Arbela sent Bram inside in Agnes' care with strict instructions to feed him and allow Toros to remain with him. Dubh and another soldier flanked Agnes and Bram, protecting them, allowing Arbela to follow her brother.

Donal glanced up as Alex and Arbela burst into his solar. Slapping his quill to the desktop, he shoved his chair back and rose, meeting them before they were halfway across the room. He grasped Arbela's forearms, halting her, holding her steady for his gaze. He looked her up and down, then sent Alex a stern look.

"What has happened?" he growled.

Arbela took a breath. "We have been betrayed. MacGillonay appeared at Dunfaileas yester eve, but instead of the peace he promised, he insulted me, and Bram's nurse somehow assisted him in smuggling weapons and men inside our walls."

"How did ye escape? Was there fighting?" Donal asked, looking her over once again.

Arbela shrugged his hands away and paced the floor, caught between renewed memories and physical fatigue. "We escaped through a hidden passage before fighting ensued. Caelen and I had a prearranged signal, and when MacGillonay became belligerent, Caelen gave the word for us to flee. He would not send us away into the woods at night alone without a serious threat. Agnes could not keep Bram safe along the way, so I came with them." She ground her teeth at the frustration of leaving Caelen and a potential fight behind. After a deep breath, she continued.

"A couple of hours ago, MacGillonay's men caught up with us. I managed to fight them off, just as Kade and his patrol arrived."

"How many men?" Alex asked. "How did ye manage it?"

"Five," she replied. "Garen took down one—she has an injured shoulder that must be tended—a snare I set slowed another, and one has a severed leg tendon and likely will need a cane if he recovers. Two others received small wounds—but the blades were poisoned," she admitted quietly, aware her father opposed the dark arts. "MacGillonay's younger son lies dead, my sword in his side."

Alex beamed. "Good lass!"

Donal quelled him with a sharp look. "Did MacGillonay attack?"

"Attack the castle? I do not know," she replied. "When I retrieved Bram from his chamber, his nurse accused me of taking the boy from her—among other things—and indicated she had offered help to MacGillonay. She knew him, as she had come to Dunfaileas as Ruthie's maid from Langa Castle, MacGillonay's stronghold.

"MacGillonay purposely taunted and insulted me," she said, words calm though the anger roiled anew. "I believe he was trying to provoke Caelen to a fight, so he could say he'd broken the bonds of hospitality."

"MacKern dinnae defend yer honor?" Donal thundered.

Arbela offered a wry smile. "I believe he was more concerned with keeping me from slitting our guest's throat. MacGillonay offered to beat me—something I said annoyed him, though I did not like what he called me—and *I* offered—politely—to let him try. I settled for reminding him I would mention the manner of snakes bordering your land the next time ye and I spoke."

Donal's brow darkened. "What did he call ye?"

Arbela tilted her head and tapped a finger. "Disrespectful." She tapped another finger. "Barbed-tongued." She slid the count to a third finger. "And a Saracen. Thrice."

She turned serious. "Father, I do not know what happened after I left the hall. With MacGillonay's men on our trail and none from Dunfaileas, I fear the worst. Ye must ride with me and set this to rights."

Donal nodded. "I will rally my men, and send a party tonight to assess the situation."

"Assess . . .? Father, I have told ye what happened."

"No, ye have spoken only of what ye know. What ye suspect is another thing altogether."

"We cannot leave them to MacGillonay's mercy overnight!"

"And I will not risk my men in the dark when we know not what we are getting into." Donal nodded to Alex. "Send Farlan to me. Tell Kade to order a scouting party."

Arbela fumed as her father's gaze swung back to her. "If MacGillonay discovers we have reached Morvern, Caelen's life will not be worth a piastre."

"What is the first rule of offensive warfare, daughter?"

"To know your enemy, Father," she replied, unable to keep the frustration from her voice.

"I do not know if MacGillonay even holds Dunfaileas, though, arguably, if he does not, it will cost little more than the trek north. However, I will know how many men to take and the weapons needed once I understand the situation. Does he have captives he will use as hostages? If he has already burned the castle and turned for home, I will take a shorter route, arrive on his beach, and destroy him there."

Donal paused. "I understand yer care for yer new husband and clan. I will go as fast as is wise." He laid a hand on her shoulder. "Dinnae fash. I willnae let this go unpunished."

Arbela bristled. "And if it was mother? Would ye wait until morn?"

* * *

Arbela lurked in the passageway, waiting for Alex to exit their father's solar. He had returned with Farlan while she checked on Agnes and Bram and changed her clothing. Her loose trousers and cropped tunic were mixed shades of deepest gray and black, as if the person handling the dye had been a mere novice, blurring the various shadings. But the fabric had been specially ordered by Arbela's uncle and given to her as a reward for skills well learned. Tonight it would suit her purposes.

She had spent a short time with her injured dog, inspecting Garen's wound and instructing the kennel master on her care. Certain she had food, water, and clean, dry bedding, Arbela moved to the stable where she requested a fresh horse saddled. Returning to the hall, she paced the floor outside the chamber where her father, Alex, and Farlan pieced together strategy for the upcoming battle against MacGillonay.

Alex rushed from the room, swiveling about in mid-stride as Arbela caught his arm. With a wave of her hand, she bid him follow, and she pulled him into an alcove, out of sight and hearing.

"I will not wait," she said urgently. "Caelen will be dead by morning."

"If he isn't already," Alex pointed out, not unkindly.

"I will not sit here, brother. I am going back to Dunfaileas tonight."

Alex perused her clothing. "There is naught I can say to change your mind? Bid ye caution?"

Arbela shook her head. "Nae. I only ask ye not speak to father of this." She stared at the wall behind his shoulder, tears stinging the back of her eyes. "Take care of Bram. He is a good lad, and I know he looks up to ye."

"Now ye are talking nonsense," Alex scoffed.

"There is little chance this will end well," Arbela warned.

"Och, that I know well. Especially if ye go alone." His teeth flashed in the darkness. "That is why I am going with ye."

Arbela nodded once, immensely relieved to have his company—and support. "I will fetch provisions and have a horse saddled for ye and await ye in the stables. Fetch yer weapons and dress for speed."

"Tell me something I don't know," he drawled, sending her a condescending look over his shoulder, already on his way to prepare.

Arbela spun on her heel and strode to the kitchen. Cook showed surprise at her arrival but didn't question her when she asked for bannocks and dried meat. Arbela collected the bag she'd brought from Dunfaileas and sped to the stable, where she set a stable lad to saddling a horse for Alex. Gnawing on a piece of hard, dry oat bread to restore her strength, she washed it down with watered ale as she hung filled waterskins on each saddle and checked the girths.

Alex entered the stable as she finished, dressed in leather armor and a black, weathered cloak. No chain mail to weigh him down. "Are ye certain about this, Bella?"

She nodded and mounted her horse. "I'll not leave that vile man in charge one minute longer than I have to. I spoke vows to my husband and intend to keep them."

With a light thump of her heels against her horse's sides, she rode away, slipping her hood over her head to escape recognition by the guards at the gate. Alex trotted to catch up with her.

They rode through the village at a brisk walk, careful to draw little notice.

"What vow did ye make, sister mine? Gutting the man's former father by marriage?"

Arbela shot Alex an impish grin that quickly disappeared. "The man threatened to take Bram and begged for a fight. I'll not disappoint him, nor be surprised if he loses his life this eve."

Alex regarded her thoughtfully. "MacGillonay does not know the fate he has unleashed upon himself."

Arbela's face turned grim. "MacGillonay should set a guard on his western wall."

Chapter Twenty Three

The near-moonless night slowed their progress. Neither Alex nor Arbela wished to risk their or their horses' necks on a tumble at great speed, and alternated between a canter and a trot, carefully weighing the benefits of allowing the horses to rest against the need to reach Dunfaileas as quickly as possible.

Weak moonlight glistened on the loch, alerting them to the end of their journey. Arbela reined her tired horse to a stop and dismounted. She and Alex tied their mounts to low limbs, giving the horses enough freedom to graze and offered them water. Grabbing her bag from the saddle, Arbela joined Alex as he crept over the crest of the hill.

"Kade and his patrol should be close," Alex murmured.

Arbela nodded, alert for any sign of the eight men her father had sent to gather information on MacGillonay and the fate of Dunfaileas. Clouds raced across the sky, counterpoint to the heavy fog gathering on the surface of the loch. The night grew silent, muffled in its misty shroud.

A faint jingle of metal resounded like an ill-formed chime. Arbela glanced at her brother.

Horse? MacGillonay or MacLean? Spoken words unnecessary between them.

Alex shrugged and crept toward the sound, his passage a mere sigh through the grass. Giving him room to maneuver, Arbela waited a few moments, then followed. They crested a low ridge as the moon's rays broke through the clouds, sending a cluster of saddled ponies into sharp detail against the pale rocks a few lengths away. Steel clanged faintly as a horse stamped a foot on the ground, striking a small rock.

MacLean. Alex nodded to the shadowed form of three men, cloaked, facing the castle. Arbela understood. MacGillonay patrols would face away, guarding the approaches.

They slipped past the horses, reassuring them with a light touch. One beast tossed his head, a light snort peppering Arbela with moisture. She and Alex froze. They waited, ears straining for some indication they'd been discovered.

"I know yer tricks, Alexander MacLean."

Alex and Arbela dropped into a crouch as they spun about, hands hovering above their sword hilts. Kade's eyes flashed beneath his cowl. "Why are ye here? Has something happened at Morven?" he asked.

"Father gathers his troops," Arbela replied as she straightened. "What have ye learned?"

Kade drew them deeper into the copse of trees, to a small overlook clustered with bushes clinging to the edge with deep roots and sheer tenacity. The parapet of Dunfaileas could be easily seen, though it would take a superior archer to pick off a guard at this distance. Arbela tested the wind. It could be done.

"There are now two ships in the harbor." Kade pointed to the loch. Arbela thought back to the single ship she'd seen the previous night. Recounting the number of oars, it had been the smaller of the two.

"I counted a dozen men with MacGillonay when he demanded hospitality," she said. "If he left a guard—perhaps two or three men—on the beach, they may have numbered a least fifteen or sixteen all told." She inclined her head to the larger vessel. "That ship carries double that number easily."

Kade nodded. "There is a small fire on the beach, though it has burned down now. Earlier we counted six men. Enough to mount a defense if attacked. That means MacGillonay has mayhap fifty men within the castle." He frowned. "I was about to send Dubh and another to yer father with the news. Will ye take the report to him?"

Alex shook his head. "Nae. We are not here to carry messages."

Arbela shook her head, determination on her face. "We are here to liberate the MacKerns."

* * *

There was a fine line between admitting he did not know where Bram and Arbela were—and making MacGillonay believe it—and keeping him on a lure just enough to avoid execution. Once MacGillonay decided Caelen was not going to confess where his wife and son hid—or how they escaped—Caelen knew his life wouldn't be worth a silver penny.

Nor would the lives of his men.

The MacKern soldiers had given a good accounting of themselves against surprise and superior numbers, nearly beating back MacGillonay's bold attack. But Caelen would not ask them to pay further when the end was plain. It was only a matter of time before MacGillonay's patrol returned with Arbela and Bram. MacGillonay would keep Caelen alive only long enough to force him to watch whatever he planned for Arbela— fire blazed in Caelen's veins at the thought—and to make certain Caelen knew Bram was forevermore in the clutches of his depraved, malevolent grandsire. A spot in hell would seem a mere nuisance after such torment.

"Do ye recollect any hidden passages from this pit?" Rory asked.

Caelen shook his head, wincing anew at the dull pain the movement cost him. "Once da tanned my hide for what he termed *betraying the clan* after he caught me playing in the one in the laird's room, I lost all interest in seeking out such passageways. I am surprised MacGillonay hasnae discovered the way out."

Rory shrugged, a black form against deeper darkness. "Is there any possible way Arbela and Bram have made it to MacLean Castle? Can we expect help from that quarter?"

"Ye know as well as I 'tis twenty miles distant. Some of that will be traveled in the dark, and all of it on foot. Alone, Arbela could mayhap elude capture and with luck come across a MacLean patrol before

MacGillonay's men caught up to her." His jaw locked and he was unable to voice the rest of his thoughts. That Bram was only five. That he could not make the journey without frequent rests, or with any speed. That MacGillonay's men would be relentless in their pursuit.

That he would kill the next MacGillonay he got his hands on.

Voices rang out above, growing closer. "I dinnae know where yer son is, Laird," one voice claimed, his tone placating. "He willnae return until he has scoured the routes between here and Morven and captures the Saracen bitch and yer grandson."

"Ye fool!" MacGillonay's voice rose. "There is but one road from here to Morven, and we are talking about a wee lad against mounted men. How long should it take to chase them down? *Shite*! I shouldnae have entrusted the mission to Maon. He is likely to botch the task."

"He named his son Maon? *Hero*?" Rory asked softly, not bothering to hide his mirth. "I needed something to laugh about. I confess I've never seen a more cowardly *hero*. Though I only met him on the butt of his sword. 'Twas a cowardly gesture to hit me from behind."

"Ye saw him?" Caelen asked, flexing his fingers as though on his sword's hilt at the sound of MacGillonay's voice.

Rory rubbed the back of his head. "Aye. Though a bit too late to do anything about it. I'd noticed him once or twice tagging at Ruthie's heels years ago, though I dinnae know his name, and I learned early to keep my questions to myself with that lass—begging yer pardon. I also remember he'd walked into Dunfaileas yester eve next to MacGillonay as if he owned the place, and was puzzled to turn about and see him prepared to strike me. Undoubtedly, his da instructed him to take me down with as little trouble as possible."

"Ye must admit he did an adequate job."

"Aye. Though 'twas still a cowardly act."

"I agree. But it scarcely surprises me."

The grate overhead clanged and scraped across the stone above.

"*Shite*," Rory commented, ducking his head against the nerve-shredding sound. "He's making enough racket to wake the dead."

A flickering torch lit MacGillonay's face as he peered into the pit. "Drag yerself up, MacKern," he called, malice lacing his voice. "'Tis time we spoke further."

* * *

Kade halted in a shadowy nook at the base of the castle wall. "How likely is it MacGillonay has discovered the hidden passage?"

"If there is no guard at this end, could he have set a trap at the other?" Arbela countered.

Kade and Alex exchanged looks. "'Tis possible," Alex said.

She cast a look to the faint glow of coals on the beach. There was no sound of feet treading the parapet above. Either the guards did not consider an approach from the loch to be a threat—a somewhat sound idea with guards already nearby—or MacGillonay deliberately kept the guards away, hoping to lure an unwary foe inside.

Skirting the heavy brush growing along the foundation of the castle, Arbela led Kade and Alex to the hidden door. She glanced at the slender limb she had lain against the panel when she had exited previously. It remained at its peculiar angle, indicating no one had opened the door from within since she placed it there. She caught Alex's speculative gaze. Grasping the limb, she tossed it to him.

"No one has disturbed this. I believe MacGillonay has not discovered the passage."

"After ye, sister," Alex bade, pointing to the opening. Her bag secured over her shoulder, Arbela stepped inside.

Instantly, the pall of dust and decaying rodent droppings struck, and Arbela wrinkled her nose. She hesitated, allowing her eyes to adjust to the near-total darkness, and to get her bearings.

Alex and Kade followed her inside. Striking her flint on a bit of tinder from her bag, Arbela lit the candle she'd left behind. Alex closed the door. She held the flame aloft as they followed the tunnel beneath the curtain wall to the level of the castle. A small landing marked the beginning of the long climb to the laird's chamber.

The upper corner of a dark rectangle caught her eye and Arbela stepped to one side.

"Another door," she whispered. "I had not remarked this before. If my calculations are correct, however, this may lead to a storeroom beyond the kitchen."

"Do we take it and risk discovery here? Or climb to the entrance ye know?" Alex asked.

"And risk guards in the laird's chamber?" Arbela tossed back at him.

"I doubt he has guards there. Ye do not believe they allow Caelen to recline in his chamber whilst they search for ye and Bram?"

A cloud swept over Arbela as she considered Caelen's likely fate. "We are less likely to meet MacGillonays in a storeroom than on the stairs," she stated. "Let us give this door a try."

The ancient leather hinges creaked softly as Alex and Kade tugged at the door. The room beyond was a slightly paler shade of dark, another door on the far side of the room outlined by a light source beyond.

They moved to the far door, and, to their surprise, it opened, revealing a mass of barrels stacked three and four high. Light trickled in from a torch burning in a sconce further along the passageway, outlining the rotund obstacles.

"Without a lot of effort—and making a great deal of noise—we will not be able to clear the passage," Kade noted. "We must find another way to let the MacLean's soldiers into the castle."

Arbela strode past him, slipping through a narrow space between two barrels. "Once I'm finished, ye can let them in the front gate."

Slurred cries of drunken revelry punctuated the air. Arbela's hand went to the hilt of her sword, furious at the liberties being taken in her home. Alex rested a heavy palm on her shoulder.

"They will not forget this night, sister," he assured her. "We will right this wrong."

She swallowed, drawing a settling breath, relaxing to center on the job ahead.

A low screech of indignation caught her ear. The darkened form of a woman, platter in her hands, assisted across the passage by a swat to her bottom, followed the sound. A man loped behind her, mouth to her ear, promising things Arbela did not want to consider. The pair disappeared into the hall.

"Follow me," she whispered. Snaking around the stacked barrels, she wound her way down the darkened passage, pausing at the entrance to the kitchen. One breath in through her nose, out through her mouth, she then slid silently around the framework. Her gaze took in those in the kitchen, both women she recognized—Cook and her assistant, Dona. The caps on their heads sat askew, their aprons smeared with grease from more than a casual wipe of messy fingers.

Dona glanced up, her face pale. Eyes widening, she opened her mouth, but Arbela silenced her with a shake of her head. The woman reached to Cook beside her, tightening her fingers over the other woman's hand. She glanced up sharply, a frown on her face. Following her friend's gaze, her eyes lit on Arbela.

Arbela offered a reassuring smile, gliding soundlessly to the women's side as Alex and Kade joined her in the kitchen. "We have returned to retake the castle," she murmured. "Will ye help?"

The two women nodded, and in short course, Arbela emptied half the contents of a container of wolfsbane into a vat of whisky.

"The oafs discovered the laird's supply, and have been quaffing it in staggering amounts," Cook reported, disgust plain for the swilling of good whisky. "They willnae notice the bitter flavor." She filled two pitchers with the tainted liquid. "This should settle the louts in the hall—those still able to drink," she amended.

Dona took the pitchers and set them on the long table, then paused, sending Arbela a troubled look. "Praise God ye are here, my lady," she said. "I wish ye well."

"MacGillonay took the castle, but our men put up a tremendous fight," Cook said, an approving expression on her face. "Killed a few of those vermin before they were beaten. Ye'll find the MacKerns who remain in the pit. I dinnae know how ye will release them without a fight from the guards." She placed a hand on Arbela's forearm. "Ye have saved the lad, aye? He is safe?"

"Bram is with my father," Arbela reassured her.

"We thank ye for yer help and for yer information," Alex said. "We will settle our accounts with MacGillonay before the day is out."

"Bless ye, sir," Cook replied. "Ye'll be sending them to their just reward, and that's the truth."

"Finish here, then hide in the storeroom," Arbela told the women. "We will find a way to let ye out of the castle as soon as we assess the number and placement of guards. We mean to empty the castle of all but those who can wield a sword."

The women nodded. Cook waved an iron skillet. "I may not heft a sword, my lady, but there's few can withstand a whack of my skillet!"

With a nod of readiness, Arbela, Kade, and Alex disappeared into the dimly lit hall, their clothing blending into the shadows.

Chapter Twenty Four

The stench of unwashed bodies and spilled whisky, and the roar of men well on their way to knee-walking drunkenness assaulted Arbela's senses as they peered around a pillar at the entrance to the great hall.

"I count nineteen men in this room," Kade murmured.

Arbela squinted against the glare of torchlight. "Seventeen," she countered.

He leaned close. "See four feet sticking from beneath the overturned bench." He grinned. "My guess? Their snoring annoyed someone."

Arbela rolled her eyes. "Assuming near fifty men with a handful killed, that leaves fewer than two dozen unaccounted for. Mayhap a dozen on the walls, half that number guarding the pit."

"So, a few roaming the halls?" Alex looked to the other two for confirmation.

"Aye. They should be easiest to dispose of," Arbela said.

"What do ye propose, sister?" Alex asked.

She arched a brow, fighting the tug at the corners of her lips. "I have a few surprises in my bag," she admitted.

Alex elbowed Kade. "I knew it. Father doesn't like to remember the two summers she spent with our uncle whose castle—unbeknownst to Da—boasted a training camp for the Hashashin order. I wager Arbela has a few unconventional ideas in mind." He jerked his chin at Arbela's bag. "What do ye suggest?"

She motioned them to a small alcove and swung her bag from her shoulder. Opening the drawstring closure, she peered inside. "After we ensure a room is clear, we can leave these just inside the doorway." She hefted a bag that clanked faintly. "I scattered some in the entry to Bram's room, so take care. They will pierce a boot and the barbs make them exceedingly nasty to remove from your foot."

"Caltrops," Alex said, impressed.

"Whilst I am remembering, I also set a splinter on the wooden latch of Bram's door." She shrugged. "And coated it with a poison that will likely give someone hives and a racing heart—'twas a small dose—so take care if ye go to his room."

Kade's eyebrows shot up. "I'd heard rumors of why yer da brought ye home a wee bit early one summer, but he has done well to keep the reason quiet. This is why?"

"Aye," Arbela grinned. "Those of the Hashashin order are hated and feared—and for good reason. But as I am not likely to best a hardened warrior in hand-to-hand combat, I saw no reason not to learn a more subtle approach."

She gave each a handful of items. "Stretch these thin ropes across passageways, slightly above ankle height. And we will grab one of Cook's large pots and set it atop the door to the privies." Briefly, she outlined her plan. With a nod of understanding, the three separated, slipping down the halls of the beleaguered castle with no more noise than the first fall of a summer rain.

* * *

Caelen rolled to his feet, fingering the scabbed line over his stomach where MacGillonay's sword had nicked him during the fight. A slight stickiness told him it still oozed and needed bandaging, but the pain of the wound was overshadowed by the ache in his head. A form blocked the scant light spilling into the noxious pit, and Caelen halted, anticipating the ladder lowered for his use.

He mounted the rungs, mentally urging himself to endure the climb as every muscle screamed from the abuse MacGillonay's men had inflicted on him earlier. But out of the pit was one step closer to freedom. If

214

freedom wasn't an option, he would take as many of the bastards down with him as was humanly possible. And he'd include the MacGillonay himself if he could.

His slow ascent allowed his eyes to adjust to the light as he broke free of the pit. His left eye was still swollen, allowing only a glimmer through the slightly parted lids. The torches affixed to the walls warmed the room, and a few held aloft lit the guards who had little to do other than keep others away from the hole. Once inside the dark confines, there was no way out. A battered table, its surface cluttered with empty dishes, leaned against the wall, out of the way in the small room. The builders of Dunfaileas Castle had wasted little space enclosing the pit. Caelen's ancestors apparently had scant mercy for wrongdoers.

"Hurry," MacGillonay sniped. "I dinnae have time to spend coddling yer injuries. Ye brought them upon yerself, so grit yer teeth like a man and come face me."

Caelen *did* grit his teeth, but in anger, not against the pains of his body. At the moment he was fairly certain he'd sell his soul for a sword and a few moments alone with MacGillonay.

"How may I be of service?" he mocked as he stepped away from the edge of the pit. "Do ye wish to set yer men against me again?" He clucked his tongue. "Och, but I am awake this time and able to defend myself. State yer business, MacGillonay. I have a riveting game of scatter the rats going on below."

And I'd enjoy a similar game here. His frown deepened.

"Ye will tell me how yer brat escaped the castle," MacGillonay demanded. "I have neither time nor patience to send out another search party without better knowledge of where they were headed."

"The wee lass I married slipped past yer soldiers?" Caelen mused, his words laced with mockery. MacGillonay's fist fell before Caelen's partially blinded eye perceived the movement. He staggered beneath the blow, but remained on his feet, peering at the laird in disgust.

"Always taking advantage of others, eh, MacGillonay?" Caelen spat, noting the tang of copper on his tongue as he registered the split on the inside of his mouth where the blow smashed against his teeth.

"Mayhap I should give ye a hearty meal and a bed to rest in before I dispatch ye?" MacGillonay countered.

Caelen shrugged. "Uncertain as I am that I would eat anything served by yer command, a bit of food wouldnae go amiss. Though I find the company below far better than among the vermin scurrying about up here."

"Tell me what I want to know!" MacGillonay shouted.

Caelen sent him a look of disgust. "I wouldnae tell ye even if I did know," he growled. "What benefit is it to attempt to protect what is mine if I tell ye the how of it the first time ye ask?"

"It is not—!" MacGillonay spun about, waving his arms at the soldiers gathered about. "Bring me the wench!"

Caelen stiffened as two guards rushed from the room. Several moments passed before one returned, skulking in the shadows.

"Well?" MacGillonay demanded. "Where is she?"

"We dinnae know, Laird," the man replied. "She wasnae in the room."

"This is how ye coax a bit of cooperation between men, MacGillonay?" Caelen taunted. "Frightening women to force the issue? I'd say that pulls ye right out of the category of worthy opponent—and directly into that of coward."

"Shut up!" MacGillonay roared. He advanced on the hapless soldier. "Ye mean to tell me she has escaped? Was there no guard on her door? Or could at least one of ye not keep yer trousers on long enough to keep watch?"

"There is no guard," the man answered, drawing deeper into the shadows. "Neither in the room nor out."

MacGillonay pointed a trembling finger at Caelen. "Chain him! I will deal with him in a moment."

An uproar surged through the narrow passage into the small room as three soldiers rushed inside. One scratched himself fervently, reddened areas clearly evident on his skin. Another limped haltingly, scarcely placing one foot on the ground. The last dripped a liquid from his plaide onto the floor the others were careful to avoid.

"What is the meaning of this?" MacGillonay snapped, eyeing his soldiers.

"There is a dark spirit at work, Laird," one gasped. "I searched the lad's room as ye instructed, and have incurred the wrath of a Saracen spirit now eating at my flesh!" He dug his fingernails into his skin.

"I did as ye ordered," the second avowed. "But as soon as we entered the room, I stepped on some trick the woman left behind. It pierced my boot and even now digs into my foot. I cannae remove the boot without great pain, for the barbs have dug deep."

"And what of ye?" MacGillonay asked, waving fingers at the third soldier.

He stepped warily across the floor. His plaide glistened. "I ran to this one's assistance," he admitted. "I stepped into oil spilled across the doorway and skidded several feet before I lost my balance." His eyes flashed angrily. "I lay stunned for a time before I rose." He gestured to his clothing. "The wool soaked up the oil quickly."

"Bring the kitchen staff to me," MacGillonay growled. "Their carelessness will cost them dear."

Carelessness? Caelen considered the plight of the three men. *Would Arbela have thought to set a snare on the floor of Bram's room? And what torments the first soldier? Poison?* He snorted. *I can account for my men who fought and died or are incarcerated with me. I cannae account for the wee lass I married.*

* * *

Drunken revelry exchanged for bleary-eyed soberness left the men in the hall holding aching heads and an assortment of other ailments not necessarily brought on by a simple excess of whisky. Arbela, Kade and Alex paused at the entrance to the hall, carefully avoiding the smear of oil and scatter of small metal beads on the floor.

"I believe we can leave these lads for a few moments," Alex said, noting the state of the men seated at the tables or sprawled on the floor. He nodded to Arbela. "Nice work. Most of them will not be able to lift a sword with any force or accuracy for some time."

"We must take out those who guard the postern gate," Arbela replied. "And any along the parapet who may be close enough to notice their absence." She reached into her bag and withdrew a slender tube and a small sack. "Have ye seen a dart tube in action?"

Kade and Alex shook their heads, clearly astonished. Arbela smiled. "Ye will."

Keeping to the shadows, Arbela led the way up the stairs to one of the openings to the walk along the top of the curtain wall. Three guards stood between them and the narrow gate. She waved Kade and Alex behind her, then slipped silently onto the parapet, crouched low, her stained cloak blending into the pattern of stones.

The first guard faced away, clearly unconcerned with a possible threat from the stair, trusting, perhaps, his fellow soldiers in the hall below.

That was your first mistake. Arbela crept closer. The man kept his eyes trained on the fire on the beach. *And that is your second.*

Knowing he would not be able to see her for several moments while his eyes adjusted to the darkness, Arbela stood and raised the tube. Placing the dart inside, she took a deep breath then placed her lips against the end of the tube. With a quick expulsion of air, she sent the scrap of wire, fletched with a bit of rabbit fur and tipped with poison, winging across the short distance to the guard.

He clasped the side of his neck, turning toward the source of the attack. Arbela stood motionless as the poison quickly did its work and the man slumped to the floor.

Kade and Alex leapt from their hiding places, not bothering to check the downed man as they quickly dispatched the next two guards. They left one propped against the wall, his profile visible to satisfy any glancing check.

Pulling a rope from her bag, Arbela tied it about the dead guard's waist, using his weight to hold the line steady as she slid quickly to the ground below, Kade and Alex following. Quickly slicing the tough leather hinges of the postern gate, she rendered it unable to be secured, then dropped six caltrops to the ground.

"Find all six before ye open the gate," she warned. "They are for any who attempt to repair the gate, not us."

Alex and Kade gave her wry salutes as they turned together and made their way back to the hall where chaos greeted them.

MacGillonay stood, hands fisted at his waist, surveying the scene in the hall. Though Arbela saw him from behind, she would never mistake the stocky figure, bristled beard visible even from this angle. He would not leave Dunfaileas alive, she would see to that. But there were still too many soldiers on their feet to protect him. A dozen or more to three was not her idea of fair odds.

"Follow me. I know a back way to the kitchen," she whispered. Bending low, the three slipped down a walkway leading to the herb garden. She eased open a narrow door and peered inside. Wreckage of the trays laid out by Cook and her assistant littered the prepping table surface and much of the floor. Only a faint flavor of whisky scented the air.

"I imagine they sought Cook after they ran out of whisky," Alex whispered. "I am glad ye thought to send her and Dona away."

Arbela nodded. "Drunken men never have good thoughts on their minds. I am also glad we hid the serving girl away and discovered the one being held in the room beneath the hall." Fire blazed anew in her veins at what hell the MacGillonays had put the poor girl through before they'd rescued her.

Her gaze moved beyond the debris to what she sought. "There. We will smoke the bastards out of the castle."

While Alex and Kade grabbed armloads of dried gorse stacked beside the bread oven and piled the kindling into one of Cook's largest pots, Arbela tapped warily on the door to the storeroom, well hidden behind another row of stacked barrels. Hearing no noise within, she cautiously unlatched the door, nudging it open with the toe of her boot.

"'Tis Arbela!" she hissed loudly. The dark stain hovering overhead descended without damage and Cook stepped to the light, her heavy skillet lowered. Three other women followed timidly behind.

"Glad I am to see ye, my lady," she breathed, her normally rosy cheeks pale with the burden of the past hours. "We've heard naught since ye sent us to hide in here. Have ye run the bastards from the castle?"

"We have hindered them, and opened the postern gate for the MacLean soldiers once they arrive. Alex and Kade are about to create a good amount of smoke and flush some others out of the hall. Come with me. It will be safer sending ye and the others out the side gate than to remain in here where the fire could be a hazard."

She had them linger a moment whilst she dabbed soot on their pale faces and bid them cover well with their dark cloaks. With the four women following her like the drag of a lizard's tail, Arbela led them to the postern gate as soundlessly as if they did not exist.

"Excellent job," she complimented them. "Hasten around the castle to the west. A MacLean patrol awaits on the bluff just beyond. Stick to the shadows until ye find them, and do not scream. By my count, 'tis unlikely any MacGillonays patrol the area beyond the castle. Ye will be safe once ye are in the forest."

"Thanks to God for ye, my lady. Ye are certainly a blessing from above," Cook said as she pulled Arbela into a quick embrace.

The three other women each gave Arbela quick hugs before disappearing into the night. Arbela breathed a quick prayer for their safety and fled back to the kitchen where Alex and Kade awaited.

Dumping several linen squares into the sink, she poured water over them then squeezed out the excess moisture. Alex and Kade dragged the iron pot filled with faggots to the entrance to the hall. Firing a brand from the coals inside the oven, Arbela followed them and plunged the lit end into the pile of gorse which caught instantly.

Laying the damp linen carefully around the burning branches, she anchored them with larger pieces of wood. The damp cloth smoldered, reluctant to burn. Taking a dry cloth from her belt, Arbela waved the smoke away, watching it drift into the hall. It took a few minutes for anyone to notice.

"Fire!" The words rang a mere instant before muffled beneath the scrape of benches across the stone floor as men scrambled, knocking things about in their haste to avoid the newest disaster.

They trampled a man on the floor, though judging from the bandage wrapped about his head, he was likely oblivious to the new injuries. The large rock Alex had set atop one of the privy doors had apparently found a target. Others limped heavily in the wake of the more sure-footed, obvious victims of the snares they'd strung across the passage to the privies. Arbela heaved a breath of satisfaction.

"Wait!" MacGillonay bellowed his anger. "Something is afoot here."

"Aye!" a soldier agreed as he hobbled past. "A Saracen witch has bespelled this castle. Save yer soul and flee!"

"Argh!" MacGillonay shouted, spilling his frustration into rising fury as his men shoved past him and smoke billowed into the room.

"The castle is not bespelled, ye fools!" He cast his angry gaze around the room, palm to the hilt of his sword as he searched for the source of the uproar.

Arbela stepped into the room as the smoke died down. It rolled about her feet, its fingers drifting upward to steal her breath. She draped a thin strip of damp linen over her nose, hiding the lower half of her face. MacGillonay halted, eyes wide with surprise before they narrowed with rage.

"Ye!" He coughed as he advanced. He drew his sword, a mighty breath expanding his chest as he prepared for battle. He coughed again, rattling into his fist as he struggled for air. "I will see ye dead before I allow ye to escape again."

Arbela flexed her hands and balanced forward on the balls of her feet.

"As I invited ye earlier," she said. "Ye may try."

Chapter Twenty Five

Alex and Kade appeared ghostlike on the edge of the room, watching, protecting, keeping the few remaining soldiers from racing to their laird's aid. MacGillonay swung his sword in an arc, flexing his shoulder and wrist muscles.

Arbela studied his movements, her stance loose, her focus now entirely on the laird, trusting her brother and Kade to hold the others at bay. He circled to her right, a slow stalk, pushing, forcing her to move. Arbela accepted the advance, stepping easily to her left to keep him at a distance. With his greater weight and strength, if he managed to close on her, things would end quickly. And very badly.

With a flash of steel, he lunged at her, sword thrust forward in a classic strike. Arbela dodged the blade, taking a step back.

"Where is yer weapon, Saracen?" MacGillonay taunted. "Ye cannae use yer mouth to defend yerself against a blade. Must I teach ye fighting as well as yer manners?"

Arbela judged her target. The way he shifted his weight easily from one foot to the other. The way his body swayed slightly, anticipating an attack. Slipping a throwing blade from her sleeve sheath, she balanced it lightly in her hand. In a flash of movement, it was gone from her fingers, and she whirled out of his following line of attack, coming to rest several feet away.

MacGillonay's face blanched then bloomed blood-red, a snarl on his lips. Her blade missed the juncture of his neck, the handle protruding from the thick muscle above his collarbone. A painful hit, but the blade did not penetrate deep enough to do serious damage.

With a shout of anger, MacGillonay tore the blade away, flinging it aside to clatter across the stone floor. He burst forward in a flurry of attacks, using his greater bulk and strength as a battering ram. Arbela was no longer where he expected her to be, and his charge carried him past her. She countered with another dagger. Targeting his lower back, it struck the upper edge of his wide leather belt, defeating her aim at his kidneys, but the sharp blade slashed deep across his flesh.

"The wee witch has teeth?" He faced her, his grin mocking as he shifted his sword to his left hand and slipped a dagger from the sheath at his boot. "Ye may throw a blade, but ye cannae win a fight against a man."

Arbela drew her sword, the long sigh of its travel from the sheath an echo of her reluctance to engage MacGillonay at close quarters. The smoke worked in her favor, for MacGillonay coughed again, disrupting his focus on her for a brief moment. She had inflicted two wounds, which, while not fatal, caused blood loss, which would soon fatigue her enemy. How long before the cuts made a difference? She had no doubt she could outlast him, but she had to remain out of his reach until the edge of his brute strength faded.

"I do not see a man before me," she replied, circling him, her sword creating slow patterns in the air before her. "Ye are an arrogant son of Satan who thinks nothing of taking what he wants, heedless of others."

"Ye are too soft," MacGillonay replied, countering her moves, twin blades of sword and dagger flashing in the torchlight. "Ye are naught but a woman, and a woman doesnae understand these things."

Arbela tested his defenses with a light attack. His sword clanged on hers as he deflected the blade. Arbela danced lightly away, forcing him in a circle, then pressed forward again. He stepped back, then again, the backs of his knees striking an overturned bench. He staggered. His snarl of rage ripped through the air, all pretense of play gone. He charged her, but again Arbela anticipated his move, and his blades flashed by her, making a crisp whistle in the empty air.

A swell of shouts disrupted her concentration, and she angled a feint to MacGillonay to turn him once again. She risked a fleeting glance past

MacGillonay's shoulder, finding Alex and Kade engaged against several soldiers. More men entered the hall, swelling their ranks. Arbela swore beneath her breath. This was not how their plan should work.

She parried another attack, noting MacGillonay's timing had slowed. Another quick glance at the fight in the hall grabbed her attention fully. She gaped, astonished to see Caelen, swinging his blade like a scythe, scattering the men about him as he entered the room. Other men followed, quickly routing the MacGillonay rabble. It was once again Arbela and the MacGillonay laird as Caelen stood several feet away, weaving on unsteady legs, gaze fixed on Arbela.

"Pay no attention to that lout ye married," MacGillonay coaxed through his sneer. "After I finish with ye, he will hand the castle back over to me."

"Brave talk for a man already condemned," Arbela replied. "I will not best ye with brute force, but that is the only path ye know, whilst I have other options to choose from."

MacGillonay clicked his tongue. "Ye must have had a different tutor than I," he said, sheathing his dagger in a smooth sleight of hand. "In my world, a good fight is a short fight. Brutal and clear who the winner is." He charged Arbela, sword aloft in a high guard. Within the first step, the sword came crashing down, its only goal to cleave Arbela in two. She countered, bringing her shorter, lighter sword up and to the side, channeling the energy of MacGillonay's attack away.

Struggling to recover from the fierce blow, she returned the attack in a series of lightning-fast strikes. Her shorter reach allowed no fatal blows, but she made contact with MacGillonay's bulk each time, parting his flesh in bloody stripes. Panting heavily, MacGillonay came to a halt, his sword now barely held in a low guard. He squinted and blinked his eyes, his face flushed, sweat rolling down both sides of his face.

Arbela, fatigued from parrying the force of his attacks, found her second wind as she noted MacGillonay stagger, blood dripping steadily from his numerous cuts. She pulled the thin piece of damp linen from her face, a surge of triumph in her veins.

MacGillonay lurched to one side but righted himself, planting his feet wide as he adjusted the grip on his sword. Drawing his sword hilt level with his ear, MacGillonay braced, sword tip aimed at Arbela's throat.

She bobbed on the balls of her feet, swaying lightly, ready for his attack. He exploded in a flurry of movement and Arbela arced her sword to the right. Changing his angle of attack, MacGillonay swept beneath her guard, knocking the sword from her hand as the tip of his blade raced along the inside length of her forearm.

Fire burst from the wound in her arm and blood spilled freely from the gash. Lightheaded from the sudden, fierce pain, Arbela slumped, grasping blindly for support. The flat of MacGillonay's sword struck the side of her head, sending her tumbling through the air. Dry reeds drove their broken ends into her cheek as she sprawled across the floor. Instinctively, she rolled to her feet, shaking her head to clear her blurred vision. A dark stain before her grew larger and she snatched a throwing dart from her belt and slung it at the menacing form.

A grunt told her she'd hit her target. Her vision partially cleared and she watched MacGillonay drop to one knee. His glassy-eyed stare bored into hers. His mouth opened and closed, but he did not speak.

Eyes on MacGillonay, Arbela sliced a strip of silk from her tunic and tied a hasty tourniquet about her arm below her elbow, pulling the knot tight with her teeth. Her breath came in short bursts as she swayed drunkenly as blood continued to drip with ominous speed from her fingertips.

A large form loomed behind MacGillonay and wrenched the man's beard upward. Blood splashed onto the floor.

Voices roared indistinctly in Arbela's ears. She tried to fight the hands that grabbed her, but her body would not respond. She felt herself falling, deeper. Darker. Silent.

* * *

The air in the cool room was heavy with moisture from the recent rain, water pooling along the window sill. Caelen rested his palm in the puddle, slick on the stone. Bleary-eyed, he stared at his hand, his mind scarcely registering the sensation.

Slender fingers settled on his arm and he angled his head to peer at the slight woman at his side.

"Ye need rest," Zora admonished him softly. "I will watch over her."

"Ye should close the shutters," Caelen murmured, his mouth parched. He couldn't remember the last time he'd eaten or drunk. "She doesnae like the cold."

"The fresh air will help keep the fever at bay," Zora soothed. "A stifling room breeds disease." Tugging gently at his arm, Zora led him to the doorway.

"Go. Eat. Play with your son. He misses her, also."

Caelen dropped his gaze to the floor, unable to look at the woman who resembled Arbela. His heart twisted, knowing she was right, but leaving Arbela's side seemed like desertion—something *she* would never do.

The door opened as he lifted a hand to the latch and Rory ducked his head into the room. Caelen did not miss the subtle shake of Zora's head in answer to Rory's unspoken question.

"Bram wanted to know if he could come up," Rory said, glancing from Zora to Caelen as if uncertain who to ask.

"He may come sit with her after his meal," Zora replied. "But I believe the laird needs a bit of fresh air and the rain has ended. Mayhap he could take Bram outside?"

"Dinnae coddle me, woman!" Caelen growled. He pushed past Rory and stalked down the passageway, his captain on his heels.

"It has only been three days," Rory offered. "And dinnae fash at Zora. Ye have been under her care as well."

"I know how long it's been," Caelen replied, bleakness coloring his voice, ignoring Rory's reference to wounds which were no longer of consequence. "MacGillonay's blade opened the vein in her arm from wrist to elbow. Another few minutes and she would have lost too much blood to survive. As it is, we only wait for a fever to take her."

"Something her aunt isnae going to let happen," Rory assured him.

Caelen whirled. "Ye think her a better healer simply because she keeps the windows open and brews drinks I've never heard of?"

Rory rocked back on his heels. "Nae. I believe she is a good healer because she takes care to use only freshly boiled bandages and washes her hands, something that strikes me as sensible, though I've not seen it before." He tilted his head. "And a nasty brew usually helps, in my experience."

"Och," Caelen snorted as he resumed his journey to the hall. But his row with Rory had restored some of the balance he'd lost since Arbela had collapsed on the floor of the hall in a rapidly widening pool of blood. He strode into the hall, startled as several men rose to their feet, benches scraping against the floor. As if pulled by strings, others also rose, staring at him expectantly.

Caelen shook his head and everyone reluctantly returned to their seats. Alex and his father remained standing. Bram's eyes stared at him fearfully. Caelen managed a slight smile as he lowered himself to his chair, patting Bram's hand reassuringly.

"There is no change," he said.

"She's still asleep?" Bram asked.

"Aye. 'Twill take time for her to heal. I believe she likes hearing yer stories, though."

Bram's smile wavered with uncertainty. "She doesnae speak to me."

Caelen pulled Bram into his lap. "She will, Bram. She will." Though he was beginning to believe it wasn't true.

* * *

"Do ye truly think she hears me?" Bram asked as he sat at Arbela's bedside.

Caelen stared thoughtfully at his wife. "I believe she does," he replied. "I believe she is simply too tired to wake. A healing body takes time and effort. She needs to know ye are here."

Bram sighed then leaned forward, his hand on the mattress. "I ate my veg-ables," he told Arbela's silent form. "Aunt Zora says the eggsplant willnae be ready for a while, so I help water them. They're getting bigger. Like me."

He peered at Caelen. Caelen nodded solemnly and retreated to a chair in the corner of the room, out of the way, but positioned where he could see the bed. His heart ached for the woman who'd risked her life to save his son and home. And him. Alex had given him the details the first night they'd held vigil at her side.

She fought like a lioness defending her young—bold, heedless yet using her strengths, knowing her weaknesses. Even if Caelen hadn't broken away and slit MacGillonay's throat, the man would have died from the wounds she'd inflicted. Death of a thousand cuts, Alex had called it. Perhaps there were not a thousand cuts on the man, but they were well placed and MacGillonay already had one foot in his grave when Caelen struck him down.

He recalled her words the first time he'd mocked her use of strength against a man. She'd agreed honestly.

I cannot compete with ye on such a physical level. I have other skills—

His lips twisted in a half-smile. Kade had reported two MacGillonay captives with broken skulls from heavy objects braced on the top of doors, a few with broken bones from sliding in the thick cooking oil she'd spread on the stone floors—which had taken hours to clean—and numerous more with those damned barbed wires in their feet. *Caltrops* Alex had called them. A few MacGillonays exhibited mysterious illnesses which had more or less resolved, which had caused Zora to arch a brow, but she'd declined to explain her thoughts on the matter.

Bram's voice pulled him reluctantly from his musings.

"Da says ye can hear me, so I made up a new story. It's called Bela and the Dragon." He shifted his weight on the mattress and Caelen noted Bram had moved from his chair to the bed and seated himself comfortably against a stack of pillows.

"There was once a really f'rocious dragon called Gillonay. He lived in a loch that dinnae have a name 'cause the water was so bad, no one wanted to live there. He had two dragon sons as mean as he was, and he wanted to kick them out of the house, but they dinnae have anywhere to go, so he decided to steal the MacKern's land."

Bram patted Arbela's hand. "The MacKern was a fierce warrior with a brave son named Bram. He was only a lad, and when the mean dragon Gillonay charged down out of the skies, the MacKern told his beautiful princess wife, Bela, to save their son. Bram dinnae want to leave, but she insisted, and he went along to help protect her.

"They met and fought with other dragons and f'rocious beasts along the way to her da's castle. Bela was verra strong and brave—just like Bram. After Bram was safe, she went back to help the MacKerns fight off the evilest dragon."

Bram paused for a moment and Caelen wondered what would come next, his interest piqued.

"The dragon was old, but he was big—long as five horses and tall as a tree. His breath stank like he ate dead things, and his big teeth had bits of his rotten supper stuck between them."

His voice fell to a whisper. "Bela is the bravest ma and she dinnae want the dragon to ever hurt Bram or his da again. She fought him and even the evil men Gillonay had brought with him. She killed the dragon, but one of his long nails cut her and she fell into a deep sleep, like a faerie princess. Even though she dinnae move, she could hear Bram when he told her stories, and one day she opened her eyes and smiled."

Bram sighed. "Ye have to wake up, Bela," he said, his voice matter-of-fact. "I really need a ma. And I'm certain Da misses ye as well. He looks really sad, and I havenae been bad once since ye were hurt.

"I've thought about it and decided it would be nice to have a little brother or sister soon, but I dinnae think ye can have one unless ye and Da talk about it first."

Caelen choked on a startled breath. Another child? He'd told Arbela he did not wish other children, though that was a door he'd closed considering how little chance they stood of ever desiring a family together—or even desiring each other, for that matter.

"Da is doing warrior things with me now, but ye and I can still have a lot of fun together. He's turning out to be a great da and I think my sister or brother would really like him. Bela, I wish ye'd wake up and get to know him better."

Tears spilled down Caelen's cheeks. He'd based his opinion of women on his first wife's spoiled behavior, avoiding a second emotional entanglement and swearing all women were petty, grasping creatures. He'd been too wrapped in his self-righteous opinion to even have more than a passing thought for the woman he'd married. She'd carried out her duties well, and Bram clearly adored her. It was too late to consider he did, too.

Chapter Twenty Six

Arbela sat at the small table near the window, musing over the events of a fortnight earlier, though they remained somewhat cloudy in her mind.

Bram touched the black threads running in a line along the inside of her arm. "Do they pain ye?"

Arbela smiled. He had been quite attentive since she woke a bit over a sennight ago. Whenever Caelen permitted, Bram entertained her with his stories and reports of life at Dunfaileas. "Nae. They do not. Aunt Zora is very tidy with her needle and the wound is nearly healed."

"I'm really glad ye woke," Bram said. "Da was beginning to worry."

"The pair of them were ever in my way," Zora noted dryly as she folded the blanket at the foot of the bed.

Zora had arrived less than a day after they retook the castle—so Arbela had been told. Arbela found her aunt's presence comforting, though not as light-hearted as Agnes. Arriving to such chaos and a seriously wounded niece likely hadn't left Zora much time for cheerfulness. But her calm reassurances and intolerance for medical practices that did not meet her standards, relaxed Arbela and ensured her injury healed as quickly as possible.

Even if it did mean Arbela was obliged to remain in Caelen's room where she'd been taken after she'd been wounded. Zora had appropriated the extra bed in Bram's room for herself, and not only was there not another room to move her to, but Arbela couldn't find it in her heart to admit to her aunt she and Caelen occupied separate rooms.

"She says they can come out tomorrow," Bram enthused, tapping the line of neat stitches, drawing Arbela's attention once again. "Can I watch?"

"Ye may help," Arbela said, eliciting a gasp from the boy. He drew his hand back, uncertainty on his face.

"It will not hurt," she laughed. "Though it may tickle."

Bram beamed, obviously relieved.

"Dinnae tire Arbela," Caelen chided as he entered the room. "Ye and I have a sword lesson to attend to, lad. She needs her rest."

Rest was the last thing Arbela had on her mind. Weak and tired for the first few days after her injury, she had remained in bed, but light exercise had her back on her feet and impatient to be about her normal routine. Zora and Caelen scolded her each time she left the room, claiming to have her best interests at heart. It was past time to ignore their good intentions. And past time to confront Caelen about their living arrangements.

Bram slid from his chair, grabbing Caelen's hand eagerly. "I'm really good," he assured Arbela. "Da says so. Can Toros go?"

"If your father agrees, ye may take Toros," she said. "Thank ye for taking over Bram's lessons," Arbela added, catching Caelen's eye. "He enjoys them. He enjoys spending time with ye, also."

Caelen's gaze skittered away, and Arbela wondered if the remark embarrassed him.

"I'll come back when I'm finished," Bram assured her as he skipped at Caelen's side, Toros at his heels. Silence filled the room as Caelen closed the door on Bram's chatter. Arbela dropped her robe to the back of the chair and, refusing to meet Zora's disapproving gaze, dressed in her favored tunic and trousers. She pulled on her boots, then opened her weapons chest.

"The lad clearly dotes on ye," Zora commented as she straightened the bedclothes. "He is relieved ye have wakened, but he still worries."

"Do not use Bram to order my actions. I am restless and 'twill do me good to spend time outside. In any case, he is too young to worry." Arbela made a rippling motion with her fingers, brushing away Zora's notion. She slipped a dagger into an empty sheath in her boot. Casting a glance about the room, her gaze settled on her aunt's questioning look.

"I agree he is growing up. I merely wish to give him better things to do than worry. Especially about me. I will be fine."

"Ye very nearly were not *fine*, as ye say." Zora's lips pinched in a narrow line. "Ye worry me, *im dustry*." *My daughter.* "It is time ye relaxed your warring ways and spent time in serenity. Planning a nursery."

Arbela met Zora's arch look with one of her own and ignored the fluttery motion in her belly. Zora sighed.

"Bram is not too young to have spent hours at your bedside, telling tales I imagine he heard from ye these past weeks," she said, returning to her original statement. "I will remind ye his father also sat at your side until I ran him off each day—which was not an easy feat. He was devastated."

Arbela's breath caught on an inhale for an instant at Zora's words. She could not imagine the bull-headed man she'd married devastated over anything less than the loss of his son. Certainly not over her, the unappealing woman he'd been bribed to marry. She was under no delusion Caelen valued her for anything more than her ability to protect Bram. Of course, the necessity of replacing her would possibly worry him. Nothing more.

With a cleansing exhale, she dismissed Zora's declaration as a woman desirous of a great-nephew or great-niece, now that her charges were grown. Surely Alex would settle down one day and provide her with babes to spoil.

Giving Zora a quick hug of apology, she whistled for Garen to join her and headed to the stable.

* * *

Bram sat at ease atop Ari's back as they circled Caelen in the pen beside the stable. He prodded the pony to a faster pace, leaning forward slightly in encouragement. His face lit with happiness and success as Ari lifted his feet over the logs spaced in a row on the ground, the first semblance of learning to ride over obstacles.

Love for the boy quivered in Arbela's heart. She savored it, changing her focus to the larger picture of Caelen spending time with his son. Warmth slid heavy and sweet as honey through her breast, but the sensation fled before she could examine it.

"Nicely done, Bram," she called as he reined his pony to a halt. Caelen stared at her for a moment, then spoke to Bram who scrambled off Ari's back and darted across the paddock to her.

"Da says we could ride outside the pen if ye'd come with us." Bram squinted his eyes beseechingly. "Please?"

"I do not see the need—" Arbela began, glancing up as Caelen stepped near.

"The need is to get the lad used to guiding his pony places other than this pen," Caelen answered, tossing Ari's reins over the top rail of the fence. "Ye are a good horsewoman and he can learn a lot by watching ye."

"I meant, I did not see the need for him to receive instruction from the both us—at the same time," Arbela corrected, her tone slightly formal after being interrupted. She couldn't imagine a companionable ride beyond the walls with her taciturn husband. Certainly not one where she was expected to instruct the boy in a skill where their approaches were dissimilar.

"I'll not gainsay yer instruction on riding," Caelen assured her. His eyes flashed. "Mayhap I could learn something as well. Or mayhap I simply wish a few moments of yer time."

Arbela gave him a startled look. "I am happy to speak with ye when necessary as we have done before."

Alerting a stable lad with a jerk of his head, Caelen sent him off to saddle Voski. He caught Arbela's elbow and guided her to the stable. "After Bram is abed, I wish to speak to ye of yer thoughts of Voski covering a few mares next spring," he said. "'Tis never too early to plan these things."

"Do ye seek Voski's approval or mine?" she asked, an impish smile tweaking her lips.

Caelen snorted. "I hardly need to ask his," he replied. "He does not quietly accept the mares being serviced by the other two studs. He seems to be of the opinion the mares are his."

"He is young," Arbela warned. "And untried in such things."

"*Such things* are often instinctive," Caelen returned, his voice dropping to a low murmur. "And often improve with practice."

Arbela's cheeks heated. *What happened to our conversation? Are we speaking of horses or . . . ?* "Mayhap this is best determined later," she demurred. "I see a lad leading Voski—and another with too many questions on his face." She slanted her gaze to Bram standing between them, rapt attention on his face.

Caelen laughed and Arbela's heart skipped a beat. "Do not say I did not warn ye," she scolded. "Lads tend to question their fathers on the most puzzling matters."

Caelen settled abruptly, turning his attention to checking Ari's girth, and Arbela smothered a smile. He handed Bram his pony's reins and Bram led Ari to a small tree stump nearby. From there, he climbed onto Ari's back, facing them with a triumphant grin. Arbela's heart warmed again to see the boy so much at ease with the pony.

"Give us a moment, Bram," Caelen called. "We will mount up and take our ride." He turned his attention to Arbela. "Are ye well? Can ye ride without discomfort?"

Taken unaware by his deeply solicitous question, Arbela grasped for words. Words to keep him at the distance they had both stipulated in their marriage, yet something to acknowledge his kindness.

"Yes." It was inadequate and she knew it. She grabbed Voski's reins. "Thank you," she added, leaving it to Caelen to decide if she spoke to the stable lad or to him. She stepped easily into the saddle, a twinge in her arm reminding her it had been grievously injured and little used in the past fortnight. She flexed her fingers around Voski's reins and glanced at Caelen and Bram.

"Are ye coming along?" she sang out. Toros and Garen barked happily as they joined her.

Bram kicked Ari's sides enthusiastically and Caelen vaulted onto Addis' back, setting him back on his haunches as they wheeled to join Bram and Arbela. Her heart soared as they rode through the gates into the late morning sunshine, their horses' hooves scattering leaves damp from an earlier rain.

She wasn't certain how it had come about, but her dreams could be found in this instant. Or, at least her hopes. She doubted Caelen would ever become a thoughtful, romantic man. But was that what she truly desired? Strong and encouraging would be better. Steady. Agreeable. She darted a look to one side. His composure was best described as focused, and his clansmen seemed to find him agreeable.

He had been solicitous of her health earlier. Caring? Or desirous of avoiding a weary woman on his hands? She shook her head. Caring too much would only lead to his desire to control her, to form her into his image of a dutiful wife—safe and dull. An image she could never fulfill.

"I wanna race," Bram complained as Ari plodded beside the larger horses. Breaking into a trot as their longer strides outpaced him wasn't enough to satisfy Bram's boundless energy. Half an hour of bouncing about hadn't taken the edge off his excitement.

Voski's antics hadn't helped. Arbela had been obliged to take off shortly after they'd begun their ride. He'd danced on weightless hooves, bobbing his head as he champed his bit. Agreeing with his desire for speed and the wind in her face, Arbela made her apologies and, finding a suitable stretch of land, urged him to a run. She and Voski were now more relaxed and settled, but Bram's petulance at not being included was her forfeit.

"Why do ye wish to race?" she asked as Ari's head bobbed at her knee, his sturdy hooves beating a rapid tattoo to keep pace.

"So I can fight dragons," Bram replied. He waved a fist in the air, mimicry of a wielded sword. "Ari isnae fast enough to leap out of the way, and I need to teach him."

"Remember what a brave pony Ari is," Arbela said. "He has fought off a wolf, and I daresay he can fight off a dragon."

"But I wanna race," Bram repeated, a note of petulance creeping into his voice.

Arbela caught Caelen's gaze over Bram's head. "I could take Voski to the opposite side of the glen and Bram and Ari could practice between us."

Caelen remained silent for a moment, and Arbela could tell he entertained the notion. His eyes swept the ground and he pointed to a spot slightly to Arbela's left. "That way has no obstacles I can see. They should be safe here."

She reined Voski to the side, giving the dogs a command to remain at the edge of the glen.

Safe. Is safe always the best option? She sighed. The child needed to stretch his wings a bit. At least Caelen allowed Bram this freedom outside the walls. He could have insisted the boy only ride within the paddocks, protected by the new curtain wall and guards striding the parapet.

A burst of happiness swelled to recall Laird MacGillonay had met his death a fortnight earlier, making this jaunt outside the protection of the walls of Dunfaileas possible. Suddenly the air seemed fresher, the sun, peeking from behind wispy clouds, brighter. The man who'd sought to kidnap Bram no longer ruled their lives.

"Come on, Bram!" Arbela called. "Ask Ari to show ye some speed."

Bram whooped and leaned low over Ari's neck. The sturdy pony gamely picked up his hooves, breaking into a roughly rollicking canter. He headed unerringly to Voski's side and trotted jarringly to a halt. His face beaming, Bram tossed side to side as Ari settled.

"I did it! Did ye see me, Bela? Ari was as fast as the wind! As fast as *two* winds!"

Arbela laughed. "I am not certain how fast two winds are, but ye definitely have an outstanding pony. Turn him about and head back to your father."

They repeated the route until Ari's good ear began to flatten. "I believe he has had enough," Arbela noted. "Shall we give him a rest? He certainly deserves it."

Bram sighed. "He is a grand pony, aye?"

"The very best," Arbela assured him.

She and Caelen rode with Bram to the edge of a nearby burn and let their ponies drink once they'd cooled. Garen and Toros waded through the clear water.

Dismounting, they tied the horses loosely and Arbela offered bannocks and a sip from a waterskin she'd grabbed in her trek through the kitchen an hour or so earlier. Bram stuffed an oatcake into his mouth and scrambled over the rocks, searching for the best stones to skip across the placid surface of the water. His shouts rang in the sun-dappled glen and Toros leapt about excitedly.

Arbela took a step after Bram, but Caelen halted her with a touch on her arm.

"I havenae thanked ye for the remarkable job ye did when MacGillonay took Dunfaileas," he said. He motioned for her to have a seat, and she perched atop a low boulder, its surface warmed by the sun. Garen lay in a nearby patch of shade, panting lightly.

"Ye do not need to," she replied. "Dunfaileas is my home. I did what I deemed necessary to gain it back."

Caelen grunted. "Ye did more than most men could do or would have thought to do. I wouldnae have considered setting traps to lessen the enemy's numbers." He scratched his head. "Yet, a bold approach wouldnae have served ye so well."

Arbela smiled. "I do not believe the *bold* approach served anyone but MacGillonay. He completely dishonored your hospitality. Some—my father," she admitted, "would not approve my strategies, but they were, in this case, necessary."

"Tell me of yer tactics," Caelen urged.

Startled to find someone other than Alex interested in methods learned in her *Hashashin* tutelage, she hesitated.

"Is this something ye dinnae wish to discuss?" he asked.

"No. 'Tis something many see as dishonorable. Most favor brute force over . . . other skills."

"Saving Bram can never be dishonorable," Caelen assured her solemnly.

A painful knot thickened in her chest. *I saved ye, as well.* Not a brag, not an arrogance. Pain at the thought of losing him. Was he tied that tightly to her love for Bram? Or was there something more?

"I wanted to discuss our bedroom," she blurted. Heat instantly blossomed in her neck and cheeks. Caelen's startled look became amused, and it sobered Arbela to see the sparkle in his eyes. "Ye may have yer bed back and I will take the cot," she said firmly. "There is no need for ye to sacrifice your rest on my account. I realize we have no extra room for Aunt Zora, and I apologize for the inconvenience. But I am healed, and there is no reason I cannot move to the cot."

"Ye assume I wish ye out of my bed," Caelen noted.

"I was not invited, nor is this part of our agreement," she reminded him. *Mother Mary save me from falling into such a trap!*

"It doesnae have to become a torture chamber merely because we both inhabit it. As ye pointed out, space is limited at Dunfaileas, and I would not wish to inconvenience my wife." He shrugged as if her decision was of no consequence.

"Ye dinnae have to decide this day," he added. "Think on it. Let me know if ye can tolerate my presence in yer bed." Caelen strolled back to the horses, a tuneless whistle on his lips, while Arbela stared after him, a thousand questions running through her mind, and all of them leading to the image of his naked body, kissed by firelight, a memory she had been unable to dismiss.

Chapter Twenty Seven

Bram outpaced Arbela to the high table.

"Look!" he exclaimed, snatching something yellow from Arbela's place. He spun about, thrusting a flower toward her. She slowed her pace to a halt, puzzled at the offering.

"What a beautiful flower, Bram-jan," she said. "Who left it there?"

He shoved it into her hand and, abandoning the topic with a shrug, climbed into his chair. "Come on, Bela," he said impatiently, motioning to her seat. "I'm hungry."

Offering a nod of appreciation for his remembering to wait to eat until she was seated, she took her place and quickly blessed their food. Bram plowed into his stack of oatcakes, dribbling honey over them before passing the platter to Arbela.

"Are ye certain ye do not know where this flower came from?" she asked, fingering the flat yellow petals with the darker raised center, much like a tiny bowl nestled atop a delicate golden plate. The sturdy stem was long and devoid of leaves.

"He doesnae know . . . but *I* do," Caelen murmured near her ear as he took his seat.

Arbela sent him a startled look. He grinned at her, his eyes dancing merrily.

"I know ye said ye arenae like other women and dinnae like flowers, but I saw this one and thought ye might like it. 'Tis the last of its kind until next spring."

"I . . . thank ye," Arbela stuttered, remembering the only other occasion he'd given her flowers. "I like flowers," she amended. "I simply wished for ye to speak to me, not indulge in empty flattery."

"'Tis naught but a flower, Arbela," Caelen said. "And I thought of ye." He motioned for the platter of oatcakes which had managed to make its way down the table, turning his attention to his morning meal.

Arbela accepted the food he placed on her trencher and dipped her oatcake in the loch of honey floating on Bram's plate. Bemused by her husband's unusual gesture, she slanted Caelen a glance. He talked and laughed with the others at the table, paying her no particular attention, but her heart warmed just the same.

I may enjoy the flower and the harmony it evokes. She chided the tiny flame of resistance that threatened to spoil the moment. *A single flower does not indicate a list of conditions unmet.*

Standing the flower upright in her empty mug, she directed one of the serving girls to add water—and bring another mug.

"It brightens the table," Caelen commented as he finished the last of his meal. He rose and leaned close. "As does my lovely wife."

He was gone before she recovered her wits enough to form a single word.

* * *

Caelen relaxed against a cleft in the rock and pulled a strip of dried meat from his sporran. Around him, others who had accompanied him on a hunt for fresh meat for the table reclined, taking the opportunity to eat a light meal.

"Do ye believe we will see any wolves today?" Rory asked.

"I had hoped we would. Coll's complaints that something made off with two of his sheep last week makes me think one roams the hills. But our party makes enough noise to frighten the beast away."

"Och, it hasnae hindered our hunting," Rory noted with a nod to the pack horses waiting patiently beneath a sprawling oak tree. Each sported numerous rabbits and a hind strapped to their trappings. Enough to feed the clan for a week or so.

"Yer wife has been a boon, Laird," a man offered from his patch of shade. "I dinnae only mean the wherewithal to repair the wall or the help and knights that came with her."

"Nay," the stocky man a few feet away added. "She has a rare way with the weans. My Ewan said she set the lads straight on her heritage a few weeks ago."

A collective laugh swept the glen. "I'll not lie to ye. 'Twas a relief to know she is a Christian," the first man said. "I was a wee bit disturbed to find our laird married to a lass who had lived among the Saracens all her life."

"Och," the stocky man interjected, waving his waterskin in the air. "She's a fair hand no matter from where she hails. I've noted a bit more respect in my lads of late, and a hustle to get their chores done of a morning. Despite her outlandish dress, I believe ye picked a bonny bride."

"I thank ye for yer approval." Caelen laughed. "'Tis good to know my wife meets yer standards."

"She has all but destroyed our standards," Rory noted. "'Tis a rare treat to find beauty, courage, and wisdom in one woman."

The conversation turned to the attributes of women, giving fair nod to the remarkable women they'd each married. Caelen listened with half an ear, his mind on the fact that Arbela had married him. He knew he was no great catch. His clan was poor, though the view from Dunfaileas was unparalleled—in his opinion. His people were warm and caring, though she had not known that when she'd accepted his offer.

What could she possibly see in him? He was above average height, his muscles largely in his shoulders and back, and he'd long ago adopted a close-shorn head rather than deal with the mass of hair he'd been born with—that tended to curl, which he'd never admit. No one would mistake him for handsome.

He was at ease with his men, and courteous with their families, but close attachments were something he had never experienced. His father

244

had considered it a kindness to mold Caelen into the tough, fearless man he felt necessary to lead a clan. He'd shaped him with scorn and a decided lack of acceptance, denying Caelen's mother an opportunity to offer her reassurances—or love.

Caelen drew the end of a slender stick through the soil at his feet, nonsensical patterns that were nothing more than an outlet for the endless energy he felt. It had been a punishable sin to sit idle before his father, and the habit of constant motion had waned little. He smiled when he thought of how he saw this part of himself in Bram.

"I wouldnae give a pinched penny for our lives, had Arbela not come back as she did," Rory declared. The men laughed.

"How did it feel to have yer wife rescue ye, Laird?" one tossed out.

"I'd be embarrassed that a wee slip of a lass managed to best a man ye've spent the better part of six years feuding with," said another.

"Will ye be taking lessons from her, then?" chimed in a third.

Rory sent Caelen a long-suffering look. "To think of all the advice I could offer—yer bonny wife awaiting ye at home, yet here ye sit with men who will show ye no mercy."

"What are ye hinting at, Rory?" Caelen asked.

Rory shrugged. "If she were my wife, I imagine I'd have a bairn on the way by now, or at least making certain we knew how 'twas done. Though I admit, she might be a wee bit formidable to the wrong man. The flower was a nice touch at this morning's meal. Makes me hopeful wee Bram will have a brother soon."

"Or sister," Caelen returned without heat, choosing to ignore Rory's meddling. He wasn't certain why he'd chosen to pick a flower for Arbela this morn whilst out checking the mares and foals in the far paddock. The daffodil, the last in a pile of what was quickly becoming little more than thick grass, struck him as the way Arbela stood out among other women. Women who no longer held any interest to him.

He could hardly credit his action to his immense gratitude for her timely entrance to the castle as MacGillonay's anger had peaked and the lives of all remaining MacKerns hung in the balance. Tactically, her attack was brilliant. He'd never thought on such practices as those she'd brought into play, but they'd served her well. Served them all well.

Nor could he lay his sudden interest solely in the fact she'd first protected Bram. She had agreed to this in their first talk of marriage. It had been one of the most important points as far as Caelen was concerned, and he had no reason to fault her dealings with the lad. If he was entirely truthful, there was perhaps the expectation she would fail in her promises to him. Ruthie had.

Caelen swore under his breath. He should know better by now than to compare Arbela to his deceased wife. Arbela was strong, undemanding, clever, and loved Bram unconditionally. Caelen had promised her space to live her life as she pleased, reaping far more from this marriage than he gave.

And now he found himself attracted to her. Curse his luck. Against his better judgement and the intent to never give a woman a permanent place in his life again, somehow he'd done just that. His wife had made her expectations known. Changing them would be a challenge.

One he was willing to accept.

* * *

Arbela glanced up as Caelen entered Bram's room. Bram gave a shout of pleasure and rushed to his father's side, excited by his unexpected appearance so late in the evening. A full day had passed since he'd given her the flower, and she could scarcely account for the flutter of her heart now. The simple gift should not affect her so.

"Is it not time for yer bedtime story?" Caelen asked, giving Arbela a wink over Bram's head. Her heart tripled its beat. *Foolish.*

"Can I stay up later?" Bram asked, his voice sliding into a pleading whine as he leaned back, swinging at the end of his da's arm. "I dinnae wish to go to sleep now that ye are here."

"I dinnae come here to disrupt yer routine," Caelen chided gently. "I happen to know Arbela tells the best stories, and ye should be grateful for her attention."

Arbela lifted an eyebrow and Caelen nodded. "Hop into bed, Bram. Yer ma is waiting."

This time her heart squeezed tight, and tears prickled her eyes. She forced a merry smile.

"Jump in, Bram-jan. I have a special tale of an ungrateful tiger for ye this night."

It took less than a moment for Bram to realize he was outflanked, and he scrambled onto his bed, leaping about as if he was the tiger. He batted at the covers with riotous growls and eventually allowed himself to be tucked beneath the plaides.

"There once was a village beset by a ferocious tiger," Arbela began. "The people got together to discuss what they should do. *I am too fearful to allow my children out to play*, said one woman. *We're all frightened*, said another. *And he ate one of my legs!* a man cried. It was at last decided they would dig a deep hole and trap the tiger. The people dug several pits along the village path, then went inside their homes and waited.

"The next day, a young man decided to visit his uncle who lived in the village. As he walked along the road, he heard a great commotion. *I wonder what that is about?* he thought. *Whatever it is, it does not sound very happy.* He left the path in search of the reason for the noise, and found a tiger at the bottom of a deep hole.

"*Help me!* the tiger cried. *I cannot get out of this pit! Why should I help ye?* the young man asked. *O, please help me*, the tiger said. *I would be very grateful. I do not wish to remain here.*

"The young man was a kind person. He found a large stick and shoved it into the hole, allowing the tiger to scramble out. *There ye go*, he said. *Nicely done. I'll be on my way.*

"*Not so fast!* growled the tiger. *I am going to eat you.* The young man was startled. *But ye said ye would be grateful if I let ye out. I am very grateful*, the tiger replied. *But I am a tiger and people dug this trap for me. Now I will eat you. Wait!* The young man cried. *Let us ask for someone else's opinion if it is right for ye to eat me.*

"Tiger agreed, and they soon came upon a small rabbit and told him their tale. Rabbit wrinkled his nose. *Before I can say yea or nay, I must see exactly what happened.* So, they walked back to the hole where Tiger had been imprisoned. Rabbit peered over the edge. *Ye were down there?* he asked. Tiger nodded. *Show me*, Rabbit said. Tiger, eager to eat the boy, leapt into the pit. *Was the limb there when the boy walked up?* Rabbit asked. *No*, the boy replied as he pulled it back out.

"Rabbit leaned over the edge. *It is my decision it is not fair for the tiger to eat the boy. Just because ye are angry with the people who dug the pit does not mean it is fair for you to eat him. Ye should have been grateful for his help.*

"And with that, the rabbit hopped away, and the boy hurried to the village, leaving the tiger howling in the pit."

Bram clapped his hands. "Funny rabbit! He tricked the tiger back into the pit."

"Aye," Arbela replied, leaning over him to kiss his forehead. "Do ye believe it was right for the tiger to want to eat the boy because he was angry someone had dug the hole?"

Bram snuggled beneath his blanket. "It wasnae the boy's fault the tiger was trapped. The tiger should have been kinder." His eyelids fluttered.

Arbela patted his head and rose, indicating Caelen should leave the room with her.

"He will sleep," she murmured as she closed the door. "He settles as long as Toros remains at his side. And Aunt Zora is there should he need more."

"Ye are a rare woman, Arbela," Caelen said. "What ye have wrought in Bram is remarkable."

"He is a wonderful boy," she returned. "I can hardly claim credit for his natural curiosity and the manners already instilled in him."

Caelen scowled and shoved a palm over his head. "Ilene—"

Arbela held up a hand to halt his words. "I was told she has been sent away. Kinder than a traitor's death, though as infatuated with Bram as she was, she may feel otherwise."

"She had kin who would take her. I doubt she has many years left. She can do no further harm."

"Thank ye for stopping by this eve," Arbela said. "Bram is always happy to spend time with ye." She angled her head. "Did ye have another reason?"

Caelen shifted his weight then leaned against the wall, his shoulder on level with her head. His scent drifted to her, and she realized he'd taken time to bathe.

"I wished to speak with ye. We've had little chance these past weeks to spend time together."

"I would not take it amiss if we repaired to your room," Arbela said. "There are often unseen ears in passageways."

Caelen pushed from the wall and crossed to his door. "Please," he murmured, motioning her through the open portal. "Ye know this is our room, not merely mine."

"Clearly, I misspoke," she murmured, still uncomfortable in a bed she had taken from its rightful owner. She did not consider the issue between them settled.

"One bit of business is rather serious," Caelen stated as they settled into seats by the hearth. Arbela raised an eyebrow, inviting explanation. "There appears to be a wolf in the area. A few sheep have been taken, and the shepherd is understandably upset."

CATHY & DD MACRAE

"I can offer Toros and Garen for a few days. They are bred as protection for a flock. Though they will not track a wolf down, they could mayhap deter one until he moves on to easier prey."

"A solid idea. I will mention it."

"I have one for ye," Arbela countered. "Da had offered ye a place in his shipping business, and all that remains is to discover what we can offer as trade goods. I had thought on this earlier, but when I arrived through the kitchen storerooms and found the barrels of whisky, I realized what ye have in plenty that others will want." She smiled. "Minus whatever the MacGillonays drank, that is."

"Ye believe we can turn a profit on our whisky?" Caelen asked. "I would like that, indeed."

"I see no reason why not," she replied. "We can discuss a name to sell it under, and mayhap a brand stamped in the barrel heads would set it apart."

"Ye are a talented woman," Caelen murmured. "I see so much more to ye than that day I offered for yer hand. I know we did not marry under the best circumstances." He leaned forward, his gaze intent.

"But I am glad I married ye."

250

Chapter Twenty Eight

The fire in the chamber burned low, but Arbela's cheeks burned.

"I scarcely know what to do or think," she admitted, hating the sensation of being in a position not of her control.

"What have I done to cause this?" Caelen asked. "What makes ye hesitant to take up my offer?"

"Things have changed," she replied, though she hated the vagueness of her words.

"We are the same people who said our vows nearly two months ago," Caelen argued. "Tell me what has changed."

"We are *not* the same," she disagreed. "Ye have done things of late I am at a loss to explain."

"Mayhap ye could tell me," he encouraged, "and I can offer insight."

"Ye have complimented me," she began.

"Unforgiveable," he murmured as she took a breath.

She cast him a quelling look and the upward quirk at the right side of his mouth smoothed away, though the twinkle in his eyes remained. "Ye thanked me for simply doing what I agreed to," she added. "Gave me a flower. Assisted in Bram's bedtime routine the past few nights. And offered to share your bed and room in the nicest terms possible."

She sighed. "I asked ye once to speak plainly, and I would offer ye the same courtesy. In light of the changes ye have wrought, pleasant though they may be, I must ask if ye expect me to change my end of our bargain."

Caelen rubbed his chin, appearing lost in thought. Just as she imagined she'd be reduced to tapping her toe on the floor in impatience, he turned a quizzing gaze on her.

"In all the things ye enumerated to me, of which I admit I am guilty, there is one I have neglected."

"Oh? Pray tell me what it is," she invited.

Caelen took on a thoughtful mien. "Ye accused me of complimenting ye, and I admit I did. However, ye deserved it as I cannot remember a lass who has done so much and received so little in return."

Arbela opened her mouth, but Caelen held up a finger, silencing her, though it went against her nature to let the point pass.

"I told ye why I gave ye the flower. It brightened our table—almost as much as ye did."

Arbela's face heated, remembering the way he'd phrased *that* particular compliment.

Caelen continued. "Bram is my responsibility as well, and I enjoy hearing yer tales. So, attending to his bedtime is hardly a point in my favor. As for sharing my bed, ye were brought here initially for nursing after yer injury, and I fully agreed. Now that yer aunt is here, 'tis only seemly we continue to share the room. There wasnae expectation beyond sleep involved when I made the offer. Ye do remember our agreement, aye?"

Insufferable man! He knows quite well I remember our agreement. Arbela gave a curt nod, not giving him the satisfaction of waxing poetic on *that* point as well.

He stepped closer. "There is one thing, however, that ye dinnae accuse me of, and I apologize for being so remiss that ye failed to notice."

"Oh? What is that?" Arbela wracked her brain to remember, unwilling to give him the upper hand.

His fingertips barely grazing her chin, he tilted her face up to his.

"I admit to wanting to kiss ye," he murmured.

His lips moved softly against hers, questioning, seeking. Arbela drew a shallow breath, all her lungs would hold, and pressed upward on her toes as sparks raced through her body. Though she'd tried to forget, told herself it was futile to dwell on the disappointment of their wedding night, she could not deny the pleasure of his touch.

Caelen's hands clasped her waist, pulled her close. His lips slanted hungrily, a soft growl low in his throat. Arbela slid her hands between them, palms against his chest. Caelen broke the kiss, but would not let her pull away.

"Where does this take us?" she murmured, relishing the feel of his arms about her despite her misgivings.

"I believe 'tis a grand thing for a husband to love his wife," he offered.

Arbela leaned back. "Are ye prepared for where this could lead?" she asked.

"I believe I am aware of how this works," he commented wryly.

Arbela shook her head. "We pledged a marriage in name only. One in which I am free to act and dress as I please. One in which I have your protection, but not your regard. Your authority, but not your presence."

Caelen winced. "Arbela, I will admit when I first met ye, I thought ye an arrogant young woman who was much doted upon by her da. Yer clothes were outlandish, and ye flaunted a king's ransom of jewels about yer neck with scarcely a thought to their worth. Ye were outspoken and no one gainsaid ye."

"'Tis a wonder ye married me," Arbela quipped, trying desperately to cover her disappointment at the picture he painted.

"Listen well, Arbela," he said. "Since I have come to know ye, I understand ye arenae arrogant, ye are confident. Ye dinnae lie and ye admit when ye cannae do something. Yer da dotes on ye, but because he is proud of ye, not because he cannae handle ye any other way. The clothes ye wear are part of who ye are. I confess I can sometimes scarcely take my eyes off ye." He laughed softly and shook his head. "And though ye are outspoken, ye are honest, kind, and use yer words to inspire, not destroy. I would never knowingly do anything to change ye. I am hardly worthy of ye, and yet I ask ye to give us a chance to know each other."

Arbela laid a hand gently on his arm. "Ye are an honorable man, Caelen. Of that I have no doubt. I will not cause ye grief or shame. However, I am not certain a change of rules at this late date is in my best interest."

"My attentions are a burden to ye?" Caelen asked, almost keeping the tang of bitterness from his voice. Arbela sighed.

"I have naught to compare your attentions to," she reminded him. "But I will not sell my freedom for the sake of what is best left in the past."

* * *

Arbela dropped a large drawstring bag to the ground in the corner of the keep beyond the blacksmith's forge. The single tree cast a patterned shade on the grass. Bram flopped beside the bag, peering at it in interest.

"I know your father is teaching ye to use your sword," Arbela said. "He has mentioned more than once what a fine job ye did creating both sword and targe."

Bram grinned. "Da says I'll get a real sword when I'm older."

"Aye, your practice will earn ye that privilege in time. Howbeit, I think 'tis time to teach ye to use a bow."

Bram's face fell. "I'm not big enough," he said. "Da's bow is twice as big as me. Bigger than ye!"

Arbela smiled. "That is true, Bram-jan. But *my* bow is much the right size." Reaching into her bag, she drew forth her curved bow. Bram's eyes grew big and he leapt to his feet.

"I remember!" he exclaimed. "Ye bested Da with this bow! Can I try it?"

"That is precisely why we are here." She handed him the lightweight bow. Unstrung, it resembled a large 'C' and Bram grasped the center, holding it backward as he aimed it at imaginary foes.

"It needs a string," he noted.

254

"Aye. Watch as I string it, for it will turn back on itself, making it very strong." She demonstrated as Bram watched, his curiosity unbound. Showing him the finished product, she then loosed the bow and had him repeat the process until she was satisfied he understood and could accomplish the feat.

She pulled a tattered piece of linen she'd glued to a small wooden square from the bag and propped it against the tree. Giving him a brief lesson on fletching, she then fired a single arrow. Eager to try his hand at shooting the bow, Bram studied her every move. His excitement peaked as she secured a thin leather bracer about his left forearm.

"I'm a real archer!" he exclaimed, waving his arm about.

"Aye," she agreed. "I made this so ye would not suffer burns on yer arm from the bowstring. That is why *real* archers wear them."

With Arbela's coaching, Bram fired arrow after arrow at the target. And missed every time. He scowled.

"The bow isnae too big, but I cannae shoot it right," he complained.

"Shooting a bow is not like wielding a long sword," she agreed. "There is a finesse, a oneness with the bow that only practice will accomplish. Ye must focus on the process until ye no longer have to think through each step. It is a part of ye. The bow will become an extension of your arm, the arrow a reflection of your thought as ye send it to your target."

Bram stared at her and she waited to hear his decision. As she'd expected, his jaw squared and his eyes glinted as he accepted the challenge. He was so much like his father.

"Can I have a bow like yers?" he asked.

"Ye will tell me what ye think mine is made of, and then we will find the necessary items to make your very own bow."

Bram was quick to study the strangely made bow. Its size and shape made it perfect for firing from horseback and was fitted for Arbela's short stature.

"People in the Levant do not use the longbow such as is done here," she said as Bram traced a finger over the layers of ram's horn and wood that made the bow strong and flexible. "When ye have mastered hitting the target from the ground, I will show ye how to use it from astride your pony."

If she'd thought Bram excited with the prospect of making his own bow and learning to shoot it, he could hardly contain his delight at this new treat dangled before him.

"Ye are the best ma, ever!" he exclaimed. "Do ye mind if I call ye ma sometimes?"

Tears clogged Arbela's throat and she could only nod. With this marriage contract, he would be the only child who ever did.

* * *

Caelen struggled to stay angry. Not that he'd shown his disappointment—which had slowly turned sour—to Arbela's decision as they'd each sought their rest. But he'd tried to show his interest in her and had spent an entire two days thinking up things Arbela would like. And all for naught. He was completely adrift on how to win his wife's favor.

He couldn't compete with her wardrobe—and wouldn't know where to find such cloth as she preferred—and she had jewels the like of which he'd never seen before. He was slightly mollified to note the ring he'd placed on her finger at their wedding was never gone from her hand.

She liked words. And mayhap actions. Certainly, she preferred straight talk to flattery. But when he praised her—she became suspicious. He grunted. It was as if the lass had never heard a compliment before.

"How do ye woo a lass who doesnae wish to be wooed?" he mused.

Rory glanced up from the blade he was sharpening. "Ye speak of the agreement?" he asked, voice low to keep from drawing attention to their conversation. Noises at the smithy tended to drown out unshouted banter, but who knew when an idle ear would make the effort to listen.

Caelen nodded. He slid a look about the area beneath the shed where several men carefully honed their weapons. He rose, jerking his head for Rory to follow. A few curious glances followed them, but quickly returned to their exacting tasks.

"Ye have decided, then, to change the contract between ye?" Rory asked.

It was scarcely a question, and Caelen gave a slight shrug. "I confess the lass has captured my attention."

Rory grinned. "'Tis about time ye realized it. She can scarce keep her eyes from ye, and ye have been hanging about like a moonstruck calf these past weeks."

"Weeks? Nae. Mayhap a few days."

"Ye have been making eyes at her since before the debacle with MacGillonay," Rory declared.

"Do ye believe she can be convinced to give up this notion she has?" Caelen asked.

Rory's eyebrows shot up. "Not if ye take that position," he declared. "Ye told me 'twas a mutual agreement, that neither of ye cared to involve yerself with the other. Simply because ye have changed yer mind doesnae mean ye can now deem it a poor idea."

Caelen scratched his jaw. "I dinnae know how to make things different. I gave her flowers, complimented her. What does a lass like her want?"

"My guess is respect," Rory replied. "Though that will only make yer life easier, not necessarily get her in yer bed."

"My life is already easier because of her. I want her willingly in my bed."

"Give her something no one else has," Rory advised.

Caelen sent him a scathing look. "Ye have seen our coffers. They dinnae lend themselves to extravagant purchases. And I cannae top my wife's jewel collection. She has stones the like of which I've never seen. A few appear to have been laid by a rather large, garish bird."

Rory laughed. "She willnae blink an eye at gems, unless they adorn the hilt of a new sword. And I've seen her weaponry. 'Tis matchless." He halted and Caelen swung about to face him. Rory turned serious.

"Spend time with yer wife," he said. "Ask about her life in the Holy Land, what the world is like there. She has seen things ye and I can only dream of and has likely seen more of battle, as well. Share with her more than simply the clan problems. Tell her of yer life as a lad in the Highlands. I'd wager she'll be interested to hear the tale.

"Make her understand she's of more value to ye than her dowry and ability to keep yer home. A man who seeks only his wife's joining in the bedchamber but not in the rest of his life, soon will receive the same half portion he gives."

Caelen grunted. "And where did ye gain such knowledge of women, my unmarried friend?" He recognized his sarcasm was a poor way to hide his own ignorance of keeping a wife, but the obvious difference in Rory's advice and his own experience humbled him.

Rory offered a sanguine smile. "The men in my family value their women as more than a ready vessel to slake their lusts and bear their children. They are careful who they tie themselves to, then commit to forging a true partnership much like a smithy combines iron and coal in his forge." He arched a brow. "And I will be as careful when it comes time for my wee sister to marry," he added.

Caelen realized the truth of Rory's claim as he recalled the couple he'd considered a second set of parents, now cold in the grave. An odd sensation clutched the center of his chest as he recognized the grief of not being able to consult the wisdom of his elders. Their clan had lost more to the epidemic than he'd initially realized.

"How do I go about forging such a bond when I've nae but bitterness to draw upon from my past marriage?"

Rory shook his head. "Ye ever see a goal and plow ahead, not minding the tender plants ye trample along the way. The men call ye Bull of the Highlands for good reason, my friend. In wooing yer wife, move only a step at a time. Give her something ye value and have never shared with another," Rory advised. "Give her something of yerself."

Chapter Twenty Nine

Zora unfolded her feet from the seat of the wide chair, stretching her toes toward the hearth. Arbela sent her a questioning look, reluctant to retire to her room even if her aunt showed signs of restlessness.

"Ye have married a thoughtful man," Zora murmured. "I wonder why ye linger by the fire when your husband awaits ye."

Arbela sighed, dragging herself from the pleasant drowsy state she'd fallen into after she and Zora had put Bram to bed. "My husband will not miss me." The admission stung.

"Those are not the words of a woman in the first weeks of marriage," Zora noted. "I understand these things can take time, but it pains me to see the two of ye have drifted so far apart."

"Do not make an issue of this, please," Arbela bid. "Ye cannot see my heart."

"No, that is true. But I can see the sadness in your eyes, and I think the two are not unrelated. Is there a reason ye have not spoken of what keeps you from his bed?" Zora leaned closer. "I see no signs of physical abuse, and I have had the care of ye for nearly a sennight. Though ye collect bruises as most young women collect embroidery thread, I did not see anything unusual. Has he berated ye unjustly? Words can create deeper wounds."

"No," Arbela replied, a ghost of a smile warring with her morose thoughts. "I believe he understands raising a hand to me would be a very bad idea. And his words are ever polite."

"Only polite?" Zora asked. "His actions speak of more."

"I am happy ye see him so," Arbela said, not wishing to enter into this conversation with her too observant aunt.

"Arbela, I believe there is more to this than ye will admit. Though it has been many years since I shared my life with a husband, mayhap I have a modicum of advice to share. Or at the very least, a sympathetic ear."

Arbela sent a glance to Bram's bed, reassuring herself he slept. "I have a perfectly agreeable marriage, *morak'uyr*." *Aunt*.

"That would explain why neither of ye spend any time in the other's presence," Zora mocked softly.

Arbela sighed, wishing she was not tempted to share her dilemma. But the thought of extending her vows to a marriage bed chilled her aching heart, and she knew of no one else to whom she could speak. She could not explain the sinking feeling as she discovered her husband's changed attitude. Many women would enjoy Caelen's attentions. Why could she not accept what he offered?

Because she did not know how deep the hook was buried.

"Caelen and I agreed to the marriage for two reasons," she began. "He needed my dowry as well as someone to care for and protect Bram." She sighed again. "I wished for a marriage where there was no expectation for me to change. He had no desire for me, nor I for him, and we promised to live amiably, though separate."

Zora remained silent as Arbela waited for the disagreement she felt certain would follow her admission. When Zora said nothing, Arbela added to her defense.

"I have seen women swallowed up in their husbands' expectations. No longer free to do anything other than submit to a common list of broodmare, household chores, and being available for their husbands' whims."

"Some women crave children and their own household, though I see this does not interest ye." Zora shifted again in her chair, leaning a bit closer. "But what of relationship? A marriage based on nothing more than fulfilling a shallow role often leaves the heart cold. But if a wife and her husband care for each other—and tend this relationship with affection and trust—all else will fall into its natural place."

"Isn't *natural place* another phrase for *women's work*?" Arbela drawled. "I have been accused of many things, but desiring woman's work is not one of them."

Zora's soft laugh confused Arbela. An impression plagued her . . . one that told her she'd missed something important in the fight to maintain her freedom. The sensation was *not* a pleasant one.

"There is a time and a place for everything, *im dustry*. Giving of oneself grows your heart. Caring for someone else enlarges your capacity to receive love. If a husband and wife truly have regard for one another, raising children and caring for the home offers many opportunities to show their esteem. Simply because ye and Caelen have some of the same strengths does not mean neither can offer help where a weakness is perceived."

"Nowhere in my marriage is there a place for that sort of regard," Arbela noted. "Merely an understanding that each will perform their duties, negating the need for interference from the other."

Zora's head tilted sadly to the side. "My poor child. Have I not loved ye enough over the years? Has your father or brother not shown ye how much they respect the skills ye have?"

Arbela gave Zora a startled look. "Of course ye have loved me— cared for me and given timely advice. Father has always loved me—with only a small dislike of some of my more suspect skills," she added with an attempt at humor. "And Alex—he is my brother and prone to teasing, but he has always championed me."

"Then why do ye assume your husband cannot also do these things?"

Arbela laughed to cover her unease. "My husband was nicknamed *Bull* years ago for his stubbornness. He loves Bram in his own way, and has applauded my skills, though as they were used in his defense, that is only fair. But he steadfastly refuses to give a woman a role in his life. And after hearing rumors of his first wife, I believe there is just cause."

"He cares for ye, Arbela," Zora insisted softly. "I had no illusions he married ye out of love, and I am certain ye did not think such a foolish thing. Stubborn he may be, but I do not believe he is hard-hearted. My only experience in his presence has been since I arrived here nearly three weeks ago. I have observed many small acts of kindness on his behalf. Unless there is more I do not see, I would suspect your husband is falling in love with ye."

* * *

Cold water sluiced over Caelen's neck and head. He straightened, shaking his head, sending the excess moisture flying. Dark eyes framed by a mass of midnight hair stared at him from the other side of the trough, the body beneath clothed in a tunic of the shimmering dark red silk his wife favored. He blinked through the prismatic water droplets in disbelief, but Arbela's form remained.

He quelled his body's sudden surge of interest and rubbed the linen square briskly over his head before draping it across his shoulders.

"To what do I owe this pleasure?" he asked. A swift ripple of concern sent his heart racing, but returned to a normal beat at Arbela's steady gaze. *This isnae about Bram.*

Arbela moved toward him, her body swaying gently at her hesitant step. She paused, a fingertip on the edge of the horse trough as though testing its balance.

"I have had an interesting discussion with my aunt," she said. Lifting her gaze to his, he saw something wary lurking in the dark depths. "I have mulled her thoughts over since then, and believe I should discuss this with ye."

Caelen swept the linen cloth from his shoulders and gave a slight bow. "By all means, I am anxious to hear what ye—or Zora—have to say."

Arbela's cheeks flushed. "These are my thoughts, though prodded by something she said." She fell into step with him and Caelen considered yet another aspect of his wife that was unexpected. Other women preceded him, or perhaps fell a pace or two behind. Arbela maintained pace with him, at his side.

He liked it.

Rory's words came to mind abruptly and he halted. Arbela sent him a questioning look.

"Shall we go someplace private?" he asked. "I deem this is more than a discussion of the state of the pantry ye have in mind."

Arbela nodded and turned with him to the gate. He waved off a silent offer of a discrete guard to accompany them, a slight grin tugging at his lips at the thought his wife wasn't protection enough. He'd watched her closely enough to know she never carried fewer than five blades hidden on her person. Her eye was quick and she would not fall apart at the first hint of danger.

What could he not accomplish with a dozen men of Arbela's skills and intelligence?

They strolled toward the beach, but took the sloping rise to the south, the same route Arbela had traveled nearly a month earlier as she fled—and then returned to—Dunfaileas. Doubling back on the castle, they approached the walls from the southern ridge.

"I was in this spot with Alex," Arbela murmured. She paced from Caelen's side to the sheer drop that overlooked Dunfaileas. She stood there a moment before facing him. "A good archer could pick off the men on the wall."

Startled, Caelen moved beside her, judging the distance. A soldier, his body indistinct lines and shadow, walked the parapet.

"'Tis too far," Caelen asserted.

Arbela shrugged. "I do not have my bow or I would test my assertion. As I said, it would take a good archer, mayhap an excellent one. And poor weather would destroy his aim. Something to consider."

"Though I appreciate yer insight on the castle's defense, I brought ye here because it was a favorite place of mine when I was a lad."

Arbela sent him an interested look and it warmed his heart. Emboldened, Caelen continued. "My da was a harsh man and dinnae abide idleness. Yet, there were times I needed a spot out of his sight and knowledge, a place that was mine alone." He jerked his chin toward the small bay. "The view from here is good, aye?"

Her face lit with the lowering sun's rays as she faced the vista. Caelen steeled his body against the enchanting sight, her skin golden, the threads in her tunic sparkling as the light wind molded the cloth to her body. He tried seeing the bay through her eyes, the single tower of Dunfaileas rising from behind the wall, reflected in the placid waters of the loch. Framed by overhead boughs, the boats returning from a day's fishing appeared as no more than a lad's toys.

"In autumn, when summer's heat is gone and the leaves change color from green to an array of red, orange and yellow, 'tis truly spectacular," he said.

Arbela shook her head. "I do not know if it is the thought of *this* being summer's heat, the idea of such a colorful view, or the fact that I find an artist's heart in yer warrior's body that challenges me the most."

The awkwardness of speaking his thoughts—those from his heart which he'd hidden deep—slipped away beneath her gentle words. "Tell me of summer in the Levant," he invited.

Her eyes closed as though to help retrieve the memories. "Heat, enough to dry your bones, seeps through your skin. Batroun is in the mountain passes only a few miles inland, but enough to temper the summer sun. The wind is hot and dry, though the air is quite humid along the coast."

"And no rain?" he teased.

Arbela opened her eyes. "Ye have more rain in a week than we do in a year," she replied, a smile lifting one corner of her mouth. Caelen's heart stuttered and he found he could not break his gaze away from the soft curve—so inviting. He stepped closer, fingertips drawing gentle lines down her cheek. Her face tilted upward and he touched his lips to hers.

So soft. So incredibly soft. They parted, allowing his tongue a small foray against hers. Arbela's breath caught, but she did not draw back. Caelen slid a hand around her waist and pulled her close, catching fire with a jolt as her body touched his. Battling his flaming response, he broke the kiss on a sigh and touched his forehead to hers, drawing on unknown reserves of strength to keep from encircling her with his arms and crushing her against him.

"What did ye wish to speak of?" he asked.

She slipped her palms over his chest. "This."

* * *

The touch of his lips on hers sent her world spinning. It wasn't an obligatory *kiss the bride* peck, nor a hesitant fumble between two people who didn't know each other and were reluctant to take the relationship farther. It fell short of demanding, but Arbela sensed he held back, giving her the power to accept or withdraw. It was her decision where the kiss led, her decision whether to kiss him at all.

She placed her palms at the points of his jaw and pulled his face closer. She nibbled his lower lip and instantly felt his pulse leap beneath her hands. There was power in the kiss—her kiss—and the knowledge nearly swept her away.

Heat rushed through her, pooling low in her belly. She drew back, startled at the sensation. A month earlier she'd had no desire for his touch, and the consummation of their vows had driven one point home. She would lack nothing if he never touched her again.

"What has changed?" she breathed, then stiffened, startled she'd voiced the question aloud.

"I care for ye," Caelen responded, his voice a whisper.

"Why? Ye cared for naught more than my dowry when ye married me." She truly wanted to know why he sought her favors now. Why he seemed to want her in his life. Why her aunt appeared to be right.

"I dinnae know ye, and to my shame, decided ye wouldnae change my mind about women—ye were too outlandish for that."

"We have ever struck sparks from each other," Arbela replied. "But they were angry, for I did not want a husband and ye did not want a wife, yet we had no recourse."

"I find ye utterly fascinating," Caelen admitted. "Must there always be an explanation?"

Arbela smiled gently. "In evaluating an enemy, in planning a defense—aye. It must be explained. In the heart? I do not find it so easy to define."

"I wish to savor this newness," Caelen said, brushing the pad of his thumb across her lower lip. "I dinnae wish to spoil what we have before us. Mayhap we should take this one step at a time."

Relief swept over her. Relief that a kiss or touch would not end in a distasteful tumble on the bed—or on the ground. It was too soon to consider the fullness of marriage, and exploring their relationship seemed a good place to start.

Arbela cupped his cheek in her palm. "I would like that."

Chapter Thirty

"Why can't I teach Toros to be a war dog?" Bram asked, right on the heels of complaining about weeding the garden. Arbela took the change in subject in stride, as she had all morning.

"I could teach him to hunt dragons," he insisted as he unenthusiastically dug a weed from the soil with the end of a stick. Slinging dirt as he modified his garden implement into a dragon slayer, he leapt down the carefully turned row, shouting his challenge to an imaginary foe.

"Back, ye dragon bastard!" he cried.

"Bram!" Arbela rapped out. He whirled, question in his eyes. "I have told ye before. That is not a word ye shall use. What do ye suppose will help ye remember?"

His face fell, and he stared at the ground, swatting his stick back and forth in ill-humor. Finally, he shrugged. "Da uses it."

"And I shall speak to him about it," Arbela assured him. "However, 'tis not a word I wish to hear from ye again. Do I make myself clear?"

Bram nodded reluctantly. "It feels good on my tongue," he admitted.

Arbela smothered a laugh.

"Then we shall come up with ten other words ye can use in its place. I will start." She tilted her head. "What about, back, ye foul swine?"

Bram giggled. "Back, ye cowardly beast!"

"Back, ye craven lizard!" Arbela shot back.

"Back, ye . . .." Bram huffed a breath, at a loss. His eyes lit as inspiration struck. "Ye big poop!"

Arbela rolled her eyes. "I think we'll go with one of the others, aye?"

Bram laughed. "Aye. I will try not to say bastard again."

Arbela leveled a stern gaze at him. His hand flew to his mouth, covering half his face.

"Why don't we take Ari and Voski for a ride?" Arbela asked, redirecting his attention from his indiscretion. Immediately diverted, Bram nodded vigorously.

"Yay!" he shouted, dropping his stick to the ground.

Arbela surveyed the half-weeded garden. "As soon as this row is finished, we will go to the stable. We cannot leave all of the work to Cook's helpers. I'll race ye to the end."

Bram snatched up his stick and dug up the remaining weeds with gratifying speed and at least some attention to the garden plants. "Hurry, Bela!" he said. "Ari is waiting."

Arbela gathered the handful of weeds into a pile to be collected later and darted after the excited boy. She felt Garen and Toros' absence acutely, but they had gone out again with Rory and the shepherd after reports of another missing sheep.

Bram struggled with his saddle, lean muscled arms not quite up to the task of heaving the chunk of wood and leather up to his pony's back. Arbela gave him a quick hand, then tacked Voski. The golden horse nipped at her with his thick lips, ears flattening in challenge when she scolded him.

She sent Bram to the small pen for a brisk warm-up, taking Voski to the larger paddock to give him space to stretch his legs at the end of his lead rope before she matched him against the pony. Bram quickly grew bored with the confines of the pen.

"Can we ride to the loch?" he asked.

Arbela considered the risk. No boats had been seen on the loch since MacGillonay's defeat, but it was still the best approach for an attack. They'd ridden there several times in the last week, but always with Caelen and often two or three other soldiers in attendance. Today, the men worked to barrel whisky for the Dunfaileas portion of MacLean's first shipment abroad. Privately, Arbela doubted the whisky would make it as far as the Mediterranean, and would likely create a market much closer to home. But it was the first of many such shipments, and Caelen had worked hard to get it right, even to the stamp which the blacksmith had created showing a castle and its mirrored image, adding impact to the name Dunfaileas—*reflection fort.*

"We cannot ask your father to go with us today, Bram-jan. Mayhap we could ride to the burn instead."

His puckered lips said he'd rather race Ari in the lapping waves of Loch Linnhe, but he agreed without further protest. With a quick glance to the sky and a short prayer to keep the gathering clouds at bay long enough to give Bram a bit more time outside, Arbela led the way through the gates of Dunfaileas.

Ari was in a bright mood, kicking up his heels as he gave his young rider a lesson in balance and tenacity. Full of energy, Bram whooped his delight as he clung tight to the pony's back.

Her thoughts drifting far from the boy and his pony, Arbela lifted her face to the elusive sun, relishing its furtive touch. Not as much as she found herself enjoying Caelen's caresses, she admitted to herself with a secret smile. Who knew he could be so patient? So interested in what pleased her, what she had to say. Warmth stole through her as she remembered the stroke of his fingertips as they lay abed the night before, speaking softly of Voski's ancestors, how he would fit into the bloodline Caelen wished to create. She'd described the horses of her homeland, something she fortunately could do without much concentration, for Caelen's lazy fingers had completely destroyed her conscious line of thought. With a laugh and a brief kiss, he'd bid her sweet dreams before tucking her beneath his arm and falling asleep.

At least, she thought he slept. She certainly had not as the lingering sparks he'd ignited took what seemed like hours to fade. His chest had risen and fallen rhythmically, a light snore on his lips, but the tented sheet below his waist had remained, tempting her to explore, though she hadn't been ready for the potential consequences.

The absurdity of her situation hadn't struck her until she'd woken alone this morning, curious about the cautious path to which she found herself clinging. As a young girl, she'd wondered what it would be like to have a man admire her for herself. Not for her father's wealth, or for her ability to strike a target with an arrow at fifty paces. Nor for her thick hair or full figure—things her friends assured her drew a man's eye. But simply because she made someone's heart sing.

She'd finally come to the realization she'd married a man who showed true interest in her, though that had certainly not been his original intent. In the past few days he'd given her his time and attention, spoken to her as if she was his equal, and kept his promise of not pushing her into marital duties faster than she was willing to go. If he was not what she'd originally expected in this marriage, was it a bad thing?

Why did she dig in her heels? Was she a coward? Granted, she had been unimpressed with her wedding night, but did that mean it could not be improved upon? Her heart tripled its beat as she considered pairing the actions of lovemaking with the shivers and sparks of his exploring hands and kisses.

Dappled shadows trailed across her face and arms, pulling her attention to the treelined path as they entered the forest. Bram rode ahead, bouncing lightly on Ari's plump back. Voski's ears twitched side to side. The hairs on the back of Arbela's neck prickled. The warm lassitude vanished, replaced by the cold awareness that something was amiss.

Green leaves rustled. The scent of water rushing over stones and damp soil and mosses assailed her nose. Light bounced across the ground, leaping between the leaves dancing in the breeze. Bram's chortles of glee rushed back to her. She looked up sharply, seeing the swish of Ari's dark tail as he rounded a curve in the trail.

"Bram!" Arbela called, sudden concern shrilling her voice. Hooves thudded on the trail ahead. Ari jarring to a stop? Or another horse and rider? She thudded her heels against Voski's side, sending him racing over the ground, her ears straining, seeking Bram's voice. Silence.

Voski closed the gap in moments, dropping his shoulder as he rounded the curve at speed. Arbela clung to his back, hands fisted in the pale golden mane that whipped her face, her body tucked against the curve of his neck and withers, eyes glued to the trail ahead.

Ari braced motionless, legs locked, head lowered to the boy at his feet. His front hooves all but cradled Bram's head. Reins trailing, he nuzzled Bram's cheek. Arbela pulled on Voski's reins, dropping to the ground before his hooves skidded to a stop. She checked her speed, shoving her anxiety deep inside to keep from spooking Bram's pony.

Ari flicked his good ear and nuzzled the boy again. Bram rolled his head and coughed once. Instantly, Ari stepped gingerly away, leaving Arbela a clear path to the boy's side. Bram sucked in a deep breath and turned wide eyes to Arbela, his lips working to form words.

Arbela fell to her knees at his side, touching soothing fingertips to his cheek. "Took a tumble?" she asked mildly, hiding her fear from the boy as she surveyed his body for obvious injury. Relief sliced cold through her as she noted straight limbs and clearing eyes. Bram struggled to sit and she placed a palm on his chest.

"Let's check ye over, first," she said as Bram settled back to the ground. One by one, she had him move his limbs, watching for any flicker of pain. Satisfied he was whole, if a bit winded, she helped him to his feet.

"I fell off," Bram admitted, his voice a bit hoarse.

"Tell me about it," Arbela invited.

A faint blush tinted Bram's cheeks. "I heard ye call me, and it startled me, so I pulled back hard on the reins. Too hard," he admitted. "Ari stopped and I dinnae. I think I flipped over his head."

"It happens to the best riders," Arbela said. "Though I am certain Ari would appreciate less of a tug on his delicate mouth in the future. And I am sorry I startled ye. Something has me worried."

272

"What?" Bram asked, peering into the forest. Arbela's gaze lit on Ari. The pony stared into the shadows, ear pricked forward, the lines of his sturdy body poised for flight. He stamped a hoof.

"I'm not certain," Arbela hedged, not wanting to alarm Bram further. She placed her hand on the hilt of her sword. Wolf? A stranger on a horse unfamiliar to Ari? Voski's alert gaze followed Ari's. Arbela listened for an answering stamp to Ari's challenge, an action nearly impossible for a rider to quell.

Leaves rustled. Arbela grabbed Bram and flung him into his saddle. She shoved the reins into his hands as she met his startled gaze. "Do not stop until ye reach Dunfaileas," she ordered, dragging the pony around to face down the trail. She smacked her palm against Ari's ample rump and the pony leapt forward, Bram clinging gamely to his back.

Knowing Voski would not follow the pony without her, she faced the forest, balancing lightly on the balls of her feet, weight slightly forward. Every nerve in her body tingled, aware of every flashing mote of light, each sway of shadow. The deep, earthy scent of churned, rotting leaves from the forest floor separated sharply from the tang of pine needles. The gurgle of the burn a counterpoint to Voski's staccato breaths as he drank in the air.

Branches crackled with a *swoosh* of leaves. Arbela vaulted onto Voski's back. He danced a step, lithe between her knees. Hooves crunched the debris of the forest floor a short distance away in a rhythmic tattoo, the sound fading as the animal hurried away.

Whirling Voski to follow Bram, she sent him racing back to Dunfaileas.

She reached the gates as Caelen swung Bram from his pony. His head jerked toward her as Voski thundered into the keep, his brow furrowed.

"What has happened?" he barked, his gaze sliding to his son whose excited chatter riddled the air. Caelen grabbed Voski's reins as Arbela quickly dismounted.

Men paused in their duties, their hesitance filling the air with expectation. Arbela brought her apprehension-charged breathing under control.

"We may have encountered someone on the trail," she said, loud enough for her voice to carry to the anxious ears. "Though we saw no one."

With a quick glance to their laird, the clansmen drifted slowly away, relief almost palpable.

"Why did ye send Bram racing back without ye?" Caelen asked, his voice taut.

Arbela gave Bram a smile to smooth over the accusation in his father's question, then turned to Caelen. "We rode to the burn, but something did not seem right. I called to Bram to halt, and when both our horses insisted there was something in the forest, I sent him away from the possible danger, though I lingered a moment to see if I could determine what it was."

"I fell off Ari!" Bram exclaimed, tugging on Caelen's arm.

Arbela sighed. It wasn't that she did not wish Caelen to find out Bram had fallen from the pony's back, and it was clear he'd sustained no injury, it was simply not the time she would have chosen to broach the subject.

Caelen's gaze snapped to his son. "What happened?" he demanded. Arbela winced at his tone, but Bram was too caught up in his tale to notice.

"Arbela shouted at me and I told Ari to stop," Bram said, glossing over the fact he'd sawed heavily enough on the reins to cause the pony's abrupt halt. "And I *flew* over his head and *slammed* into the ground," he added, emphasizing each action with raised voice. "I couldnae breathe!"

"The fall knocked the breath from him," Arbela interjected calmly in an attempt to downplay Bram's somewhat embellished story. Caelen gave her a sharp look then knelt before Bram, relieving Arbela of her worry he'd rage over the details. At least not in front of Bram.

274

"Always grip with yer knees, lad," Caelen said. "Did the fall injure ye?"

Bram swayed his upper body from side to side as he chewed his lower lip thoughtfully. "Nae. Arbela checked me. I dinnae need to see the healer."

Caelen ran his hands lightly over his son's arms and peered into his eyes, then chucked him under his chin. "Then take yer pony to the stable and give him a good rubbing. He was brave to bring ye home so quickly and deserves an extra handful of oats. But no more," he admonished, waving a finger before Bram's face. "Ye dinnae wish to give yer pony a sour stomach."

Bram nodded and stepped toward the stable, Ari following placidly. Caelen watched the boy's progress for a moment, then turned to Arbela.

"Tell me what you found."

Somewhat taken aback by his calm tone and surprised he did not immediately accuse her of putting Bram in danger, Arbela hesitated, shifting from thoughts of Bram to remembering what she'd noticed in the forest, shying away from the guilt fluttering through her that she'd taken her attention from their surroundings by daydreaming instead of protecting Bram with every ounce of her being.

"As soon as Bram was away, I noticed the quiet. No birds, though we'd made enough noise to silence them. But they did not resume with Bram's absence. Both horses had alerted to something in the woods, though I could not determine what it was. Voski continued to scent the air and after several moments, hoofbeats pounded on the ground only a short distance away. I had originally wondered if we'd encountered the wolf, but I am now certain it was a rider who did not wish to be seen."

Caelen absorbed Arbela's words without comment. A moment of silence stretched between them, then he nodded. "I will send someone to search the area. I am glad ye and Bram are safe."

Caelen's hard gaze changed before her eyes, from hardened warrior, inflexible laird, and solicitous father into something warmer, inviting, encompassing her in a wealth of caring—and the flutter began anew in Arbela's belly. Leaning forward, Caelen lowered his head and kissed her.

Chapter Thirty One

Relief, panic, and desire slammed through Arbela, completely overwhelming her, overriding the intentions and beliefs she'd clung to in terror of losing herself. Had Caelen been arrogant, brutish, or demanding, she could have resisted him—and had, for well over a month. A month in which he'd been no more than distant, polite, and undemanding. The past weeks of unexpected change, however, had worn away at her resistance—softly, insistently, as one polished a cherished object to coax a reluctant shine.

His lips skimmed hers with a gentleness that took her breath away. Warmth, like sunlight after a cold rain, shimmered hot beneath her skin, and she eased upward on her toes to deepen the kiss. Caelen's mouth slanted across hers in acceptance, then slid slowly across her cheek.

"I believe we should discuss this further where there are no prying eyes," he murmured in her ear. His breath stirred against her skin, raising hensflesh on her neck and shoulders. Realization of where she stood quickly doused the prickles, but the accompanying heat hummed insistently through her veins.

Caelen cocked his head. "Mayhap ye could impose upon yer aunt to engage Bram in a game or two of *Fierges* whilst the rain keeps him inside?"

A roll of thunder punctuated his thinly veiled question. A drop of rain landed on her nose and others kicked up puffs of dust in the ground around them. Arbela nodded. "I will see to it." Her cheeks flushed hotly at the faint rasp of her voice.

Bram scampered across the yard as thunder rumbled yet again. "Dinnae get wet!" he shouted as he passed, heading into the hall. Arbela's head spun, torn between chasing down her stepson and attending his sire.

With a low chuckle, Caelen pulled her against him.

"Five minutes, no longer," he whispered, then released her with another fierce kiss.

Arbela's breath grew shallow as she hurried into the keep. The enormity of the step she anticipated loomed before her. She wound her way up the stairs, scarcely feeling the stone beneath her booted feet, and found Zora bent over a piece of embroidery in Bram's chamber.

"Could ye . . . that is, Bram . . .." Arbela stared at her aunt, her tongue in a hopeless tangle. Heat twisted in her core and she dropped her gaze to the floor. Embarrassed.

"Shall I mind the boy for ye this afternoon?" Zora asked mildly, setting her sewing aside. She rose and glided to Arbela's side, lifting her chin with a gentle touch of her fingers. "I will be happy to do so. He is an engaging child." A small smile played about her lips. "Mayhap 'tis time for another."

Arbela bit her lip, stifling her protest. To deny Zora's assumption would be naught more than a convenient lie.

Zora tilted her head. "I will entertain him below stairs whilst ye prepare yerself. Take whatever oils and such from my belongings as ye wish."

"He said five minutes," Arbela blurted. She clamped her mouth shut as new heat flamed in her cheeks.

Zora laughed. "Take at least ten, *im destry*. 'Twill be worth it." Without waiting for Arbela's reply, she swept from the room in a rustle of silk and the delicate chime of bracelets.

Arbela shook herself and spun on her heel, crossing the hall to Caelen's—*their*—room where she quickly divested herself of her stained clothing. She set the latch in the door to hinder interruptions and poured water from the ewer into the basin, adding a few drops of rose oil. Breathing in the scent, she swiftly bathed, then toweled dry as she stared at the garments available to her. Choosing the heavy brocade robe, she belted it loosely about her waist then unbraided her hair, combing through the long strands with her fingers.

Her toilette firmed her mind on the path she'd chosen and relief settled over her, freeing the burden of indecision, leaving her almost giddy. The door latch rattled, pricking Arbela's mood. Rather than entertain the nagging doubt that rose at the sound, she quashed it beneath a surge of excitement spreading sweet as warmed honey.

She released the latch and opened the door. Her blood heated at the sight of Caelen's damp, bare chest, evidence he'd also taken time to sluice off sweat and grime. Clearly, he thought this moment to be important. Her heart soared with unexplainable joy.

"I'd prefer to stare at ye from *that* side of the door," he murmured with a nod inside the room.

With a swirl of her robe, she stepped to the side and granted him entrance. Caelen pressed the latch home with a *snick*. Arbela's pulse raced wildly. Should her wedding night have been like this? Excited to be in her husband's presence, anxious to have his arms about her, longing for his kiss? Quite different from the calculating desire to engage in the proper motions to seal their marriage vows.

She met Caelen's gaze, and the bottom dropped out of her stomach.

Dinnae muck this up. Caelen stared hungrily at Arbela, glad he'd managed the calm words to get him inside the room, for at this moment nothing above his waist functioned properly. Her eyes sparkled, and if he'd drunk a barrel of whisky, he'd not feel more disoriented—or euphoric.

Even after acknowledging the lass had captured his interest, and after a week of fumbling about, attempting to garner his wife's notice, and after an additional week coaxing her to trust—and hopefully accept—him, this was the first time he'd looked his fill at the woman he'd married. And the first time she'd stared back with such frank interest—and invitation.

"I'll—" Caelen halted and cleared his throat, smoothing the rough edge of his voice. "I accept all ye offer, Arbela. And ye may say yea or nae as ye will."

A lift of a dark brow asked a silent question. Caelen's grimace at his bumbling words pressed into a half-grin.

"I wish ye to have choice over what happens. Not doubt or remorse afterward," he attempted to explain.

Arbela's lips softened and one hand rose to the belt of her robe. Caelen took a step toward her. "No," he breathed, and immediately chided himself for the look of confusion on Arbela's face.

"May I?" he asked, reaching for the thick silken tie. He chanced a look at her face, relieved to find the pale dismay replaced by heightened color in each cheek.

"Aye," she murmured, relaxing her hand to her side.

Caelen stood close enough to feel the heat from her body, scent the aroma of roses that wafted from her skin. He captured her waist and drew his hands around the full curve of her hips, then back to the trailing edge of her belt. He gave it a quick tug and the knot slithered apart. Arbela caught her breath on an inhale. Caelen fingered the edges of her robe.

"Something bothers ye still," he murmured. "Speak plainly so we may work this through."

"I wish to do this," Arbela replied, "but the concern lingers I will lose myself as I become, not Arbela, but the laird's wife."

"And if I said I dinnae wish to lose Arbela?" Caelen asked. "That she and my wife could be the same?"

Relief smoothed her brow. "Ye do not wish to change me?"

Caelen shook his head. He could not imagine a worse fate. "Nae."

A smile flashed in her eyes, and a blow of desire struck Caelen's chest, thrusting outward, hardening his body. He gripped the edges of her robe, whitening his knuckles.

"If I remain Arbela," she warned, her voice soft, "I will not become a biddable woman who chatters constantly about babies and household gossip."

Caelen's bark of amusement rang. "By St. Andrew's crooked nose, I would hope not! I'd not risk changing ye into a woman who reminds me of my dead wife." His humor fell. "I want ye—Arbela. And all that entails. Will ye have me as yer husband?"

"If I take ye as my husband, I will give in to the temptation to do this," she murmured, raising a hand to cup his cheek. He turned his face into her caress, dropping a kiss to her palm.

"Ye may touch me however and wherever ye wish," he rasped, his voice betraying his passion.

"And ye will touch me?" Arbela's voice fluttered.

"Mayhap we could discover what ye do and dinnae like."

He loosened his grip, drawing the edges of her robe apart, spilling her breasts to his gaze. Kneeling before her, he cupped her breasts, pressing them gently together. Arbela gasped as he opened his mouth, drawing the tip of one breast inside in a slow, suckling movement. His fingers kneaded her soft flesh, his tongue rasping across the tight peak. Arbela grasped his shoulders, fingers biting hard into the muscle, bracing against the sway of her legs.

Caelen slowly released her breast and stood. "I happen to like that. Quite a bit, actually. Though, if ye dinnae, I would not . . .." He grinned. "I would *try* to not do it again. 'Twould be difficult, but I would attempt to honor yer wishes."

"Nae," Arbela croaked. "I like it, as well."

Laying his palms against her shoulders, Caelen slowly swept her robe back, and Arbela let it fall to the floor. "This is also what I like," he murmured. "Yer skin is warm, kissed by the sun." His hands fell to her full breasts, down the slender expanse of her waist, and over the swell of her hips. "I could lose myself for hours in yer curves."

His kisses feathered across her skin, spreading henflesh in their wake.

His blood ran hot and fast, but he remembered their wedding night, and resolved he would somehow change her opinion of lovemaking from a burden she endured to a pleasure she was willing to pursue.

Taking her hand, he led her to the bed, sweeping back the coverlets, steeling himself against the outburst he prayed would not come. Ruthie had hated lovemaking, and though he'd eventually found his release with other women, nothing had ever been as important as forging this link with Arbela. She both excited and humbled him. If she bolted, he would not ask again.

Arbela slid onto the bed, her dusky skin a contrast to the sun-whitened sheets. Caelen felt certain he'd never seen anyone so beautiful. She shattered every notion he'd ever entertained as to a comely lass, rebuilding his ideal to her exact, perfect proportions. He unbuckled his belt, dropping his plaide to the floor, then lay next to her, smoothing curls of hair from her face. She reached an arm about his neck and drew him to her, her lips lightly brushing his.

"I like this," she said.

"And this?" he asked, drawing the flat of his hand from her hip to breast, lingering to fondle the fullness. At her murmur of approval, he gently caressed her curves, kneading firm muscle, noting how she relaxed in his arms.

She countered his caresses with innovations of her own, matching his boldness, slowing to a rhythm that had his blood thrumming in his ears. He dropped his palm to the curls between her thighs, encouraged by the heat and dampness he found there. Arbela jerked her hips once as he slid a finger against the swollen skin. He continued his careful exploration, gritting his teeth against the answering thudding pulse of his body.

"Have I found any places ye dinnae like to be touched?" he asked, nipping playfully at her belly to cover his apprehension of her answer. Her gasping giggle brought him up short.

"Ye find my lovemaking amusing?"

"Nae," Arbela replied. "Ye found a sensitive spot."

"A *ticklish* spot?" He sent her a devilish grin before testing the soft skin just beneath her ribs.

"I have never been ticklish in my life," she retorted, though the wary look in her eyes told him otherwise.

"Ye wouldnae lie to yer husband, would ye?"

She shook her head.

"Then we will save this for another time," he murmured, his cock heavy with desire, denying time for foolery. He rose above her, a hand on either side, touching her core lightly. Her eyelids closed as her lips parted. Fighting the urge to give in to the need to sheath himself fully, he teased his way, marveling at how her body adapted to his. Arbela tightened about him, then cried out, pressing herself against him. His arms trembled as he held himself still, but she caught his flanks in her strong hands, forcing him to move. And move. And move.

Her breathless cries added fuel to the fire raging inside him. She arched against him, arms flung wide. He fought against his release and lost, carried away by her passion. His breath roared in his ears, nothing else existing but the tight warmth rippling over him in never-ending waves. Depleted, he still continued, sending Arbela into another spiral of pleasure. His breath rasped in his chest, but her response hardened him again, and he took her again, reaching his second climax quickly.

Weightless, yet too heavy for his arms to support him any longer, he lowered himself atop Arbela, resting his head in the crook of her shoulder, not missing the opportunity to nuzzle her breast. Her heart raced beneath his ear, and she smoothed her fingers over his head as her chest rose and fell with each ragged breath.

"I believe I liked that as well," she whispered.

"Both times?" he asked.

"Aye."

Caelen couldn't have stopped his grin had he tried, but he hid it from her view as he rolled lazily to his side and tucked her against him.

"When I wake, ye can see if there are any touches I dinnae like," he offered.

Arbela's soft laugh sputtered as Caelen drifted off to sleep.

* * *

Sunlight slipped a long, thin edge across the wooden floor. Arbela's mind bolted to wakefulness at the sound of footsteps on the floor, though her eyes were slow to follow. She blinked her heavy lids, bringing Caelen's face into focus as he loomed above her.

He kissed the tip of her nose. "My bonnie wife is awake," he declared. "I will have a tray brought up so ye can break yer fast."

Arbela scrambled to a seated position against the scattered pillows. "Nae. I will eat in the hall."

Caelen grinned. "Ye have missed the morning meal, my love, though Cook has set a tray aside for ye—provided ye are hungry before she serves the noon meal."

Arbela jerked her gaze to the angle of the sunlight. "I have overslept," she said, her thoughts flying over the things she had not done that morning, her skin heating as her wayward mind recalled the things she *had* done in the pearly light of dawn.

"Why the sudden frown, Arbela?" Caelen asked, seating himself on the edge of the bed, one finger tugging lightly at the edge of the sheet she clasped to her breast.

"'Tis naught ye have done," she said, patting his hand—though whether to distract him or reassure him, she was not certain. "I have missed much by lying abed."

Caelen's grin returned. "No one in the castle begrudges ye the sleep." His voice teased, but Arbela flinched.

"They all know what we've been doing?" she asked before she could stop herself.

"Och, aye. And with a long, rainy afternoon, I would suspect many of the others were doing it as well." He brushed his lips across her cheek. "Though surely none as thoroughly nor as pleasurably," he whispered.

He rose to his feet and held out a hand. "Come. If ye insist on rising, we can go down together. I am certain yer aunt has come close to the end of her tether with our son. He has proclaimed his need to practice his archery skills with ye this day."

Arbela's head spun. *Our son.* Her body tingled at his words—and his casual, loving touch. She scrambled from the bed to stand before the reflecting glass Caelen had ordered hung on the wall a sennight earlier. Her long hair lay tousled about her shoulders, and a blush stained her cheeks. The same overly rounded form, short legs and dark-rimmed eyes she knew and recognized reflected back to her in the glossy surface.

She was still Arbela. And yet, the inside, the part no reflecting glass could reveal, felt different. More alive. Loved and cherished in a way she'd never experienced before. Certainly more sensitive, she admitted as Caelen's arms folded about her. He leaned his chin on her shoulder, staring at her in the mirrored surface.

"I like seeing ye thus," he murmured. "Howbeit, if ye wish a bite of food before taking on Bram's antics, I would suggest ye dress yerself. Otherwise, I cannae be held responsible for what might happen."

Her skin prickled, warmth spreading through her limbs. Arbela turned within his embrace. "Mayhap I wish to feed a different hunger," she said, and answered the fierceness of his kiss with one of her own.

Chapter Thirty Two

Bram nestled contentedly between Caelen and Arbela, his eyelids fluttering downward only to snap open as his head sagged. Arbela shot Caelen a smile over the boy's head. He responded with an upward wiggle of one eyebrow, sending sparks swarming through Arbela's veins to cluster low in her belly. She ducked her head to hide the blush heating her cheeks. The low noise of late evening in the hall, as people concluded their day and prepared for their beds, surrounded her in a cocoon of comfort.

"I believe 'tis your bedtime," she murmured, brushing a curling lock of dark brown hair from Bram's brow. Bram struggled to a sitting position, a scowl on his face.

"I havenae had a story," he reminded her, rubbing his eyes with his fists.

"A short one, then," Arbela agreed. A few heads swiveled in her direction, for her tales were well liked, and in the absence of a bard for an evening's entertainment, few chose to miss Arbela's stories.

"Tonight I shall describe for ye animals in the land where I was born," Arbela said. "Ye have many beautiful creatures in your land of Caledonia, but I have seen many fantastic animals in my travels.

"The lion, whose story I told ye once before, is a beautiful beast, with a mane gracing his neck. He is known as *sher* in Persian or *asad* in Arabic, and sometimes *singha*—meaning *courageous lion*—is added to a name to show the person has much courage." Arbela chucked Bram beneath his chin. "Bram MacKernsingha," she demonstrated. Bram laughed softly, fighting sleep to hear Arbela's tale.

"There is a large, catlike animal called a cheetah, which can run faster than the wind. His speckled fur allows him to blend into the rocks and grasses as he hunts his dinner. The hyena appears after the lion or cheetah finishes their meal, scavenging for leftovers. Their doglike bodies are misshapen, legs longer in the front than in the rear, and their fur is striped and coarse. But their bite is amongst the strongest of all animals, allowing them to break large bones and seek the marrow within.

"Oryxes are larger than your cattle, and have horns that stick nearly straight up from their head. Their horns are sharper than the finest blade, and the oryx has been known to kill lions with them. They are beautiful and tasty, but very dangerous."

Bram's body slumped against Arbela's side, and she pulled him close, caressing the soft skin of his cheek. "For ye, my son, there is the caracal. Twice the size of the tabby that roams the upper hall, it is a wild creature that some have been able to tame. Its preferred prey is birds and the caracal can leap from its hiding place and snatch them from the air. They are graceful and intelligent and make admirable hunting companions."

"Can I have a crackle?" Bram mumbled, eyes closed.

"Someday when ye are older, if it is your wish, we will travel to the Levant and ye may choose a caracal," Arbela agreed. "Though ye have many wonderful things to see and do here as well."

Bram nodded, satisfied, his body at last limp as he lost his battle with sleep.

Caelen carefully gathered the boy into his arms and carried him to his chamber as Arbela made certain the fire was damped on the hearth.

"Shall I remain with him until Aunt Zora retires?" Arbela whispered. Caelen laced his fingers through hers and tugged her close.

Dropping a kiss to her lips, he replied, "Nae. We are but across the hall should he have a need. A lad of his years shouldnae require a nurse much longer. We will see to a private room for yer aunt should she wish to remain here."

Arbela hugged Caelen's arm. "Mayhap we could create two adjoining rooms so each could have privacy, yet Bram could still feel comforted by her presence."

"Ye dote on the lad," Caelen protested with a smile. He pressed a kiss to her forehead. "He loves ye, ye know. And he wishes we would gift him with a wee sister or brother soon."

The swirl of heat returned, and Arbela, still new to her husband's teasing, amorous ways—and her body's response—was glad for the semi-darkness that hid her blush.

"I did not know this," she replied.

"Och, the lad will be heartbroken to hear it," Caelen said, his Scot's burr deepening. "He sat at yer side whilst ye healed from yer wounds, telling ye stories no doubt he heard from ye in earlier weeks, and the day before ye woke, he explained ye should get to know me better. From what he gathered, ye and I need to be in accord in order to discuss an addition to our family."

The door to Bram's chamber closed softly and Zora stepped to the boy's side. She twitched the blanket more closely beneath his chin.

"Your husband speaks the truth," she said over her shoulder. "Our Bram wishes for a brother or sister. Mayhap the two of ye should do as he recommended and *discuss* the issue." With fluttery motions, Zora shooed Arbela and Caelen from the room.

Tossing a bold grin to Caelen, Arbela tugged his arm and they left quietly lest they wake Bram. The moment the door closed behind them, Caelen drew Arbela into his arms, slanting his mouth across hers hungrily. Only a few feet from their room, the hall lit by torches scattered along the wall, Arbela softened, leaning her body into his. Caelen's hands slid up her sides to cup her breasts and she moaned.

"A thundering herd of horses wouldnae interrupt ye," a deep voice noted. "And did I have a less urgent matter to discuss, I'd toss ye into yer room and latch the door."

Arbela gasped. Caelen shoved her to his side, a hand sliding toward the dagger at his belt. Her gaze fixed on Rory, his wild hair and stained clothing proclaiming his hurried travel.

"I have just arrived," he commented, "and met with Gordon at the gate. It seems he was reluctant to interrupt his laird this late at night, but it willnae wait."

Ice water could not have doused Arbela's ardor more affectively. Gordon, one of her father's knights, trained and tempered on the Crusades, did not have fanciful notions. She straightened, cold reason replacing the heat within. "What is it?" she asked.

Caelen sent her a narrow look which she returned. "I am not to be coddled," she reminded him. His scowl disappeared almost as quickly as it rose, and he turned to Rory.

"Tell us," he said.

"There is a light on the cliff behind the castle," Rory said. "Gordon thought he noted it yester eve, but found naught when he searched save a bit of charred wood as from a campfire. Though off the main trail, he figured 'twas a traveler—until it repeated this night."

"A single fire?" Caelen asked, already striding down the passageway. Arbela clung to his heels, the broad shoulders of the two men leaving no room for her betwixt them.

"Aye—as best he can tell, and I looked as well before I came for ye." Rory cast a glance over his shoulder. "I wouldnae interrupt without good cause."

Arbela had never been on the receiving end of even veiled ribald jokes before, and her skin twitched uncomfortably. Surely what passed between her and Caelen was private. On the other hand, the production of children was in the best interest of the clan, and therefore, their efforts—or lack thereof—was likely noted. And apparently speculated upon, perhaps even wagered upon, the thought of which caused embarrassed heat to burn her skin.

She grimaced. What she had given Caelen she would share with no other. Somehow, she must learn to counter the bawdy comments with grace—and possibly humor—to separate inquisitiveness from the sanctuary she and Caelen attempted to create behind closed doors.

But she had insisted on being counted one of the men and apparently this was the price. She shoved the indignity deep and focused on the possibility of a threat to all she held dear.

She arrived on the parapet with Caelen and Rory and closed her eyes for a moment to dispel the effects of the torchlight. After a moment, she peered into the inky blackness and spotted a glow that flickered in the dark, yet remained in place.

A campfire.

In a low voice, Caelen sent four men into the night. Their shadows faded into the darkness as torches on the wall were shielded for the moments it took the men to blend into the forest's gloom. Time passed as those on the parapet awaited some sign from the scouts.

Arbela strained her senses, unable to trust her eyes to tell her what she needed to know. Was it a simple traveler? More than one? Was the campfire a feint designed to attract their attention whilst mayhem was enacted elsewhere? A signal of unknown importance?

She sniffed the air, detecting only the faintest trace of smoke. The wind blew from the north, and likely carried sound away as well. Noting Caelen and Rory paid no attention to her, she strode the parapet, passing soldiers along the way. Each gave a brief nod, but did not turn their gazes from their duty. When she reached the section of the wall overlooking the loch, she stopped, staring at the dock stretching across the water, its wooden arms sheltering the clan's small boats.

The waning moon cast little light, but cold white pinpricks bobbed on the inky surface of the water. Black shadows and cold illumination dominated the nightscape. Nothing else intruded. Even the glow of cooking fires through cottage windows was not bright enough to cast their light upon the scene. Peace reigned. Whether real or illusory, it was impossible to determine.

After several long minutes, Arbela nodded to the soldier to her right and made her way back to Caelen and Rory. They seemed to be carved from onyx for all the movement they showed. Anticipation fairly crackled in the air. The firelight on the cliff winked out.

Nearly an hour later, the four men gathered in the hall to tell their tale. A single fire, prepared as though for cooking, had waited alone in a small glen above the castle. Gordon had inspected the ground as best he could whilst the other men had remained watchful. Other than scuffed footprints leading back to the main path, they had discovered nothing.

"I dinnae like travelers having a view over the castle," Caelen admitted with a glance to Arbela. She recalled her earlier note that an archer—an excellent archer—could fire upon Dunfaileas from the vantage point.

"We will create a path in the opposite direction, and a glen if we must, to encourage a different campsite. Though I dinnae care for travelers to cross our lands without permission, until we have enough men for a continuous patrol of our borders, this will have to do."

"My father—" Arbela began.

"We can care for our own," Caelen interrupted with a nod to Gordon. "Yer efforts are appreciated, but I dinnae wish to call upon the MacLean further."

"My father's knights—" Arbela's protest rose, stirring a few resentful looks from sleepy servants who huddled on sleep pallets on the floor of the hall. She tempered her voice. "They are not an affront to your ability to govern your clan. If necessary, we can house the extra help until this danger passes."

"I will determine if more help is needed," Caelen replied stonily. "For now, I dinnae believe this requires such recourse."

Arbela frowned, quelling the urge to shout at him for disparaging her suggestions. "I do not like these small troubles."

The men glanced at her. "What small troubles?" Caelen asked.

"A wolf which we have neither sighted nor killed, and now an abandoned campfire."

"Och, wolves arenae uncommon," Rory replied. "And with Garen and Toros assisting the shepherd, we've nae lost more sheep."

"Whoever lit the campfire was dinnae care to answer for their presence when we arrived," Gordon added.

Arbela sent Gordon a stern look. "Were ye so noisy?" she asked. "I would have thought to approach with caution, not announce your arrival."

"I dinnae believe the incidents are related," Caelen interjected, sending Arbela a look to warn her from further speech with Gordon. Stifling the urge to storm from the room, Arbela leaned back in her chair and regarded him evenly.

With a nod, Caelen sent the men back to their posts with thanks for their diligence. Arbela sat silently until they left the room. Firelight flickered low and a chunky candle burned atop their table. Mutiny glittered in her dark eyes.

"'Tis clear ye dinnae agree with my assessment," Caelen said, tempering his tone against his dislike of interference.

"I do not," she agreed, voice as brittle as his.

Caelen ran his palm over his pate. "The men have good instincts, Arbela," he pressed.

"As do I," Arbela interjected. "I have endured my share of sieges and should be allowed to state my concerns."

"Ye are—" *a woman.* Caelen choked back his instinctive reply. "Ye are entitled to yer opinions, but I would ask ye share them with me first."

"Oft times a man will remember better when the matter is fresh on his mind," Arbela countered. Her hands gripped the armrests of her chair. "Wasting time is never a good idea."

"The incidents to which ye refer are days apart, as well as at some distance from each other," Caelen argued. "'Tis not worth keeping men from their rest to investigate further."

Arbela shook her head, clearly of a differing opinion. "Someone is behind both these acts," she declared. "But as MacGillonay and his son died some weeks ago, ye will have to enlighten me as to who your other enemies may be."

Caelen's blood ran cold. "MacGillonay and his *younger* son are dead," he whispered. "The elder son yet lives."

Arbela rose. "I will see to the outer defenses," she said. "Mayhap ye could reassess the matter of the missing sheep. Wolves are not the only creatures capable of indiscriminate slaughter."

Caelen flinched at her biting tone. "Nae. The castle is secured. We will retire and reconsider this upon the morn."

He stood, gesturing for Arbela to precede him. He halted at her scathing look.

"I believe the clime to be softer in the stable than in our room this night," she stated. Without a backward glance, she strode from the room, boot heels clipping her anger on the stone floor.

Chapter Thirty Three

Arbela blew past a sleepy stable boy with an abrupt wave of her hand. Possessing a surprising bent toward self-preservation, the boy disappeared quickly and without comment. Voski snorted and stamped a delicate hoof as Arbela stormed into his stall and slammed the door tight.

She slumped into a pile of fresh, fragrant grass in the corner of the stall, feeling the absence of her dogs acutely with no warm, sympathetic bodies to nestle close. Voski dropped his head and nudged her side. Anger slowly fizzled and Arbela rubbed the long, bony nose with rough affection.

"Men," she muttered on a long-suffering sigh. "He knows naught of castle warfare, yet will not consider my experience on the matter. I heard the words he did not speak, and he should consider himself fortunate I did not call him out for it. In fact, I wonder why I did not."

Voski snorted gently, moving the loose curls about her cheek.

"Ye speak truth, golden one," she murmured. "I have no wish to be a widow. And at this moment I have no desire to be a wife, either."

She caressed the horse's stubbly muzzle and lapsed into thought.

Why am I the only one who sees a possible connection between missing sheep and a lone campfire? Is it because there is no wolf pelt nailed to a rack, and I am the only one who seriously believes that the reach of an archer to that particular stretch of parapet is potentially deadly?

Arbela scowled. *I will take the first opportunity to prove to these bull-headed Scotsmen that I am correct. And I will come up with a substantial wager to make it worth my while. Disbelief on their faces shall not be enough.*

Somewhat mollified with the assurance of proving her point—and reaping a secondary benefit as well—she let her hand drop to her lap. Voski moved a step away to nibble on a bit of hay, his tail swishing gently at a fly. Arbela burrowed into her impromptu bed, creating a cushioning layer of warmth around her. But sleep eluded her.

What if MacGillonay's elder son desired revenge? He had not been present when his sire had captured Dunfaileas. Did this indicate a lack of interest? Or had other considerations kept him away? Could he—or anyone else for that matter—be stealing and slaughtering MacKern sheep deliberately? Other than food, why? A band of reivers could explain it, though with the MacLean to the south and the MacGillonay to the north, who would dare trespass MacKern land?

Something deeper was at work here, she was certain. Though with only the two seemingly unrelated incidents—at least as far as Caelen and his men were concerned—she could prove nothing. Mayhap it was time to visit the shepherd.

* * *

Morning was a scant brightening of the sun in a sullen sky. Rain fell slow and thick through the trees, catching the previous drops lingering on the leaves before thudding dully onto Arbela's borrowed cloak. Not wishing to outline her plan to the bull-headed laird, she did not bother returning to her room for travel clothing, but appropriated a heavy woolen plaide from a row of other such worn garments near the door of the stable.

Voski danced along the trail, oblivious to discomfort, prancing hooves crinkling the leaf-strewn ground with little or no noise. Birds were silent, no doubt huddled together, feathers fluffed against the rain. No small woodland creatures scurried across her path, likely finding the weather a deterrent to normal activity as well. Arbela and Voski were quite alone.

The path wound through the trees and bracken, skirting boulders protruding from the side of the mountain. Arbela let Voski pick his way and speed, though the rock-impeded trail seemed to hinder him not at all.

The thatched roofline of the shepherd's cottage at last appeared over the rise, glistening wetly in the rain. But no smoke rose from the pitched roof, and no challenging barks issued forth. A faint bleating reached Arbela's ears.

Is the shepherd in the hills with the flock, a few left behind for unknown reasons? But why would he leave them unprotected? A few woolly backs gathered en masse, huddled next to the cottage, heads tucked together against the rain.

She reined Voski to a halt and perused the area from the cover of the trees. Rain pelted the ground, but Garen and Toros should have heard her. She released a low whistle. From far away, a single bark replied.

Dismounting, Arbela drew her sword, leaving the reins twisted about her saddle so they would not trail the ground. Slipping silently through the bracken, she approached the cottage. A muddy patch lay before the door, though whether churned from the recent rains or many feet, she could not tell.

A solid ball of fur exploded from the undergrowth, dragging a length of old, partially rotted rope. The beast struck Arbela mid-chest, the excited whine emphasized with frantic licks of a wet tongue. Tears stung Arbela's eyes as she hugged Garen close.

The dog's pelt bristled with scraps of leaves and twigs, and a long scratch ran the length of one light brown leg, marked with both dried and fresh blood. Arbela stooped and set the dog down. Garen's tail swept the ground, scattering leaves and mud.

"Slow down," Arbela chided. "Where is Toros?"

Garen leapt to her feet and darted away, halting to peer over her shoulder, whining breathless encouragement. Grabbing Voski's reins below the shank of the bit, Arbela followed Garen into the woods.

* * *

Caelen's head would soon burst open, he was certain. And in a perverse way, he looked forward to the event, as such an action could only provide relief from the pain thudding within, improving the way he felt this dreary morning.

"Ye dinnae look so well," Rory noted, taking his seat next to Caelen at the long table. "Yer wee wife kept ye up late?" He nudged Caelen with an elbow and ruffled his eyebrows in a comical leer.

Caelen recoiled with a snarl.

Rory's brow arched, smirk dismissed, as he took in Caelen's appearance. "Unless she challenged ye to a drinking contest yester eve, I would believe the two of ye arenae in accord."

"She challenged my decisions," Caelen growled.

"Hers differed from yours," Rory corrected, pausing to shovel a spoonful of his meal into his mouth.

"Hers doesnae make sense," Caelen replied, scowling at the petulance in his voice.

"Ye sound like Bram," Rory mumbled through his porridge. He swallowed and waved his spoon in the air. "If yer wife doesnae agree with ye, it doesnae mean she is wrong."

"When I want yer opinion, I'll ask for it," Caelen muttered, knowing Rory was right, but not liking it.

Rory shrugged and shoveled in another bite of porridge. "Where is Lady Arbela? If ye are too woolly-headed to join me, mayhap she can ride with me to check the site on the cliff in daylight."

"I dinnae know." Caelen rose, careful to not let his heels touch the ground and jar his brain loose.

Rory shot him a startled look. "She was angry enough she sent ye to the stables to sleep?"

"Nae," Caelen bit out. "*She* slept in the stables."

A choking sound erupted from behind Rory's closed fist as he hastily covered his mouth. "Then she isnae likely to be in any better mood than ye are." He wiped his mouth on his sleeve and shoved his trencher away. "Come with me. Fresh air will do ye good."

Caelen reluctantly followed his captain and best friend from the hall, squinting in the dreary glint of sunlight through low, dark clouds. He hunched his shoulders against the steady rain and crossed the yard as rapidly as his pounding head and the slick mud would permit. Rory entered the stable with a great shake of his head, slinging water in every direction. Caelen winced and regarded his night of angry over-indulgence a colossal mistake.

"Ho, lads!" Rory called heartily, apparently either oblivious to Caelen's discomfort or choosing to remind him of his blunder in a manner he wouldn't soon forget.

Tousled heads appeared over the stall doors, long lean faces with uncombed forelocks and bristly chins whether horse or lad.

"We require our horses," Rory said, approaching the nearest stall. "And fetch a clean blanket for my saddle. A dirty one chaffs the hide."

A lad set off to do his bidding, and Rory and Caelen strode deeper into the stable to the horses' stalls. Past Voski's empty one.

"Have ye turned out Lady Arbela's horse?" Caelen demanded of a stable lad busily forking the manure from the hay. The lad looked up, surprise on his face.

"Nae," he blurted. "I wouldnae send him out in such weather. My lady took him out herself around daybreak."

With a muttered curse, Caelen grabbed his saddle and settled it atop Addis's back. Within a trice he led the protesting horse from his stall and to the open door of the stable where rivulets of rain dribbled from the eaves.

"What has the wench done?" Caelen growled as Rory drew alongside.

"Yer *lady wife* no doubt has questions we were unable to answer for her last night," Rory replied, stressing Arbela's title only faintly, a worried look on his face. "Astride that ferocious beast of hers and likely armed to the teeth, I would imagine she is in little danger. Not to mention the weather which even the darkest scoundrel wouldnae venture out in."

298

"One broken leg," Caelen muttered. "Just one is all it would take to make her an easy target."

Rory lifted a brow. "Do ye refer to the horse's leg or yer wife's?"

Caelen led Addis beyond the low eave and swung onto the stallion's back, wincing as he made jarring contact with the saddle. "The horse."

* * *

Arbela did not stop at the shepherd's cottage as Garen showed no interest in it, only in getting Arbela to follow. Trailing the dog to the cliffs overhanging the cottage, likely an adequate shelter from all but the worst winter storms, they climbed upward, the path now little more than a line of close-cropped grass and dirt, legacy of the sheep's sharp teeth and cloven hooves.

Arbela's breathing became labored the higher they climbed, and the cold rain lost its immediate effect as Arbela sweated with her efforts. The activity hindered Garen little, though Voski tossed his head as his hooves slid in the loosened pebbles.

At last they reached a tiny croft the shepherd likely used as shelter when returning to his cottage was not convenient. The circular stone building appeared scarcely large enough to hold a single pallet, though any shelter would be welcome when unexpected storms struck.

Garen disappeared inside and Arbela followed cautiously, hefting the comforting weight of her sword. She paused, giving her eyes a moment to adjust to the windowless gloom. A whine to her right pulled her attention. Garen lay curled protectively around Toros's body, her head across his neck. Arbela's heart lurched.

Toros thumped his tail weakly on the packed earth and Garen lifted her head with a soft croon. Arbela stooped beneath the low lintel and crept inside. The odor of nameless filth assailed her and she suppressed a gag. A low moan, not from Toros, told her she was not alone.

Her heart steadied to note Garen did not flinch, and she peered into the darkness. A roughly dressed man, bearded and lean, lay atop a bed of rags.

"Are ye the shepherd?" Arbela asked.

The man's fingers partially closed as though seeking the grip of a weapon, then relaxed, the effort apparently too much to complete. Garen rose and stepped to the man's side, nuzzling his beard. He groaned and lifted a hand in a faint gesture, and Garen returned to Toros's side.

Torn between assisting the stranger and Toros, Arbela knelt beside her dogs, caressing Toros's head. Making a quick assessment, she discovered he was tied to a large stick that had been driven into the earth, so tight he could scarcely move. And even if loosened, his broken foreleg would not carry him far. She made short work of the ropes, freeing him, but other than to lick her hand in gratitude, Toros did not move.

He seemed content to stare at her, as if her presence was all he required, and, humbled, Arbela turned to the stranger. Placing a hand on his forehead, she did her best in the close quarters to remain out of his reach. His eyes fluttered open.

"I am the shepherd," he rasped. "There isnae wolf."

"Hush," Arbela urged him. "I did not believe there was. We will get ye to the castle, and ye can tell the laird what ye know."

"Hurt . . . too bad," he wheezed. "Yon dog took blows . . . meant for me. His mate . . . she protected the lass . . .."

"They are a good pair," Arbela agreed soothingly, wondering if all shepherds referred to their sheep as *lasses*. "I will get ye water and dress yer wounds. Ye are likely to fare better waiting for my return here than to ride exposed to the rain."

"Ye must find her . . .." The shepherd's voice cracked.

He grunted and waved a hand at her, but Arbela had no time to worry over sheep. She fetched the waterskin from Voski's saddle. The shepherd slurped greedily at the water then lay back with a sigh at Arbela's renewed reassurances. With as much care as she could, Arbela searched the man for wounds, grimacing at the sight of a long tear in his abdomen, the other myriad cuts and bruises comparatively of little importance.

She leaned back on her heels and stripped the damp plaide from her shoulders.

"This should help with the cold," she said, tucking the warm, dry side about the man carefully.

"I will return as quickly as possible with a litter. The healer will see to your wounds. And I will make certain someone finds the lass," she added, capturing the shepherd's frantically waving hands in her own, silently commending his fervor in keeping up with a lost sheep, but placing his singular concern below his need for immediate care. "I will also leave both dogs with ye. Neither are in any condition to keep up with my horse, and they may be of use to ye whilst I am gone."

She searched both dogs again for treatable wounds, but found little else than what she'd already observed. She patted Toros's head. "I am grieved to leave ye, but ye must wait a bit longer. And ye, lass," she said, rubbing Garen's ears, "have done an excellent job this day. I ask ye to remain on guard another hour and I will bring men to take the task from ye."

Garen whined, but did not move when Arbela half-rose to leave the tiny hut. She scanned the edge of the forest for signs of danger, and seeing none, crept to Voski's side. With a leap, she gained his back, crouching low as she thumped her heels into his side. The stallion reached his full stride in a bound, soaring over stones and downed limbs as if born to the mountains.

Wind whipped the golden strands of his mane into her face, and Arbela swiped at the tears. Someone was targeting Dunfaileas, and when she next spoke to Caelen, he would listen to her reason.

Chapter Thirty Four

Arbela caught sight of Caelen as she approached the open castle gates. He looked like hell. Hunched over the front of his saddle, reins dangling from his fingertips, his scowl was enough to deter all but the most determined. The stable lad toeing the dirt in a nervous circle before him did not meet his gaze. Whatever he'd said clearly displeased his laird. Arbela urged her bedraggled horse into the bailey and swung down, instantly on the defensive against Caelen's dark mood. She was cold, anxious, and in no frame of mind to have her actions questioned.

He glanced up, meeting her look. His frown fled, his brow smoothed. He slid to the ground, narrowing his eyes in a brief wince as his feet hit the ground.

"I have need of a litter and the healer," Arbela said, forestalling whatever angry words he might harbor.

His look of alarm startled her. "Not for me," she added in a calmer voice. "The shepherd is badly wounded and I could not bring him here on Voski."

With a crisp nod, he gave orders to a nearby soldier who took the steps to the stable in two hasty bounds. Caelen stepped closer to Arbela and laid a palm on her shoulder.

"Ye are certain ye are not harmed?" he asked.

"Nae. I am cold and wet, but the rain has ceased, and I am anxious to return to the croft. Toros has been injured and leaving him and the shepherd behind was not easy."

"Tell me what ye discovered," Caelen ordered, his voice warm with interest.

Arbela met his words with a raised brow. Caelen winced. "*I* have discovered not listening to my wife is bad for my health," he quipped. "I should have given yer opinion the respect it deserved."

"Thank ye," Arbela replied softly. "Though yer words are kind, ye must realize that at your first opportunity to listen to what I said, ye dismissed me—for no good reason other than I am a woman."

Caelen's eyes narrowed. "I dinnae say that."

"'Tis easy enough to hear what is not said, as well as what actually leaves your lips," Arbela noted grimly.

"Will ye tell me now?" Caelen asked. "I regret my bull-headedness, and realize we willnae always agree. That is nae reason for us to go to bed angry. I missed ye fierce last night."

Arbela could not quite contain the smile tugging at the corner of her lips. "Whisky is a poor comforter, aye?"

The soldier returned, interrupting them as he directed a stable lad to attach a sturdy litter to a stocky horse's harness.

"I will tell ye what I found as we ride," Arbela said, anxious to return to the croft. Caelen nodded and flung his cloak over her shoulders before mounting his horse. The solid warmth of the cloth, heated by Caelen's body, nearly stole Arbela's breath and she laid a trembling hand on Voski's neck.

She and Caelen exchanged looks. Her thanks for the comfort of the cloak. His silent request she remain behind and tend her health with a fire and mug of hot cider. Her appreciation for the thought, and further gratitude for not insisting she retire tamely to a chair by the hearth.

Without exchanging words, Arbela and Caelen swung into their saddles. Three other soldiers rode up, forming protection around Arbela as the group left the yard and began their journey to the shepherd's croft. Aware of the men's concern, she allowed their excessive protectiveness.

The sun had wrested control over the sky by the time they reached their destination. Garen darted from the tiny croft, tail wagging a greeting before she disappeared inside again. Leaving the others to prepare the litter, Arbela ducked beneath the lintel, her eyes scanning the dark objects in the gloom. To her relief, Toros raised his head and thumped his tail. She patted his head reassuringly then turned to the shepherd.

His chest rose and fell, but so shallowly it was several moments before Arbela noticed the movement. A large shadow blocked the narrow rectangle of light at the door as Caelen entered the shelter. He patted Toros then knelt beside Arbela.

"He lives," she said with a nod to the shepherd. "But his injuries are dire."

"I will carry Toros out so he is not in the way, then we will load Coll onto the litter," Caelen said. He hesitated a moment, gaze fixed on the shepherd. With a single muttered word Arbela did not catch, he touched the man's shoulder, then turned to Toros.

Arbela cradled Toros's head in her palms as Caelen lifted the injured dog. Toros whined, his eyes anxious. Arbela cut a strip of heavy wool from her cloak then carefully wrapped it about his broken leg, stabilizing the limb, and relieving much of the pain. Toros licked her hand.

"Place him before me on Voski," she directed as she mounted her horse. Caelen gave her a cautious look.

"When necessary, Voski is calm and gentle," Arbela reminded him. "He will carry us back to Dunfaileas without a misplaced step."

Caelen gently laid Toros across her lap and Arbela tucked the edges of her cloak about him, creating a sling of sorts. Garen watched intently from the ground.

"All will be well," Arbela said, as much to reassure the dogs as herself.

Caelen and two others mounted up. "Rory, take the others and search the area. Report back with anything ye find."

The trip back to the castle was long but uneventful, balanced between speed and the shepherd's comfort. The healer, anxiously awaiting them at the gate, took over the shepherd's care, leaving a basket of bandages, poultices, and splinting slats for Toros.

By the time they arrived, the morning meal was long past and Bram paced the bailey, no less fretful than Zora for their return. At Bram's cry of dismay on seeing Toros's wounds, Caelen was compelled to carry the dog to his son's chamber for care. Zora set to cleaning and setting the broken limb with Bram her helper.

"It doesnae look as if we are needed. I will check with the healer in a bit and hope the shepherd can tell us what has happened," Caelen murmured, settling a hand on Arbela's waist. She nodded.

"I would like nothing better than a hot bath and dry clothes," she answered.

"Nothing else?" Caelen asked, a glimmer of hope in his eyes.

"Mayhap some rest," she added, surprised to find her earlier anger and resentment gone, and willing to go along with his teasing. "I did not get much sleep last night."

"Nor did I," he admitted ruefully. "All I have is the memory of ill-advised indulgence and a sweet wife to whom I must apologize."

With gentle pressure on her waist, Caelen guided Arbela into the passageway and to their room.

"There speaks a man with regret for turning to drink," Arbela said. "'Tis plain your head still pains ye, for there are few who consider me *sweet.*"

Caelen closed the door with a click of the latch. He leaned one palm against the wall above Arbela's head, the other hand still at her waist. But she did not feel trapped, for there was no menace in his stance, only sincerity and intensity for his next words.

"I ask ye to forgive me, Arbela, and I will ask ye again before the same men as I disparaged ye before yesterday. But I wish to tell ye in private that I dinnae know how to respect a lass before ye came into my life. Och, respect her body, aye. I wouldnae impose myself where I wasnae wanted. But ye are different, Arbela. Someone to admire for more than her sweet form and caring ways. And I am truly sorry I dinnae listen to ye yesterday."

He scanned her face and familiar warmth stole through her, though the henflesh on her arms reflected the cold, damp clothing she wore, not anticipation of his kiss.

"I did not enjoy my night away from ye," she admitted. "And I will not allow it to happen again, save for illness or legitimate absence. Howbeit, I know we will disagree from time to time, though that can be healthy when done with respect."

Caelen quirked a brow. "Will ye take me to task if I run roughshod over ye?"

Arbela leveled an uncompromising look. "I will gut ye like a fish if ye do so again."

Caelen caught her as she fell forward into his arms, laughing or sobbing, he wasn't certain which. He hugged her tight, thankful she had consented to hear him out and hadn't drawn her sword against him. Though it appeared she still might if he dinnae change his ways—at least a bit.

Arbela lifted her face from his chest, eyes merry. "I believe ye are warmer than a bath," she whispered, drawing fingertips across his cheek. Caelen's interest piqued.

"I have heard removing wet clothes will make ye warmer, faster," he noted with an air of sincerity. Arbela unlaced his leine, then slid her hands slowly down his chest to the buckle of his belt. She had it undone in a trice and the leather fell away, leaving his shirt tail hanging free. Her hands worked their way beneath the cloth, smoothing their way over his abdomen and chest.

"Is it working?" she asked.

Caelen shook his head to clear it of the fog created from blazing desire. Once again, his brain lagged behind, his body registering little more than the magic of her touch.

"Let me show ye," he murmured. He unfastened her long leather vest, its surface spotted unevenly from the rain. Pushing it from her shoulders, he addressed himself to the many tiny buttons gracing the front of her knee-length silk tunic. Arbela's shoulders shook.

"Only a few are necessary," she said, demonstrating as she drew her head through the opening of only a half-dozen buttons. The rest of her garments fell away with little difficulty and Caelen's hands slid freely over her chilled skin, noting the rising warmth.

Grabbing a couple of blankets from the bed, he tossed them to the floor before the hearth. He drew Arbela to their comfort and wrapped a third about her, leaving her only long enough to stir the fire. It leapt to life with a crackle and he fed it another block of peat.

Satisfied with the heat rolling from the hearth, he turned back to his wife.

* * *

Sometime during the afternoon, they retreated to the bed, allowing the fire to die down. Tangled in each other's arms, they did not heed the room's chill.

Arbela turned lazily to face Caelen, hooking a leg over his thigh.

"What will your clan think of its laird laying abed most of the day with his new wife—again?" She drew a fingertip over the lines of his lips, remembering the play of them against her skin.

"They are aware their laird has lost his head to his pretty new wife. And they likely are pleased ye seem dedicated to bringing more children to the clan," he murmured, moving his lips only enough to speak. With a swift move, he captured her finger between his teeth. Arbela squeaked in surprise but did not draw away.

Meeting his steady gaze, she arched her body against his, desiring him once again. His cock thickened beneath her hand, and a knowing smile flickered across her lips. Caelen rolled to his back and pulled her over him enough to transfer his attentions to her breasts, drawing them into his mouth with a smooth suckling motion.

After long moments of such pleasurable torment, Arbela pulled away, sliding down his flanks, trapping his solid heat between them.

"I have mentioned this before, but it bears repeating, I think," Caelen said as he pushed with his hips, urging her to settle atop him. "I am verra glad I married ye."

Braced over him, Arbela grinned as she moved enough to take him an inch inside but no more. "Ye never said *verra glad*," she corrected him, mimicking his burr.

Caelen countered her move with a thrust, winning another inch. "Verra, verra glad," he amended. Arbela clenched about him as a tremor wracked her body. She steadied with a shaky breath.

"I am *verra glad* as well."

* * *

"Did ye fight the Saracens?" Bram asked, shoving his wooden spoon into the air as though the curved surface had magically become a well-struck sword. "Did they fling themselves at yer castle?"

Arbela observed him with languid amusement from her nest in Caelen's lap, her shoulder buried against his shoulder, idly thankful the laird's chair was such an impressive piece of furniture to seat them both. "It does not appear two days cooped inside the castle agree with him," she remarked with an indulgent laugh.

"The confinement certainly wore me to a frazzle," Caelen teased, placing a kiss atop her head.

Arbela laughed again and snuggled closer, noticing the relaxed mood of the people lingering in the hall. Many had made an effort to speak a word or two to Caelen during the meal, often pressing a hand to her shoulder in unspoken approval before they moved on.

"Tell me about Batroun," Bram demanded as he settled into his chair, his trencher cleared of the vegetables he'd fussed with earlier. Arbela stole a look beneath the table where Garen crouched at Bram's feet. Toros was unable to navigate the tower stairs, but had claimed a thick blanket before the hearth in Bram's chamber with plenty of treats from Cook and the instant attentions from a young maid when the dog's inability to go outside presented a problem.

"In Batroun, all young boys ate at least five bites of vegetables before weapons practice each day," she stated. "The weapons master said he'd never seen such strong young men—so agile were they from their excellent food."

Bram cast her a look of scorn mixed with uncertainty, flicking a glance to his empty trencher. Arbela smothered a laugh.

"Not long before I left Batroun to sail for Scotland, a devious Saracen attacked the castle not once, but thrice."

"How did ye know 'twas the same?" Bram asked. "Did ye get a good look at him? Was he scarred and ugly?"

"I did not see the leader of the force that attacked Batroun, for we never captured him, nor spoke terms with him." She quirked an eyebrow at him. "I knew it was the same man because he never set his forces at us in the same manner twice."

"Why?" Bram wondered. "What do ye mean?"

Caelen ruffled Bram's shaggy curls. "Listen to yer ma, lad. Strategy is what she's known for."

Bram turned his eager attention to Arbela.

"Batroun is known as a very secure castle," she began. "It has guarded the pass to the sea for many years, and travelers have often taken shelter within its walls.

"The castle has been attacked, for it is also known that the baron is a wealthy man, and not only his wealth, but his power would pass to any who became its ruler. *This* man," Arbela noted with a raised finger for emphasis, "used strategy rather than brute force—which would not have worked in any case—to ascertain Batroun's weakness."

"What weakness?" Bram wanted to know.

Arbela smiled. "There is none—at least none as yet discovered. Rather than waste his soldiers in a full attack, the Saracen cleverly set a series of attacks. As soon as one was deemed a failure, he withdrew for a day, mayhap two, before creating a different attack or diversion."

Caelen stiffened beneath her, and Arbela came instantly alert. *A diversion.*

She cast a look at Caelen, noting his inward gaze, his quickening breath.

Could MacGillonay's elder son be attempting a distraction? Drawing the dogs, who served as protection for her and Bram, and men they could not spare into the forests looking for a wolf that did not exist? And setting a fire upon the cliff at night, again drawing men away from the castle to seek the cause of the blaze?

She opened her mouth to ask Caelen if he thought the same.

The clatter of booted feet snatched her attention as Rory rushed across the hall, brow furrowed in concern.

"Another fire has been lit on the cliffs."

Chapter Thirty Five

Arbela launched from her chair and was halfway across the hall before the scrape of bench legs on the floor died down, cursing her decision to wear a gown to supper in an effort to please her husband. Until the alarm had been raised, she'd found the flowing lines of the draped cloth echoed the sinuous line of pleasure she'd experienced in Caelen's arms, liking the way the luxurious fabric caressed her skin—a sensation lacking in the leather trews and well-fitted vest she commonly wore. But suddenly the gold embroidered brocade and diaphanous silk were nothing more than an impediment to her movements—and betrayed her lack of sword and bow accoutrement.

A stride or more ahead of the men, Garen at her side, she snatched her skirts in both hands and thundered up the stairs to the parapet, darting around a guard and pulling up against the stone wall at the rear of the castle. On the cliff's edge a fire glowed, the red flames dancing in the brisk night air. A sudden gust of wind brought the scent of approaching rain, and the tension streaking through her eased.

"'Twill rain soon and put it out," Caelen said from behind her as though reading her mind. He rested a hand reassuringly at her waist, his warmth seeping through the layers of clothing, but Arbela could not escape the thread of cold alertness tugging at her senses.

"There has to be something else," she stated, pushing aside the frustration, seeking a place of calm where she could fit the pieces of the puzzle together. "Ye have made certain 'tis not simply a traveler's fire."

"Aye," Caelen answered. "Though I havenae set a watch over it." His voice dropped. "We havenae the men to spare."

"Has the shepherd roused?"

"Nae. He battles a fever from the wound in his abdomen. I dinnae know when I will be able to question him—if ever."

"What does Rory say?" Arbela questioned.

Caelen shrugged. "He viewed the two sheep whose carcasses the shepherd had discovered, and determined 'twas best to leave Toros and Garen as requested as protection against further loss. He is of the opinion there is a lone wolf at work."

Arbela gave a curt nod, still lacking some important bit of information. The actions did not fit together—yet. "I would counsel against sending men out to check on the fire."

"I disagree," Rory said as he joined them. "We must discover who is behind this, and the only time is at dark when the fires are lit."

"A single fire does naught but cause aggravation," Arbela countered, the idea of a diversion nagging her. "'Tis not enough reason to split our forces."

"I still say we make the attempt. Mayhap only two men instead of a larger force." Rory turned his words to Caelen. "Can we not spare two men?"

"Two?" Arbela asked, drawing the word out in disbelief. She faced Caelen and Rory, ignoring the crowd beginning to form about them. She dismissed Rory's request. "Too easily ambushed."

Rory sent her a deprecating look. "Our men know the area well. They were born here and have hunted the forests. They know every tree and rock."

Arbela lifted a brow, the unease growing inside her. "And how long since the fires began? Whoever it is has been lurking in our woods for at least a fortnight. I would wager he is quite familiar with the land by now as well."

Caelen raised a hand between them. "We will not allow ourselves to be drawn out tonight," he said firmly. "Tomorrow we will make a plan of action to settle this once and for all. Though 'tis only a single fire, 'tis clear it divides us."

Rory sighed. "I admit it fashes me something fierce to know someone taunts us so."

"And from a position only a superior archer could claim as significant," Arbela added. "Though we know this, and Dunfaileas has ever been safe from this threat, it vexes us all."

Caelen's eyes glittered in the torchlight. His nod of agreement settled Arbela's tension further.

A rumbling sound like the sudden rush of wind reached their ears. A guard shouted from the darkness.

"Laird! Look!"

Caelen shoved through the crowd, Arbela and Rory following. They rounded the corner of the wall and skidded to a shocked halt. A fire raged on the beach, engulfing one arm of the dock.

"Tell me," Caelen rapped out, eyes glued to the scene below.

"There was naught," the guard stammered. "And suddenly a whoosh—and flames."

"Burning oil," Arbela said, the thrum of battle beginning in her veins. She touched Caelen's arm. "It would catch quickly and burn fiercely. If the oil soaks the boards, the fire cannot be put out. The oil will burn until the wood is gone."

"But we can save the rest of the dock," Caelen replied. "And the vessels tethered there."

Casting a cool look to Arbela, Rory nodded. "I agree."

Caelen turned to the men at arms. "To the beach!" he called. "Save what ye may. Be wary."

Arbela shook her head, knowing their efforts would have little effect, but choosing to follow Caelen's lead. "I will change out of my gown," she said, knowing its billowing cloth would be a danger to her near the fire. But none heard her as they gathered arms and buckets, shouting to each other as they spilled from the open gates of Dunfaileas.

With a sigh of aggravation, Arbela fled the parapet and hurried through the hall, Garen on her heels, brushing aside the shrill queries from servants seeking news. A quick glance told her Zora had removed Bram from the room—a thoughtful move as the boy would undoubtedly wish to help, and she did not have time to spare keeping him out of the way.

She pounded up the stairs, heedless of the noise, bleeding off a bit of frustration with her actions. Slinging the room's heavy door open, she tugged ineffectually at the dozens of tiny jeweled buttons of her gown. She gave the fabric an impatient tug, disregarding the need to replace buttons and torn cloth later, and a half-dozen buttons exploded from their silken moorings with a scatter of refracted light.

Tugging the heavy brocade tunic over her head, Arbela managed to make short work of the rest of her clothing, emerging from the chamber only a few minutes later dressed as usual in trews and tunic, sword strapped about her waist, buckling an arm sheath, its slender dagger clenched in her teeth. Garen crossed the hall with a whine at Bram's door.

Arbela slipped the dagger into the sheath, giving Garen the command to follow in an impatient gesture.

"Do not bother the boy," she chided the dog. "He cannot come with us and I do not have time to spare arguing with him."

She took the stairs two at a time, haste lending length to her stride. Weaving her way through the hall, she crossed the bailey, softly cursing the people crowding the way, voices excited, heads craned to see the docks where flames leapt ever higher in the night sky.

Garen paused, sniffing the skirts of an old crone who pulled her tattered cloak close, her face completely invisible in the blackness of her cowl. Aware of Garen's interest from the corner of her eye, Arbela grabbed the dog's collar.

"Leave it," she ordered, giving the dog a tug as she skirted the old woman. Garen whined, a low growl rumbling in protest. Arbela picked up her pace as she left the castle grounds, Garen once again at her side. She ran down the wide road to the beach, eyes scanning for a glimpse of

Caelen. With a sigh of relief, she caught sight of his shorn head, silhouetted darkly against the red-gold of the fire, and she hurried to his side.

* * *

Caelen wiped his brow with his forearm, staring into the inferno that defied their best efforts to douse the flames. "What devilry is this?" he growled. "The water only spreads the fire further."

"Ask yer wife," Rory grumbled, dropping a bucket at his feet in a gesture of surrender. "She seemed to know."

Recalling Arbela's earlier words, Caelen glanced about, but did not spy his wife, though it was difficult to identify the dark forms pacing the shore, as impotent against the blaze with their buckets as if they'd done naught more than spit into it.

"She dinnae agree with our actions, and I believe she stayed behind," Rory muttered, a commiserating grip on Caelen's shoulder. "Though I will be interested to hear what she has to say when we return."

"I am here." Arbela's voice came from behind them, slightly breathless as if she'd run from the castle.

Rory's grip tightened and Caelen whipped about at the combination of unexpected pain from Rory's fingers and the sound of Arbela's voice. He glanced at his captain as he shrugged from beneath his hold, startled to note the man's face seemed to have drained of all color.

"What are ye doing here?" Rory rasped, his voice harsh, accusing— and Caelen could see no reason for the man's confrontational tone.

"Dinnae speak so to my wife," he said, low rebuke in his words. Arbela's eyes widened, clearly startled by Rory's tone.

Rory whirled, strain on his face discernable even in the glare of the fire. "She shouldnae be here! She should have remained with Bram." He staggered a step toward Arbela, shaking his fist in the air. "Damnable woman!"

Arbela dodged the angry man with a step to the side. Garen snarled a warning, advancing on Rory on stiffened legs.

"Halt, Garen," Arbela commanded, and the dog stopped, her eyes fixed on Rory.

"What are ye thinking, man?" Caelen growled, grabbing Rory's arm. Rory shrugged him off, eyes blazing.

"She was supposed to protect Bram," he shouted, his face only inches from Caelen's.

"Protect him?" Caelen's blood ran cold despite the waves of heat rolling from the nearby fire. "Protect him from who?"

"The crone—" Arbela's voice rose. "The old woman I stumbled into in the bailey. Garen growled at her." She sent Caelen a horrified look. "Bram was not in the hall when I left. I did not check his chamber."

Caelen gripped her arm, heedless of the warning from Garen for presuming to touch Arbela in anger. "Who was the crone?" he demanded. "Did she have Bram?"

"Do ye believe I would have left had I thought she had him?" Arbela raged. She jerked from his grip, her eyes blazing her fury at his question. "Garen, come!" She whirled and jogged swiftly up the road.

Caelen whirled on Rory. "Come with me. Ye have more knowledge than ye should. Ye will help me get my son back—even should it kill ye."

With a bleak nod, Rory accompanied Caelen without protest.

They overtook Arbela in the bailey, sending Garen off with a word to search for Bram. The dog immediately cast about for scent and Arbela turned to Caelen and Rory.

"Do not interfere," she barked, holding both men at bay with a flip of her hand. "Unless ye can describe for me what it is ye know of Bram's safety," she amended with a fierce look at Rory.

"Ye should have stayed with him," Rory said, repeating his earlier claim stubbornly. She silenced him with a glare. Caelen grabbed Rory's shoulder, whirling him about to face him.

"Ye are my milk brother and my captain. Ever have I trusted ye. But I will kill ye myself if harm comes to Bram."

Rory inhaled a deep breath, shaking his head as if attempting to dislodge memory or knowledge he did not want. "It wasnae supposed to happen like this. If Bram had been protected, Keith Dubh would have been killed or captured—and Brinna set free."

"Keith Dubh?" Caelen thundered. "Ye have treated with MacGillonay's son? Damn ye, Rory!"

A single bark interrupted. Arbela cast a look about the bailey for Garen and spied her plumed tail several feet away, her nose to the ground as she wove through the crowd.

"She has found the trail," Arbela said, grabbing Caelen's arm. "Come. She will lead us to Bram."

Both men started after her and Arbela briefly wondered about the wisdom of allowing Rory to accompany them. But her immediate concern was in finding Bram. She would deal later with the traitorous Rory herself.

Garen streaked through the gates. Arbela retraced her steps, keeping the dog in sight, afraid she would lose her in the darkness as Garen left the torchlight and broad road and slipped into the forest. The underside of her furry tail flashed light brown, a faint beacon in the gloom. Arbela darted after her, praying Bram was uninjured. She did not know if she could endure seeing the boy reduced by fear.

Heavy footsteps in the brush behind told Arbela Caelen and Rory still followed, and she immediately dismissed the sound as unimportant. Garen slowed, the fur on the back of her neck ruffled forward, her gaze fixed on a spot ahead.

Reaching the dog, Arbela dropped a hand to the silken head with a silent command to wait as she peered through the trees. Garen's low rumble protested the halt, but she remained at Arbela's side. Four dark forms, three a good bit taller than the fourth, gathered in a tiny glen. The scent of horses drifted to Arbela, though she could not see them.

A slight shuffle of leaves behind her alerted Arbela to Caelen's presence. His breath warmed her ear as he spoke in a low undertone.

"I left Rory some yards back with a sore head, though it willnae bother him until he wakes. What is this?"

Arbela held up four fingers, then turned her hand sideways, forefinger and thumb extended as she slowly narrowed the open space between them. Her voice sighed softly.

"Bram."

Chapter Thirty Six

Caelen's heart thudded in his chest.

"They have horses," Arbela breathed. "We must not allow them to mount."

Garen growled again and leaned forward against Arbela's hand. Voices in the glen rose in anger. Arbela placed her hand on her sword. Garen leapt from the brush as a thin cry cleaved the air. The dog streaked across the deep grass, her sable body a blur in the dark. The small figure turned, wrenching free of the robed shape next to him.

"Garen!" Bram cried.

Without checking, Garen leapt straight for the throat of the one dressed as a crone. The man dropped his robe, revealing his true form, frantically thrusting his arm upward in protection from the dog's attack. A second man staggered backward, stumbling in his haste to avoid Garen. A third, shorter man grabbed at his belt, the glint of steel bright. He seized Bram from behind with a shuffling motion, yanking the boy hard against him. Caelen rose, poised for battle. Arbela laid cautioning fingers on his forearm.

"Call off yer dog!" the short man shrieked.

Garen darted and slashed at the man who'd dressed as a crone, the roaring sounds of her fury terrifying. Bram's cry tore Caelen's attention from the dog's attack. The man's blade winked beneath Bram's throat and the boy's eyes shone wide with fear.

Caelen fought Arbela's restraint as if he'd stepped in a trapper's noose. His entire focus centered on getting Bram away from the trio, but he forced himself to accede to his wife's strategy. Nothing had ever been more difficult.

"Garen—halt!" Arbela shouted, stepping into the small clearing. The dog ceased her attack, but backed only a few feet away, still snarling and snapping her willingness to slay the man who dared touch Bram. Caelen struggled with the same emotions, eager to destroy Bram's kidnappers, and the taut lines of Arbela's body told him of her barely restrained fury.

In the clearing, two men—one grasping his shoulder, blood staining his fingers—stood back to back, swords visible in their hands. The third, shorter and perhaps their leader, gripped Bram in a strangle hold. A vivid scar, visible even in the scattered moonlight, twisted the left side of his face.

Unable to remain still, Caelen moved to Arbela's side, entering a small patch of pale moonlight. "That is MacGillonay's elder son, Keith Dubh," he murmured with a nod to the scarred man. "More than his face bears evidence of his shame."

Arbela gave a slight nod of understanding.

"Let the lad go," Caelen commanded, voice raised.

"Ye killed my family!" the smaller man screamed. "Da, my brother—my sister."

"That is incorrect," Arbela replied evenly. "*I* killed your father—and your brother. Let the boy go."

It was clear to see the young man hovered close to striking a fatal blow—and Bram was his chosen target.

"You have no cause to harm the boy," she continued in the same firm voice. "'Tis I ye are after. This can be between ye and me alone."

Caelen grasped Arbela's wrist painfully. "Dinnae be a fool," he rasped. "Three to two is fair odds. He will let his guard down and 'twill be over. Ye needn't bait him."

The wiry man's gaze darted from side to side. "Caelen has been a thorn in our side since he took Ruthie from us," he declared. "He is a treacherous bastard. How do I know ye dinnae have others hiding in the shadows?"

"Ye do not," Arbela replied, ignoring the press of Caelen's hand. "Ye

320

will have to trust me."

"The lad is mine!" the man shrieked. "Fair payment for the lives ye have taken from me."

"What do ye propose?" Arbela asked, raising her voice. "To raise him as a MacGillonay?"

It was too much. Caelen stepped forward with a snarl. It was Arbela's turn to pull him back.

"I want ye to pay!" the small man cried. "Pay in blood for what ye have done to my clan!"

"And taking a small lad is the best ye can do?" Caelen roared, anger blinding him to little else than the sight of his son in the disfigured MacGillonay's hands. His hand gripped his sword hilt, half-pulling the blade from its sheath.

"S-stop!" the man stuttered. He gestured with his dagger. "The lad is Ruthie's son—though MacKern blood runs in his veins. I will trade ye the lad for the lass."

Without hesitation, Arbela slung her sword to the ground before her. She shook off Caelen's grip before he could do more than stare dumbfounded at her. Her stride carried her across the glen, shedding daggers as she went. They glinted on the grass, marking her path with a twinkle of moonlight.

"Arbela, no!" Caelen shouted. His step forward halted at a cry from Bram as the man twisted him about, blade again at his throat. Garen barked savagely, but remained in place.

"Bram, now!" Arbela cried over the melee in the glen. The boy lifted his booted foot and brought it down heavily on the inside of his captor's foot. The man howled and doubled at the waist, bringing his knee up as he grasped his lower leg. He hovered above Bram, the lad's shoulder tucked beneath his arm, trapping him against his shallow chest.

His hands tied behind him, Bram appeared unable to do further damage, but without hesitation, he leaned slightly forward then threw his head backward with all his might. Releasing Bram, his captor grunted, a gargled sound as blood cascaded from his broken nose. Buckling his legs, Bram fell to the ground, landing on his bottom. He rolled back, drawing his knees to his chest. With but a moment to take aim, he launched the power of his legs forward, his boots catching his captor square between his legs as the force sent him staggering a dozen or more feet away.

The taller man launched himself with a roar at Bram. The boy struggled to his knees, then rolled aside to avoid being captured again. Coming up against a large fallen log, he scrambled into a small hollow in the dirt beneath it, out of reach at least for the moment.

The third man, abandoning concern for his injury, rushed toward Arbela.

Caelen leapt forward, intent on putting himself between his defenseless wife and the two armed men. Yanking his sword from its sheath, he lowered his head, adding momentum to his speed. He passed Arbela and, snaking an arm about her waist, lifted her off her feet. She did not waste time railing at him, but went limp in his arms, landing on her feet as he set her behind him in a swift, twisting move.

She would make him pay for his actions later. At the moment, he did not care.

Caelen raised his sword high and brought it down on the nearest man's shoulder at an angle, cleaving him to the waist. Spinning about, he caught sight of the scarred man rising to his feet, his dagger in hand. Face covered in blood, he launched himself awkwardly at Arbela who had lost little time in recovering her speed or direction.

She blocked the short man's wrist with her forearm and shoved upward, deflecting the blow. Slight though the man was, his arm strength surpassed hers, and he slowly brought his bladed hand down, then jerked free. Arbela whirled about, dodging his next attack, hands spread wide for balance.

"Da!" Bram's voice reached Caelen's ears and he turned as his son burst from his hiding place. Bram sped across the short distance, off-balance with his hands tied behind his back. He stumbled and fell, and Garen was on him instantly, using her body to stand over him protectively.

The third man had met Garen's teeth before and shied sideways, turning his attack to Caelen. A dark figure sped across the glen, raising the hairs on the back of Caelen's neck.

How many more were there?

Caelen's attention was split. Having shed her weapons, he knew Arbela was in no position to protect herself. To his astonishment, a slender blade glinted in her right hand as she wove it back and forth before her assailant's eyes. He'd seen at least four blades fall from her hands. That she carried a fifth should not have surprised him.

Arbela lunged lightning swift toward Keith Dubh. With a vicious swipe of her blade, she laid open his upper arm. Keith's eyes widened in shock and his dagger slipped from useless fingers as he crumpled to the ground, screaming as if the devil had taken hold of him.

Caelen jerked his sword up instinctively to meet the third man's attack. But the dark figure he'd seen a moment earlier crossed between them, taking the brunt of the blow on his own sword.

Rory.

With a roar, the MacKern captain made short work of the man who'd attacked Caelen. Turning about, Rory caught a flying blade to the upper chest, the force flinging him backward. He staggered then braced himself against a tree. Dropping his sword to the ground, he surrendered.

Caelen's gaze swept the glen, silent now except for the sobbing cries of the injured MacGillonay.

Bram crept from Garen's protection and ran to Caelen's side. With a slash of his dagger, Caelen released Bram's bonds and the lad gripped him about one leg with all the force of a frightened lad. Caelen seized Bram's shoulder in a tight grip, sliding his palm to the lad's back in reassurance.

Arbela straightened, surveying the scene as she wiped her palms down the length of her thighs. Rory slid to the ground beside the tree, groaning in pain. Plucking the short dagger from his shoulder, he tossed it to the ground next to his sword. His face shone pale, sweat beading on his brow. Clutching a fist to his wound, he pressed hard, doubling over. A moment later, he straightened, turning anguished eyes on Arbela.

The leader of the small band writhed on the ground, hand gripping the deep wound in his arm. Arbela stepped to his side and snatched the blade from his reach, wiping it on her vest to remove the blood. The man continued his contortions, his screams thin and frantic.

"Scorpion poison," Arbela explained with a shrug, sending Rory a remorseless look. A swift kick to the side of Keith Dubh's head silenced him abruptly. "He'll thank me for that later. Ye may sweat yers out," she informed Rory, voice tight.

The other two men who had kidnapped Bram required no further attention save burial, though Caelen was disinclined to worry overmuch about that.

He shifted his gaze to Rory.

"Talk."

* * *

The moon hung low in the sky. Rory clenched his teeth, sweat pouring down his face.

"The poison will not kill him," Arbela noted, not bothering to hide the disappointment from her voice. Rory had, after all, assisted Keith Dubh in kidnapping Bram. Poison was too good for him.

"But he may wish it would in the next several hours," she added on a slightly happier note.

Caelen seated Bram on a nearby rock, standing behind him, arms on either side so Bram would feel comforted. Arbela paced the grass, finding it difficult to be still.

"After my parents died from the pestilence, only my wee sister,

324

Brinna, was left." Rory sucked in a labored breath, rolling his head on his neck, unable to escape the pain of the venom streaking through his chest.

"I couldnae bring her to the castle—death was too strong there. I sent her to the shepherd who lived far enough away as to be unaffected by the *mezils*. He was our great-uncle."

Arbela and Caelen exchanged glances. Though they would hear the full tale from Rory, things began to make sense. A shudder ran down Arbela's spine. The shepherd hadn't been seeking a lost sheep when she found him gravely wounded at the croft, but a lost girl.

"I was worrit when Coll sent word of missing sheep a fortnight ago. I took Toros and Garen with me, hoping 'twas naught but a wolf, and for Brinna's protection should it prove otherwise." Rory panted. "I knew Keith Dubh would likely not take his father's and brother's deaths lightly. But he is a scarred ruffian, not liked well enough by his clan to take control of the MacGillonays. Angry he might have been, but I doubted many would follow him. 'Twas a miscalculation.

"I found naught that first day. But the second time I visited, Coll had been tied to a chair in his croft, and Brinna forced to wait on Keith Dubh and his toadies." Rory gasped as a particularly bad spasm of pain struck. "She is but twelve!" he hissed. Arbela's heart lurched.

Rory closed his eyes and for a moment Arbela thought he had fainted. His low, shuddering breath reassured her he had not.

"I wouldnae betray Bram, but Keith Dubh had Brinna and alone I could do naught but pretend to go along with his plan. I knew ye were wary of sending men away from the castle to inspect Keith Dubh's diversions. And ye were right. But I had to ensure ye wouldnae leave Bram unprotected." Rory opened his eyes and stared angrily at Arbela.

"Ye came to the dock! Ye left him! Ye should have killed the man sent to kidnap Bram, and I would have . . .." His head rolled back, his arms limp at his side. "God, Brinna!"

The glen was silent save for Rory's light moans.

"Ye dinnae think to speak to me?" Caelen asked. "I could have helped ye."

Rory clutched his shoulder and leaned forward. "I couldnae. He promised if I did, I wouldnae see Brinna again—save to bury her. After he finished with her."

"Ye know as well as I he cannae harm a lass—not, at least, in that way."

Rory's eyes shone bright with pain. "His two men were more than able—and Keith Dubh more than willing to watch." He turned his gaze to Bram. "I am truly sorry my plan failed. I wouldnae see ye in harm's way. I will ever be indebted to ye, Caelen. And will endure whatever punishment I have earned."

Arbela's stomach heaved. "Tell me where he kept Brinna."

* * *

The outline of an abandoned hunter's croft, outlined against the pale streaks of dawn, loomed in the darkness. Arbela slipped from Voski's back and hurried o the single door, her path lit by the glow of torches carried by Gordon and six other men-at-arms. A heavy beam settled in new iron bolts contrasted to the utter disrepair of the small building, and it took two men to heft the rough-hewn timber away.

Arbela was the first through the door.

Faint embers glowed on the hearth, but the young girl huddled within the hut shivered with the cold. Golden hair straggled free from her braid, and her silver eyes glowed huge in her pale face. Arbela checked her pace.

"I will not hurt ye," she soothed. "Your brother told me where to find ye."

Brinna crumpled to the floor, her eyes screwed shut, tears flowing. Arbela sat beside her, pulling the girl's head to her chest, encircling the thin shoulders with her arms.

326

"They said they would return—and take me with them," she whispered. "I dinnae wish to go."

"Of course ye did not," Arbela replied. "And ye must not fear them, for they are dead."

Brinna drew back and met Arbela's gaze. After a moment, as though satisfied, she nodded. "That is well, for my brother would have dealt harshly with them. Is my uncle well?"

Even in the diminished light, Arbela saw the girl's lip quiver. With gentle fingers, Arbela swept a lock of hair from Brinna's face. "Why don't we go see him together?"

* * *

Gulls wheeled overhead. The piercingly blue sky reflected in refracted light on the rippling surface of Loch Linnhe. The dock bobbed lightly, its charred timbers rising like battle-scarred knees from the water. Alone with her memories of the previous night, Arbela soaked in the sun. Her body was sore from the battle and her heart ached with the fright of almost losing Bram—and betrayal.

Booted feet crunched on the pebbles and Caelen dropped down behind her and drew her body between his raised knees. Wrapping his arms about her, he placed his cheek against her hair.

"Bram is still sleeping, as is yer aunt and Brinna. The healer says the bumps and bruises will heal quickly."

Arbela nodded, placing a hand atop his. "I wonder if the deeper wounds will ever heal? Would things be different had I understood the shepherd's concern? Could I have prevented Bram's kidnapping?"

Caelen sighed. "Ye cannae think that way, Arbela. Looking back only helps if ye learn, not if ye simply pile blame on yerself." He shook his head. "So many ifs could have changed so much. I cannae argue with Rory's desire to protect his young sister—whom I scarcely remembered— but it angers me he couldnae bring himself to confide in me."

"If only he had brought her to the castle after his parents died," Arbela mused.

"Death was strong here. He was right. She would have fared better at the shepherd's croft in the open air, away from so much sickness. Rory was later reluctant to part them, to bring more grief to the lass."

Arbela considered Caelen's words. "'Tis easier to hear this after the danger has passed," she noted. "I would have been at a loss to find my twelve-year-old sister suddenly in the hands of a madman who demanded I betray my laird."

"The shepherd confirms Rory's tale. He woke early this morning from his fever and though weak, says Rory has given us a cleaner version of what transpired after Keith Dubh arrived."

Arbela shook her head. "Rory deliberately picked a fight with me last night so I would stay behind. He went along with Keith Dubh as long as he could, but could not bring himself to follow through with MacGillonay's final actions. I was supposed to guard Bram."

"He was confident of yer abilities, my love," Caelen said. "Though he could not be certain which man would attempt to kidnap Bram, he'd hoped it would be Keith Dubh—and that ye would kill him."

His words mitigated a small amount of the guilt tearing at Arbela. She nestled against him and sighed.

"I do not believe Rory is a bad person, though my anger over his actions will linger a time. And I suppose I should be remorseful for striking him with a poisoned dagger, though I am not." Caelen's chuckle warmed her ear. "I certainly do not regret using poison on Keith Dubh."

This time Caelen laughed.

"What will become of Keith Dubh?" Arbela asked.

"He will be punished," Caelen replied. "He should have been little threat to us. After his da's failed attempt to take Dunfaileas, and with the knowledge any repeat attempt would be met with the wrath of the MacLean, we should not have heard even a peep from him." Caelen shrugged. "With his past history, it seemed unlikely he could mount any serious attack or gain the following of his clan, his two toadies who met their deaths last night notwithstanding. I am fairly certain he would not have been awarded the lairdship."

Arbela tilted sideways, turning her head to meet Caelen's gaze. "What history?"

"Och, he was the worst of the MacGillonays. But he met his match when he raped the daughter of a powerful laird—Cameron, I believe it was. Rather than kill the lad, the Cameron scarred the lad's face so he'd never attract a woman again, crippled his leg so he'd never acquit himself in battle, reducing his appeal as MacGillonay's heir—and fed him his severed manhood so he'd never prick a woman again." Caelen shrugged. "'Tis likely why he wasnae with his da when they broached our walls nearly a month ago."

"No wonder he was slight of frame and did not resemble his father or brother. Such a thing would stunt his growth."

Caelen sighed. "I forget ye come from a place where such things exist. 'Twas a harsh punishment, but the Cameron was in a cold fury and likely saved other lasses a similar fate. Keith Dubh was known far and wide as a blackguard."

"Hence his name, Keith *Dubh*?" Arbela asked.

"Aye, named Keith for his da, Dubh for his black heart."

"I would advise sending him to my father for sentencing and punishment."

Caelen nodded slowly. "An excellent idea. 'Tis the baron's responsibility to handle such a matter. To take it into my hands would only strengthen the feud between MacKerns and MacGillonays. This would smack more of justice than vengeance."

"Father has presided over many cases in Batroun, and King Alexander gave him the right to do so here." She was silent a moment. "I predict he will sentence him to be hanged in the MacGillonay courtyard and left for a sennight to warn against further treachery."

Caelen hugged her tighter, but did not reply.

"What will become of Rory?" Arbela asked.

Caelen sighed. "He has been my brother since we nursed the same breast as bairns. I trusted him with my life. I can sympathize with his dilemma, but 'twill take time to rebuild trust between us. I have already replaced him as captain. He understands. 'Tis my belief he will work hard to overcome his mistake, and 'tis my hope we will be companions again someday."

A shriek startled them, sending Arbela and Caelen bolting to their feet. Bram raced down the road, Garen at his side, Gordon at his heels. Bram threw himself into Arbela's arms. Tears stung her eyes as she held him close.

"I fighted the bad men, Bela," he crowed. "Just like ye taught me. And it worked! I was too scared at first to 'member, but ye 'membered for me."

"Ye were very brave, Bram MacKernsingha," Arbela said, chucking him beneath his chin. "Ye were as brave and as fierce as a lion."

"I couldnae gainsay the lad from joining ye," Gordon grinned. "It seemed best he get the excitement out of his system."

"He is ever welcome," Arbela reassured him.

Caelen wrapped his arms about Arbela and Bram. "Almost always," he whispered as he nipped her ear playfully.

Arbela's blood warmed and she turned her head for a decent kiss. In Caelen's arms, his child held close, was where she belonged.

Epilogue

Dunfaileas Castle
Late Spring 1223

Bram chortled with glee as the bairn grabbed at his finger. "He'll be a braw warrior," he declared approvingly.

Arbela laughed. Zora handed her a soft woolen blanket to ward against the chill air, draping it about her shoulders and the bairn. Caelen thought his wife had never looked lovelier. Her cheeks pink, her eyes sparkling, and the bairn in her arms, she completed the image Caelen had longed for. From time to time he was still caught by surprise to discover that this strong-minded, dusky daughter of the desert held his heart. But he would not have it any other way.

"Ye inspect the lad's grip already?" Caelen asked, striding to Bram's side and placing an arm about Arbela's shoulders.

"Och, aye," Bram replied in all seriousness. "He must be able to wield a sword."

"He is but a bairn," Caelen chided. "There is plenty of time."

Bram nodded. "But I have so much to teach him. And I have all but outgrown Ari, though 'tis nae problem as I will keep him fed and brushed until wee Tomas can ride him."

Arbela smiled and ruffled Bram's hair. "This is not the time for swords and ponies," she said. "This is the time for stories."

Bram climbed into the chair next to her and laid his head on her shoulder, one small arm protectively about his brother. "Ye will like Ma's stories," he said. "Hers are the best."

Caelen's eyes misted. "Which is yer favorite, Bram?"

Bram thought for a moment. "Tell him the one about St. George and the dragon."

~The End~

A Note from the Authors:

We hope you enjoyed Arbela and Caelen's story. We found it fascinating to bring you a tale deeply rooted in history, with differing cultures and religions. Many of the places and people in The Highlander's Crusader Bride really existed. If you'd like to know what happened to them, read on.

Donal MacLean is fictitious (more on the MacLean clan later), though in our story he took up the cross and traveled to Outremer with King Richard, who was, of course, king of England in 1190, and who spearheaded the Third Crusade. Donal hired on with Bohemond IV of Antioch & Count of Tripoli, another historical figure, in 1193 after Richard headed back to England. Donal was soon made Baron of Batroun, and, in our tale, fostered Phillipe de Poitiers (Phillipe I of Antioch, Bohemond IV's son, who truly lived, though his early personal history is scant) at Mseilha Fort (castle in our story) on the road between Tripoli and Beirut in St. William's Pass. Such a place did exist, though reports differ in its origins, and it guarded the pass, giving safe passage to travelers and merchants through the area.

Bohemond IV, Prince of Antioch, was actually known as *le Cyclope*, and for the reasons stated in our story. When Donal and his family are recalled to Antioch Citadel in 1221 and receive word they are to return to Scotland, Phillipe is given the news that he is to be married to Queen Isabella of Armenia the following year. This also, to Phillipe's detriment, is true. He cared little for the Armenians or their religion, which differed in its style of Christianity from that of the Holy Roman Church, and, when forced to marry Isabella, became quite arrogant, riding roughshod over their culture, and was eventually assassinated by the people he ruled. However, after digging deeper into Phillipe's history, we discovered an interesting twist, and decided to bring you an altered version—one that *could* have happened—in The Prince's Highland Bride, due to release in 2020. Stay tuned.

Donal MacLean will bring back to Scotland all the trappings, foods, spices, and customs of a Middle Eastern Court, as many crusaders did. Spectacular jewels and outlandish clothing that had never before been seen in Scotland will make Arbela suspect—questioning her morals and religion. Leave it to Arbela to be both uncompromising and charming, winning hearts and acceptance in due time.

Donal MacLean's ship, **Falcone de Mar**—or the *Sea Falcon*—is an interesting blend of a medieval cog, already in use for hundreds of years with its sturdy square sail, and the Italian Cocca—which we could find no evidence of until the 15th century—with its innovative triangular lateen sails. Those lateen sails had been in use in fishing boats around the Mediterranean since the 2nd century CE, allowing fishermen to sail 45 degrees into the wind.

The period between the cog and the cocca is where our story lies, and a shipbuilder certainly didn't simply wake one day with the idea of the cocca in his head. These ships evolved over time, and resulted from the needs of the winds and seas where they originated as well as the ship's general use. The Crusades were a time of great opportunity for the Italian City States, such as the Venetians, as they had to transport men, horses and supplies from Italy to the Holy Land. These circumstances prompted innovation in ship construction.

The *Sea Falcon* represents a missing link with its lateen sails allowing it to tack across the Mediterranean, regardless of the wind direction. The large square sail caught the wind when it was 90 degrees to the vessel or at its back, moving it at great speed. The ship's size allowed it to carry cargo as well as passengers, and Donal's plans to create a trading company from MacLean Castle in Scotland, would soon come to fruition.

The Saracens who attacked from the North African coast, on the other hand, would have commanded sleek, wave-skimming dhows, lateen-rigged ships propelled by both rowers and trapezoidal sails. The pirates from the Outer Hebrides, by contrast, used square-sailed birlinns with 12 to 16 oars.

Arbela's horse is an **Akhal-Teke**, an ancient breed from Turkmenistan still used today as show jumpers, in eventing, and dressage. Dating back centuries in origin, they were known as the Heavenly Horse. The hairs of their coat are clear at the tips, giving their coat a glistening sheen which is unique to this breed.

As with all our books, there is a canine (or occasionally feline) character. For Arbela's dogs, we chose the **Aidi** breed which is an average-size, moderately coated dog, with its origins in Morocco. It is known as a livestock protector and also has good scenting capabilities.

Arbela's character was the product of a Scots father and an Armenian princess mother. Visiting her mother's people was often a perilous undertaking, and her father insisted his daughter be trained in weaponry skills in an effort to keep her from meeting her death as her mother had at the hands of bandits. He was displeased to find Arbela had spent two summers in Armenia at an uncle's castle where devotees of the **Hashashin** order met and trained. As a small woman, well-aware of her limitations in hand-to-hand combat, Arbela was fascinated by the skills they exhibited which used cunning instead of strength, and combined weapons such as poisons, traps, blow guns, use of pressure points, and acrobatic skills. They also honed their skills in disguise, equestrianism, the art of war, linguistics, and strategies. The Hashashin order arose around 1090 and existed until 1296 when they were utterly destroyed by the Mongols.

At the time of the MacLean family's arrival in Scotland, King Alexander II was king and had recently married Joan of England. He was 23, she was 11.

Finally, the first person to sign himself Maclean, was Gilleain na Tuaighe, born c. 1210, and known as the first MacLean chief. However, there was a strong presence of his ancestors in the Inner Hebrides and

Western Highland regions of Scotland, traceable back to Gilleain na Tuaighe's great-x-34 grandfather, Tuirmhich teainrich righ Eran, who died c.320B.C. Tradition states he was a King of Dálcuinn. (Clan MacLean History Project). We felt secure placing MacLeans in the area of Loch Aline in 1222 AD, and giving them a fairly long history there. Though the MacLeans were notably aligned with the Lords of the Isles and the king of Norway, our MacLean, in a bid to assist his shipping trade, made an alliance with the king of Scotland, though he carefully balanced his position between the cultures.

According to the Clan MacLean History Project (link above), Gilleain na Tuaighe means 'Gilleain of the battle-axe'. Gilleain means 'servant of St. John', and Maclean translates as 'son of Gilleain', or 'son of the servant of St. John.'

Thanks for joining us on our tour from Scotland to the Holy Lands and back.

~ **Cathy & DD MacRae**

Acknowledgements:

A huge thank you to all who read through this story as it evolved and gave us such encouragement: Dawn Marie Hamilton, Cate Parke, editor Liette Bougie, and our great beta-readers, Ann Leeson, Barb Massabrook, Donna Finley, April Renn, Raine Clarke, and Sharon Frizzell.

I'm pleased to say Dar Albert once again worked her magic on the cover art.

If you enjoyed Arbela and Caelen's story, please consider leaving a review.

About the Authors:

Cathy MacRae lives on the sunny side of the Arbuckle Mountains where she and her husband read, write, and tend the garden—with the help of the dogs, of course.

You can visit with her on Facebook, or read her blogs and learn about her books at www.cathymacraeauthor.com. Drop her a line—she loves to hear from readers!

To keep up with new releases and other fun things, sign up for my newsletter! There's an easy form on my website. (You'll find DD's news there, too!)

Other ways to connect with Cathy:
Facebook: Cathy MacRae Author
Twitter: @CMacRaeAuthor
Pinterest: AuthorCathyMacRae
Instagram: Cathy MacRae_Author

DD MacRae enjoys bringing history to life. Research is one of the best things about writing a story! And with more than 35 years of martial arts training, DD also brings believable, breath-taking action to the tales.

You can connect with DD through www.cathymacraeauthor.com. It's always exciting to hear from readers!

More books by Cathy Macrae

The Highlander's Bride series
The Highlander's Accidental Bride (book 1)
The Highlander's Reluctant Bride (book 2)
The Highlander's Tempestuous Bride (book 3)
The Highlander's Outlaw Bride (book 4)
The Highlander's French Bride (book 5)

De Wolfe Connected World series:
The Saint
The Penitent
The Cursed

The Ghosts of Culloden Moor series
(with LL Muir, Diane Darcy, Jo Jones, and Melissa Mayhue)
Adam
Malcolm
MacLeod
Patrick

More Books by DD Macrae
(Contemporary Romance)
The Italian Billionaire's Runaway Bride

Read an excerpt from The Prince's Highland Bride

Chapter One

The Mediterranean coast
Early winter
1224 AD

"Halt!"

The shout from behind echoed off the rocks, punctuated by the *shush* of steel against leather and the thunder of the mounted pack. Phillipe urged his horse to greater speed. Surrender was not an option.

To his left and right, his guards bent low over their horses, grimly determined to outpace the men in pursuit. They were past reckless banter, beyond the boasts that they'd make it to Tripoli. All attention was on the dangerous footing ahead and in assessing the manner of men who chased them. The road from Sis to Tripoli was often fraught with such danger, and bandits were not unknown. However, if Phillipe was placing bets, his would lie squarely on Baron Konstantin.

The darkness that had hidden their departure from Sis Castle was no longer their ally but rather their foe as they sped over the rutted road. Torchlight twinkled in the distance, marking the city ahead, taunting them with safety.

If only Father received my missive. If he's sent men to help . . ..

But Phillipe knew help would not be forthcoming. The road ahead lay silent. Failure loomed, tightening like a physical noose about his neck.

I am the King of Cilicia! They have no right! Rage burned side by side with indignation at the injustice. Grand Baron Konstantin, formerly regent to the young queen, Phillipe's wife, cared for nothing but furthering his own power—and Phillipe stood squarely in his way.

340

Phillipe's steed stumbled, his shod hooves clattering over loosened stones.

"Damn!"

As if in answer to his irreverence, his horse pitched forward, falling abruptly to its knees. Phillipe lost his grip and plummeted over the animal's neck, landing hard on the packed ground. With a grunt of effort, Phillipe rolled and sprang to his feet, body low, sword in hand. A swift glance at his horse told him it would prove no further use in evading capture. Its sides billowed, head low, one foreleg toeing the ground as though it could no longer bear weight.

Pain flashed through Phillipe's skull. He winced and shook his head as his vision cleared. Four men shot past. They wheeled their horses in a spray of dust and gravel. Phillipe felt rather than saw his two guards, men he trusted—Hugh and John, men who, like him, called Antioch, not Cilicia, home—align his flank him.

Like giant black birds, cloaks swirling about them, the bandits—if that was what they were—circled Phillipe and his men. Moonlight glinted off the long curves of deadly *kilij*, the weighted, curved blades of the mounted warrior. Phillipe flinched. A single downward stroke would slice through him with little effort. If either he or even one of his men faltered, they were doomed.

He made a beckoning gesture with the fingers of his left hand, lips curled in a feral grin.

The black-clad men faced Phillipe and his guard, the ends of their turbans wrapped to conceal the lower halves of their faces. Moonlight glinted dully on chainmail coifs protecting their necks and shoulders.

These were no ordinary bandits.

Damn. He resisted the urge to exchange glances with his guards. Phillipe gripped his straight-bladed sword, raising it aloft in a high guard. Hugh and John lifted their swords waist-high, clearing their saddles, prepared to strike.

The bandits charged side-by-side. Phillipe backed against John's horse's flank, sticking close as his men met the charge. John ducked a swing meant to take his head and countered with a swing that bit deep into the bandit's torso. Phillipe blocked a downward attack and rammed his shoulder into the villain's horse, causing it to veer to one side. The rider grabbed the reins with both hands, dropping his guard. Phillipe thrust his sword through his foe then pushed him from his saddle and mounted the steed.

A shout from Hugh made Phillipe whirl his horse and rush to his aid. Hugh's sleeve darkened with blood as he valiantly fought the two remaining marauders, but was rapidly losing the fight. Phillipe brought his sword up for a head strike then sliced low when the bandit raised his guard to parry. The force of Phillipe's swing unhorsed the man. He landed awkwardly on the hard, rocky ground and did not rise.

Hugh dispatched the remaining bandit then sagged forward, his wounds taking their tithe.

"John, bring wine and bandages," Phillipe shouted as he dismounted to help Hugh to the ground.

Hugh waved him weakly away. "Go, my lord. Ye expose yourself. I will just slow ye down." He grimaced as Phillipe helped him to sit.

"I'll not leave ye to die in this place," Phillipe growled. "Not after ye risked your life to protect me."

John knelt beside them, placing a stoppered flagon on the ground along with a length of cloth. He split Hugh's sleeve, exposing a deep cut the length of the man's upper arm. Blood welled steadily from the wound and the white of bone could be seen. Already Hugh's skin appeared tinged with gray.

John shook his head. "He's right, m'lord. We should run whilst we have the chance. Antioch is but a few leagues away."

"I'll not leave him to die alone."

"Then let me tend his wounds and ye go ahead. I will see to it he makes it to your father's palace."

Hugh groaned. "Go, m'lord. John will patch me up and ye can send your father's men to escort us back."

Torn between loyalty and duty, Phillipe kicked a rock with frustrated violence then mounted the horse he'd won in battle.

"Very well. But I command ye both to follow as soon as ye are able."

"Aye, m'lord."

Phillipe guided his horse into the shadows and was only a short distance away when the sound of horses again thundered behind him. Wheeling his mount, Phillipe drew his sword and raced back. Encircling Hugh and John were ten riders dressed the same as the deceased bandits, swords pointed at their heads.

A tall man, his face angular, his nose as sharp as a falcon's beak, kneed his horse between his soldiers. His eyes narrowed in the barest hint of pleasure. He jerked his head toward Phillipe.

"If he resists, kill the others."

Phillipe spat on the ground. "'Tis like ye to sit back and command others to do your work, Darius. Konstantin's actions have rubbed off on ye."

Darius fluttered the fingers of one hand in a bored manner and shrugged. "I prefer not to soil my hands with the likes of thieves."

Phillipe startled, caught off-guard by the accusation. "Thieves? Ye have the wrong king." A sneer dragged at one side of his mouth. "Crawl back to your master. Ye have no authority over me."

"Oh?" He nodded to someone beyond Phillipe's shoulder. The man held Phillipe's lame horse with one hand, a leather satchel in the other.

"Look what I found, Sardar." The soldier opened the leather bag and reached inside. Moonlight sparkled in his hand in flashes of red and white, and a twinkle of gold.

"What . . .?" Phillipe tried shaking his head, but the unexpected sight of the jewels befuddled his mind even more.

Darius smirked, his condescending manner infuriating Phillipe—as it always had.

"We are taking ye back to Sis to stand trial, my King." The title dripped acidly from Darius's lips.

"On what charge?" Phillipe demanded. A sick sensation hollowed his stomach.

"Why, theft of the Crown Jewels of Cilicia, of course."

* * *

The Prince's Highland Bride, Book #6 in The Hardy Heroines series, available 2020.

Made in the USA
Las Vegas, NV
31 May 2021